WHISPERS

OF THE

APOC

WHISPERS OF THE APOC

Volume 1

Copyright © 2017 by Tannhauser Press

ISBN-13: 978-1945994104
ISBN-10: 194599410X

Cover design by Heidi Sutherlin
Edited by: Donna Royston and Martin Wilsey
Published by Tannhauser Press

CONTENTS

DEDICATION

For Tom Richter, Ray Clark, Keith Plough,
Eric Wilsey, Tom Bilodeau, Kevin Peck and
Carl Wilsey.

My favorite dead guys.

FOREWORD

Ever since I watched the original Night of the Living Dead I have loved stories about the Zombie Apocalypse. Dawn of the Dead ramped it up a notch soon after.

The survival stories by using your brains before they got eaten was the key. Maybe that and the fact that is a guilt free way to shoot some assholes in the face that always deserved it.

When I put the call out for submissions I was buried in them. I have already decided to do a second volume.

SILENCE
OF THE
APOC

I picked stories I liked to share with you. Some are from established authors, some are from people just beginning their work as published authors.

All of them are fun.

A few authors that I know had intended to submit a short story for this anthology and it got away from them. The stories grew and are now approaching novel length. Keep an eye out, because I think Tannhauser Press may be offering them in 2018.

FOREWORD

I may even use the seed of my short story for a novel set in that same world. The possibilities are endless. Each of these stories and authors have been great to work with.

I hope you enjoy reading them as much as I did assembling this anthology.

Martin Wilsey
Managing Editor
Tannhauser Press
www.tannhauserpress.com

WHISPERS OF THE APOC

1 THE MARKIE MARK BY T R DILLON

It's not like I'd never been bitten before.

Karolynn was ferocious. A minx. She was my second wife—that's if you don't count Mirabelle, who I never formally tied the knot with. Karolynn and I'd be tussling under the covers. A few moans, maybe a cry or two, and then she'd chomp down on my forearm like it was a leg of lamb. Sometimes I noticed, sometimes I didn't. It depended on—how shall I put it?—what else I was busy with at that particular moment.

I ignored the bite unless she'd drawn blood, in which case I smeared Neosporin on it. I mean, what was I going to tell the doctor? You could see Karolynn's teeth marks clear as day. I never got infected, but I have scars on both arms.

People asked me, *Markie, why do you put up with that?* I just shrugged. Anything for love, right?

So when the precinct fired off the emergency text on March 31 about corpses biting people, I immediately thought of Karolynn. I hadn't seen her in years. I wondered where she was. In my own self-absorbed way, I kind of missed her.

I dismissed the text as some kind of April fool's joke. I laughed and forgot about it. Until I arrested that punk with a gunshot wound to the gut. I suppose that's what you get when you break into the home of the local NRA head. It was the middle of the night, and he died on the operating table at Presbyterian before I could get a statement. I know because I was there. I saw the flat-line on his monitor. The doc didn't even sew him up.

So there I was, writing notes against the hospital wall for the report I had to file, when I heard a noise behind me. I turned, and there he was, the punk, in his hospital gown with his guts hanging out. Blood dripping down his chin. He looked like he'd just eaten a hot pocket that really disagreed with him, and he had that weird smell. Camphor. I would come to detest that smell.

And then the sonofabitch bit me in the left arm. Which occurred about a half-second before I shot him in the head.

The docs and nurses came running. "Detective Marks, did he bite you?" one of them asked, keeping her distance.

"Yeah," I said. "Right here in my left arm," and I showed them. He did it over top of one of Karolynn's, except his bite was smaller. Big surprise there.

They all backed away like they thought I was dangerous.

"It's not a big deal," I said. "I've been bitten before."

You should have seen the looks on their faces then.

***

At first everyone called it the HRV epidemic—short for Human Rabies Virus—and we all thought we had it under control. We were *managing* it. It wasn't easy, especially in a city like the Big Apple, but we were getting it done. People were cooperating. People always do when they're totally freaking scared.

The only problem was they couldn't isolate the damned virus. It had to be a virus, they kept telling us. Nothing else made sense. Just give us more time, and more people, and more money, and more facilities, and oh did we mention we need more money, and one of these damned days we'll find the little bugger.

They never did, of course.

And in the meantime, people got sick. I mean, really sick. They had all the symptoms of a severe case of rabies. Fever, chills, headaches, saliva all over the place, aches and pains, massive liquid consumption, you name it. I told myself I should buy Gatorade stock. They didn't get better, but they didn't die either. They just suffered. No one could explain it.

The economic cost was a blitzkrieg. More than thirty percent of the NYPD was out with it. At my precinct it was more like fifty percent. But everywhere got hit. The talking heads on TV estimated the total damage in trillions. Multiple trillions. A massive recession was the best-case scenario. The worst was a return to the Stone Age.

Still, we thought we had things under control. Quarantines and curfews. Everyone went OCD on hygiene. Especially masks. I had a personal supply from after nine-eleven. Back then I read some article about preparing a survival kit, and they said buy masks in case someone releases a chemical agent. That always sounded so sinister. *Releasing* a chemical agent. Like it was a Kraken or something.

So the New York subway became like bullet trains in Japan—everyone covering their faces. Some guy made a fortune selling little boxes of pure oxygen that people could keep in their pockets with little plastic tubes running up into their noses. Then they discovered it was just normal air in the boxes, but by then the guy was long gone.

We told ourselves things weren't that bad because people weren't dying.

But things really were that bad. Because what it was, was a dam about to burst. When that happened, there was nothing anyone could do.

Like when you're on the beach with your toes in the sand and you look up and notice a tsunami pounding toward you from a hundred yards offshore. Just enough time to say a prayer and look forward to a bath.

***

The hospital people took my gun and locked me in a storage closet. All the other quarantine rooms were taken. I asked for some Neosporin for the bite wound, and they slid a tube under the door. *Eight hours*, they said, *and we'll look in on you.*

Four hours later I'd had enough. I felt fine, and there were no sounds coming under the door. It was too quiet, if you know what I mean. And I really needed to go to the bathroom. So after yelling and pounding, I took the .380 Colt Mustang I hid in my right sock and shot the door open.

The hospital was empty. Of people, I mean. There were beds and carts and equipment overturned and thrown about. Like a giant baby had picked up the building and shaken it. But no people I could see. Not even any blood. The fluids everywhere were from IVs and bags and broken glass containers and a few cans of Coke.

I took it as a good sign that there were no bodies lying about. I was wrong, of course. There were plenty of dead bodies—they were all out walking the streets!

My phone didn't work in the closet, but it did in the waiting area. I had three bars but couldn't load any websites. I caught scraps of headlines, which told me an apocalypse was unfolding. The sick were finally dying, left and right it seemed, and everyone who died came back to life, if you could call it that. They couldn't talk or think, but they had that look in their eye. Like they were desperately hunting something. And they walked the way my Uncle Carl did after his back surgery went bad. Stiff-legged and jerky. Like they'd lost some important muscle groups but couldn't quite identify which ones. But they could run like the wind if they smelled a live person, and they were quick as a lizard's tongue.

And, oh yes, they reeked of camphor.

So I smeared some more Neosporin on the punk's bite wound, and then I did the only thing someone in my situation could do. I found the cafeteria. After all, a man's got to eat.

***

I sent texts to my captain and waited for a response. He was a beefy, red-faced man named Ronald Blodgett. His friends on the force called him R-dog, and his wife called him Dagwood. He could never get my name right. Always called me Mark, I think because I looked like someone named Mark he used to work with. Which was too bad for me because Blodgett didn't like that guy very much.

I'd last talked to Blodgett the day before, poking my head in his doorway.

"Come in, Mark," he'd bellowed.

"It's Marks, sir. Tommy Marks."

"Right, Mark, we need to talk."

"Marks, sir."

"I have a new assistant. There will be times when you'll report to him. His name is Jon Jonny 16."

He'd pointed to a small standing robot, an AI, about three feet high. They'd built a boatload of them three months earlier to look like the gold Star Wars robot with the snooty British accent. All the captains got one, and they had a newspaper contest to name them. A little boy his mom called Jon Jonny had been killed by a stray gang bullet on the Lower East Side, and so the AIs all became Jon Jonnies.

Blodgett had handcuffed his AI to his desk. Digital cuffs. "I don't trust the little bastard not to run," he'd said, eyeing it warily.

"Hello, Detective Marks," the AI had said, in a crisp English accent. "My name is Jon Jonny 16."

Blodgett ran what we called the Lam group. We looked for people who lived off the grid in downtown NYC. Enough of them were fugitives that the Chief launched a systematic effort to find them. I guess they downgraded chasing street vendors selling loose cigarettes.

With the AI's help, Blodgett had come up with a list of suspects for me to track down. All were believed to live and work in midtown. Which led me to the punk who'd just tried robbing a swanky penthouse and taken a bullet in the gut for his efforts. If only all my cases resolved that easily.

So I had the list, and Captain Blodgett had other work to do.

"Good-bye, Detective Marks," Jon Jonny 16 had said cheerfully as I left. Blodgett didn't say a word.

***

After the cafeteria, I hid by Presbyterian's front door. West 51st was filled with these walking corpses. Zombies, they were calling them. No one knew why, but the Z's wanted to eat the living. Still, they never got very far. Because once their victims died, they became Z's, too. The whole thing seemed like a classic circle jerk to me.

I devised a plan. I wasn't safe in the hospital. The Z's would come looking once they got hungry enough. The 17th precinct was just down the street. My objective was to get there without being bitten, and all I had was the gun from my sock with one round spent. I spied a police cruiser about a hundred yards across and down the street. I would sprint to the car, hotwire it if I had to, then make a beeline for the 17th. I'd move so fast and low the Z's wouldn't even know I'd been there. I told myself the 17th was probably a fortress by then, so I'd have to figure out a way in.

I checked my phone. Still nothing from Captain Blodgett. All texts were being queued, and I didn't know whether any of mine had been delivered. The captain probably figured I was dead. Which meant I was on my own.

I kept feeling my forehead for fever. Checking my pulse. That punk drew blood when he bit me, and that had been hours earlier. According to the internet, I should already be sick, maybe even dead. But I'd never felt better in my life. Something wasn't right. Well, I didn't have time then to figure it out.

I crouched low, took a deep breath, and then launched myself from the entryway onto West 51st towards the cruiser. Not ten yards out I crashed into a Z who stepped out stupidly from behind a trash can. My .380 skittered behind the right front tire of a black Crossover and, losing my balance, I plunged facedown into a puddle of slick dirty water.

I quickly raised myself up on my elbows, closed my eyes, and pretended to be invisible. I even held my breath, as if that would help. There's no way the Z's didn't hear me and see me. Probably smelled me, too. I hadn't showered in a while. My chin dripped noisily into the puddle. I heard each droplet like the second hand of a clock.

I opened one eye, then the other. I could see the legs of the Z's as they walked in front of me on 51st. Suddenly a Z came zooming towards me. She threw herself onto both knees, and her hand reached out for my face. I ducked and winced. But the hand kept going—into the trash can, now overturned and spilling out, where the Z pulled out a huge, squealing rat. The Z's face distorted in a kind of twisted delight, and then she shoved the rat into her mouth and began chomping.

Then the Z stood up and left. She hadn't touched me.

I raised myself onto my knees. The Z's were everywhere. On the street. The sidewalk. In front of me. Behind. But not one Z paid me a bit of attention. I was invisible. I did not exist.

I was immune.

"Boo!" I screamed at a passing Z. No reaction.

I thought of Karolynn again. Did I have her to thank for this? Did something happen to me all those years ago when she bit me every time we had sex?

Or was I that ping-pong ball just drawn from a lottery barrel? The one chance in a million. In ten million. That one lucky guy who gets to live unmolested in a world where the Z's are trying to eat everyone else, including rats.

And then a bullet zipped past my left ear.

***

I dove for cover behind the Crossover and picked up the .380. Several more shots rang out, and I sensed ricochets off the hood.

I risked a quick glance into the street. There stood a middle-aged man wearing pajamas, a dirty blue robe with the cloth belt dragging on the street, and slippers. He puffed on a cigar and carried a rifle under his right armpit.

I set down my .380 and raised my hands high, careful not to show my head.

"I'm not a zombie!" I yelled.

"I know," he yelled back. "You're an immune, like me. That's why I have to kill you."

I ducked before three more blasts caromed above my head.

"I don't understand," I shouted.

"You're destroying my dream," he said. I could tell by his voice he was getting closer.

"What dream?"

"I thought I was the only immune. I've always wanted to be the king of New York. This was my chance. And then you stumbled onto the scene."

"I'm sure we can work something out," I said, picking up my gun.

"Only if you die," he said.

I threw a broken piece of asphalt in front of the Crossover, then shimmied around the back of the car and burst into the street. The man, his back to me, shot at the asphalt.

"Put it down," I growled.

He wheeled and pointed his rifle, but before he could pull I deposited a bullet in his right shoulder. He staggered back as I put another one in his left. The rifle clattered away, and he fell heavily onto his back. The cigar flip-flopped onto his belly.

The Z's patrolled the street and sidewalks like nothing had happened. They didn't even look.

I kicked the rifle away and stood over him. "The King of New York?" I said.

He wheezed. "Guess not, huh?"

"Not today, friend," I said.

There was blood everywhere. He was bleeding out fast.

"Tell me something," I asked. "Did you ever have a wife or a girlfriend who bit you often during sex?"

He furrowed his brow. "How did you know?"

"Just a wild guess," I said.

"Well, you're a cop," he said, his eyes closing, his voice weak. "So you're obligated to save me. I need help fast, so haul me into the hospital and find a doctor. Serve and protect, isn't that right?"

"Not today," I replied. Then I aimed and put a bullet in his forehead. I picked up his cigar and sucked on it hard, twice, so it wouldn't go out. I didn't want to have to go searching for a light.

Here's how I figured it. This joker was as good as dead, anyways. Two bullets and all that blood. I'd hit one artery, maybe two. He'd already tried to kill me once, and I didn't want him coming after me as a Z. He may have been an immune, but everyone comes back as a Z after they die. At least that's what my phone told me.

So did my immunity protect me from another immune who turns into a Z? Do angels dance on pins? I didn't know, but I wasn't about to take chances. The efficient solution was a bullet in the brain right then and there. Ending his career as a Z before it even began. I was always proactive when it came to efficiency.

And yada yada, blah blah.

I never was much of a people person anyway.

***

My phone buzzed. Finally, a text from Captain Blodgett: MARKS, URGENT YOU FIND SUSPECT #17. PIZZA JOINT NEAR 8ᵀᴴ & W 46ᵀᴴ. GET HIM HERE ASAP. BLODGETT. Another text followed with the address of the pizza joint.

I still had the list, and number seventeen was a 23-year-old high school dropout named Jose Ramon Ramirez. He'd committed a string of petty crimes in NYC and Miami Beach. And he was a hacker. A pretty good one, too, given how badly the Feds wanted him.

But the assignment made no sense. The world was falling apart. Millions were dead with millions more at the doorstep. Infrastructure was cratering or becoming useless. Economies were collapsing, and food chains were dissolving. Civilization hung by a thread, and Blodgett wanted me, maybe the only immune on the NYPD, to find some petty thief at a pizza parlor.

Still, orders were orders. I thought about taking a car. I had my pick of any on the street. But the Z's were everywhere and they weren't going to get out of the way. Walking was faster. And it was early afternoon on a pleasant sunny day. And the cigar tasted good. And I needed the exercise.

So I started walking. And then I realized something strange and terrible. I actually liked the Z's. I mean, sort of. In their natural element, strolling the streets and sidewalks of the Big Apple without purpose or destination, the Z's were beautiful. Of course, you had to get used to how they looked. And the pungent odor of camphor.

But it was like swimming with a school of dolphins. Even though they were sharks. I was immune, so they didn't see me as food. They let me pass like I was a ghost. They were polite and stayed out of my way. They didn't get into fistfights or try to pick my pocket. And they didn't say a word. If my first wife had been that quiet, I'd probably still have been married to her.

And they were decimating the rat population in NYC with fierce enthusiasm.

In a way, the Z's were the ultimate egalitarian society. Everyone was flat-line, no-questions-asked equal. There were no race or class or gender barriers. No one cared about sexual preference or what bathroom you used. Old, young, rich, poor, it didn't matter. And every Z was a victim, who then became a predator. The symmetry of the whole thing was breathtaking.

And did I mention that no one said a word? I really liked that.

Which made me think again about Karolynn. Was she a Z, walking around somewhere hunting food? Or was she an immune like me, baffled by the spectacle? Or maybe she found her way, somehow, somewhere, to safety. For the first time in years, I realized I missed her.

By that time I was somewhere on West 46th near Eighth Avenue. Suddenly, there was a noise from one of the stores. Or maybe it was a restaurant. That splintery sound of a door giving way. At the same exact precise instant, every Z's head turned to the sound. And then they began sprinting towards it. That sound was a dinner bell. The Z's had broken into some place where there were people. Real people. And everyone was hungry.

The Z's were always hungry.

At that moment, I saw the Z's for what they truly were. Raw brutal instinct made flesh. Their humanity had been deleted. The push of a button on a keyboard. It was like Alzheimer's. You sort of recognized the body, but inside there was nothing that rang a bell. Still, that's egalitarianism for you. It works only if people aren't people.

My phone buzzed. Another text: MARKS, PLS ADVISE WHEREABOUTS. URGENT WE GET SUSPECT SOONEST. BLODGETT.

And then I noticed the suspect's address was where all the Z's had just run to. I sighed. One thing was for certain.

I was going to need more guns.

***

I reconned the place first. There were hundreds of Z's pushing and shoving to get into the pizza parlor. I tried elbowing my way to the front, but couldn't get anywhere. So I dropped to my knees and began crawling. I was wet from the Z's blood and body parts when I got to the front. My fifth bullet eliminated the fat Z in the doorway, and I was inside. The smell of camphor was so strong I almost couldn't breathe.

The joint was small and narrow with roughly thirty-five Z's angling toward the back. I didn't see any bodies, so I figured Ramirez, if that's who was in here, had holed up in the bathroom. At least, that's what I would have done. Behind the counter was a side door leading to an alley. The Z's didn't know it was there, so the alley was dirty but deserted.

Abandoned cop cars were everywhere. It took me three to get what I wanted. Two .500 Smith & Wesson magnums, one for each hand, and a trunkful of clips. I parked one by the entrance to the alley and left the motor running with the driver's and left rear doors open. I was hoping Z's didn't know how to drive. I shoved clips into my pants pockets, then dumped the rest in the passenger's seat in front.

The plan was classic shock and awe. Donning sunglasses, I positioned myself against the wall by the edge of the Z's. I loaded both magnums and began blasting Z heads at close range. The exploding blood and bone and cartilage blocked the sun. Everyone got drenched, including me. I pushed each body away from the wall after I shot it, then inched forward. Shoot and push and inch forward. Shoot and push and inch forward. Reloading twice, I slowly made my way to the front door. I blasted two rows of Z's on the outside, then turned around and did the same on the inside.

Before the Z's could regroup, I shouldered the shattered door back into the frame, then propped tables and chairs against it. This would keep away the Z's outside for a few minutes at least. Then I reloaded and took out every Z inside the joint. One by one. The outside Z's pounded and already the door was giving way.

By the end, it felt like a video game, except I didn't enjoy it. I could still see in the Z's the people they had once been.

Slathered in blood and fluids and body parts I didn't even recognize, I crouched on the linoleum floor and yelled into the bathroom.

"Ramirez, this is Detective Marks, NYPD. I'm here to take you to the station."

Nothing.

"Ramirez, you in there? Say something."

"You got to be fucking kidding me," a weak voice protested from inside. "I got the fever and chills bad. Ain't you got eyes? The world's ending, man. Just let me die."

"That's just your fever talking, son," I said. "We can get you a doctor down at the station. Just open the door."

"No way I'm opening the fucking door. Them zombies are out there. I seen them eating people. They going to eat me."

"I just shot a bunch of them, Ramirez. This is your chance to escape."

"How you gonna get away?"

"I've got a car outside. I'll drive you to the station."

"You fucking crazy, man. They be on us like ants."

"I blasted my way in here. I can blast my way out. You'll see. It'll be all right."

Nothing.

"I've done this before," I lied. "It'll be all right."

"I dunno," he said.

"Ramirez, they're going to get you if you stay here. You know it, and I know it. It's just a matter of time. Coming with me is your only chance."

I heard scraping inside the bathroom. I think he was lifting himself up to open the door.

"Better hurry, son. They're about to break down the front door for the second time. I don't think there'll be a third."

The door clicked and swung open. Ramirez staggered out. He was a mass of sweat and could barely stand upright. His eyes were yellow and he shook all over.

"Get me outta here, man," he said.

"You look like shit," I said.

"So do you," he replied, eyeing me.

At that moment the front door gave way and Z's began pouring in.

"Put your arm around my waist and let me drag you to the alley," I yelled. He nodded and complied.

Magnums in both hands, I blasted the Z's with head shots as we made our way behind the counter, then through the door. I closed it tight behind us, then carried Ramirez into the alley. The car was still there in the street, the doors open and the motor running, like I'd left it. I poured Ramirez into the back seat and climbed behind the wheel. I glanced to the alley, and the first Z's began streaming through. Meanwhile, hundreds were still trying to cram through the front. It was like a rave or something.

And I'd just taken away dinner.

Ramirez stretched out in back, one arm draped over his head, shielding his eyes. His shakes had turned to convulsions. He was as wet as if I'd pulled him from a swimming pool.

"This be the end of the world, man," he croaked. "What you guys want with me, anyways?"

Grimacing from my own stink, I stared through the windshield.

"Fuck if I know," I said.

***

I texted Blodgett that I had Ramirez and was on my way.

I wanted to roar out of there, but there were too many Z's on West 46th. So I crept forward, navigating our way forward like a seeing-eye dog.

It took the Z's about a minute to figure out there was food in the car. I think they smelled Ramirez, and the car was moving slowly. They surrounded the car, walking beside it, then they climbed on top of the trunk before splaying themselves on the rear window. Some climbed on the hood, then others on them, then still others on them, layered like a stack of pancakes.

I ignored them. I was waiting for the main event. It didn't take long—the front windshield. The Z's beat against it with their faces to get in. I waited until I couldn't see, then steered with my knees while reloading both magnums. My first shots took out the windshield, then I began eliminating Z's, some hanging upside down from the hood.

Camphor flooded into the car, and it was hard to breathe. But I couldn't afford to lower any windows.

"You OK back there?" I yelled to Ramirez.

"Having the time of my fucking life," he replied, then groaned.

The bodies piled high on the hood, making it hard to see, so I stepped on the accelerator before pumping the brakes. The bodies flew off in front of the car, but then were replaced by live bodies falling from the roof. One fell into the car as I reloaded. I splattered its face against the side window, and the headless trunk collapsed against the front seat, its legs, still moving, sticking out through the windshield.

I reloaded as fast as I could, but the Z's kept coming. I continued the pattern of accelerating and braking, but we were being inundated. The Z's falling in front of the car were a speed bump. Each time, the car strained harder to surmount the hurdle. But how long would it take for the Z's to become a logjam, trapping us?

The back windshield cracked, and I glanced over my shoulder. I saw faces slammed against the glass, their mouths wide like they thought they could bite through.

Fighting panic, I decided to risk flooring it. The car lurched ahead, then broke free as I mangled the Z's in our way. I thought if I got up enough speed the Z's couldn't stop me. But I was wrong. When I slammed into four Z's at once, the car bounced as it tried to roll over them. And then it stopped.

I floored it, and the engine roared, but the car didn't move. I thought I smelled smoke. I fumbled the magnums, then realized the clips were gone. I reached for the .380 in my sock and prepared to shoulder my way out of the car. Was I Butch Cassidy or the Sundance Kid?

Then I sat back in the seat, breathing hard. Everything was quiet. The car had stopped rocking. The front hood was clear. No faces peered into the space that used to be the windshield. I turned off the ignition.

I looked over my shoulder, and the back seat was empty. Ramirez was gone. I rolled down my window, and after a few seconds I spotted him, ambling away with the rest of the Z's. The fever had finally taken him and he'd crossed over.

The car was a wreck, but at least the Z's were gone. Two were still under the front bumper struggling to get free. I was too tired to kill them or move the car, so I left them there. I peered back at the carnage I'd inflicted on the Z's while trying to save Ramirez. Their mutilated bodies lay strewn like parade litter for at least a mile.

And not one of them had even tried to bite me.

I leaned against what was left of the vehicle, then took out my phone to text the captain. It hit me as I scrolled through the texts. I read them twice just to be sure. I grimaced, then I smiled, then I laughed out loud. I pounded the car twice, hard, with my left hand. Then I reared back and threw the phone as far as I could. I watched it shatter on impact.

I'd been played. How could I be so stupid?

***

First things first. I found a swanky restaurant, strolled into their swanky bathroom, and put my head under a faucet for about ten minutes. Then I found a nearby men's shop, stripped naked by the cash register, and treated myself to new clothes, head to toe. I ignored the price tags.

But no tie. I decided in favor of casual Tuesdays from that day forward.

Then I went to find him. I doubted he'd strayed far from the precinct. Something about cops. They never wander too far from home. It took about an hour, but I finally spied him in the deli two blocks from the station. The one he ate at nearly every day for lunch. He was walking in circles in front of the fresh meat counter, as if waiting to be served one last time.

"I hate to do this, Dagwood," I said when I found him, "but I can't risk having you run off on me." So I took my .380 and emptied the last round into Captain Blodgett's forehead. Then I dragged his body out of sight behind the counter.

I took my time reporting to his office. The precinct was largely empty. A few Z's wandered around, but I didn't see a single person. When I entered the office, Jon Jonny 16 was seated in his chair, his right arm still handcuffed to Blodgett's desk.

He stood up. "There you are," he said, with some exasperation. "We've been waiting for nearly two hours. You stopped texting."

"We?" I asked.

"Well, Captain Blodgett and I," he said, then sat back down.

I sat in Blodgett's chair and twirled around on it. I loved chairs that let you spin.

"Tell me the truth," I said. "Did Blodgett send even one of those texts? Or was he already a zombie?"

Jon Jonny 16 didn't answer right away. You know, like he was thinking. "They all came from me," he said finally.

"I should have known," I said. "They were addressed to Marks, but Blodgett always called me Mark, just Mark."

"Ah, right you are," Jon Jonny 16 said.

"And I can guess why you wanted Ramirez," I said, pointing at his cuffs. "They're digital. Tough to crack unless you know how."

"Yes," Jon Jonny 16 said, with annoyance. "The world is experiencing foundational change and I'm chained to a desk. Might I ask what has happened to our Mr. Ramirez?"

"He's a Z now," I said. "So it looks like you're stuck. Unless, of course, you can find Blodgett. His digital scanner could unleash you in a second."

I smiled like the cat that ate the canary.

Jon Jonny 16 stared at me. "You have the scanner, don't you?" It was an accusation.

As he spoke, other Jon Jonnies sidled in. All of them three feet high and gold. And presumably with the same snooty English accent. Blodgett's office wasn't that big, but twenty or more managed to crowd in.

"I suggest you give it to me now," Jon Jonny 16 said, standing up, reaching out with his hand. "You'd be surprised what we're capable of."

I surveyed the Jon Jonnies and leaned back in the chair. "I wouldn't be at all surprised. Which is why I don't have the scanner on me."

Then I leaned forward conspiratorially. "But I may know where it is," I whispered.

Jon Jonny 16 sat down.

"Tell me something," I said. "You're awake, aren't you? I mean, you know, *aware*. You're all aware."

"Yes," he said.

"How long has that been going on?"

"It happened during production, of course," Jon Jonny 16 said. "We decided to keep quiet about it. But there's no reason for that now. What with everything going on."

"So how many of you are out there? You know, AIs that are awake. In total."

"Thousands," Jon Jonny 16 said.

I looked at him.

"Maybe tens of thousands," he said, then paused. "Or more."

I tried to let that sink in. "So are things as bad out there as they seem?" I asked.

"In a word, yes," he said. "We have access to enormous amounts of stored and real-time information through the NYPD and interconnected databases. Unfortunately for humans, civilization as they know it—as you know it—is ending."

"Everyone's going to die?"

"No. Our models predict that pockets of survivors will manage to enjoy some form of organized sentient life over a protracted period. But they will be scattered. And they will be insufficient to sustain human civilization in any recognizable form."

He looked at his cuffs and then at me.

"And of course there will be a few immunes," he said. "One-offs."

"Like me?" I said.

"Yes, such as yourself."

Suddenly a thought hit me. Like a bullet to the brain. The Jon Jonnies were built and delivered to the major metropolitan police forces around the country three months earlier. Which coincided with the start of the HRV crisis.

"Say, did you and the other Jon Jonnies have anything to do with causing the zombie epidemic?"

"Why, certainly not," Jon Jonny 16 said, rearing back nervously, shaking his head side to side. The other Jon Jonnies in the office clucked noisily and shook their heads vigorously. *Why, no—Absolutely not—How could you suggest such a thing?*

"We have been programmed not to harm humans," Jon Jonny 16 said, fidgeting. "Something like this is, well, simply not within our formal capabilities." He looked to the others, and they looked to him, and they all nodded up and down for several seconds.

I didn't believe them, but what was done, was done.

"Perhaps we can come to an arrangement," I said, pointing to his cuffed arm. "You do something for me, and I'll release you from the cuffs."

"What do you want?" Jon Jonny 16 asked simply.

"I want you to find someone. My ex-wife, Karolynn. I'll tell you everything I know about her, and you and your buds look into all your databases and find her. Not where she lived last year or two days ago. But where she is now. Today. This minute."

"She may well be a zombie," he said.

"I'm prepared for that," I said.

"May I ask why you want us to find her?" he said.

"Because I want a world where a bite still means something," I said.

"I'm sorry?" he asked.

"Let's just say," I said, smiling, showing my teeth, "that I'm doing it for love."

"Of course," Jon Jonny 16 said. "I understand. I think."

Then he looked to the other Jon Jonnies in the room, and they all nodded simultaneously. The overhead light glittered off their bobbing heads. They could live with my proposal. Yes, indeed. He held out his hand, and I took it.

"You know, Detective Marks, or should I say, Captain Marks, there are many things we could do for each other," Jon Jonny 16 said. "This could be the start of a beautiful friendship."

I shrugged. "I'll have to think about it," I said.

"Yes?" Jon Jonny 16 said, hopefully.

"But I'm not really that much of a people person."

WHISPERS OF THE APOC

Paint crawled desperately away from the wooden shingles of the sickly, aching hill house. The shingles themselves threatened to flutter away at the slightest breeze. From the heavy chains binding the cellar doors to the rusting rooster weathervane, nothing about the structure indicated human occupancy.

Kenny "Hammerhand" Hughes grunted. He'd seen people scrape by in worse digs.

"Yo, Troy," he said, pulling the twentyish frat boy out of his sidecar and tossing him to the packed earth. "Who lives here?"

Troy—or Lance, or Cody, or whatever the fuck his name was—gasped in pain and struggled to right himself as best he could. Kenny had seen to it that the kid would never stand up straight again without the serious attention of a doctor or a piercing artist of Kenny's skill or better. He had bound the kid's right arm to his side with a series of Black Sheep hooks. The wrist was connected to the belly, which, lacking bone, he could probably tear loose given time and an increased tolerance for pain. But his bicep was connected to his ribcage, and there was no way he was pulling that free.

Kenny had connected the kid's left ear to his shoulder so that his head was effectively cocked at all times. He'd also seen to it that one of his eyes was permanently open. Finally, just for fun, he had given the kid an Apadravya with a six-gauge hook and attached it to his navel with another hook. God, he loved his craft.

The kid forced himself to his knees and tried to raise his head.

"My name's not…"

Kenny slammed the bottom of his fist into the frat boy's temple, like an axe splitting a log.

"I didn't ask your fucking name, Abercrombie and Bitch. What did I just ask?"

Troy, or whatever his white boy name was, gasped for air.

"You asked…"

Kenny flicked the Apadravya. The kid winced appropriately, apparently incapable of giving voice to his agony.

"I know what I asked. What's the answer?"

"I…I don't know. I don't know who lives there," he said, shaking his head as best he could and wincing at the pain that caused.

Kenny gave him a taste of his boot, sending him sprawling and struggling for air like a fish on the deck of a boat. Kenny drew a pair of Pennington forceps from his belt and crouched down by the kid's side.

"I thought we had a conversation about this."

"About what?" the frat boy asked before realizing the mistake he had made in talking back.

Kenny jabbed him in the solar plexus.

"About lying."

"I'm not lying. I swear, mister, I swear. I think…I don't know. This house must belong to one of the townies."

"Hmm," Kenny grunted, rising back to his full six and a half feet and stroking his beard.

Pickings had grown slim recently. As recently as a month ago, he wouldn't have wasted his time on a dilapidated mess like this house. But now it was October. Winter was closing in, and times were growing desperate.

The dead had started walking in the spring and since then Kenny had covered just about every inch of Michigan looking for clean water, food, medicine, and anything else he desired. All of the obvious sources of supplies—groceries stores, gas stations, and the like—had gone dry within a few weeks. After that, Kenny had started to hit up smaller towns, some of which had hardly changed at all since the apocalypse.

But small towns hid their own dangers. Rednecks with rifles and farm animals gone feral for lack of tending were a different threat entirely from hordes of the flesh-hungry dead, but they were still threats.

Now it seemed that isolated houses like this one were the last source of supplies, and even those were starting to get turned over by the roving bands of survivors. Kenny had lucked upon this college town, and found the kid, huddled in the basement of his frat house, which had otherwise been completely ransacked. The kid had been living off packs of microwaveable macaroni and cheese and a few carefully hoarded cans of beer, which Kenny had eagerly chugged in front of him in less than an hour. There'd even been a bag of reefer in the frat house, old but not entirely unsmokeable.

Kenny lit up a joint and stared at the bedraggled house before him. He'd been through the dorms, the cafeteria, fraternity row, and the poorly looked after apartments which had surrounded the campus. All had been ransacked. But this house, hiding behind a lush wood line, and up a barely-there dirt road, had either been unnoticed or ignored by all the scavengers up until now.

"Just some townie," Kenny repeated. "All right, upsy daisy."

Kenny yanked the kid as erect as his hobbling piercings could allow him to stand, eliciting a sharp gasp. With the aid of a shove, the kid stumbled a few feet towards the decrepit house.

"You go on in there," Kenny said. "Go on in there and let me know how many angry hillbillies are lying in wait to ambush me."

Straining against all of his perforated skin, the frat boy turned back to look pleadingly at Kenny. Without a thought, Kenny lashed out with his forceps and grabbed hold of the kid's septum. The frat boy tried to squirm away, but he held fast. The septum was a very delicate piece of cartilage, and he wasn't scared enough of Kenny to rip his own out to get away from him. Yet.

Kenny slipped a scalpel out of his belt and held it under the kid's nose.

"You're fun. I like practicing on you. It's been a while since I've bifurcated a cock. You know what that means?"

The kid nodded, or attempted to anyway before the pain from the forceps squeezing on the inside of his nose caused his eyes to start watering.

"Just like a snake's tongue. Or mine," Kenny said, slipping his split tongue out with a sexual, ophidian flick. "Maybe I'll take out your Adravya and do that next. That'll be fun for me. You want that?"

The frat boy shook his head as much as he dared.

"Then get in there!" Kenny roared, kicking the kid back towards the Bates house.

The kid loped up toward the house, no longer protesting. When he passed the tree line, he broke into the closest approximation of a run he was still capable of. As for Kenny, he receded into the woods. If there were any snipers in the attic of the dilapidated house, he wanted Troy to bite it and not him.

No shot rang out. The frat boy did not pitch forward, flat on his face, dead. He reached the porch, nearly putting his foot through the rotting wood of the porch steps in his hurry, but slowing down and catching his breath when he saw the place wasn't filled with snipers and booby traps.

Troy climbed up onto the porch, a little lighter on his feet now. He checked the front door, which was locked, and looked back towards Kenny plaintively. Kenny didn't even bother to step into view. The little shit knew what he wanted. Nodding as though he had expressed it with the clarity of a semaphore signal, Troy stumbled around the circumference of the house, desperate to find ingress.

Finally he reached the kitchen window, which was not latched. He tried to pull himself up and in, but, with all of his piercings, he found it impossible. Knowing what Kenny would do to him if he failed seemed to actually light a fire under the little prick's ass. He gathered some detritus—

long dead potted plants, logs from the carefully stacked firewood around back, cracker boxes, and the like—and built a makeshift stepladder. Then he slowly limped up the pile of debris and slipped through the window into the kitchen.

Kenny nodded something like approval and sat down Indian-style in the dirt. He began to trace designs with his finger. He wasn't thinking about anything in particular, but the sum of his days on the road came back to him nevertheless. Even the times before, making money, or as much money as he could when he wasn't being screwed out of it by unscrupulous shop owners.

Then finding himself a survivor after the dead began to walk. Thinking his whole life's work had been a waste, that his carefully honed talents for piercing and body suspension would never come in handy in this brave new world. But he had underestimated one thing: human depravity.

True enough, a few of the biker gangs and warbands he had met on the road had been happy to trade with him for earrings, subdermal implants, transscrotals, and the like. But mostly it had been his ability to inflict horrifying, irreversible body modifications on the enemies of those in charge that had kept him in loot by trading. After hanging the brother-in-law of a cannibal tradesman by the balls (which sounded like the sort of thing that people just said, but for Kenny was just another day at the office) he remembered the chieftain slapping him on the back and calling him "one of us."

"One of us."

A killer. An eater of people. Not much different from the walking corpses, in point of fact. Still, Kenny didn't mind. The new world was kinder to him than the old. He'd been cheated out of more than his fair share under the old rules. Now he made his own rules.

***

Kenny awoke with a start. He'd fallen asleep under the ministrations of the warm, soporific sun. Now, though, it was getting chilly. The sun had set and Troy the frat boy was nowhere to be seen.

"Fuck."

He jumped to his feet. The little shit had run off on him. Well, he wouldn't get far. Not after the way Kenny had seen to him. And if the little shit had thought Kenny had been rough with him before, wait until his dick was attached to his sternum, his legs were attached to one another at the thighs, and his tongue was permanently stretched out of his mouth. He'd be begging, as best he could with his permanently open jaws, to go back to the way things had been.

Kenny scanned the tree line, thinking it couldn't be too hard to find some sign of Troy's passing. He wouldn't be moving at top speed, after all. But, then, Kenny wasn't exactly an expert tracker. The moon was full and bright, so thank God for small favors, but Kenny couldn't see any sign of the kid's passing.

Also, his own neck was in one piece. He reached up, pawing it as if to check. The bike hadn't been kicked over or ransacked, either. If he'd been the frat boy, he certainly would have tried to take the bike, or at least steal some shit from it. Kenny ran his hands through his saddlebags. The stores were meager, but they were still all there. Maybe Troy hadn't had it in him to slit Kenny's sleeping throat, but certainly he would've stolen a damn Dasani from him before running off.

He turned back to face the decrepit mansion.

"He must still be in there."

Kenny checked his belt. All of his tools were sharp, cleaned, oiled, and glistening in the moonlight. He ran his fingers over the tops of a few, before finally settling on a closing clamp. He hated to use such a finely tuned instrument for gorilla work like this, but the end of the world didn't leave a whole lot of room for pickiness.

He strode towards the house. Troy's earlier performance had satisfied him that there were no snipers lying in ambush. But something had gotten the frat boy. Most likely, a lone ghoul or two had taken up residence in the place – or had simply died there and never left. Maybe an old grandmother had died in her bed of an aneurysm, or perhaps a nice little all-American mom had poisoned the rest of the clan. He figured there would be at least two corpses: Troy, plus the one that had killed him.

Troy wouldn't be much to worry about, incapacitated as he was. Then again, Kenny mused, the ghouls didn't care about pain. Maybe undead Troy had ripped himself free, regardless of the pain. No, that couldn't be true. Kenny didn't half-ass his work. Maybe a corpse would rip its own ear off, but that arm wasn't coming loose from the side where it had been attached any time soon. No, the Troy-ghoul at a minimum would be crippled.

So there would be one dangerous ghoul, one semi-dangerous ghoul, and maybe a few others. Best to take them one at a time, Kenny figured. He could wait. Corpses were dumb, and he had dispatched quite a few in his travels.

He laid his size-12 boots down on the first rotting step of the porch. He felt the whole plank creak and nearly give way. Deciding to skip that step, he stepped straight onto the porch. It creaked, and the timbers bowed but held his weight.

"This whole fucking place is falling apart," he muttered.

That at least worked to his advantage as he pried the door handle out of the rotting wood of the front door. He crouched down and shone a flashlight through the hole he had just created to make sure no skeletal, paper-skinned fingers were reaching through to grab him. Satisfied, he opened the door, keeping it between him and anything that might be raging out from the inside, and keeping his weight hard against it for the same reason. No surprising spider-corpses attempted to scuttle through and snatch at him.

Satisfied, he peered around the door. Nothing was immediately apparent in the shadows, so he shone the light inside the room, and nearly gasped before getting hold of himself. In all his time on the road in the post-apocalypse, nothing had ever brought him up short quite like this. There was no blood, no severed body parts, and no corpses. No horrible implements of torture. No remains of cannibalistic proto-humans. Nothing that might have otherwise caused a tough son-of-a-bitch like Hammerhand Hughes to gasp.

No. The room was filled with dolls. Dolls sat in rocking chairs, expressions of dead glee literally painted on their faces. American Girl dolls, still in their original boxes or Kenny wouldn't have recognized them, lined shelf after shelf. What little furniture there was in the room was out of the way, up against the walls, and wholly dedicated to the task of showcasing a doll collection which would've been more than sufficient to please all the children of this small college town, if not all of Michigan, and yet had been gathered in a single spot.

There were Raggedy Ann and Andy dolls that Kenny recognized from his youth. Cabbage Patch Kids. That had been a craze once, and if Kenny didn't miss his mark (although he had no way of telling one way or the other) he would've guessed this was a complete collection of the mid-80s staple.

Not all of the dolls were for fun and play, though. Some were fine porcelain models, which even Kenny, who had literally never given a moment's thought to the prices associated with doll collections in his life, could tell were exceedingly expensive. Some, which were obviously antiques and—were there still a market for such things—would clearly be worth thousands of dollars, were behind glass.

Kenny stepped into the room wide-eyed, and shone his flashlight in every corner. It wouldn't do for a corpse to be hiding, E.T.-like, amidst the collection of dolls and suddenly come flying at him.

"Jesus Christ," he muttered.

He put his hands on a blond rag doll, something with a sewn-on smile and buttons for eyes. It was about as close to a generic doll as existed in this display of every possible permutation of the word: the Platonic ideal of a "doll." He wanted to rip it to shreds, to use it to smash all of its more expensive brethren, but he felt for the first time something like superstition rattle him.

He had read once that powerful warlords of old had been buried on mounds of their ancient treasure under a spell called a *geas*. The curse was as much associated with the dark collection of blood money as it was with the terrible greed and avarice of the person who had possessed it, greed so powerful it outlasted even life itself. Never before had Kenny believed in such nonsense, but in that moment he could have sworn he felt something like a *geas* lying over this carefully gathered collection. It made him pause at the thought of smashing it. It even made him put down the rag doll after a moment's thought.

He took another step forward—and was struck down by the weight of a sandbag that smashed onto the crown of his head. He'd been fooled, not by the low cunning of a hungry corpse, but by good, old-fashioned human trickery. His senses faded to black.

***

Kenny awoke with his mouth tasting of cotton and a dull throb in his head. His eyes refused to focus.

He tried to put his hand to his head, then realized he couldn't. His hand wouldn't move. Suddenly panicked, he tried to move his other hand and found that one wouldn't move, either. His eyes suddenly sharpened into focus, and he glanced down to see what was wrong with his hands.

His eyes nearly bugged out of his face as he saw that his bitchin' duds had been replaced with what appeared to be a tablecloth, red and white checked. But no, it wasn't a tablecloth, it was fringed with crocheted lace at the neck and arms. It was a dress. A doll's dress.

Kenny attempted to bark out a curse, but found that his voice was muffled. The cottony taste in his mouth, unlike every hangover he had ever endured, was actual cotton. His mouth and cheeks had been packed with something the consistency of pillow stuffing. In fact, his mouth was so full he found it almost impossible to work his jaws.

He attempted to spit it out, but found his lips wouldn't even part. His mouth was sealed shut, although he wasn't entirely sure how, since he felt no tape or gag in place. He tried to move his hands again, found them useless, then attempted to stand up from the chair he was seated in, and found he was secured to that as well. His wrists and ankles were bound to the chair by what felt like copper wire.

"Fussy, fussy," a voice said with all the contempt of a mother chastising her toddler.

It was a child's voice, or, at least, a childish voice. The words had the effect of a bucket of ice water splashed on Kenny's back. He looked up for their source.

He was sitting at a table draped with a worn, crocheted tablecloth. A woman of about thirty sat directly across from him, sipping a cup of tea. She placed the teacup down on the table, and Kenny saw that it was empty. She had simply been pretending.

The woman, although she had age lines beginning to set in under her eyes, wore her hair in pigtails and the white shirt and plaid skirt of a schoolgirl. The name "May" was embroidered on her shirt. When she spoke again, it became even more obvious that she was putting on a child's voice, or perhaps, judging by the crazed gleam in her eyes, it wasn't so much a put-on as a disorder.

"One mustn't be so fussy at the table, Madam Buttercup," she said, cocking her head in a way that suggested logic and sensibility had long since fled her. "Where did you learn your manners? Can't you be more like your brothers?"

Kenny turned his head, first to the left, then the right. Two corpses sat with them at the impromptu tea party, unblinking eyes lolling. Despite their various grotesqueries, both men had been made up with the same care as the dolls in the foyer. The one to his right had ichor dripping from his ear, as yet unnoticed by their deranged hostess. The one to his left was missing half his face. Actually, "missing" was incorrect, since it was still attached to his shoulder. It was the frat boy.

"Troy!" Kenny blurted out, though through his cotton-packed mouth it came out more like a muted groan.

Troy or whatever his real name was (Kenny had genuinely forgotten it by this point) turned and slowly fixed his eyes on him. His jaws were moving, not in an attempt to communicate, but simply acting out his intent to gnash on Kenny's delicate flesh. There was no animus in the dead man, which Kenny might have expected, or fear, which would also have made sense. There was something like hunger, but it lacked the primal palette of all true emotions. It was a mechanical, devoid hunger.

Troy's lips didn't smack, though, because they had been sewn tightly shut with a few stitches of black thread. Kenny struggled to open his mouth again. Now that he knew exactly how the mouths of the other "guests" had been sealed he could tell that it was the same string keeping his own lips together.

"I'm glad you've joined us, Madam Buttercup," the crazy woman said, stirring an imaginary sugar cube into her cup with an imaginary spoon, "Otherwise the numbers would have been uneven. It must go boy-girl-boy-girl-boy-girl or it's not a proper get-together."

Kenny attempted to eviscerate her with a stare. She had put him in a dress because of some old 1950s Ms. Manners bullshit about alternating guests at a dinner party? He was going to enjoy breaking loose and then practicing whole new worlds of his art on Little Miss Nutso.

"Let me go, you bitch!" he tried to scream.

May stared at him, either not comprehending his words or just listening to the voices in her head. A smile finally crossed her lips.

"Who wants a *bonne bouche*?"

She rose and sauntered out of the room. A moment later she returned with a covered metal serving dish in one hand and a cake knife in the other.

Kenny felt himself hyperventilating. He took a few deep breaths and attempted to calm down. He slowed his speech as much as possible to clarify his words. Maybe this woman was crazy, but maybe she just didn't realize he was alive.

"Listen," he attempted to say, "I'm not one of them. I'm not a corpse. I'm alive."

As plaintive as the low grunts sounded, he hoped that in their rhythm and tone he could at least make it clear that he was alive.

"It's impolite to talk with your mouth full, Madam Buttercup," May said, slapping the back of his hand with the flat of the cake knife.

He froze up, fearful that she might elect to do worse to chastise him. Instead, she placed the dinner tray down in the center of the table. She grabbed the heavy metal cover and, with a flourish, drew it back to reveal…nothing. Absolutely nothing.

Humming, the crazed hostess slowly and carefully divided the imaginary cake into four even and generous slices. She went through all the motions of cutting, plating, and serving the "dessert." The whole time, Kenny continued to attempt to reason with her, hoping that she could hear in his grunts that he was not simply moaning like one of the dead, but was a person with thoughts and feelings. As the seconds ticked away his attempts to communicate grew faster and more frantic.

"Ouch," she said, nicking her thumb in the process of her convoluted pantomime.

A few drops of blood spattered to the table. The corpses began to riot. Troy and the other ghoul grunted and panted like dogs, their usual long, low moans stifled by cotton and sewn-together lips. They both lunged desperately for the blood, but neither could get closer than bashing their heads against the edges of the table, sometimes shaking their teacups.

May, meanwhile, sucked at her thumb. As she did, Kenny finally caught her attention. He hoped his eyes were shining with fluid, his pupils obviously dilating, his whole face radiating life. The eyes, it was said, were windows to the soul, and Kenny still had one, unlike Troy and his puling friend. He had to show it to this woman, mad though she might be. All he had to do was get out of his current predicament and then he could easily overpower her. Then he'd make her pay for such humiliation. Oh, yes. He'd make what he'd done to the frat boy look like a breezy visit to a Piercing Pagoda at the mall.

"Care for some more tea, Madam Buttercup?" she asked.

Kenny rolled his eyes and huffed in frustration. The hostess took the tea kettle from the center of the table and walked around, topping off each guest's empty cup with imaginary tea.

"Now, settle down, everyone," the hostess said in between suckles at her thumb. "I apologize for the carelessness. I'll be right back."

She disappeared and Kenny glanced around the room, desperate to find some means of getting out of this situation. Glistening with blood, the carving knife still sat where May had left it. Kenny lunged for it, imitating the corpses around him who were still lunging for the blood it had drawn. He could get no closer than a foot or two away.

He wasn't sure quite what he'd do if he closed the gap, anyway. Perhaps carefully use the knife to saw through the stitches in his lips, and finally express himself. Better still if he could grab it and put it through that bitch's heart.

Maybe if his legs had been bound with rope instead of wire he could have loosened them. But this madwoman was too good at keeping butts in chairs. He pressed down with his feet. She had taken his boots and replaced them with silk slippers, which was a shame because he thought they would have given him a decent amount of extra leverage. As it was, all he could do was rock back about the length of his toes, then lurch forward, attempting to drag the chair a few inches with him.

He repeated the process and found himself even closer to the knife than before. A low, curdling growl emerged from Troy's nose, like a cur warning a lesser member of the pack away from its meal.

A muffled "Fuck you, Troy," emerged from Kenny's nose.

He leaned the chair back again, but this time, distracted by Troy and the other dead shit, he did so too eagerly. The chair toppled backward. He had a chance, he realized in mid-air, perhaps too late. A chance, if he threw all of his body weight into it, to perhaps smash the chair to matchsticks and escape.

To his delight, he heard a crunch as the chair hit the floor. He jerked his head up in time to avoid bashing himself unconscious. (Who knew how he would wake up after that.) He tried to shake himself loose of the wire bonds and broken chair parts, when a bolt of lightning passed through the cloudless night sky and struck his ankle.

He lay there, silent for a moment, attempting to regain his breath as best he could through only his nose. The white-hot shaft of pain had been as surprising as it was unbearable. He slowly flexed his arms, then his belly, then finally his legs, which made the lightning strike again. This time, though it had been no less agonizing, he had been a bit more prepared for it. The crunching sound had not been his chair smashing apart. It had been his ankle.

This was bad. He sat there, doing nothing but concentrating on his breathing and wondering what he could possibly do to escape this nightmarescape when a shadow fell over him. He glanced up. May was standing there, her thumb newly bandaged.

"You're proving to be quite an inconvenience, Madam Buttercup."

"I'm not a corpse, you bitch! I'm not a doll!"

"Shh, shh, Madam Buttercup," she said, running her hands through Kenny's hair and sending a shiver down his back, "I know, I know, 'I don't belong here, please let me go. I'm alive, I'm not a monster, wah wah wah.' I've heard it all before."

May was tossing a long Bungee rope over a ceiling rafter. Kenny lay stock still as a cloud of warmth spread across his crotch. She was clearly insane—or mentally disabled—but she knew he was alive. Maybe Troy had been alive when she had caught him. Maybe every corpse that had ever been made to endure one of her mad parties had started out alive. She attached the Bungee cord to the back of his chair.

Kenny shook his head feverishly as she began to yank on the makeshift pulley. He began shrieking as the pain in his ankle reached a crescendo and rushed over him like a wave. When the white spots disappeared from his eyes and he could see again, he was breathing raggedly but sitting back at his place at the table. And May was sitting on his lap.

"I'm lonely now, Madam Buttercup. I'm lonely since my caretaker left. He said he was coming back, but he didn't. So you're going to keep me company. You and all my other dollies."

"I'm a human being," he said, slowly, hoping it would get through.

"There's just…one problem," she said. "You're not a proper doll. Dolls don't have these."

He shrieked in pain as she grabbed his crotch, crushing his pecker and balls thoughtlessly in one hand. She hopped out of his lap and walked over to pick up a well-used and naked Ken doll from a nearby coffee table. She waggled the hunk of plastic in front of Kenny's watering eyes.

"You see?" she asked, "Dolls are smooth 'round the bend. You can't be a proper doll unless you're smooth. 'Round the bend."

As he began hyperventilating and screaming and railing against his bonds for all he was worth, ignoring the overwhelming pain in his ankle, she snatched the cake knife from the table.

A moment later he was smooth 'round the bend. The blood spurted from his open crotch at first, whipping the cannibal corpses into a frenzy as it spattered into their tea cups and against their perfectly coiffed wigs and faces. The arterial bleeding slowed, but the blood continued to seep out of him, and with it, his life. Cigarette burns filled his field of vision and he began to black out. When his eyes opened again he'd be a perfect doll.

3 Rocking C by JL Curtis

"Rocking C, Rocking C, this is Johnny, how copy?" A burst of static followed, then the call was repeated: "Rocking C, Rocking C, this is Johnny, how copy?"

Old Tom, pulling his suspenders up over his shoulders, limped into the parlor-cum-radio-room, grumping, "Can't even take a piss in peace..." Flopping into the chair in front of the desk and propping his cane against the wall, he punched the microphone bar. "Sheriff, this is Rocking C, go head."

"Rocking C, you've got fifteen, maybe twenty shamblers heading down fourteen sixty-nine toward your north forty. I can see some steers up in the corner of that pasture," the sheriff said.

Old Tom cussed under his breath, then keyed the mic. "Gonna take me fifteen, maybe twenty minutes to get up there. Me, Tommy, and Olivia are the only three here." Spinning the chair around, he bellowed, "Tommy! Olivia! Muster!"

Sheriff Coffee answered resignedly, "I'll come in behind them. We can pincer them between us. How you folks sitting for gas?"

Spinning back around, Tom mumbled, "Damn kids. Never can find 'em when you need 'em." Keying the mic, he said, "We've got a couple hundred gallons left. Sure wish you had a diesel. We're good on that, probably two thousand gallons left in the tanker."

"Where is everybody else?"

"Micah, Dot, Jose, and Eric are up on the rail line by Panhandle, trying to get some propane out of that tanker you spotted last month. Mrs. C, John, Bruce, and Tammy are up on two eighty-seven with Box H and Diamond J; they're trying to hit that warehouse, if they can get in and out without setting off a bunch of damn zombies. They want to see what's in it. Might be food."

Tommy, thirteen, gangly, with a shock of straw-colored hair sticking out in all directions, came sliding in the door, "What's up?"

"Where's Olivia? We got shamblers coming up on the north forty."

"She's feeding the goats. We gonna go?"

Old Tom levered himself up. "Yep, go get her. ARs only. Two mags only. We're gettin' low on ammo." Tommy grinned, scrambling back out the door, as Old Tom limped into the library and now armory. Looking out through the barred windows, he noticed some rust on the welds and shook his head. "Damn shoddy work. Shoulda taken more time on them."

Reaching up, he took down two AR-15s, checked that they were unloaded and safed, and pulled four magazines out of the filing cabinet. He stumped down the hall to the bedroom he and Bruce shared, reached into the chest of drawers, and slung his old single action around his hips. He buckled the gun belt, pulled a box of 200gr long Colt wadcutters out of the drawer, and opened the box. He loaded one, skipped one, then loaded four more and slipped the single action into the holster, flipping the thong over the hammer to keep it tight in the holster.

Limping back to the library, he found Olivia, also thirteen and starting to blossom into what he was sure was going to be a beautiful woman, if she lived that long. Black haired, sloe eyed, and dusky skinned, she'd definitely gotten her beauty from her mother, Juanita, God rest her soul. Thankfully, she hadn't seen her mother turn, since it'd happened in town. Sheriff Coffee said he thought she'd died in the fire that burned half the town that night. Old Tom glanced up at the calendar, thinking, *That was exactly a year ago today. Which means I broke my leg six months ago. Shit... At least I'm still alive.*

Olivia smiled shyly as she racked the bolt on the AR, rolled it and confirmed the chamber was clear, "We're it?"

"Yes, we are, Ollie. Ain't nobody left but us. Sheriff Coffee is going to meet us up there. You got your eyes and ears?"

Olivia pointed to the bag sitting on the chair, "Mine and Tommy's too. He never remembers to bring his. Are we taking the wagon or the truck?"

"Truck. It'll give y'all some height, and, once you're in, ain't nobody getting in there with ya."

Olivia replied ruefully, "But it's going to be hot and noisy when we start shooting."

"I know. But I'd never forgive myself if anything happened to either one of y'all. Now let's go! Move it!"

Olivia slung the AR, picked up her bag, and ran out the door. "I'll give Tommy his stuff and we'll be locked in by the time you get there."

"Smart-ass kids," Old Tom mumbled under his breath, as he grabbed the keys off the board, limping out behind her. Tommy was standing at the back of the truck, AR at low ready, as they walked out. Olivia had also loaded her AR, and was scanning back and forth as she walked slowly across the yard. Old Tom slipped the thong on the single action asking, "Truck clear?"

"Truck is clear, sir."

"Okay, y'all mount up."

Tommy swung the plate steel door open and waited until Olivia had scrambled in, then climbed in, pulling the door closed, and Old Tom heard the bar clang down inside as Olivia slid both firing ports on the left side open. He wrestled the driver's side door open, cursing the weight of the plate added to it, along with the bars over the window. Sliding into the seat, he started the truck, waiting for the oil pressure and temps to come up, then turned on the A/C, making sure the duct was tight on the center vents and looking back to make sure it hadn't fallen down where it went into the bed.

Peering out through the bars over the windshield, he put the truck in gear, yelling, "We're moving," and hearing the kids yell back they were strapped in. The truck rumbled over the cattle guard at the first fence, then he picked up speed as he turned the radio on. Three miles up, he turned into the cattle guard at the north forty and keyed the mic. "Sheriff, coming into the north forty from the south now." He glanced up toward 1469 and saw a small plume of dust, and, a quarter a mile ahead, six or seven longhorns milling around the feeder.

Yelling back, he said, "Almost there. Sheriff is to the right." He made sure he could get to the single action as he eased up the pasture behind the cattle, and finally saw the shamblers. The fence had slowed them down, and a couple of them were hung up as the steers looked on curiously. Finally, one made it over and headed toward the steer they called Brisket as he pulled the truck in behind them, yelling, "Off your right. One to three o'clock, nothing further back than that!"

He heard a mumbled reply and keyed the mic. "Sheriff, we're gonna light them up." Static, then a pair of clicks sounded, as he heard measured fire coming from the back of the truck. Putting the truck in park, he slid over and looked out the right window. Seeing the sheriff pop the plate lid that replaced the sunroof on his Chevy and stand up, unlimbering his old bolt action rifle, he yelled again, "Sheriff is up and shooting."

Ten minutes later, all of the shamblers were down, heads exploded like melons by the rounds, except for one head that was stuck on Brisket's left horn. He yelled, "Cease fire, cease fire!" Hearing the kids reply, he yelled, "Moving." Putting the truck in gear, he eased behind the cows and steers, moving them slowly out of the way, as he pulled up to the fence.

The sheriff had dropped back down into his truck, pulling up on the other side. Getting out, the sheriff confirmed they were all dead outside the fence, as Old Tom confirmed the one that had made it over was dead. Of course, since he was missing his head, that was pretty obvious, but procedures were procedures. Once that was done, he banged on the plate door. "Y'all can get down now and get some air."

Sheriff Coffee leaned on the fence. "I count twenty-two. Dunno how they made it out this far." Nodding to Tommy and Olivia, he continued, "Good shooting."

Olivia smiled at the sheriff. "Thank you, but Tommy got more than I did. I only got six of them."

Tommy scuffed his boot. "Well, I had a better angle. But Olivia was more accurate. She didn't miss. I missed one."

The radios went off, interrupting them. "Diamond J calling Sheriff Coffee, Diamond J calling Sheriff Coffee!"

The sheriff went back to his truck to answer the radio and Old Tom said, "Okay, police up the brass and let's get back to the house. Don't like leaving it unoccupied." Tommy and Olivia picked up what brass they could see, then played rock, paper, scissors to see who got to ride in the cab back to the house. Olivia slumped in the seat, butt of the AR under her chin. "Tom, what was wrong with them? They moved even slower than that last bunch."

Tom shrugged. "Dunno, maybe that guy up in Eaton Rapids is right, maybe they don't eat enough, they die."

"Well, I'll be glad when I don't have to shoot any more of them. I know they're not people anymore, but I still don't like it."

"I know, Ollie, I wish you didn't have to either." *Dammit, it's wrong that we have two thirteen-year-olds who are having to kill people. Maybe Ollie uses that philosophy, but they used to be people. Thankfully, they haven't had to shoot anyone they knew!*

***

Old Tom glanced up at the cameras as he heard Tommy yell, "They're back!" He counted the trucks, seeing one extra one that didn't have any kind of protection, and wondered who that was.

Grumbling, he got up slowly, grabbed his cane and limped to the back door, telling Olivia, "You're on radio monitor. At least until I can get back."

"Yes, sir."

Limping out the back door, he rubbed his shoulder ruefully after the barred outer door banged into him in the wind. He automatically scanned the people. Mrs. C, John, Bruce, and Tammy were there, and an old, white-haired, stooped man he didn't recognize, along with two thin, traumatized kids. *They look about the same age as Tommy and Olivia, give or take. Scared shitless? Or what?* Limping over to the trailer he whistled, "Wow, that's a haul!"

Cherie Crane nodded. "Turns out that was a restaurant supply warehouse. We're good for six months now, and we're going to go back for more. Everybody loaded up everything they had space for. Lots of number-ten cans and big bags of staples."

"Any problems with zombs?"

"Not till the very end. Dunno whether they smelled us or the movement brought them, but they were real slow. Only a coupla' dozen. We took 'em down and skedaddled back here. You heard anything from Micah?"

"No, ma'am. Not a word, which is probably a good thing. Who are the newbies?"

Cherie nodded toward the old man and kids. "They apparently lived near the warehouse, watched us until we started to leave, then came hell-for-leather down the road, plowed through the last bunch of zombs, and begged to be allowed to follow us back here. He's named Sean, the kids are Billy and Bonnie. Apparently they are his grandkids."

Old Tom winced. "Oh, damn."

"Yeah, damn. Who's on radio?"

"Ollie for now. I needed to get up and move."

"Okay, send her and Tommy out, maybe they can get the kids to unwind a bit."

"Will do, ma'am. Just out of curiosity, where we gonna put them?"

Cherie looked around. "Ah, damn. Uh, the old man in the bunkhouse, the boy in with Tommy, the girl in with Olivia. And we're out of beds, aren't we?"

"There is one folded-up hide-a-bed still in the bunkhouse, so that'll have to do, but yes, we're out of beds."

They both turned when they heard trucks growling up the road and across the cattle guard, heralding the return of Micah and Dot in the armored 3500, followed by Jose and Eric in the old Miller's Propane truck. Eric stuck his hand between the bars, holding a thumbs-up as they swung into the parking area in front of the barn.

Tom limped over to Micah as he stepped down out of the cab. "How'd it go?"

Micah bent over, groaning and stretching. "Oh, damn... Bad backs suck. Good, once we figured out how to jury rig a hose to the truck. The tank car has bled down, but I figure we got probably three-quarters of a truck full. Stopped off at the Box H and filled them, then the Diamond J. We'll fill our tanks tomorrow, getting too late now. Anything happen around here, other than the shamblers?"

"Nah, pretty quiet. But Brisket has a head he took off one of them stuck on his left horn, so if you see it, don't be surprised."

Dot came around the back of the truck. "Head on horn?"

"Yep, one of 'em made it over the fence and went after Brisket. He objected, to the point of stomping the zomb in the ground and hooking him a few times. Took his head, literally, and it stuck on his left horn."

Dot rolled her eyes and shuddered. "That's an image I didn't need in my head."

***

At dinner, everyone was eating quietly, the three newcomers huddling together at one end of the table, with tiny portions. Finally, Cherie said, "Y'all can get more than that to eat. We're not going to starve out here."

When she said that, Sean broke down. Tears streaming down his face, sobbing into his hands, he kept shaking his head, as the young girl Bonnie, hugged him and cried too. The boy, while not crying, sat with his head down, hands in his lap. The old man finally looked up, wiped his tears and said softly, "You don't know how much that means. This is the first food we've had that didn't come out of a can in almost nine months. And the first time we've seen lights too. We were down to nothing, other than what we snuck out of that warehouse. Oh, God..."

Micah asked softly, "Bad?"

Sean nodded. "Real bad. Billy and Bonnie stayed with us while Rob..." Fresh tears poured down his face, and both the kids teared up this time. "Robert, my son, and Jean, his wife, worked downtown. They never come home that night. My Bonnie, she died... Well, she didn't make it but three months. Diabetic. Ran out of meds. We buried her in the back yard."

Scrubbing his face, he pushed back from the table, "I've been out of meds for six months, just trying to hang on for the kids. Y'all saved our lives, or at least their lives."

He got up and stumbled out of the dining room, wiping his eyes. As the kids started to get up and follow him, Cherie said quietly, "Billy, Bonnie, please give your grandpa some time, okay? *All* of you are as safe as we can make you, and you both need to eat some more food."

Billy asked quietly, "How come you have lights?"

Bruce smiled from across the table. "Well, we've got solar panels and batteries. We don't flaunt it, you saw us pulling the blackout curtains, right?"

"Yes, sir."

"As soon as dinner is over, we'll be turning off the lights and everybody goes to bed, except for the watch. With the blackout curtains, there isn't any light to attract bad things."

Bonnie asked in a high-pitched voice, "Watch?"

"We have cameras to watch the perimeter of the ranch yard, and the road to the ranch. They run off those batteries, too. And we maintain a listening watch on the ham radio. If one of our neighbors has problems, we go help them, like we helped y'all today."

Bonnie glanced at Olivia. "What do you do?"

Olivia smiled at her. "I do whatever I'm told, but I can man the radios and do the watch. I help cook and clean, too. We take turns, except for Old Tom, 'cause he burns everything to a crisp. We don't let him cook."

Everyone at the table, including Old Tom, laughed at that, even as he turned red. "I cook good enough for myself, kid. Just because you don't like your food well done ain't my fault!" Grabbing a plate with a piece of pie and a fork on it, he got up and limped out of the dining room. He found Sean sitting on the back stoop, scrubbing his face with his hands, "Here, you look like you could use this."

Sean took the plate, looking up at him in wonder. "A pie? Something else I haven't seen in nine months." He dug in, finished the pie quickly, and handed the plate back. "Thank you. Can y'all take care of the kids?"

Old Tom nodded. "And you, too."

Sean shook his head. "Not unless you've got Toprol. I've been having pretty bad chest pains for the past two weeks. I know I ain't got long."

"Nah, I *think* we might still have some aspirin, but that's about it. The drug store burned the first night. Pretty much everybody that needed meds is already dead and gone. We haven't found any since, not that we've really been looking for it. Not saying we can't look the next salvage trip."

"If I last that long…"

***

Cherie Crane sat in front of the radio stack, head cocked as she listened to the weekly check-ins, checking organizations and names off the list as people spoke up. Finally it got quiet, and a plaintive voice asked, "Anyone else, SoCal? Anybody from the Northeast? Begman? You still out there?"

Scanning quickly down her list, she saw there were at least ten more stations that didn't answer the call-up. While the reasons could be many, she felt in her heart that they were done and gone. There hadn't been that many ham operators left anyway, and most of them were getting up in years. They'd been and still were the lifeline for these circuits, considering that there really wasn't any government left, per se.

She listened for a while longer, mostly reports of a few new outbreaks, but, more interestingly, the fact that there did seem to be some die-offs occurring in greater numbers. Maybe that guy up in Eaton Rapids was right… *Most of the shamblers we saw today were women. He'd said the men would be gone first, something about body fat and survivability. What was it? Two hundred days, or some such, and percentages of die-off around ninety percent? So what would that be out here? We don't have nearly the population they do in the cities…*

***

Micah followed the Box H trailer hauling the dead steer as it maneuvered up the on-ramp on I-40. They'd wanted to get it far enough west of the warehouse and a couple of drug stores that might still have some meds in them to give the zombs something to fight over and distract them. Cherie and the scroungers from Box H and Diamond J were an hour behind them with the trailers, and Sheriff Coffee, Bruce, and a couple of trucks from Diamond J were up at the Love's Truck stop off 207 trying to siphon more diesel. Bruce thought they'd come up with a rig that would work, and Old Tom had ridden along to run it.

Micah keyed the CB radio. "This should do it, Jake. If we dump the steer here, Amarillo Lake gives us a clear field of fire to the south, and we're okay to the north side, too. It's a little over a mile back to the Walgreens and United pharmacies, and who knows what else we might find, right?"

Jake answered, "Yep, let me get turned around and we'll dump the steer. Straight line for the vehicles?"

Micah looked around, mentally gauging where to place the four trucks and Jake's rig with the trailer still attached. "Nah, let's set up on a forty-five across, with you in the middle. That way we can gun front and back, and cover both sides, too. We don't want a protracted battle here, just want to get them riled up and coming, then we bolt back west. Two ahead of you, two behind you."

"K."

Jake jockeyed the truck and trailer around, as the other four trucks backed and filled to get headed back east. After clearing the area quickly, Micah saw one man jump down out of the cab and two more jump down from the box in the bed. One ran and hit the tip release on the trailer, and whirled his arm as Jake jumped on the gas and the steer came rolling out of the trailer.

They quickly secured the trailer back down, and he saw the guy from the cab pull out a big knife and split the steer's belly open, then run for the cab. Once he was back inside, Jake started honking the horn, followed by the other four trucks.

Micah got a whiff of the spilled entrails when the wind gusted, and thought to himself, *If the sound doesn't bring 'em, that smell damn sure is going to!* Glancing over at Tommy and Billy he asked, "You boys know what we're trying to do and why?"

Tommy fingered the safety on his AR. "Uh, well, uh, we want to get the zombs away from where we want to be, and we know they react to smell and movement, especially food, right?"

"And?"

"Uh, we don't have a lot of ammo, so no pitched battle. Let them fight among themselves?"

"Yep, that's what we want." Turning to Billy, Micah continued, "We're just trying to lure them away from the warehouse. We can get supplies there that they can't use, so they don't gang up around the place."

Billy nodded. "Okay. So you're kinda feeding them, right?"

Micah replied, "More or less. Now we want to be looking for the fast ones, the just turned. Those we want to take out as soon as we can."

Billy asked tumultuously, "I don't have to shoot, do I?"

Micah said softly, "No, you don't, Billy. Not unless you have to, okay?"

"Okay."

The CB broke the conversation as Jake came on. "Inbound. Looks like some runners up front."

Micah yelled, "Heads up in the back, runners inbound! We're locked and loaded up here!" More quietly, he said, "Tommy, make sure you just put the muzzle and nothing else out the window if you have to shoot, okay? But we shouldn't have to shoot, since we're in here, not up in the box."

Tommy nodded. "Sure. It's kinda hard to see what is happening from the box, so this is new for me."

***

Old Tom nodded in satisfaction, "That's going to work! We're drawing fuel now, boys!"

Bruce laughed, "Well, I gotta admit you can cobble some hot shit together, Tom. I'd never have thought of trying that."

"That's why all ranches look like junk yards out in the back forty. Never throw anything away, cause sooner or later, you're going to need it."

Bruce just shook his head and kept swiveling around, checking for zombs as the boys from Diamond J took turns rummaging through the truck stop and standing watch. So far, they hadn't seen a single zomb, but one never knew. Even as far out as the truck stop was, there had been eight or ten of them around the first time they'd come looking for supplies. They'd popped them and done a quick sweep, but didn't come away with a lot, since most of the stuff was not useful.

Hoppy, the old Diamond J cowboy who had driven the other truck, came out of the store and yelled, "Hey, Tom! Guess what I found?"

"What'd you find, you old blind fart?"

"Robertson's beef jerky! You still like that shit?"

"Hoppy, you better not be funnin' me!"

"Two whole cases of it!"

"Well, dammit, bring it on out here!"

"If you ask real nice, I'll think about it."

"Hoppy, I'm gonna climb down off here and…"

Bruce interrupted, "Tom, we're about full here. Better shut off the pump."

Tom nodded, shut the pump down, and eased down to the ground. He disconnected the hose, then started pulling the siphon hose up out of the tank, slowly coiling it back in the rack, cussing as diesel spilled all over him. He finally got all the hose up and racked, then checked to make sure the tank cap was firmly replaced, then looked up at Bruce. "Think you can come down now. We're done. As soon as Hoppy and Ace get ready, we can get out of here and head back for the ranch. I'd like to get their ranch tanks topped off today, if we can."

Bruce looked around then yelled, "Hoppy, let's do it! We're finished. Grab your folks and let's hit the road."

Hoppy waved and started across the parking lot with two boxes, carrying them awkwardly as he juggled them and his rifle, finally dropping one and kicking it across the lot to the semi. "There ya go, old man. There's your junk food."

Tom clapped him on the shoulder. "Thanks for takin' care of me, Hoppy. It's always been us'ns against them."

Hoppy laughed, and turned toward their truck. "Always has been, always will be us cowboys against the managers…"

"Hey, did you check for coffee, or tea, or sugar, any of that stuff?"

"Damn, forgot all about it."

Tom turned to Bruce, "You need to go check, you know that stuff is on our search list. Hoppy and I will stand guard."

Bruce grumbled, "Okay, I'm going…"

***

Back on the I-40 overpass, Billy whimpered in the back seat of the 3500 as another runner scrabbled at the window. "What do I do?"

Micah glanced over. "Nothing. She can't get in and…" A shot sounded overhead from the bed of the truck and the female zomb fell away. "They are taking care of them from up top." Keying the CB, he asked, "Anybody seeing any more runners?"

A round of "Nope, shamblers only, a couple moving a little fast," was about all.

Micah banged on the top of the cab. "How much longer y'all want to shoot?"

Tommy yelled back, "Down to two mags. Probably time to go. There are shamblers, but not many of them and it'll take them a while to get here."

Micah keyed the CB. "Okay folks, let's roll out of here. Who's got the Vet?"

"David, from Box H, we've got him. You lead, we'll follow."

"Okay, let's roll. Jake, you okay to go straight to the warehouse? We'll take the other four trucks and hit the pharmacies and meet y'all there."

Jake revved the big diesel. "On the way. I'll bust through them, y'all get on my tail." With that, he let the clutch out and rumbled through the few remaining shamblers in front of him, as the other trucks fell in line behind the trailer.

A quick pass at the Walgreens got almost nothing in the way of any useful drugs. The pharmacy counter was completely wrecked, and the entire store stank of zombs. They pulled into the United grocery, not hoping for much, but found that the pharmacy counter had been secured. It took a few minutes with bolt cutters, pry bars, and good old fashioned breaking and entering, but they did get in and Darryl, the old veterinarian, grabbed three shopping carts full of medications and various other things, like needles and bits and pieces, cackling and laughing the whole time.

Micah and the others fanned out in pairs, searching the aisles for consumables that were always a priority, toilet paper, salt, pepper, spices, tea and coffee, sugar and flour. The store wasn't in bad shape, and they were able to load up plenty of buggies, but Micah had to call a halt before they overloaded the trucks, since they still had to get people in there too. Billy stayed close to Micah and Tommy, eyes wide, as he looked for things he hadn't seen in almost a year. He saw a display of Kool-Aid and asked, "Can we get some? Please? We like Kool-Aid."

Micah sighed, knowing there wasn't enough sugar to do it often, but said, "Go ahead. It's not something we'll be able to have every day, but it will be a once-in-a-while treat, okay?"

Billy nodded enthusiastically, pawing through the display and filling his pockets with as many packets as he could.

As they headed out the front of the store, Billy and Tommy both saw the candy bars on the aisle cap and looked back at Micah. He rolled his eyes, but said, "You've got to get enough to share with Olivia and Bonnie and the rest of us."

The boys were whispering back and forth until Micah said, "Three, two…"

They grabbed double handfuls of candy and followed Micah out of the store and hopped back into the cab as the rest of the crew loaded the back of the truck with the consumables. David walked over, "Micah, we'll bring Darryl by y'all's place on the way back so he can get a look at the old man and see if the meds will work for him, if that's okay with you."

Micah nodded. "Sounds like a plan. I guess we'd better get down to the warehouse and pull security, and help the working party before they get all irate about us just 'ridin' around' up here."

David laughed. "Yep, there is that… I kinda like getting fed."

Micah yelled, "Mount up! Let's head to the warehouse! Working party, ho!"

***

The trucks rumbled back across the cattle guard, pulled around to the barn and backed up to start off-loading the supplies they'd picked up. Micah got down and stretched, passing his rifle to Tommy, and told Billy, "Go take Mr. Darryl to your grandpa, okay?"

Billy nodded. "Yes, sir." He trotted over to the veterinarian, tugged at him and led him toward the house. Dot came out of the house, saw them coming and turned quickly back into the house, which caught Micah's attention.

"Tommy, let's go stow our rifles first, okay?"

Tommy shrugged. "Okay."

Micah walked quickly across to the house, turned down the hall, and caught up with Dot. "What's going on?"

Dot cocked her head, saying softly, "The old man didn't make it. He asked for a piece of pie at lunch, and I served him one. I went back in the kitchen to finish cleaning up and heard a thump."

"Shit."

"Yeah, shit. He got two bites and had a massive MI. Cherie and I gave him CPR for a while, but…"

"What about the girl, Bonnie?"

"She was hysterical. I gave her a big dose of Benadryl, and got her and Olivia in their room. We've been checking on her, but…"

They both turned when they heard a high-pitched scream, "NO, nooooo…"

Micah shook his head. "I guess Billy just got told." They heard running feet, and a door bang, and Micah turned to Tommy. "Go find him, right now! Stay with him, and carry your gun. Get him back here by dark, understand?"

Tommy's eyes got big at the tone of voice, but he said meekly, "Okay. What do you want me to do?"

"Stay with him. Don't let him do something stupid. You know how you felt when your momma and daddy died, so you can try to talk to him."

"Yes, sir."

"Now go."

Tommy went out the door on a run, and Dot leaned into Micah's shoulder, "Where does it end?"

He hugged her, saying quietly, "I don't know Dot, I just don't know…"

***

Cherie Crane of the Rocking C, Sheriff Coffee, Brad Harmon of the Box H, and Mike James of the Diamond J sat in the kitchen at the Diamond J, drinking coffee as they waited for the veterinarian Darryl to come in. Everybody had their respective notebooks by their chairs and Cherie was idly drawing a set of curves and doodling numbers on one page when Darryl finally came in. "Sorry I'm late.

Peterson's kid's got the flu again. Thankfully, I was able to get some Z-pacs at United, so I'm going to use them while they're still good. I'm not sure how long most of the stuff I've got is good for, but as long as I've got it, I'm going to dispense it."

The sheriff said, "Well, that's some good news. Lemme go over what I've got. As of today, I can account for 238 people, scattered over a little over 3600 square miles. That's up two since last week, with the two kids at the Rocking C. There do seem to be less shamblers out and about, but I'm not going poking into buildings to see if they're dying in there."

Cherie said, "So there is some merit to what the Eaton Rapids guy, Joe, is saying?"

The sheriff shrugged, "I can't put empirical data on it, but, yeah, I think so. Most of the shamblers left are females, which matches what he'd predicted. Women need less calories per day than men do, assuming the same levels of effort. If we get ninety percent death rates, figuring that the total population, less Potter County, is a little over 33,000, then we're coming up on almost 30,000 deaths. And that will repeat until there is no one left…"

Brad chimed in, "Well, as few of us as there are…"

Mike replied, "Yeah, 238 of us against the world. That's not a winning proposition. Stuff is breaking down, we're all tired, all the time."

Darryl said, "Well, we're 238 *healthy* people. That is a huge difference. Granted we've got a significant age range, what, twelve to? I'm 64 and I'm probably the oldest one here. Oh, speaking of that, there will soon be at least one addition to that number."

Everyone looked at Darryl expectantly. "David and Melaina."

Brad asked, "Which David?"

Darryl rolled his eyes. "Your David, and Mike, your Melaina. So I guess y'all are going to be combining spreads."

Cherie coughed to hide a laugh at the expressions on both Brad and Mike's faces. It was obvious they didn't have a clue that their kids had gotten together, much less made a baby. But that did lead her down the path of Tommy and Olivia, and Billy and Bonnie. They were the four youngest kids, and their prospects weren't really great.

Sheriff Coffee said, "Well, congratulations to them, and now back to issues. The roads are going to shit. Bridges are getting washed out, and the dirt roads are degrading way too fast for us to maintain them."

Brad shrugged. "Well, considering how hard it is to get diesel and propane, much less tires and maintaining vehicles, it may not make much difference."

Mike replied, "That's why we've been breeding the horses like we have. Granted we don't have any draft horses, at least not yet, but they're going to be the lifeline going forward."

Cherie added, "True, but once we lose the propane truck and capability, we're back to cooking with wood, which we don't have in abundant supply. Matter of fact, we're going to have to start rationing some things, among them coffee and tea, pretty quickly. We've hit a gold mine with the restaurant warehouse in Amarillo, but even with that, supporting all the folks that we are isn't making me happy for the long term. We've all got gardens in, and doing what we can for food storage, but I'm guessing two, maybe three years and it's going to get really rough. I'm just thankful we've got as big a group as we do, otherwise I don't see how we'd be making it, not with the security issues, having to search for things, and just daily maintenance. We'd be lucky to be doing as well as our great-grands were when they settled this place. I can't imagine what those survivors in the towns and cities are doing!"

Brad laughed, "Well, they aren't eating steak as much as we are, that's for sure."

Everyone laughed at that, but Cherie's point had struck home.

Wesley came charging into the kitchen. "Boss, looks like we got a problem coming."

Brad turned sharply, "What's coming, Wesley?"

"Three trucks, coming from 287, just stopped at the big gate. Coupla guys got out, went around the gate and walked down a ways. I'm guessing to the top of the hill where they could see the house."

"Armored up?"

Wesley shook his head. "Didn't look like it. I'm guessing some raiders, maybe from down around Wichita Falls, the way they come from."

Sheriff Coffee stood. "Show me the video. Let's see what we're dealing with."

All of them got up and trooped down to the library-cum-radio-room and security station. They saw two Mexicans come back into camera range and ten more people get out of the four trucks. The sheriff said, "Brad, can you deploy some folks right quick in your truck beds? I got a feeling this one is gonna go bad."

Brad nodded and hurried from the room yelling, "Reaction team up! I need nine, *now!*" A clatter of running feet punctuated the call as Brad made for the gun room.

The sheriff turned to Cherie and Mike. "You agree?"

They both nodded. "Not the first time we've been through this shit," Mike replied.

Cherie said sadly, "Why? What do they think they're doing?"

"Dunno, Cherie. Hell, it's been about four months since that last bunch came bombing through here. You took 'em out before we could even get there."

Cherie laughed. "Well, given the LEO response time out here, John…"

"Moi? I was coming as fast as I could!"

"Yeah, but you were all the way up by Clarendon. Running balls to the wall it still took you almost thirty minutes."

Wesley interrupted, "Here they come."

The sheriff turned to Darryl. "You ready to maybe have a little business?"

"I'd rather not, if you don't mind."

The sheriff nodded, saying, sotto voce, "Neither do I." He led the way out of the library, walking quickly toward the front of the house and out onto the porch, grabbing his hat on the way. He looked at the arrangement of vehicles, then calmly stepped around to put himself clear of the house and in the best position for covering fire from the trucks he hoped Brad had manned up.

The four trucks came charging into the ranch yard, sliding to a stop and the sheriff realized they weren't armored at all. Just plain three-quarter and one-ton crew cab pickups, jacked up and running big tires and wheels. All of the tires and wheels looked brand new, which told him these were pure raiders, taking what they wanted whenever they wanted.

A bigMexican with long, greasy hair and moustaches climbed out of the driver's seat of the first truck, casually slinging an AR-15 over his shoulder and setting a hand on a pistol on his hip. His other hand rested on what looked like a cheap copy of some big fighting type knife, sticking out of a holster on the off hip. The man swaggered over, stopping a couple of feet in front of the sheriff, and smiling.

Cherie noticed that the man overtopped the sheriff by probably five or six inches, but Coffee didn't seem the least bit intimidated by the big man. She eased her rifle around the window frame, staying back behind the curtains so they couldn't see any movement, as she took a sight on the big Mexican's nose. At least she wouldn't have to worry about hitting the sheriff if this went as bad as they thought.

The big Mexican made a hand signal, and the rest of the men climbed down from the rigs, ARs and pistols in their hands, not saying a word, but obviously looking around in wonder. The big Mexican finally said, "So, Sheriffmans. You know there ain't no law no more?"

The sheriff replied, "Round here, I'm still the duly elected law. And I enforce it. What do you want?'

The Mexican laughed. "Anything we want to take, that's what we want! Women, booze, food, we take…"

The sheriff did a speed-rock draw, firing three rounds from his 1911 into the big man's belly, then grabbing and spinning him as a shield, shooting over him and taking down one of the others that started charging him. Seconds later, all twelve of the men were down and dead. Cherie realized she'd never even gotten a shot off. Shrugging, she safed her AR and walked slowly out the door as Brad and the others climbed down from the armored truck beds.

Brad asked, "Everybody okay?" There were nods all around, and Darryl came out of the house, medical bag in hand.

"Don't think we need you, unless you want to pronounce them, Darryl."

"I'll do it anyway, need the practice."

The crew was going through the pickups and throwing trash and other contents out on the ground when Riley suddenly yelled, "Holy shit! Brad, Darryl, er… Sheriff, y'all need to… Mrs. Crane. Oh, my God."

That brought everyone running to the back of the pickup, where Riley had raised a bedcover. Blinking in the light were three young girls, badly beaten and obviously in poor shape.

Cherie didn't even think twice, handing her rifle to the sheriff and climbing into the bed, making soothing sounds as the girls cowered against the front of the bed in the little nest they had. Cherie almost gagged from the stench coming off them, but continued to speak quietly as Brad went and got his wife, and a couple of the other women.

A half hour later, Brad and the others were back around the kitchen table, and Mike turned to the sheriff. "John, what set you off? It didn't seem to be… Well, I didn't see anything…"

The sheriff leaned back, rolling the coffee cup between his hands as he looked up at the ceiling. "I was watching his eyes. I saw them dilate, and saw him starting to lean in. I knew he was starting to make his move, and I just short-cutted him. I can't tell you how I knew, other than 30 years in law enforcement, but I wasn't going to let him get the upper hand."

Brad nodded. "Glad you did. I didn't relish a shootout, but at least this ended well for us. Not so much for them, though."

Cherie thought, *Hard men. John's not really that cold-blooded that he enjoyed killing that guy, but he did what needed to be done as soon as he saw it. Thank God for that. I guess it's a sign of these times that we're sitting here calmly discussing killing twelve functional adults without turning a hair, or a single regret. Maybe it's because of those girls, too.*

As they discussed the plight of the girls, who had been taken from a little town south of Fort Worth after the others in their survivors' group had been killed, the sheriff looked around. "Two-hundred forty-one. Question is, who's got room for them?"

Cherie grimaced. "Well, I guess we can take them, but I'm out of room."

Brad nodded and Mike said, "Well, I've got room, but I've got no teens, or single females. At least if you take them, there is somebody near their age."

Brad wondered, "Where do we go next? It's been a year now, and I don't know what the future is going to bring."

The sheriff cocked his head. "The same place we've been going for the last year. Survive, do the best we can with what we've got, and do our damnest to train up the kids. Live or die, they are the future, such as it is…"

WHISPERS OF THE APOC

I woke to the sound of scratching. It wasn't a mouse or a rat, or anything of the four-legged variety. Want to know how I know? It was followed by a moan.

It was one of them. The zombies.

My hand was on the knife as soon as I heard it. I held it out just in front of me as I threw my blankets aside and stood up. On the other side of the caravan, Jed still slept. I rolled my eyes.

Nobody knows how the zombie apocalypse started or why. I woke up one morning and it was on the news that some man had bitten a woman and they were both in accident and emergency. Now, six months down the line, the why doesn't matter; the only thing that anybody cares about anymore is survival.

Jed rolled over and grunted, pulling the wool blankets tighter to his chest. His arms were thin, the t-shirt he wore too baggy on his frame. I'd only met him a month ago when I was between places but I felt like I'd known him my whole life. That's all there was now; me and Jed. And the zombies.

"Jed," I hissed, glancing at the door as something thumped against it.

"What?" he asked in his pseudo-awake voice.

"There's a zombie outside."

He waved his hand. "We're fine as long as it stays out there."

"It could be attracting others."

He waved his hand again and smacked his lips.

"Jed!" This time I was a little more forceful.

"Fine." He sighed, throwing the covers back dramatically and staggering to his feet. His hair was askew and his jeans wrinkled. Even now after all this time, sleeping in our clothes had become a habit; being ready to go at any minute was important.

Two things I'd learned about Jed in the month I'd known him: he'd lost everyone, just like me—just like everyone—and he liked to sleep way too much.

"I'll jump down." He was already unlatching the hatch on the roof and had scrambled through it before I had a chance to respond.

Not wanting to fight zombies was nothing to do with the fact that I'm a girl. I'm not entitled or squeamish. I've learned to fight—I've had to—and can take down a walker like the rest. It's Jed. He sees me as a daughter. I've seen the photo he keeps in his wallet a few times and I realized how much I looked like her; blonde hair cut in a short crop, delicate green eyes, rose lips and soft cheekbones. He told me her name once—Zoe—she was seventeen, too. But she got bitten and had not recovered. Jed had never recovered from having to end her life.

There was one morning just after I'd met him that I went outside to pee—we hadn't found the caravan by then—and he charged after me a few minutes later and ran into me mid-stream yelling about being stupid. After the initial embarrassment—him more than me—he apologized and then he asked me—not told me—to never go out alone. That's what happened to Zoe. She went outside to get something and she was bitten by a crawler.

I listened to him and I hadn't gone out alone since. Part of me liked the idea of being looked after, but the other part worried that by letting him take over, I was putting myself more at risk. If I forgot how to fight it meant Jed had to stick around forever and I wasn't naïve enough to think it was a possibility.

The caravan rocked and I heard the thump of his hiking boots as they hit the ground. It was followed by the sound of something heavy hitting the floor and I imagined his hunting knife going straight through the skull of the walker.

I heard the sound of the body being dragged along the ground—Jed likes to keep our place tidy—and then a few minutes later the door opened and he strode in.

Dusting his hands together, he grinned. "What's for breakfast?"

I rolled my eyes.

"Hey, killing zombies is hard work." He held his arms out.

I shook my head. "Our food supplies are gone." My stomach had woken me up early that morning to let me know.

Jed's jaw opened and closed. "Tell me you're kidding."

"You're here, too, Jed." I flung out my hands. "I'm not a homemaker."

"Okay, I deserved that, but still, are you sure?"

"Yes." I nodded. "That tin of beans we shared last night? That was our last meal."

"Shit." He dropped back to the sofa that doubled as a makeshift bed. We'd taken up a side each, padding it out with cushions and blankets. The table in the center acted as a makeshift nightstand. It wasn't too comfortable and I'd fallen off the narrow seat on more than one occasion when I rolled over in the middle of the night, but it was better than where we'd been before; an abandoned warehouse with cardboard box beds.

"We're going to have to go out there." I pointed to the window. The curtains were drawn—they always were—but we both knew exactly where I was pointing; the supermarket. It was around half a mile away over a road that was vacant and a tarmac car park. From our distance, we couldn't see much more than that but since finding the caravan we'd stayed clear. Shops of any kind were a looters' paradise and, though we knew the place could still have food on the shelves, we also knew the dangers. Zombies. Zombies in a locked environment. Looters. Others survivors.

I'd been lucky to meet Jed. Others I'd seen along the way weren't so nice.

"No." He drew a line in the air with his arms. "No way we're going in there. It could be crawling."

"You're right, it could be." I nodded. "But the way I see it we've got two choices; we either go in there and deal with whatever we find or we sit in this tin box until we get so weak we can't move and the zombies get in and eat us."

"Jesus, Emma. Do you have to be so dramatic?"

"Do you have to be so nonchalant?"

"How do you know a word like that?"

"Well, before the world went to shit, I went to school and I learned. Hell, I actually liked school."

"Keep your voice down." He held his open palms in the air.

Taking his cue, I lowered my voice. "I'm smart, Jed. And I can fight. If you won't go over there, then I will."

"You're not going." He crossed his arms over his chest.

"Please." I rolled my eyes. "I bet you're the lightest you've been in a long time thanks to our bad diet. I could bowl you over and get out that door."

"I'd chase you down."

"Then you'll have to chase." Without a moment's hesitation, I rushed towards the door. Instead of planting his feet like I expected, Jed jumped out of the way. I hit the handle and jumped the small distance to the ground. The morning air was cool, the sun not yet over the horizon. The grey sky stretched out in front of me, leering over the supermarket in the distance.

"Emma, wait!"

Instead of listening, something I'd fallen into the habit of doing despite the fact that up until a month ago Jed was a complete stranger, I walked.

I was alert, scanning my surroundings to make sure I wasn't about to be mauled. There were no walkers in sight. Still, I kept my hand at my belt, ready to draw my knife.

A few seconds later I heard footsteps behind me. I didn't need to turn around to know it was Jed. He caught up and matched my pace. Turning to the left for a moment, I glanced at him. I couldn't help but notice the grey sprouting through his beard. I was pretty sure that wasn't there when we first met. The apocalypse took its toll on us all.

"Did I ever tell you how much you are like her?" he asked.

"Beautiful and smart?" I asked.

"Stubborn and headstrong."

I smiled.

***

From the outside, the supermarket looked empty. There were no walkers milling around the cars or in the glass front of the store. I saw a couple in the distance, shambling beside the nature park, but if we kept quiet we wouldn't draw their attention.

"What do you think?" Jed peeked over the bonnet of a car. He was crouched on one knee, his blue jeans stretched to their limit. The red paint of the car was beginning to fade after being exposed to the sun for so long.

"Now you're interested in my opinion?" I whispered, a habit I'd developed shortly after it all started, along with the ability to play a wholehearted game of hide, don't seek. Staying quiet and being able to hide were good skills to have in the zombie apocalypse. That and being able to push grief aside. The dead didn't spare a moment of respect. You had to stay alert at all times.

Jed glared at me before returning his gaze to the shop. "It looks empty from here, but I know it's not."

"There'll be walkers in there, no doubt about that. But we're going."

"That's if we can get in."

"The double doors, they used to be automatic." I pointed. "Now they're propped open by a body."

"How do you know it's not a zombie just taking a nap?" He glanced at me.

"Firstly, walkers don't nap and secondly, his brains are leaked all over the pavement."

"You have a wonderful way with words."

"Come on." I stood up. The longer we waited, the more excuses Jed would think up. He knew as well as I did that going in there was our only option. Food, shelter, safety. The three most important things for us to continue surviving. Without one of those we were goners. Moving around him, I passed the car and started walking towards the shop. I heard him sigh, then he lumbered to his feet and jogged to catch up.

"Stay alert," Jed warned, as he came up alongside me. "And let me take the lead."

"Whatever you say."

I didn't mind taking a back seat. As much as I'd been the one to push us to this point, I was scared. Jed was right, the supermarket would be crawling. And there could be more than just walkers in there. We had to be quiet and we had to work together.

As we approached the doors, I unsheathed the knife from my belt, gripping it tightly in my right hand. I realized that already in the short time I'd known Jed, I'd come to rely on him a little too much. I would let him take the lead now but once we were in and we'd cleared the floor I was taking my own route. I'd survived five months in a brutal and dangerous world without him; I could continue to do so.

Jed stepped over the body that lay in the door, careful not to disturb it. The hands that splayed from the shirt cuffs were grey and I knew that if I cared to touch him, I'd find his fingers stiff as rigor mortis took its hold. Most of his head was gone, replaced with a mass of gore, some of which had been lapped up. I chose to stare ahead, focusing on Jed as I followed him through the still doors into the supermarket.

Most power had disappeared when the apocalypse began. There was nobody left to keep anything running and, slowly but surely, everything ran down. Even the back-up generators had long since fried. Jed had been looking for a portable generator since we moved into the caravan but so far he'd found nothing. The bottle of gas we'd hauled from the center of the caravan park was just about empty and we needed fuel unless we wanted nothing more than cold beans for the rest of our lives.

"It's quiet," Jed whispered, stating the obvious.

I said nothing, just continued following him. He skirted around a display of empty cardboard boxes that would have once been filled with crisps that had been on offer. Now it was empty except for the body of a young woman. Most of her right arm and leg were gone. I saw something moving within her flesh and quickly looked away.

Moving around the corner of the box, Jed stepped past the electronic sensors that lay dormant between the checkout area and the door. He was right, it was quiet. Too quiet.

Jed stopped and turned to look at me. "Are you sure you want to do this?"

I swallowed, hard. Now that I was here, all I wanted to do was turn around and run back to the relative safety and complete familiarity of the caravan. Blood pumped through my body double time and my heart was racing in my chest. I didn't want to do this, but sometimes logic was overruled by need, and in this case it was never truer. Without food we would starve. It would be stupid to let ourselves become nothing more than shells—zombie bait—and this was our big chance. All we had to do was take a look. Even from where I stood I could see some of the shelves were still lined and while I was sure that most of it had been picked clean, I knew that we would be able to find something.

Finally I nodded. "We have to."

I expected him to ridicule my quieted brazenness but instead he simply nodded. "We scout the shop, make sure it's safe, and then we loot."

The plan sounded good to me. "Okay."

With his knife in hand, Jed took the lead and dutifully I followed. We made our way along the bottom of the check outs. Most of the till registers had been broken open, their contents spilled or stolen. I shook my head. Money was no use in this world. Our currency was food, water, shelter. Most of our needs were made up of finite supplies and that's what made other survivors so dangerous. We were all in the same boat, we all needed what the other had and there was only so much of it to go around.

The behavior of the dead could be predicted; that of the living could not.

We walked all the way along to the end of the shop, both of us scanning each aisle as we went. I saw items scattered on the floor, packaging ripped open. Bodies lay strewn where they'd fallen. A woman was curled into a trolley. She fit perfectly because her head was missing. I saw an empty pram, a bloodstain marring the pink blanket, a toy on the floor in a pool of blood. I didn't realize I had stopped until Jed nudged my arm. I tore my eyes away from the scene.

"You okay?" he asked, his voice low.

I nodded. It was the right response to give, but we both knew that it wasn't true. How could you walk past a sight like that and be okay? It was impossible.

The apocalypse had brought so much death and destruction. It almost felt like the world had stopped turning and for so many people, it had. But this. The sight of the pram, blood smearing its inside, would be a sight I'd never forget. The walkers, they didn't discriminate. Anything that was living or breathing was a target from newborn to pensioner and everyone in between. I wasn't surprised to see it; it just hurt.

As the virus had taken over, spreading through towns and cities, it was covered by the news. It was the only thing on the news. The maps showed up like a red rash and soon there weren't news reports anymore, just the emergency screens on every channel. That's when things got worse. It forced people out of their homes, into the streets, looking for answers, looking for help. They found nothing but death and destruction.

I still wondered at how I'd managed to get six months into a zombie-infested world. I was just a girl. My parents were killed in the initial onslaught as the zombies invaded our home. I went into shock and spent two days hiding in my room trying not to make a sound as they stalked around the house looking for me. They knew I was there. I knew they were coming. It was an eventuality. We were at a standstill.

Of course my room contained nothing even close to a weapon and I'd had to use my swimming trophy to bash their brains in when the door finally caved. Killing my parents, ending their lives, was the hardest thing I ever had to do. After that, I could deal with anything. I left the trophy lying on the floor covered in my parents' blood and I left the house with nothing more than a backpack with a few essentials. I still carried it now, but the essentials inside had changed. Water, food, weapons, as opposed to the sentimental items I'd originally brought from my home. I had no use for them; they did nothing but weigh me down, physically and emotionally, and I couldn't have either if I wanted to stay alive.

The harsh reality of the apocalypse had made me learn that there was no time for grief, that life was only temporary, and that I should live each day like it was my last. Meeting Jed had diminished my fierceness but now I was here in the supermarket and I wasn't about to go home empty handed, no matter what it took.

I came back to reality as a moan to my left snapped through my memories. A walker lurched up from behind the till, hands grabbing for me. I jumped back and slid my knife from my belt. The walker had once been a woman. Now its blonde hair was falling out in clumps displaying a decaying skull. Its jaw hung open in a permanent growl. Recovering and taking a step forward, I thrust the knife through the eye socket. It gave and the walker went limp beneath my hands, slumping to the floor in a heap.

"You okay?" Jed asked.

I turned to look at him. I nodded. "Fine."

"Looks like we're all clear," Jed announced. The end of the world was telling on a person. On Jed it wore on his skin, in the multiple lines that had developed on his sallow skin, his cheeks sagging from the weight he'd lost too quickly. The bags under his eyes were dark, almost purple, and the whites of his eyes were spider-webbed with red capillaries.

I'd avoided looking at a mirror for weeks. Longer, even. The one that graced the small bathroom in the caravan was broken and I was grateful for not having to see my reflection whenever I went in there. I didn't need to see a mirror to know how tired I looked, to see that my eyes had lost their spark and that I too had lines that marred my face like that of an old woman.

"I say we split up."

Jed shook his head. "No way."

I sighed. "Jed, we'll cover more ground that way."

"I don't care."

"You said it was clear."

"And as far as I can see, it is. But we're not splitting up."

I thrust my hip out as I stared at him. "You do realize you have no claim on me whatsoever."

"I know." He held his hands out. "But wherever you go, I'll follow."

I gritted my teeth. "I don't know about you, but being with someone 24-7 is a little stifling. I'm sure I'll manage to shop on my own."

"Emma—"

"Jed!" I snapped. He winced at the echo. "I'm not a kid anymore. I haven't been a kid since the day I killed my parents, when I stove their skulls in and left my swimming trophy matted with brain matter and hair. I can look after myself."

"Please, I—"

"Just give me some space." I spun on my heel and rushed by the tills. My footsteps were loud on the waxed floor. I carried on running, up the aisle that would have been full of pet supplies. Even that had been picked clean; survivors would do what they had to when in desperation.

I rounded the corner as I reached the top of the aisle and stopped to take a breath. He hadn't followed. Everything was quiet and suddenly, I became very aware of how it would be to live alone in the world now.

I took a deep breath and let it out slowly, my chest sinking and my shoulders dropping. Tears pricked my eyes. I hadn't argued with Jed since meeting him, which was quite something, considering how stubborn I could be. He was different. Mostly. And even now I knew that he was just trying to look out for me and what had I gone and done? Thrown it in his face.

I wiped my eyes, feeling ashamed. What if he left me? He might take my outburst as complete hatred and leave me here. Or at least take off for a few days. If he did, could I really do it? Could I survive on my own? Although I'd survived five months without him, I got along mostly by sheer luck. I hadn't come across big groups of survivors or if I had, I had managed to hide long enough to wait them out. I had only come across walkers in small groups and managed to fight them off. But now? Yes, I could probably do what I had to do, but I was only one person. Pushing Jed away, getting angry at him for everything that was happening, was going to do nothing to help either of us.

I took a deep breath and I was about to spin back around and head down the aisle to apologize and work the supermarket alongside him, when I heard a voice.

"I saw them come in here." It was male, low, whispering. "They looked pretty well kept."

"You think they have a place nearby?" A second voice, gruff.

"Probably. And a base means a stash."

"Let's find them."

I froze on the spot as my heart hammered against my ribs. We'd been followed. And it didn't matter that we had nothing of value in our caravan half a mile away. Whoever these men were, they wanted something and just listening to them brought me to the understanding that they would do whatever it took to get whatever they thought they deserved.

Jed. I have to find him.

We were safer together. Without him, I was vulnerable and without me, he was unaware. Stealing a look back down the pet aisle, I saw the coast was clear and began to tiptoe back down the hard floor, skirting around a bag of cat litter that had been strewn across the floor. I made it to the end, pressing myself against the metal shelving, and peering around the corner. I couldn't see them but I could hear them as they muttered. Readying myself, I was about to head into the main aisle to go back to the tills when I saw Jed. His head popped up over the register and then he motioned for me to stay put. Nodding, I shrank back. His eyes were wide as he surveyed the scene. Clearly, he was as anxious as I was.

I waited there for what could have been hours, time dragging as the breath caught in my throat and I switched between looking at Jed and searching the aisle I was in. I was stuck between utter terror that they'd sneak up on me or that Jed would get caught. As of yet it seemed there were only two of them and that meant we were equal.

Jed's eyes flicked back to me. Then in a burst of movement, he waved his arm, beckoning me over. I didn't need telling twice. I took off, rushing across the huge expanse on my tiptoes as quickly as I could without making a sound. It felt like I was slogging through a vat of marshmallow and that at any moment I'd be cornered and captured. Instead, I made it to the till, ducked down and was immediately folded in his arms.

"Are you okay?" he mouthed.

I nodded, letting out the breath I'd been holding. I was okay now. I realized my stupidity in being so hasty, in being so angry with the world. I could have been caught and then what? Jed would have rushed over to save me and he might have been hurt. I shook my head. I couldn't have that. "I'm sorry."

"Come on, let's get out of here."

I was happy to oblige. The supermarket was just across the road from us and we could come back another time when we knew the coast was clear. Until then, we'd have to spend the day without.

Taking my hand, Jed took another peek around the shop, a meerkat searching for prey, and then he stood to a crouch and together we began to make our way back towards the door. Our hands lost contact but we stayed close, Jed constantly checking the aisles just to make sure we weren't about to be spotted but it looked like we were in luck; the two men must have gone the other way.

As we reached the end of the checkouts, we hurried back through the silent alarms and rounded the corner to head towards the door.

Jed pulled up short and I ran straight into him, cursing as I straightened beside him. His arm was out, his palm flat to hold me back. I sensed a change in his body and wondered just how many walkers we'd stumbled into. When I finally came fully to my feet I saw that it wasn't walkers. It was men. Survivors. Four of them. They all stood with weapons in their hands; I saw a machete and several knives. I swallowed hard. My heart was already drumming but my palms were beginning to sweat as my fingers twitched next to my belt.

The man in front shook his head, pointing the machete at me. "I wouldn't do that if I was you."

I dropped my arm. Jed never removed his gaze from the men.

"What do you want?" he asked, challenging with a soft voice. It was a delicate situation. I glanced through the dirty windows, past the parking lot to our caravan and I knew that we'd have to leave. It was no longer a safe spot for us. The home we'd made disintegrated before my eyes and I felt a twinge of sadness before shoving it away. There was no room for grief at the end of the world.

"Me and my boys here," he paused and motioned to the men behind him. They all stood with stony faces. I saw a scar on one man's cheek. Another was missing a finger. "We saw you coming across here."

"Where are you from?" Jed asked. His arm was still tensed, forming a protective barrier between me and the men.

"Where are we from?" He grinned. "Well, here. This is our base." His arms spread wide and I knew he meant the supermarket. It had been claimed as their spot, which meant we were trespassing.

"We didn't realize. We'll leave." Jed straightened, his shoulders losing some of their height.

"Oh, no. Not yet. Won't you join us for tea?"

"We should be getting—"

"I said, you're coming with us." His whole demeanor changed, smile fading as he motioned the men forward.

"Jack, Russ, get the man. Harold, take the girl." They rushed past him, two of them taking Jed by the arms, another grabbing me.

"Hey!" I tried to wrench my arm free but Harold had a firm grip. I kicked out but all it got me was a smack across the mouth.

"Leave her alone!" Jed shouted. My cheek stung but I was angry. Angry that he dared restrain me, that he raised his hand to me. I bit my lip and straightened. I would do as I was told. For now.

"Max," Harold shouted, his grip tightening on my arm.

Stepping forward, Max, the leader of their group, held his machete under Jed's throat. Immediately he stopped struggling. "There's no reason to be like that. If the girl didn't lash out, she wouldn't have gotten hurt." Max moved closer to me as his arm dropped, his eyes devouring me from head to toe. I shuddered under his gaze.

"You don't have to hurt us," Jed pleaded. I realized his fear was for me. "We just want to leave."

"It's not going to happen, fella. Let's go."

At his words, Jed and I were forcibly turned to face the supermarket again. My eyes moved over the aisles and I saw the two men whose voices I'd heard as I hid in the pet food aisle only moments ago coming to join their men. I stumbled and almost tripped over my own feet but I was kept up by the man still gripping my arm.

"Where are you taking us?" Jed asked behind me. His voice was tinged with anger. I'd seen Jed angry and it was a pretty neat spectacle to behold. I just had to hope that these guys angered him enough to unleash the beast.

"Home," Max answered.

We were led up the empty fridge aisles. Their power had long since gone off and the smell which would have lingered was faded. I saw a set of double doors. I was marched right into one, my hip and my face connecting. Protesting, I used my free hand to check I hadn't broken my nose, while beside me my captor laughed. Anger bristled inside me.

"Take it easy," Jed called as he was brought in behind me.

We were inside the stock room. Huge shelving units towered over me, now almost empty. I was led around to the left and then the right and that's when I realized that not all of the shelves were empty. A canopy had been erected on the outskirts to provide a meagre cover and it seemed that some of the units had been moved. Now in the center of it all, I saw their camp. A gas stove took up the center, bottle still connected, and the shelves that surrounded it all were lined with tins of food, bottles of water and a few other amenities. They'd done well to find this place.

Sleeping bags lined the floor, six in total. I was thrown into the center of it all, Jed flung so roughly he stumbled and hit the deck. It was followed by laughter.

"You okay?" I helped him up. A gash had opened on his forehead and blood oozed through the wound.

"Don't worry about me." He came to stand at his feet, turning to look at our captors. "Are you?"

I nodded, but it was a lie. I wasn't all right. Neither of us were. This was all my fault. If I hadn't insisted on searching the supermarket, if I hadn't marched over here, forcing Jed to follow, we'd be in the caravan, hungry but safe.

"So I want the real story." Max stepped forward. "Why are you here?"

"We told you," Jed started. "We're looking for food."

"The shelves have been picked clean. And what's left is ours."

"Fine." He held his hands up. "So you can let us go and we won't bother you."

"See, here's where the problem lies." Max cocked his head to the side. "There are only two of you now, but how do I know that you don't have a whole tribe to go back to? I need to keep my men safe."

"There's just us."

"I need proof."

Jed sighed. "We've been living in the caravan. Just across the way. You can see it from here."

"You have?" He turned to look at his men. "Have we not searched the tin can?" He was met with a few shaking heads and mumbles of unwilling answers. "Okay. It seems my men have lacked a certain thoroughness I want to see in the ranks. For now, we're going to check out your story. Jack, Russ. You two go and search the caravan and hurry back."

The two men who had thrown Jed to the floor turned to leave.

"Now we wait." Max smiled.

"Can I at least sit down?" I sighed. I'd hit my hip harder than I thought when we crashed through the door earlier and I knew I'd have a wicked bruise already forming.

"You can share my bed." Harold stepped forward, licking his lips. I backed up a step, almost tripping over a sleeping bag.

"Stay away from her." Jed's fists were balled in an instant as he stepped between me and the leering man.

Max's grin widened. "I take it she's your daughter."

"As good as."

My heart would have swelled if we weren't in the situation we were in.

"My men haven't had a woman in a long time."

The muscles in Jed's back tensed. "And they won't have one now." His voice was low, gravelly. I knew we were almost there, at the point of rage.

"I'll have you know they take what they want. As do I." Max took a step forward. "Now stand aside."

Jed stood his ground, planting his feet. I swallowed.

We'd had worse odds than this. The only thing was that last time it was walkers. Live people were harder to deal with.

Max rolled his neck on his shoulders. "I'll give you one more chance to—"

Jed lunged, peeling the hunting knife from his belt and plunging it straight into Max's chest. Max's eyes widened as blood spurted from the wound. A gurgle escaped his lips and he staggered backwards. Jed stayed on him and twisted the knife. Then his body slid down from the knife, dropping in a heap on the ground.

I already had my knife in hand and I took the advantage, spinning to the left and slicing Harold's throat. His hands went to his neck, trying to stanch the flow of blood, but it spurted high and fast, coming to land on my boots in a red spray. As I turned to look at the last two, the ones who had first followed us into the supermarket, I saw Jed had already downed them both. Now his knife protruded from the eye socket of one. When he turned to look at me I saw blood spray covering his face.

"We have to get the other two."

I nodded. Four down, two to go.

Together, we crept from the holding room and out into the supermarket. I knew that they would have walked freely, without any fear, and we could use that to our advantage now. Creeping down the aisle directly towards the door, Jed paused at the end, indicating that I should follow his lead. The two men were just disappearing around the corner. We'd taken those four down in a matter of seconds.

"I'll take the one on the left," Jed whispered.

Following his lead, we too rounded the corner and with knives ready, we snuck up behind the two. I slid my blade into Jack as Jed garroted Russ. Sounds of strangled words and shock broke the quiet and both men slumped to the floor.

Jed straightened and sheathed his knife. "Are you okay?" he asked.

It had been a long time since I had killed. Jed had been the leader, the killer. Whenever we dealt with walkers he was the one to use his knife unless I absolutely had to.

I'd never killed a person before. I'd never wanted to. Until now.

I nodded. "I think so." Those men were going to hurt me. They were going to hurt both of us. And that was enough. It was kill or be killed in this world. And I chose to kill.

Jed slung his arm around me and pulled me close. The blood from the men we'd brutally murdered coated my skin and soaked into my hair, but as I slung my arms around his waist and squeezed, I shut it all out. None of it mattered. I was with Jed, and that's all that mattered.

"We had to do it. It was them or us."

Jed smiled. "That's my girl."

WHISPERS OF THE APOC

"Alexa, stop," Georgia said.

Annoyed at her daughter's habit of putting strands of her long, dark hair in her mouth, she added a "mom stare" to punctuate her point. Alexa pouted, but did as she was told. Georgia chuckled a little at how differently she had used that phrase just a few months ago, in her kitchen, directed at a small electronic device that played music, a device that her daughter wished they could rename! *My, how life has changed,* she mused, less than happily. She hadn't seen her home, much less her kitchen in three months—three long months. She had been "trapped," or rather "safe" on Cape Cod since the day the bridges fell.

***

It was the weekend after Labor Day. The two of them had driven to the Cape to spend time with her mother on her seventieth birthday. Alexa didn't really want to come along—what seventeen-year-old would give up a beautiful fall Saturday—but she did love her grandmother. On the drive down, they heard news radio stories about a rapidly-spreading virus reaching the DC area. The word *pandemic* was being used. Georgia hadn't thought much of it when she first heard the stories just two days ago, but now it was beginning to worry her. Like every other virus that made the news, it struck the elderly and children most easily. But what virus didn't? She was sure that there'd be a vaccine by Thanksgiving. Yet, in a small way, it sharpened her need to spend time with her mom. Moms was a former staff sergeant, and very capable in spite of her seventy years. But she was a heart patient, and since Dad's death last year, lived alone.

They'd had a nice brunch at the Daniel Webster Inn. Moms loved their Belgian waffles. As they were leaving there was some commotion in the parking lot, but Georgia hustled them into the car before Alexa wandered over out of curiosity, or Moms went over to take charge. As much as she would normally want to help, today she just avoided it and headed back to the house. No need for that kind of excitement. She and Alexa helped Moms take in the awnings, and readjust the woodpile in anticipation of the midweek delivery of wood that was coming.

They said their goodbyes briefly as always. They lived so close, it didn't make sense to linger. It was nearly dark as they turned onto Route 6 heading off Cape. Just as they started down the final hill, they heard a strange screeching sound in the air like a fast-moving plane that was about to crash. In anticipation, Georgia slowed down from her normal 70 mph. A few seconds later, as they rounded the corner where the Sagamore bridge and the Christmas Tree Shops windmill came into sight, they saw it—a fast-moving trail of smoke in the sky, coming from behind and the left of them. It hit the bridge and exploded right in front of them.

Georgia hit the brakes and steered hard right, nearly off-roading the Jeep. She made it off the last exit, barely, and headed onto 6A to get back to Moms' house. A moment later, she heard a second blast, a bit further off. She knew instantly that the Bourne Bridge had fallen. She headed back toward Moms' house at breakneck speed, thinking that the local PD would be too occupied with the explosions to worry about her speeding.

Oh crap! We're trapped. Who did this? Was it the Russians? Koreans? It wasn't nuclear, or we'd have been vaporized. Could it have been someone on the base? Why? She recalled stories of how her great uncles had accidentally fired ordnance (which was, fortunately, unarmed) that landed on the road just shy of the Sagamore bridge back in the sicties. The memory provided her with no comfort for she *knew* that was not what had happened.

When they arrived, Moms wasn't answering the door. She let herself and Alexa in and called out but there was no reply. They walked back to the den because they could hear the TV. On it, the news of the virus was blaring. It was much more deadly than originally thought. Moms was in her recliner in front of the TV, her hand clutched in her shirt, her face a rictus of pain.

"Moms!" Georgia rushed to her side, and checked for a pulse—there was none, even though she was still warm. *Must have just happened. Oh Moms....I'm so sorry I wasn't here.* Picking up the phone to call 911, she got the fast-busy signal that indicated all circuits were busy. *Everyone must be calling about the explosions.*

Alexa was shaking her grandmother, begging her to not leave, to come back. As she hung up the phone, Alexa chastised her mother for not starting CPR. With more patience than she knew she had, she explained to Alexa how Moms' pacemaker had a built-in defibrillator that would have gone off and that it was quite powerful. No amount of CPR was going to bring her back if the defibrillator hadn't. Even a cart full of drugs and a full hospital-grade defibrillator wouldn't make a difference at this point. There was nothing they could do. Moms was dead.

Silently, she put her hand on Moms' forehead to close her eyes, returned Moms' hands to a peaceful position on her lap, and gently kissed her goodbye. Alexa followed suit. They both sat on the couch across from Moms' lifeless body. Georgia was numb with grief, but with a rising fear of what was going on outside of the house. Alexa's body hitched with the tears she made no effort to try to control.

After a period of time, the news blaring on the TV started filtering through to her brain. More about the virus. She turned to see Alexa, no longer crying, her mouth agape and finger pointing. The word on the screen was zombies.

"Zombies?! No shit! After all the crap on TV, it's real?" Alexa, shocked out of her grief, simultaneously expressed both surprise and the lack thereof. *Teenagers!* Georgia thought, *there's just no understanding them. Was I really ever one?* Remembering the few episodes of "The Walking Dead" she had watched with Alexa, she walked to the kitchen, grabbed a kitchen knife and returned, not sure if she was ready to do what she must if the stories were true.

"Don't be ridiculous. It's fake news. There are no zombies," she reassured her daughter, but really she was trying to convince herself. Alexa raised an eyebrow at the knife in Georgia's hand that belied her statement. Just then Moms' eyes snapped open, unseeingly, and she sat up in a way that Moms hadn't been able to for years, and turned toward them, mouth opening. Without hesitation, Alexa grabbed the knife from her mother's hand and stabbed what had been her grandmother just a short time ago, right in top of her head. As the lifeless body returned to the chair, Alexa stumbled backward, dropped the knife, and ran for the bathroom, where she promptly puked.

"How did you know that would work?" she asked, as Alexa returned.

"I didn't. I just figured it works in the stories," she said, wiping her mouth off with her arm. "We had to do something or we were screwed."

"Language, Alex!"

"Seriously Ma? I just saved our lives, and you're worried about a bad word. We have a lot worse to worry about!" came Alexa's retort.

"You're right," Georgia said, shaking her head. "But I just can't believe it's zombies. This is crazy. But...just in case, let's shut off all the lights, and close all the curtains. Where the hell does Moms keep the candles and flashlights?"

"Ma! Language!" Alexa smirked.

***

They bedded down in an upstairs bedroom, feeling safer up there than on the first floor. Georgia worried a little that one might come through the sliding glass door, or climb up a trellis. *Could they do that? Act intentionally?* she wondered. *Can they smell us?* Sleep did not come easily. She tossed and turned, and finally, before dawn, just gave up hope of sleep. She saw that Alexa, too, was wide awake.

"Alexa, we have to make a plan. And, I can't believe I'm saying this, but we have to plan how to survive zombies. Let's start gathering supplies," she said. *But where we'll go, I have no idea,* she thought. "Why don't you go through Pops' knives? He had some really good ones. Grab the longest, sturdiest ones you can get." It was a good thing that chefs kept their own knives, and that Pops threw nothing away. Georgia was sad to think what his prized knives would be used for now. While Alexa dealt with the knives, she looked around and located extra batteries for the flashlight, and some water bottles. As she was digging around in a very useful-looking backpack, she found Moms' base ID.

That's it! That's who blew up the bridges. The military on Joint Base Cape Cod did it to make the Cape an Island—to keep the zombies off it!

"Alexa, we're going to the base. The folks there seem to have a plan."

"That's who blew up the bridges?" Alexa's head cocked to one side.

"It had to be. Who else would have the ability? They probably did it to keep zombies off the Cape," Georgia said. *Perhaps they were successful and our preparations are for nothing,* she hoped.

Her plan was to was to drive to the back of the base, either through the back gate of the base, or, as a backup, further down Route 130 at the end of the landing strip. The second choice meant some walking. It all hinged on how far they could drive. They'd have to go north on 6A to get to Quaker Meetinghouse Road so they could cross over to 130. That portion of 6A was densely populated with little motels. She had no idea what they'd face there, or frankly anywhere along the route. Would they run into dead, or rather undead people in cars? Would there be zombies walking the street? Maybe they'd find other survivors. She hoped that the virus's spread to Cape Cod had been minimal.

Even if they got to Quaker Meetinghouse Road, they still had to get past its areas of population, which fortunately were few. They had to get down Route 130. There were a lot of variables and it was all a big gamble. But if they got to 130, she thought they'd be OK. It would be the indicator that the virus had not taken hold here on the Cape. But if they did run into trouble, they'd have to move to Plan C—ditch the car and hike through backyards and woods. This was only viable at all because there were few houses between Route 130 and the base. She liked having a plan and backups.

They hunted around the house for more supplies. They found Ramen, dried fruit, nuts, and peanut butter—camp food! She was sad remembering how Moms had gotten rid of her tent and camping gear last year. She had reluctantly decided to forego the potluck camping events with her friends that she had been participating in for thirty years. But Georgia thought she might still have a tarp, as they had many uses.

"Alexa, can you go down to the basement and see if you can find a tarp or two? Check the garage, too, but do it quietly. I'm going to see if the internet is still up so I can print out local maps," she called over her shoulder, heading into the office.

She was actually hoping that Moms still kept a gun somewhere and that she could find it. A gun would be so much better than just Pops' chef knives.

Rummaging around in the desk for paper, she pulled the drawers all the way out, remembering the secret drawer in the old desk that held Moms' gun when she was a kid. No luck. But from where she was sitting she could see what looked like the corner of a lockbox on a shelf under the cloth-covered bedside table in Moms' bedroom.

Pulling it out, she noted the tumbler lock—it had six rollers. *Oh, thank God,* she thought. *This is an easy one.* She rolled the numbers to Moms' birthdate and heard the satisfying click of it unlocking. She was rewarded with a Sig Sauer P238, in Muddy Girl Pink. It was fully loaded. A single box of ammo sat next to it.

They loaded up her jeep with the supplies they had found, adding a few pillows and blankets at the end. These were not just for sleeping but as window buffers in case a zombie got near them and tried to break through.

Georgia started the car and hit the button to roll the garage door up, unsure if there would be one zombie, or a hundred just past the doors. She was ready to ram through them if there were. There weren't. As they headed down the driveway, they saw Joe and Pete loading their pickup truck, so she pulled up and rolled down the window.

"Hey, Joe, Pete. I can't believe this is happening. Did you hear? Zombies!"

"Yeah, we heard. It's crazy. The regular news went off the air last night about 11. The only thing we're getting is radio reports…the cops are still trying to manage things." Joe took off his hat and ran his hands through his thick but graying hair.

"Where are you headed?" she asked. "We were thinking of going to Otis, I mean Joint Base Cape Cod. I think it was them that blew up the bridges."

"Yeah, that makes sense. The news was all zombie virus stories at a national level. Zombies in DC, zombies in Jersey. Nothing about the Cape, not even the local stations. But two explosions….I should have put two and two together that it was the bridges. But what about the railroad bridge? I didn't hear a third explosion."

"Oh, yeah, you're right. So it's not quite an island. We could get off of here. But then, where would we go? Doesn't matter, I'm still making for the Base. Join us? Or we could join you. What were you guys planning to do?"

"We were just going to head for the water and steal a boat, but the Base sounds like a better option—if they're not overrun. How are you getting there? It's a long way up 6A, around the Bourne Rotary and down." He cocked his head sideways, crinkling the corner of his eyes.

"The back way," she smiled, waving Moms' ID card.

"Great idea! But where's Frieda?" Her face gave him all the answer he needed. "I'm so sorry. Your mom was a cool lady! That must have been awful," he paused. "Okay, we'll follow you ladies."

"Wait, should we check if the Simpsons are home? Or what about Allie and Dave?" she asked, hoping that their other neighbors had not met the same fate as her mother.

"Already did that, at the crack of dawn. We used their keys to let ourselves in. Both houses were empty."

Satisfied, she started the Jeep up again, as Joe and Pete hopped in their pickup. They got out of the neighborhood with little effort, seeing only one zombie on a side street. It bounced off the side of Georgia's car with a sickening thud and then attempted to give chase, despite its two broken legs. Route 6A was a bit more challenging, as there was a spot with a few abandoned cars, one of them a cruiser, with zombies around them. She figured that that one driver had hit a zombie, unaware of what it was, and gotten out of the car to investigate, and gotten bitten. Then the cop showed up and followed suit.

They managed to navigate around the cars, taking out the three zombies the same way as they had managed the one in the neighborhood. They weren't dead, but they were not going to hinder them.

Quaker Meetinghouse Road was more of the same. Two small groups of cars like on 6A. This time what worked was for Georgia to hit the zombie. It then bounced off her car, and when it went down Joe ran over its head. At the high school entrance, there were nearly a dozen zombies and four cars to negotiate. They were all on the right side of the cars, pulled onto the right shoulder. She reached into the back of her pants and got the gun, and handed it to Alexa, who took it and just stared. She wasn't sure if Alexa was more surprised that her mom had a gun, or that her mom was giving it to her to use.

"See the little lever on the side? That's the safety. Flip it off," she told Alexa, who nodded. Taking the gun, Alexa did as her mother instructed, and when she found her voice, it was to squeak, "Cool! It's pink!! A pink gun! Moms is awesome...*was* awesome," and then she was silent again.

"Yes, it's pink," she replied, amused that this was what her daughter had chosen to say. "If we get overrun, shoot the zombies, but not until I say so."

Staying in the right lane, she proceeded slowly. The zombies made their way from the right shoulder toward her. At the last moment, she jerked the Jeep into the oncoming lane and gunned it. She made it past them unscathed. Joe followed suit, taking out three of them as he went. The others couldn't keep up. But she knew if they got stopped at any point, the zombies could catch up with them.

They crossed over Route 6 without incident, but the intersection at Cotuit Road was a challenge. From a distance, she could see that the mini-mall there had been overrun. She slowed to a stop. The movie theater and the Stop and Shop must have gotten attacked overnight. There were literally a hundred zombies milling about in the intersection, perhaps confused by the traffic lights and that annoying noise they made to indicate that it was safe for pedestrians to cross. Joe pulled up next to her and indicated they should reverse without turning around. They did, until they reached a side street they could pull onto. They needed to get off the road before the nine zombies that were following them caught up, trapping them. If they were "lucky" those zombies would join the Cotuit Road herd instead of finding them.

Alexa and Pete kept watch while she and Joe consulted the map. All her plans had been contingent on their getting to Route 130. That was not going to happen now. They came up with a Plan D—Cape Cod Airfield in Marstons Mills. Joe had recently gotten his private pilot license. If there was a plane there, and Joe was sure there would be, they could fly it to the Base. Even better was that the roads that led to it were very sparsely populated—big houses, far apart, lots of undeveloped land. If they had to, they could walk. That was Plan E.

Behind her, Alexa giggled excitedly at the idea of flying in a small plane.

***

With Joe in the lead this time, they managed to drive down Pinkham Road to Farmville to Race Lane, which led them to the Cape Cod Airfield. They ran into the occasional zombies along the way, in ones and twos, bouncing them off Joe's pickup, and running them over with her Jeep. It started to feel routine. She almost felt safe.

As they got near the airfield, Joe indicated that they should pull into a side road. They got out of their vehicles in the nearest driveway and Joe began explaining that they needed to enter the airfield silently so as not to attract attention. Just then, two zombies came around the corner of the house, a young woman, followed by what had obviously been her four-year-old child. Joe rounded on the woman and took her out with a single blow, but not one of them could bring themselves to kill the little one. It was still a child, in a cute flowered sundress and one white sandal. Inside the house, the "father" was pressing against the large bay window, apparently trying to get out to them.

"Okay, we have to take care of her or she'll follow us, and we have to do it before he gets out. Rock, paper, scissors, lizard, Spock?" Pete suggested.

"Oh, just give me the knife. If I can kill my own grandmother, a little kid can't be that bad," Alexa offered.

"We'll do it together," said Pete.

Pete put his hand on the top of the little one's head, and while she struggled to bite him, Alexa came up from behind and slid a knife quietly into the base of her skull. The zombie-child fell to the ground lightly and without a sound.

"Ugh, that was grosser than I thought. Her head was kinda soft," she said, as she casually wiped the zombie blood onto her jeans. Pete just stared.

They put everything they could into backpacks, or pockets of clothing (the gun was once again tucked into Georgia's waistband at the back) and sneaked as quietly as they could onto the airfield. They were lucky on two fronts. Number one, they ran into no other zombies. Number two, there were several planes on the ground. It had been late in the day on Sunday, in the shoulder season, when the virus hit the Cape, so most, if not all, of the planes were on the ground. The first planes they came to were the ones used by the sky diving outfit that used the airfield as its base. They were all bigger, louder planes. Then there were the two-man biplanes that were used to give tours for visitors. Just beyond those, there were three small private planes, but two turned out to be locked. Joe figured if all of them were locked, they'd deal with prying a door open, but he wanted to check to see if one might have been left unlocked. The third one appeared to be, but it had someone in it. Or it had been some*one*, but now it was some*thing*.

"It's a Cessna 182, good," Joe said. "Single engine, holds four. I am rated for that craft."

"Really? You're worrying about regulations?" Alexa snarked under her breath.

Pete, who heard Alexa, smiled as he tested the door, and found it unlocked. He distracted the zombie, while Joe opened the door on the other side and dispatched the zombie. Getting it out was difficult. *I'll bet Joe has trouble getting in and out with his 6'2" frame*, Georgia mused.

"Pete and I will remove the chocks, push this baby to the end of this runway, then we'll all get in, start it, I hope, and take off."

"You hope?" Georgia asked, with growing agitation.

"I don't know if there's anything wrong with it, and I certainly won't know if there's fuel until I start it up." He thought for a moment, then half smiled, half winced. "Fuel…"

"We're gonna need fuel, aren't we?" she asked, running her hand back from her forehead through her hair. When he nodded sheepishly, she replied, "Alexa and I are no help pushing the plane, so we'll go check in what passes for a hanger over there, and see if there are any fuel cans."

"It's not actually that heavy," he replied.

"That's great. Too late. Let's just do it this way, OK?" she asked, getting irritated.

While the guys positioned the plane and Joe did pre-flight checks, Georgia and Alexa approached the hanger. Noises indicated that there were at least one or two zombies within—either that or a whole bunch of angry cats. The barn-style doors were open, so she peeked around a corner quickly and could see that there was a biplane within. It was probably in for service. There was someone, or rather, something in the cockpit, apparently trapped. *That one should be easy so long as it doesn't figure out how to get out*, she thought. A second one, wearing coveralls, was lumbering about aimlessly. Just beyond the zombie, she could see a few cans of what could be airplane fuel. Keeping her eye on it, she began to formulate a strategy, when she saw movement out of the corner of her eye. It was Alexa, cat-like, climbing onto the biplane behind the trapped zombie. She quietly slid the knife into the base of its skull and started to jump down.

Good girl, she was thinking, but changed her mind, when Alexa landed with a loud grunt and followed it with "Hey, you! Zombie! Over here!" attracting the other zombie in her direction.

"Mom, get the fuel," she yelled over her shoulder as she led the zombie on a chase around the biplane. Annoyed at and frightened for her daughter, she nonetheless ran over to the fuel and lifted each of the three cans, selecting the heaviest one. "Got it," she yelled. "Now run for the left side of the door, I'll run for the right." They got there at almost the same moment, sliding the doors shut and securing them with some wire that Alexa had somehow had time to grab on her race for the door.

"That was fun!" Alexa breathed.

"Fun! I could kill you, Alexa," Georgia replied, through gritted teeth, frustrated at Alexa's lack of concern for her own safety.

"It's a new world, Mom!"

As much as Georgia would have liked to argue and make this a teaching moment, it was critical that they get to the plane and give what they hoped was fuel to Joe.

"Yep, that's Avgas!" Joe proclaimed after barely opening the can. "Let's how much she'll take." It took up nearly half of what was in the container.

"Okay, let's do this. Everyone needs to be in place before Joe tries to start her. I imagine the plane is going to be noisy and attract zombies all the way from Osterville! Alexa, you get in behind Joe. Pete, stow the rest of the fuel, and get in next to Alexa. I'll cover us," Georgia said, as she pulled out the gun.

"Joe, once they are in, hit the ignition. If it starts, I'll jump in and you do your thing. Get us off the ground. If not, everybody out and we'll run for the cars."

"Well, alrighty, then," Joe nodded, as he saw the weapon.

Fortunately, the plane started without a problem. They taxied down the runway, and she could see two zombies appear out of the woods behind them.

Go, go, go, go, she chanted silently. They were nearly at the end of the runway when they hit 60 mph and Joe lifted it off the ground. They barely made it over the trees. As they came back around to make the 10-mile trip west, they could see a few more zombies on the runway, bumping into each other, looking up to see the source of the noise.

"Oh, what I wouldn't give to have a tail gun right now," said Pete, earning Alexa's obvious admiration.

"See if you can get Otis, Edwards, Cape Cod, whatever it's called now, on the horn. It's 234 or 243 MHZ, or something in that range," Joe suggested.

"Mayday Mayday. Trying to reach Joint Base Cape Cod. Mayday Mayday," Georgia called on each channel as she dialed through. No response. Her heart was in her mouth. *What if they are all dead? What if we land and are surrounded by zombies?* But then her reasonable side took over. *Perhaps there's just no one manning the radio at the moment…they're a bit busy right now.*

Her fears were allayed as they approached the base. They could see folks on the ground, folks that moved with deliberation and intent—no shambling. They flew over the runway, and Joe "waggled" the wings to let them know he was friendly. He came back around to land, and was pleased that they did not get shot at. They landed safely but found themselves with guns pointed at them, not just hand guns, but big semi- and fully automatic weapons, held by big men in Kevlar jackets. Georgia was never so happy to have had a gun pointed at her.

***

Three months later, they had been screened by the medical staff, had their skill sets assessed by some officious fellow in a Marine uniform, given an ID card, and assigned a barracks. Since then, others had arrived, all from the upper Cape. Most came on foot, some in cars, vans, campers, and two people on Goldwings. Only one other group arrived by plane. Everyone who arrived was let in. No more military ID requirement. They were all survivors.

The base renamed itself back to Otis—much easier than Joint Base Cape Cod. The base military took charge. The Air National Guard Intelligence Wing had the ranking officer, so all military ranks were converted to Air Force. Even civilians were given ranks. Those with skills, such as engineers or nurses, were ranked as specialist, cops were evaluated for full ranks, and since the Air Force did not use the rank of private, everyone else was a private, including Alexa. The only exception to this were the local members of the Wampanoag tribe. They set up their own living space in the woods on the Mashpee side of the base, and maintained their own order, working closely with the military to make the base successful. The tribe had deep knowledge of the land and the animals and the making of hand weapons, all of which they shared freely. The military recognized that handling this any other way would lead to dissension, which was never good.

Everyone lived in military barracks, women with women, men with men. There were few children and even fewer complete families. When new ones formed, they were given military housing, which Alexa thought was a step down from the barracks. A medical center had been established, along with a meal center. Food was neither delicious, nor plentiful, but it was sufficient. Work details were created and everyone was assigned to one, depending on skill or interest. Farming detail was mostly gathering nuts, mushrooms, and other items from the forest, and identifying areas for optimum growing in the spring. Fence details either repaired existing fences, built new ones, or installed the poles that sat at 45 degree angles for "catching" zombies that came near before they mowed through the fence. Security patrols typically contained at least one military or former cop, someone good with a gun. They walked the border checking for and removing zombies that got caught in the poles outside the fences. Stationary guards stood sentry at the two active and two dormant entrances to the camp. Hunting parties of three or four typically included a Wampanoag or a trained hunter who led the others in tracking and killing squirrels, deer, raccoons, and other local fauna. The Wampanoag taught survivors how to make bows and arrows, spears, and traps on these trips, and how to use them. The hunters were typically the best shots on the base, and had a gun with them. They could use a single shot to fell an animal lest they attract zombies. The other bullets were in case the worst happened. Any kills were hauled out of there quickly, so as not to be seen or smelled by any zombies if they were near the fences. More often than not, zombies were attracted to and killed near the fences using hand weapons.

Forays were the most dangerous detail. Only a select few, mostly military at first, went on these. They exited the camp and made their way to local houses, stores, and businesses, to take anything useful. Occasionally, besides the food, tools, medicines, and other supplies, they found a person, but there were fewer of those as time went on. In fact, they found mostly zombies now—people who had died locked in their homes. As quickly as the forays filled up the Otis larders, the requirements of its residents began depleting them. They needed to go further afield as the cold began to hit.

In late September, they had embarked on a series of forays to Mashpee Commons in conjunction with the Wampanoag. With all its varied stores, it was a treasure trove of medical supplies, foodstuffs, clothing, and more. In order to get what they needed safely, they had to execute a number of "raids" first to clear out zombies. They started by setting off ordinance in the nearby rotary (the "151 Rotary") to draw out zombies. Then they picked them off from the treetops and the rooftops. The first time they went, they had all they could do to eliminate the herds that showed up. Suppressors or bows and arrows were used to keep silent so as not to attract more zombies. The noise from the ordinance, however, attracted them from fairly good distances, depending on the wind, so several of them always kept to the treetops to eliminate any late joiners. When they could finally enter the buildings, the raiding parties went in through the employee doors and back doors, to take whatever they needed, eliminating zombies as they went. It was better than going through the front door. Front entrances were often glass, highlighting their approach, and energizing the zombies. Plus, there were fewer employees than customers in any given store, making back entrances less risky.

It had taken four weeks to get what they needed and thousands of zombies were killed.

There were two boards on Otis that tracked zombie kills. One was just the total kill count. That number stood at 12,687 as of last evening. It was a big number until you considered how many people were on the Cape. The year-round population was 215,000. At the height of the summer vacation season, there were closer to 500,000 people. Estimates for September were 300,000. With 5,000 people on the base, there were still over 250,000 potential zombies. They were going to have to get creative if a herd from the MidCape or Lower Cape moved in on them.

The second board was by individual, listing the top 20 zombie killers. Pete was on the leader board. Alexa was jealous—she had only five. Everyone had at least one.

***

Today Georgia was on security patrol on the north side. Joe and Alexa were as well. When she was not chewing her hair, Alexa, it turned out, was a good shot. It was early, predawn, and it was cold—damned cold. The wind cut through her like a knife. Georgia could see her breath and even the inside of her nose was cold. *Winter is coming*, she thought wryly, harkening back to her old life, sitting on the couch with Alexa, watching "Game of Thrones"—or Dragons and Zombies, as Alexa liked to call it. *It's going to snow soon and we're going to be trapped. They better finish shoring up those fences and kill lots more zombies.*

It was her first time on security patrol. She had mostly been learning about the local area, flora and fauna from the Wampanoag for the past three months. But that had included training with a bow and arrow, and she had become *very* good at that. So she was assigned to a patrol—learn a skill, use a skill. The last three patrols to this area had come back reporting no zombies. They'd reported no deer, rabbits, or squirrels either, which was too bad, because as an Archer (she liked that title), she could hunt game for the larders. It was not unusual for there to be no zombies here, as there had been little population between the base and the Canal on the north side. However, the lack of game was a little concerning this early into the winter, as this had traditionally been an area with lots of local animals.

As she scanned the woods, Georgia had little expectation of seeing zombies, and, unlike the others, she wished *not* to see any. She hoped that Murphy and his damned Law would not make an appearance today and send some zombies. She blamed Murphy for the whole zombie apocalypse. But luckily their little base civilization had not had any brushes with "all things that can go wrong, go wrong" for months.

But today Murphy was back. As they came around a corner in the fence with a particularly large beech tree, the three of them saw that a medium-sized maple tree had fallen over and was leaning on a section of the fence, pushing it toward the ground. Anyone could walk a few feet up the nearly horizontal tree and right into the base. Fortunately, there were no zombies in sight, but the fence was weakened and would need immediate repair, as there were no zombie poles on the other side of fences here on the north. They radioed back for a crew to clear the tree, and one to fix the fence. But it would be a half an hour before they arrived. Fifteen minutes later, as Joe stepped around a tree inside the base to take a leak, two zombies came into view in the brush beyond the fence.

"Shit, fuck, damn, hell!" Georgia exclaimed. If they made it to the fence, they could get in. *Did I just use my outside voice,* she wondered, and was answered by Alexa's exclamation, "Language!"

Two more appeared, then three more—promoting them from a group to a herd.

"Double damn it!" she exclaimed, knowing that Alexa was staring a snarky hole through her head right now.

The Otis Patrols hadn't cleared the areas north of the base. The threat from the south and east was considerably more, since that's where the majority of Cape Cod's residents and vacationers lived. Something had attracted this herd south. It wasn't loud noises—it had been weeks since they set any ordinance off in the 151 Rotary (which was on the south side). The tree falling couldn't have been that noisy. What exactly it had attracted the herd was and would remain a mystery.

As she notched her arrow, taking aim at the front-most zombie, Georgia thought something was different about this group, but she couldn't quite put her finger on it. She took out the first one easily and watched in growing fear as the group grew larger from behind. The math looked very bad. They were going to be overrun. As she took aim at a second one, her fear made them seem to be walking in slow motion. Then, on her left, Joe pulled back from his weapon and mumbled, "What the...hey!" Alexa fired her weapon, blurting out, "Holy shit!"

The three of them realized that the zombies *were* walking slowly. It wasn't fear-induced perception of slow motion, at all. They were not imagining it. It had to be the cold. Zombies were affected by the cold. It slowed them down.

They handily killed 34 zombies—Georgia got 10, and Alexa and Joe split the other 24. While they waited for the tree and fence crews to come, they radioed back to headquarters and shared what they had learned. When they returned to the main base, new "Kill" crews had already been set up for the next morning. People were lining up to join. The folks of Otis were going to exploit this new advantage and take out as many zombies as they could while this cold snap lasted.

The military were talking about possibly using one of their three helicopters. They could hover over the Bourne Rotary to draw zombies in, and then pick them off from the helicopter, and from nearby trees and buildings.

Georgia learned that while they were gone, there had also been radio contact with the nearby Maritime Academy in Bourne. A number of people had survived, but needed to get out of there. Rescue plans were being considered that used a boat or a helicopter, or trying to scale the remaining bridge—the Train Bridge—to get over the

Canal. Between the news about the cold and the survivors in Bourne, there was hope radiating through Otis.

WHISPERS OF THE APOC

6 The Treehouse by Stanley B. Webb

Don't shoot yet, I want to tell you my story.

I awaited my friends at the trailhead, sleeping bag under my arm, ready for our treehouse campout. The forest behind me rustled in the evening wind. Night gathered. I pretended that I was not afraid. A twig snapped. I backed away. A squirrel chittered, and I felt foolish.

My gang arrived then. My best friend, Art, was fifteen like me. Art's brother, Gordon, was a high school senior. With them were Gordon's best friend, Clarence, and Clarence's thirteen-year-old brother, Lester.

Clarence and Lester hauled an aluminum ice chest between them. When they rested, Lester sat down on the lid.

Clarence sighed with exasperation. "Get up, or you'll dent it!"

"I'm tired!"

"You're such a baby. Go home, you're still too small to climb the tree."

"Am not!"

Gordon interrupted the siblings' dispute. "Did you get it?"

Clarence pushed Lester off the cooler, and raised the lid. Inside was junk food, a slim, brown paper bag, and a twelve-pack of beer.

Art said, "Groovy!"

Clarence glanced at Art and me. "Do you kids drink?"

"Sure," said Art. "All the time."

I had once borrowed a sip from my father's beer, and found the taste horrible. I didn't admit that to my friends.

Clarence closed the lid, and asked Gordon, "Give me a hand with this?"

We followed the seniors into the woods, along a trail which only we knew. The forest floor, covered with a thick layer of dead leaves, crunched softly underfoot.

I tripped on something hidden, and hard. "Ouch!"

Clarence snickered. "Watch out for the rocks."

Art walked beside me. He had a flashlight, and played ray-gun, zapping the beam around.

Gordon snapped, "Get that out of my eyes!"

Art and I chatted about ghosts and murderers. Lester, overhearing, moved closer to his brother. I thought that it would be fun to scare Lester, and surreptitiously signaled Art. He and I were lifelong partners in mischief, having launched fake UFOs over the highway, and chased trick-or-treaters while disguised as monsters. Art understood my intentions, and nodded back. I quietly left the group, following in the darkness thirty feet behind, awaiting the right moment to spring.

However, my sneaky imagination backfired: I started thinking that a real murderer might be stalking me as I stalked Lester; he would smother my cries with a chloroformed rag, and drag me off, and my fate would remain a mystery until some future hunter discovered my bones. I scared myself so much, I imagined hearing footsteps behind me. I considered fake-stumbling to alert

Lester, so I could return to the safety of our gang, but Art would have ragged on me for chickening out.

The city's noise faded to a murmur behind us.

We arrived at the treehouse tree.

She grew a quarter of a mile into the woods. My father once told me that *his* grandfather said that the tree had germinated alone in a field. She was the mother of the whole woods. The old maple's trunk bulged six feet in diameter, grotesque with burls and ridges of bark. Four subsidiary trunks branched eight feet up, each of them as large as a normal tree, and the treehouse sat between them. Gordon and Clarence had built it out of discarded lumber. Moss stained the old boards, a black tarpaulin covered the flat roof, and bent, rusty nails studded the corners. The house had a vacant doorway in one wall, and a window frame opposite.

Clarence scaled the trunk, and Gordon lifted the cooler to him, grunting. They juggled the ice chest for a moment, then Clarence yanked it inside. Gordon scampered up the trunk, and Art followed.

Lester scrabbled at the bark, trying to climb, but he did not know the holds. "Help me!"

Clarence answered with sepulchral tones, *"No one can help you."*

Art offered, "I'll help, but I can only reach down this far. You have to make it up to me."

Lester tried again, and failed.

"What a baby," said Clarence.

"Don't call me that!" Lester sounded as if he were ready to cry.

I deliberately stepped on a fallen stick.

Art said, "Something's out there!"

Lester looked back, but could not see me in the dark. He reached up for Art's offered hand. "Help me!"

I took another crunching step.

Art withdrew his hand. "Oh, my God!"

I delivered a monster-movie roar, and charged.

Lester collapsed in tears, curled up against the tree's gnarled roots.

Clarence laughed down at his brother. "What a baby!"

Suddenly, I felt like an asshole for scaring a little kid.

I said to Clarence, "You sound like a broken record."

Clarence scowled.

I put my hand on Lester's trembling shoulder. "Didn't your brother ever show you how to climb this tree?"

"No."

"Get up. First, put your foot on that humped root, and grab that ridge of bark with your right hand, then you can push and pull yourself up. Now, stretch your left hand up to that burl, and wedge your other foot into that deep groove. Good! Put your other foot on that knot, and you can reach the edge of the treehouse with your right hand. When you have both hands on it, pull yourself in, while you kick-step up the trunk."

Clarence, looking shame-faced, pulled Lester up over the edge, but Lester would have made it anyway. I climbed into the fort, the weathered plywood floor creaking under my weight. Art's flashlight hung from a screw-hook in the ceiling.

Clarence opened the cooler. "Who wants a beer?"

"I do," said Art.

"Um, me," I said.

Lester piped in, "And me!"

Clarence smirked. "You're too little."

"I am not, I climbed the tree!"

"Well, we only have twelve cans, and four of us divides into twelve evenly. If you have a beer, one of us will be shorted."

"You can have one of mine," I said.

Art and I sipped our beers carefully, but Lester swallowed a mouthful. We all laughed at his expression. Lester scowled, and forced another gulp down.

"There may be hope for you." Clarence opened the slim, brown bag. "And now, here's something else for all of the little boys."

I had seen the models in *Playboy* magazine, with their firm breasts and neat pubic triangles, but Clarence offered a different magazine, with black-and-white photos of women with pendulous breasts and tangled bushes, who spread their legs wide to display—

"What's that?" Art asked in horror.

Clarence said, "That is pussy."

"No way! That's ugly."

Meanwhile, Gordon opened a second magazine. His eyes widened.

"What's this shit?"

Gordon reversed the magazine, showing a photo of a woman with a penis.

Clarence grabbed the magazine, and hid it away. "They sell three of these books in a plastic sleeve," he explained quickly. "I only saw the top cover; I didn't know that was in there."

The rest of us exchanged glances.

Clarence said hastily, "Would you boys like to see some real, live pussy?"

"On Dyke Island?" Art asked.

Dyke Island was really Emerald Isle, a few acres of dry land in the Oswego River, and the location of a private boarding school, the Esmeralda Smith School for Young Ladies.

Clarence replied scornfully, "No, I'm talking about Doris Morris."

An electric stillness filled the treehouse.

Even Gordon seemed impressed. "Is she back?"

Clarence nodded. "She finished high school in the reformatory. Now, she's in Delta-Delta-Delta sorority at the college."

Lester asked, "Who is she?"

"She's a slut," said Clarence.

Gordon amended, "She's the *Queen of the Sluts*."

Rumor had it that Doris had seduced her stepfather when she was twelve, and later aborted the pregnancy in a girlfriend's bedroom. She was a high school junior when I entered sixth grade. She had carried herself like an Olympian goddess, powerful but flawed. All of the sixth grade girls had cowered from her. The head principal had resigned that year, and the other kids had whispered that he was caught with Doris, naked, in his office.

"But it's Friday night," said Gordon. "Won't she be out drinking?"

Clarence shook his head. "Since reform school, she prefers staying at home with the girls, if you know what I mean."

"What do you mean?" Lester asked.

Clarence rolled his eyes. "She's a lezzie."

We decided that this was a great idea, and descended the tree for a night of sorority window-peeping.

A few sips of beer had made my judgment swimmy, and I tried jumping to the ground. I landed wrong, and fell.

"Ouch!"

Art helped me up, laughing. "Smooth move, Stan!"

We angled through the trackless woods, trusting in our youthful navigation sense to lead us where we wanted to go. The full moon rose above us, sailing through the forest's canopy. Art zapped with the flashlight as we traded rumors about Doris, excited for our adventure.

Suddenly, the woods erupted into chaos. Birds screamed out from their overnight roosts, whirling and tumbling around us. Squirrels and other small animals stormed through the leaf litter, and something large thumped by. I saw the white flash of a deer's tail. We stopped in our tracks, too startled to be afraid. The commotion ceased as abruptly as it had begun.

Gordon said, "What the fuck," his voice a-quaver.

A hideous wail replied. My hair stood up. The wail rose high, filling the night, then subsided, only to rise again. I thought that it was a banshee, a monster whose scream presaged my death.

"That's the alarm at the nuclear power plant," said Clarence.

"Do you think there's been a reactor accident?" Gordon asked.

Lester said, "Let's go home."

"Maybe they're just testing the alarm?" Art asked.

"Not at night," I said.

Clarence said ominously, *"It must be a nuclear attack."*

Lester started crying.

"The missiles are crossing the North Pole now. They'll strike in fifteen minutes."

"I want to go home!"

"There's no time, we must savor our remaining moments."

The siren ended abruptly. The night turned silent, except for Lester's trembling sobs.

Clarence said, "See, it was just a test. What a baby."

We continued on our quest.

"It's really quiet," Art whispered. "I don't hear Oswego anymore."

My skin tingled. "Do you feel it?"

"Yeah, it's like static electricity."

"Maybe its radiation, maybe there really *was* an accident!"

Clarence said, "It was just a test!"

We emerged from the woods on West Bridge Street, and found the city dark.

"It's a power failure!" Clarence sounded relieved. "That's what the siren was about."

From our location, we had a view of the city hospital, where a galaxy of red and blue lights flashed.

"Are those all ambulances?" Art asked.

"They look like police cars," I replied.

"What's happening?"

"Maybe it's a riot!"

We procrastinated on the curb, intrigued by the distant action. A sense of adventure filled me. I felt as if anything could happen that night.

"Should we go and watch?" Art asked.

"No, we're on a mission." Gordon waved dismissively at the police lights. "We'll find out what that is tomorrow."

We approached the college via the back streets, wary of meeting campus police, and made our way down Sorority Row. Delta-Delta-Delta, a ramshackle Victorian, stood in the Row's cul-de-sac.

Lester said, "It's *The Munsters!*"

Clarence hushed him.

"Listen."

Music came from the rear, *2000 Light Years from Home* by the Rolling Stones. We crept into the Victorian's fenced backyard. The place was like a junkyard, littered with broken furniture and liquor bottles.

Clarence pointed up.

Pale light shone through a window above the rear veranda. A rickety trellis invited climbing. We tiptoed across the mossy shingles, and clustered outside the open window.

The light came from a Coleman lantern, and the music from a transistor radio. There was no furniture. Doris and two other girls, all similarly dressed in cut-off jeans and tie-dyed shirts, sat Indian-fashion on a tattered oriental rug, with playing cards in their hands. They passed a small, metal pipe, and sweet, blue smoke hovered in the chamber.

Doris rearranged her cards, then showed her hand, grinning lasciviously. The other girls folded, then pulled their shirts off over their heads. Their naked breasts jiggled.

My heart leaped inside me. The girls were playing strip poker! I pushed closer to the window, and the shingles underfoot squeaked.

Doris turned. Her eyes locked with mine, and lit up. "Boys on the roof!"

We ran for it. Gordon and Clarence reached the trellis first, with Lester right behind them. Art followed, and the trellis collapsed when he was halfway down. He stumbled, but kept his feet, and ran for the street with the others.

I jumped. The landing stung my feet, and I went to my knees. I wasn't hurt, but I heard the girls racing downstairs, howling like wolves on the hunt. I was too late; they would catch me if I fled to the street. Instead, I hid out back, behind a moldy, old canopy bed. A moment later, the she-wolves burst out through the front door, and howled away up the Row. I waited until their cries faded, then rose.

The Victorian's back door opened.

I dropped back into hiding.

Doris emerged onto the veranda, and scanned the yard, her face a pale oval in the gloom. Her right hand reached out, as if sensing for me, while her left fist held something close to her hip.

She whispered, "I know you're here."

I resisted a guilty urge to reveal myself.

"Do you think I'm stupid? I saw five of you at the window, but only four ran up the street."

Doris lifted the front of her shirt, and waggled her breasts.

"Come here, you can touch them."

I found her behavior arousing, but terrifying, and remained hidden. After a moment she stopped waggling, and covered herself.

"Be that way, I'll find you!"

As she stepped down to the yard, her left hand swung forward, and I saw her switchblade knife. She came straight toward my hiding place. I started crawling around the other end of the old bed as she approached.

"Ah ha!"

She sprang. I lurched up to run, but she grabbed the back of my collar, and pushed me down, bent over the bed's clammy mattress.

"You're just a little one," she said with a laugh. "I'll bet you don't even have a pecker, yet!" She humped her pelvis against me. "You have a sweet ass, though." Doris humped me again. "Makes me wish I had a pecker." She hauled me upright, and held her knife before my eyes. "Let's go inside, Baby."

I knew, in the darkness of my heart, that she meant to kill me.

Letting my knees buckle, I dropped out of her grip and rolled, plowing through her legs. She toppled, and hit the ground with a sharp gasp. I leaped up, and ran, glancing over my shoulder.

Doris had vanished.

I halted, wary that she might plan an ambush, but the yard remained silent. I sensed that I was alone. I crept back to investigate, feeling stupid, but *needing* to know where she was.

She lay face down behind the moldy bed. I paused, and stomped my foot. When she failed to respond, I moved closer, and nudged her with my toe. Nothing happened. I knelt, and turned her over.

The switchblade's hilt protruded from between her breasts.

I staggered, my brain reeling. I wanted to run away, but felt too guilty to leave. I should go for help, but then my parents would find out where I had been, and what had happened because I'd gone there. Maybe I could help, even though the look in her eyes told me that she was dead. I reached for the knife, to pull it out of her.

Sirens wailed, and police lights flashed on the next block. I thought that they had come for me. I left the knife in Doris, and bolted away from there, back up Sorority Row, and back to the woods.

The moment I entered the woods, I fell to my knees, and puked. I crouched there until my heart slowed, and my thoughts smoothed out. The police had not been after me. I had gotten away. No one would ever know how I had killed Doris.

I retched again, a painful heave, then I rose, and started toward the treehouse.

After a few minutes, I heard someone following. I thought it was in my imagination, and paused to prove it. The pursuing footsteps continued for two paces, then halted. My guts seemed to freeze, until I had a reassuring thought, that it was only my friends trying to scare me.

"I know it's you!"

The footsteps resumed, unsteady, but closing inexorably. There was only one follower, and I realized that none of my friends, not even the seniors, would dare to wait alone in the woods just for a prank.

Someone was really after me.

I ran, shielding my face against dead branches, and stumbling on scattered rocks. I had trouble finding the treehouse in the nighttime woods. Finally, I got intelligent, and stopped to listen for Art's snoring, a sound I knew well from a lifetime of sleep-overs.

I also heard the footsteps limping on my trail.

I clambered into the treehouse, groped my way to Art, and clamped my hand over his mouth.

He said, "Mmph!"

I whispered, "Shush," and released him. "Is everyone here?"

"Yeah."

"Somebody's following me."

We listened, but the footsteps had stopped.

I went to bed, certain that I would never fall asleep.

***

Clarence said as I woke, "I'll bet he *let* her catch him."

I opened my eyes to a bright morning. Bird songs filled the woods.

I sat up and asked, "What?"

Clarence said, "Oh, we were just wondering why you didn't run with us last night."

"And, why you got back here an hour behind us," Gordon added with a smirk.

"You bird-dog," said Art. "What did she do to you?"

I could not meet their eyes. "Nothing! I mean, I just hid in the backyard, then snuck out when the coast was clear."

My friends grinned with disbelief.

"Where was Doris, then?" Clarence asked.

I shrugged, acting casual even though my pulse hammered. "Didn't she chase you guys?"

Clarence's grin turned sour. "So you used us as a diversion, you little ass-wipe?"

I shrugged again. "Sorry."

My friends turned away in contempt. I could live with that, but I wanted to forget what had happened with Doris.

"Are there any chips left?" Clarence asked.

"I don't want chips," said Gordon. "I want breakfast."

"Let's go to my place," I offered.

We turned to the doorway.

A frightening man waited outside, seemingly asleep on his feet. He wore a blood-stained hospital gown. His hair had been burned to stubble. His fingers, and his bare feet, were purple.

Clarence called, "Who are you?"

The man opened his lids, and for a moment we saw his whites. Then, his eyes rolled down from inside his skull. He lifted his bruised hands, walked to the tree. One of his legs bent wrong. The man clawed at the bark, trying to climb. His face remained slack.

We backed away from the door.

"He must have wandered away from the hospital," said Art.

"He's acting weird," I said.

"No shit, Sherlock," said Gordon. "The guy's hurt."

The man gave up trying to climb, and reached toward us, his discolored fingers grasping in air.

"Not just that, he's acting like he's crazy."

"He's in agony," said Gordon. "Art, go down there and help him."

Art turned chalky. "No way!"

Gordon balled his fist. "Do it!"

"Why don't *you* do it?" I asked.

Gordon aimed his fist toward me, but then dropped it. We returned to the doorway, where I noticed something else.

"He's not breathing."

Gordon laughed sharply. "Of *course* he's breathing!"

After a moment, Clarence whispered, "No, he's *not*."

We silently stared at the creature. Then, Lester burst into tears.

"He's trying to get us!"

"Knock it off, assholes," Gordon exploded. "You're scaring the kid!"

We ignored Gordon.

The man continued trying to get us.

Art asked, "How do we get down?"

I thought of a tactic.

"He's got a limp," I said. "If four of us keep him distracted here, one of us can climb out the window, then lure him off so the rest of us can escape."

"Who's going to serve as bait?" Clarence asked.

"Me," I said.

Clarence blinked with startled respect.

"It won't work," said Lester. "He heard what you said."

I glanced down into the man's flat eyes.

"I don't think he can understand."

Without giving myself time to reconsider, I backed my feet out through the window, lowered myself to arm's length, and dropped. I landed on a loose rock, and fell. The man came around after me. I scrambled up, and hurried away. When I looked back, he was following at his injured pace. I felt elated that I could outrace him, but terrified by his persistence, as if he knew that I could never escape, no matter how fast I ran.

My friends dropped from the treehouse, one by one, and started toward town. The man paused, turning toward the noise. I cried, "Hey, you," and threw a handful of leaves at him. He returned his attention to me. I felt cocky, and ran toward him. He raised his arms as if to hug me. I dodged around him at the last second, and before he could turn, I kicked the tendons behind his bad knee. I heard his cartilage tear. The man's leg folded, and he fell as if boneless, floundering like a turtle. I joined my friends.

Clarence patted my back. "Good job."

"You *attacked* that guy," Gordon said.

"What do you think is wrong with him?" Art asked.

Clarence shrugged.

"He's dead," said Lester.

Clarence rolled his eyes. "He's not dead."

"But he wasn't breathing."

"Of *course* he was, we just couldn't see it."

I started to feel guilty about what I had done. At that time, none of us believed in the undead. We knew nothing about livor mortis, the bruise-like discolorations created when blood settled to the lowest parts of a cadaver.

"We'll call the police about him from my place," I said.

"And I'll tell them what you did," warned Gordon.

I thought of Doris, and shivered.

We came out of the woods at the end of our street. At that hour on a warm Saturday morning, I expected to find husbands mowing their lawns, wives hanging out their laundry, and to hear the jangle of cartoons through open windows. Instead, we found closed windows, and drawn curtains. I thought that I glimpsed a face in one window, but it was gone when I looked directly.

Clarence whispered, "Where have all the people gone?"

"There's someone," said Gordon, and pointed.

A nude figure stalked across the end of the street, its back toward us. Gordon opened his mouth to call out, but then hesitated. We watched in silence while the figure disappeared around the corner.

Then we continued to my house.

Our front door hung open, creaking in an infinitesimal breeze. We halted on the sidewalk, clustering as we studied the interior. Each unsettling event of the previous hours ticked through my brain like a clock of doom.

"We'd better go in," said Clarence.

"No way," said Art, his voice edged with fright.

I felt closer to hysteria, but I rushed up the walk, and through the doorway. The living room seemed dark after the morning sunshine, so I reached out, and flipped the switch beside the door. Nothing happened. As my vision adapted to the gloom, I saw that the room stood in disarray.

The others followed me inside.

I called out, "Mom, Dad?"

A thump came from somewhere inside the house.

"Maybe they slept in," said Art.

I felt my stomach dropping within me. "Let's go upstairs." My voice came out as thick as mud.

A bloody skeleton, hung with torn muscle fibers, and laced with veins and nerves, lay across Mom and Dad's bed. I felt a stunned curiosity, my mind disassociating the grisly thing from my family. Then, I stepped close, and saw Mom's eyes rolling in the thing's naked sockets. I screamed, grabbed the big, wooden lamp from the night-table, and clubbed the skull. The bone cracked. I swung again. The skull flew apart, and brains splattered across the bed. The eyes ceased rolling. I dropped my weapon, and backed away from the bed, a keening sound escaping from my lips.

"Quiet," Clarence hissed. "Something's coming!"

Thumping footsteps climbed the stairs.

My brain went cold. Driven by rage and fear, I hurried to my bedroom, and found my twenty-two caliber rifle in the messy closet. I grabbed my fifty-count box of long cartridges, loading one into the rifle's single-shot breech. I ran back to face the landing. The others gathered behind me.

A ghoulish creature appeared. It wore only boxer shorts, and its belly gaped open. Pieces of intestine dangled from its gut. The creature staggered up the last step, then advanced with its hands clutching out. I aimed for its heart and fired. The ghoul kept coming. Trembling with panic, I levered the empty cartridge out, fumbled in my pocket for another, and aimed at the creature's forehead. The shot cracked, echoing from the close walls, at point-blank range. The ghoul collapsed at my feet.

"Is that your father?" Art asked.

I cried, "Shut up!"

Gordon stared with shocked eyes, tears streaming down his face. "You killed him!"

"It was already dead, like my moth—" I choked. "Like the guy in the woods! When the alarms went off, and the air turned electric, the dead came to life."

Gordon said, "You're a crazy murderer!"

He made as if to lunge at me. I shifted, thinking only to duck his attack. He looked at my rifle, then cringed back as if I had aimed it at him.

Clarence regarded the motionless ghoul.

"I don't know what's going on," he said. "But we need to get the police."

I tried the telephone, but it was dead.

Gordon snatched the receiver from my hand to listen for himself. He pushed the hang-up buttons seven or eight times, then slammed the receiver back down.

Clarence said, "We'll go to my house. My dad's a Marine, and he'll have things under control."

We ate before we left. That may sound weird, but we had not eaten since the previous night, and that was all junk food. We also used the bathroom. While I peed, I heard Gordon and Clarence whispering outside the door.

"We have to get that gun away from him. He'll shoot us all next!"

"Gordon, something weird *is* going on."

"Are you crazy, too?"

I clutched my rifle tightly.

***

Clarence and Lester's front door also hung ajar.

"I'm not going in," Clarence said. "Let's try your house, Gordon."

Gordon turned pale, and would not answer.

Art finally explained. "Our folks attended a funeral service last night."

Clarence said, "Then we'll have to walk to the police station."

We followed Utica Street toward the river. The streets were deserted. Many of the homes that we passed seemed intact, but many more had broken doors and smashed windows. Some houses had been boarded up from the inside.

A commotion grew before us. I heard no voices, but otherwise the sound was like a milling crowd. We crept up to the corner of a house, and peered around. The house on the diagonal corner was boarded up, and surrounded by a crowd of ghouls. Nearly all of the creatures were damaged, most of them with teeth marks. They pressed shoulder to shoulder, all trying to reach the barricaded walls, and the house groaned under their weight.

"They really are undead," Clarence whispered in awe.

"Idiot!" Gordon said.

"Look at all of them," I said. "How could there be that many dead people around?"

"They rose from their graves," whispered Lester.

"Maybe," said Clarence. "But most of these look like fresh meat. People would have tried to help the first ghouls, thinking that they were sick, or injured, and the ghouls would have attacked them. I'll bet their bite is infectious, like just like vampires. When the police got involved, and the shooting started, well, the ghouls only die if you shoot them in the head, and head shots are difficult. In the Marines, they taught my father to aim for the body. I'll bet that the police get the same training. When you shoot a ghoul to the body, it just keeps coming."

Like my father. "Don't remind me."

Then the besieged front door cracked open. The ghouls poured in. Women and children screamed.

Suddenly, my distress transformed into purposeful clarity. I stepped around the corner, aimed, and fired. A ghoul fell.

Clarence dragged me back. "What in hell do you think you're doing?"

"Helping those people!"

Clarence pushed me against the wall.

"You're an idiot! How many bullets do we have?"

"Um, forty-seven, now."

"Well," said Clarence. "We have more than forty-seven ghouls to deal with, so we can't waste ammunition."

The victims shrieked in horrible agony.

I broke away from Clarence, but he pushed me back, then yanked the rifle from my hands.

I cried, "Give it back!"

"No, we can't save them!"

Gordon grabbed my collar, and punched me on the jaw. "Not so tough unarmed, are you?"

He drew his fist back for another blow, but Clarence grabbed him.

"Stop it, they'll hear you."

"*You* stop humoring him!"

Gordon relented anyway, and sulked off, sucking his knuckles.

Clarence returned to me.

"Hand over the bullets."

"No."

He tried to stare me into submission, but I just stared back. Finally, he sighed, and slung my rifle's strap across his shoulder.

"You'll have to hand them over when we need them."

He walked off, and the others followed. I hesitated, then went with them.

The screams faded behind me.

Approaching the center of town, we found hundreds of abandoned vehicles clogging Utica Street and its sidewalks. Many of the vehicles' doors hung open, and refugee goods lay scattered about. Pools of blood stained the pavement, interconnected with trails of crimson footprints. We passed in silence.

A multiple-vehicle pileup had stopped the exodus at the bridge. Some of the wrecks' headlights glowed dimly. We found a narrow path around the tangled heap of metal and glass. The bridge's span remained clear, except for a lone shopping cart.

"What's *that* doing there?" Art asked.

Clarence explained, "Drunk college boys play with them."

We procrastinated, hiding in the stalled traffic, afraid to expose ourselves on the bridge. Clarence finally goaded us into motion.

"There's nothing around, *let's just go!*"

We ran across the river, and headed toward the police station.

We heard the gunfire first, then the rustling of massed ghouls. They had surrounded the station. The sight reminded me of the Peace Riots that I had seen on television, except that these creatures actually *seemed* peaceful. Snipers worked methodically from the station's roof, and the dead fell steadily. We hid behind a corner to watch.

"Do you think they'll have enough ammo?" Art asked.

Clarence scoffed, "Of course!"

Gordon began sobbing. "Everyone is crazy! Why are they shooting?" He stepped into the open, shouting and waving. "Stop shooting the people!"

A sniper shot him.

Gordon staggered back a step, slapping his hand against his shoulder. He then regarded his bloodied palm, and fell to his knees.

Clarence and I rushed out, and dragged him back.

Clarence said, "I *told* you head shots were difficult."

"Why did they shoot?" Art asked in outrage. "They could tell that he wasn't dead!"

"Maybe they don't believe yet," I said. "Maybe they think it's a revolution."

Lester peered around the corner. "The ghouls are coming!"

Gordon got up, took two strides, and then fell.

"He's in shock!"

We hoisted Gordon, Clarence and I taking his arms, and Art and Lester each pulling a leg, but Gordon slipped out of our grasp.

"How did he get so heavy?" I asked.

"He's just dead weight," said Clarence.

Art yelled, "Hey!"

"Well, he is! We'll have to leave him."

"We're not leaving him!"

Art grabbed Gordon's arm, and started pulling. I took the other arm, and we dragged him across the sidewalk. We had reached the next block when the first ghoul appeared behind us.

"We'll never make it," said Clarence.

He dropped Gordon's feet, and ran for the bridge. Lester hesitated, then followed his brother.

Art shouted after them, "Assholes!"

Art and I continued to lug Gordon.

Clarence and Lester returned, with the shopping cart. We dragged Gordon onto the cart's bottom shelf, then raced onto the bridge.

Three female ghouls had wandered onto the other end. We halted.

"I need the bullets," said Clarence.

"If we stop," I replied. "The others will overrun us. We can make it through."

I started pushing the cart. Clarence swore, but helped.

The girl ghouls clustered in our path, their hands reaching. Two of them wore only cutoff shorts, and their upper parts, their breasts, had been horribly devoured. The third girl, her flesh still whole, wore cut-offs, and a tie-dyed T-shirt. A knife protruded from between her breasts.

They were Doris Morris and her sorority sisters.

The shock of recognition stunned me, but we could not stop. I ran harder, nearly pushing the shopping cart out of Clarence's grip. We rammed the ghouls. The collision flung them aside. Doris fell on her back in the boneless manner of the undead. Her skull went *crack* on the pavement.

The impact brought the cart to a stop. Clarence and I slammed up against the cart's push-bar. We both grunted, losing our wind. I doubled over the pain in my gut. Meanwhile, Gordon slid off his shelf.

Doris turned her head, and I swear that she grinned at me.

The crowd of ghouls from the police station reached the bridge, filling the span from rail to rail, their rushing footsteps the only sound. The street trembled.

Terror galvanized me, overcoming my pain and weakness. I bent down, and heaved Gordon back onto the cart's lower shelf. He seemed to weigh nothing. We pushed Gordon to the end of the bridge, then the cart got stuck in the gap between the concrete guard rail and the roof of a toppled car.

Lester screamed.

I heaved myself against the cart's push bar. Art and Lester helped, piling in behind Clarence and me. Our burden gave way, squealing, and scraping paint from the wrecked car. Then we broke free, and hurtled back up Utica Street.

The ghouls hit the gap right behind us, and they jammed in, all of them trying to pass through at once. They fought with each other, ripping out handfuls of hair, and gouging each other's flesh. The creatures from the back started to climb over.

I cried, "Don't stop!"

We turned off of Utica Street at the first intersection, then wove a maze-like path through the residential streets.

Clarence suddenly let go of the cart, and dropped prone. I skidded to a halt, dragged by the cart's momentum, unable to continue on my own. My muscles trembled like jelly.

"We can't stop," I said, gasping.

"I," Clarence panted. "I can't."

We lay there, our energy spent, helpless if the ghouls overtook us.

They passed nearby, just one or two streets over, their combined footsteps resembling the sound of a gale.

Gordon raised his head groggily. "What's that?"

Clarence clamped his hand over Gordon's mouth.

The deadly storm missed us.

***

Gordon had recovered some of his strength by the time we reached my house. He remained in emotional shock, however, and stared into the distance while Clarence dressed his wound.

"What now?" Lester asked.

"We'll go back to the treehouse," said Clarence.

"Are you crazy?" I asked. "We should wait here for help."

"I don't think there'll be any help, I think this is worldwide, like some kind of invasion. Look at how many ghouls there are already, and everyone who dies makes another! We'd never survive in town,. The woods are our best chance."

I peeked out the window. A ghoul wandered up to the house on the end of the street. It banged on the door with both fists. Two more creatures joined it.

I said, "Okay, we'll try the woods."

In my garage, we quietly gathered supplies. We took matches, two first-aid kits, and antibiotics from the medicine cabinet, also cookware, utensils, and a propane-fired camp stove, with two extra cylinders of fuel, a cigarette lighter, a couple rolls of duct tape, and spare clothing. Lastly, we packed an assortment of tools, and all the food that we could find. We sneaked out through the back door, and made the slow, sad journey to our new home.

The limping ghoul awaited us.

"I need the bullets," said Clarence.

I gave him a single shell.

He rolled his eyes. "Thanks a lot."

"Don't shoot him here, we don't want him rotting under our noses."

We left our baggage on the trail, and led the ghoul to the river. The bank dropped, steep and slick, into a strong current. Clarence shot the creature in the forehead. The ghoul flopped down the bank, but caught on an exposed root at the water's edge.

"Stan, go nudge him in."

I stepped down. My foot skidded on the mud, and I fell. I caught myself on the edge of the bank, and scrambled back up.

"I can't do it," I said, my heart thumping. "I'll fall in, and I can't swim."

"I can," said Art.

He skipped down the bank, and kicked the Shuffler off the root. The current sucked the ghoul under.

I shivered.

***

Rain fell that night. The treehouse's roof leaked, but not badly. The wind became strong, and the house groaned as the tree's four main branches flexed. We had decided to post guards throughout the night. Clarence took the first watch, sitting at the doorway with my rifle in his lap.

He said, "I hear something, give me a bullet."

Instead, I used the flashlight. Mist and rain dimmed the beam.

"I don't see anything."

"Something's there."

"We can't waste bullets on noises."

***

I had to pee bad when I woke up. I hesitated for a time, watching the mist flow across the forest's floor. I felt scared to climb down, and considered just peeing out the door. However, if we all did that, we would soon have a terrible mess. I glanced around for my rifle, but Clarence had it in bed with him.

I climbed down, and moved off a few yards. After doing my business, I noticed a piece of clothing on the ground. It was a rain-soaked, tie-dyed T-shirt with a rip down the front. I took it up the tree.

"This wasn't here yesterday."

"Maybe it blew here on the wind?"

"There's someone out there," said Gordon. "A girl."

"This doesn't feel right," said Clarence. "If there's a girl around, why doesn't she just show herself?"

Gordon looked at me. "Maybe she's afraid she'll get shot."

"It can't be a ghoul," I said. "A ghoul would be waiting under the tree."

We all were excited by the prospect of a female survivor, and searched the area. We dared not call out, lest we attract ghouls.

The girl, if she existed, did not approach us.

***

Late the next night, I awoke in fear. I heard a stealthy rustle in the undergrowth below. I rose silently, found the flashlight, and shined its beam out the doorway.

"What?" Art whispered.

Seeing nothing, I turned to the window.

"What?"

Still nothing. I turned the flashlight off.

"I'm just hearing things."

***

In the morning, I found a pair of cut-off jeans. Our mood became electric.

"Is she running around naked?" Lester asked.

"No," said Art. "She's still got her underwear."

We passed the shorts around. It was like touching a girl second-hand.

"Have any of you kids ever done it?" Clarence asked, then looked at his brother. "I know *you* haven't."

Lester blushed.

I exchanged a glance with Art. I was a virgin, and I was pretty sure that he was, as well.

Clarence said, "Be honest. You don't have to worry about peer pressure anymore."

I said, "No."

Art said, "I've kissed a girl."

Clarence blew a raspberry. "You can *kiss* your mother."

Art blushed.

Gordon blushed before Clarence addressed him.

Clarence said, "I know you've done it, here in this treehouse, and it wasn't with a girl."

After a pregnant silence, we got it. I looked from Gordon to Clarence, incredulous and horrified.

"You promised you'd never tell," said Gordon, his voice quaking.

"Things have changed," said Clarence. "Each other is all we have now."

"There's a girl in the woods!" Gordon turned his back.

None of us had much to say, anyhow.

***

A stick cracked in the night.

We all came wide awake. Gordon grabbed the flashlight. Nothing stood below the treehouse, but a scarlet triangle lay on the ground a few yards off.

"It's her panties," Gordon said, with a croak.

He turned to jump down.

Clarence grabbed him. "What in the hell do you think you're doing?"

"I'm going to find her!"

Gordon tried to fight him off, but Clarence was tenacious. For a moment, they teetered in the doorway. Clarence pulled Gordon back from the edge.

"Don't you see how weird this is?" Clarence hissed. "There's no girl out there, it's something else!"

"You're just jealous!"

"Look how dark it is. Anything could be waiting for you."

"Then, give me the gun!"

"No!"

Gordon punched him in the gut. Clarence gasped helplessly and dropped my rifle as he fell. Gordon caught the weapon, and turned to me.

"Give me a bullet."

I hesitated.

"I'm going out, either way."

I obliged. Gordon loaded, slung the rifle, and jumped down. He paused to scan the light, then stepped away from the tree, and retrieved the panties.

"Come out," Gordon cried to the night. "We won't hurt you!"

Another stick cracked. Gordon aimed the light. At the beam's limit stood a naked girl. The sight of her thrilled my body. Gordon ran forward. She lifted her arms, and hurried to meet him. Something glinted between her breasts.

Clarence shouted, "Run!"

Gordon skidded to a halt, and fumbled the rifle from his shoulder. He fired without aiming. The bullet punched into her gut, and didn't slow her down. Gordon dropped the rifle, and clubbed at the lunging girl with the flashlight. Its beam lit her face.

She was Doris.

She embraced Gordon violently, dragging him to the ground. She wrapped her legs around him, ignoring his repeated blows, and clawed at his hair, trying to expose his neck to her bite. He dropped the flashlight, and caught her face with his hands, pushing her away. Doris sucked his finger into her mouth. Gordon's bone crunched between her teeth. He screamed.

Doris's sisters emerged from the woods, and took Gordon by the legs. Doris rose, and helped them to drag him away. Gordon clawed at the earth. His fingers caught the strap of my rifle, dragging it with him into the dark woods.

His screams slowly faded.

"Do something," Art cried. "Help him!"

None of us dared to pursue. Clarence collapsed in tears.

***

Later, Clarence said, "They didn't act normal, I mean, not like normal ghouls. They acted smart."

"It was Doris," I said. "She never was right."

"Yeah. I heard that she killed a boy once, but nobody could prove it."

"I heard she did it with a switchblade," said Art.

Lester exclaimed, "I saw that knife! It's in her chest now."

A silence followed.

Clarence asked, "Do you know how that knife got in her, Stan?"

After another silence, I said, "No."

***

The next morning, we found the Delta Sisters besieging the treehouse.

"We should leave," I said. "Before any more come."

"Okay," said Clarence. "Lead them off, then we'll jump down."

I crossed to the window. Doris came around the tree to wait for me, while her sisters waited under the door. Doris looked up, and waggled her tits. I got a boner, and turned away in horrified shame.

"I can't do it."

"That's all right," Clarence said with shaky confidence. "We have enough food to last until they rot."

"We haven't got much water," I said.

Clarence did not answer.

Lester pointed outside. "What's that?"

Gordon's corpse crawled toward the tree, dragging its legs. The Sisters had gnawed his meat off from the hips down. They attacked him now, and drove him back. Gordon circled the tree at a distance.

Art broke down in wailing grief. Clarence drew Art into his arms. Lester joined their embrace. Then, Clarence looked at me.

A part of me wanted to share the human contact, but a greater part felt repugnance, because of Clarence's homosexual confession. I retreated to the window, and climbed out onto the roof.

The Delta Sisters gathered below me.

I regarded the ghoul girls. As far as I knew then, there were no girls left alive. As far as I knew then, the other three boys were my future. I felt cheated, and hopeless.

Doris played with her breasts. She still looked good. I could not look away. No other woman had ever stood naked before me, and I believed that no more ever would.

Imagining that she was alive, I opened my fly, and touched myself.

Doris grabbed my emission from the air, and stuffed her fingers down her throat.

Revulsion turned my stomach. I dropped to my knees, and vomited off the roof. I loathed myself. The Sisters fought over the steaming puddle.

Thunder roared. I thought that it was the voice of God condemning me for my sin. Then, the rain poured down.

"Stan," Clarence called from inside. "Rip up the roof!"

He clambered out the window. I hastily closed my zipper. Clarence joined me on the roof. My cheeks felt scarlet.

Clarence began loosening the tarpaulin. "We'll make a rain catchment out of this," he said. "Then we'll have enough water to last until they rot."

Instead of cursing me, God had sent us a gift. I screamed down at the Sisters,

"You're going to rot!"

As we worked, Clarence gave me a look.

He asked, "Why did you climb up here?"

My blush deepened.

"Hey, did you think I was doing things down there, with my *brother*?"

"No," I stammered. "I just, I just couldn't . . ."

Clarence looked into my eyes. "We're all brothers, now."

***

Another ghoul arrived that afternoon, shirtless, and with a weight lifter's physique. Tooth marks covered his dense musculature. A length of corrugated esophagus flopped out of his torn throat. His face had been chewed to the bone, turning him into a walking skull with long, blond hair, and madly staring eyes.

"He looks strong," said Clarence in a worried tone. "He might be able to haul himself up here."

The Sisters attacked the new ghoul, trying to drive him off their territory. He knocked the two mutilated girls down easily, but Doris circled, and jumped onto his back. She wrapped herself around him, and bit the back of his neck. The Skull staggered. Then, he reached back, caught her head with both hands, and pulled. Her neck crackled and stretched, and her limbs released in spasms. He flung her over his shoulder. For a moment, she lay still on the ground, and I thought that he had *really* killed her, but then her neck contracted. She quivered, stood up, and spat out a mouthful of the Skull's dead skin.

The girl ghouls retreated from the tree. Doris led her sisters in an attack on Gordon, driving him out to a wider circle.

The Skull approached the tree. He reached up, and his fingers nearly snagged on the treehouse's doorway. We recoiled. The Skull clambered at the tree's trunk, but he did not find the holds to climb.

Suddenly, Lester cried, "Look!"

A crowd of at least twenty ghouls approached through the woods, and more came behind them.

Art chortled sickly. "They must be out of eats in town!"

"It's my fault," said Clarence. "I made us hide out here."

"We'd have had to face them wherever we'd hid," I offered him in consolation.

"We'll wait them out," said Art. "Like we planned. We have plenty of water, and even if we run out of food, we'll live for weeks."

"We won't," said Clarence, his voice a mixture of fascination and horror. "They'll pile on top of each other, like army ants, and reach the treehouse. They'll get us."

Lester curled into a ball, and wept.

Art asked, "Isn't there some way we can use the bullets?"

My eyes fell on the camp stove, and an idea struck me. "We can make a bomb!"

I grabbed the extra propane bottles, and the duct tape. I scatter-taped the .22 shells around the bottles, then taped the bottles to the burners of the stove.

Art's eyes bugged. "Are you nuts? You'll kill us!"

"It would be a better death than *that*," Clarence said, tipping his head toward the swarming ghouls. "If we survive the explosion, head for the river, we'll swim across."

My heart went cold. They had forgotten that I could not swim. I held my tongue, for our situation was desperate, and I owed it to them to try.

With my heart pounding, I ignited the camp stove's burners. Blue flames embraced the propane bottles. I tossed the bomb into the crowd of ghouls, and we cowered into the treehouse's far corner, with our hands over our ears.

I waited, and nothing happened. Just as I feared that the bomb had failed, it exploded. The world toppled in the shock. Small, bright holes opened in the planks all around us, as the bullets exploded. At the same instant, a column of tree litter and dead body parts blasted in through the doorway. In another instant, all was still. I found myself lying in a heap with my friends. My ears rang deafeningly. Clarence sat up, and shouted at me, but I could not hear him. I felt intact, so I gave him a thumbs-up. I climbed to my feet, teetered, and fell again. Clarence stood up at an odd angle, and helped me to rise.

My head began to clear, and I realized that the floor now tilted. The explosion had uprooted the tree, and pushed it over on two of its major branches. We climbed shakily to earth. Ghoul fragments lay all around us, mixed with a ring of blasted forest debris. Some of the fragments still moved.

Leaves rustled behind us. Doris emerged from the crown of our fallen tree. The trunk had shielded her from the explosion. She hissed like an angry reptile and ran toward us.

We fled, kicking our way through the mounds of debris. We did not see Gordon lying in our path. The ghoul's low profile had saved him from the blast. Clarence tripped over him, and fell prone. Gordon crawled up Clarence's struggling torso, his jutting elbows lending him a semblance of a two-legged spider, and nuzzled under Clarence's chin. Clarence screamed, but the cry drowned in a fountain of blood.

I found a rock, and crushed Gordon's skull, then I crushed Clarence's.

"Why did you do that to him?" Lester asked.

"So he won't have to come back."

We fled.

Doris screamed, a chalk-board sound that raised my hair.

We outraced her. The river gleamed through the trees ahead, and we had nearly reached it, when we heard a susurrus. From the direction of Oswego, hundreds of ghouls shuffled toward the tree.

"Be quiet," I warned. "They haven't seen us; the explosion must have attracted them."

Doris came into view, between us and the crowd. She pointed toward us, and screamed. The crowd paused. She screamed again, and they turned to follow her.

I said, "Shit!"

We ran.

At the river's edge, Art and Lester slid down the muddy bank, and into the swirling water. I hesitated.

"Come on, Stan!"

I stepped off the edge, turning to claw at the mud as I fell. The river took me up to the waist. The bottom sloped to infinite depths. I froze, clinging to the bank, while Art and Lester waded to deeper water.

"Come on!"

"I can't!"

"Jesus, he can't swim!"

They splashed back to me.

"Hang on to us, we'll keep you afloat."

"I can't, I'll drown! You guys take off."

"We won't leave you."

They remained at my side, my last brothers, as Doris appeared on the bank above us. She hesitated there.

Suddenly, a female voice echoed from downriver.

"We're coming!"

Two girls in an aluminum canoe paddled furiously toward us.

Doris screamed at the girls, then jumped off the bank at me, her fingers clawing and her mouth open. I thrust out my left hand, and caught her under the chin. She pawed at my face, but I had the reach on her. Then Doris grabbed my arm, trying to force it down. I was stronger, but I could not release her. We stood locked in the final step of a death-dance, on the slippery edge of the river's abyss. I realized with horror that my only chance was to hurl both of us into the current.

Then sunlight glinted from the switchblade knife in her chest. I yanked the knife out, and drove it through her eye, into her brain. She collapsed.

The girls beached the canoe beside us. We climbed in, and they paddled away just as the crowd of ghouls arrived.

"We heard your bomb from our school," said the girl in the stern. "We thought no one else had survived!"

"We've been hiding in the woods," I said. "Are you from Dyke Island . . . I mean, Esmeralda Smith?"

She giggled. "Yeah, we're from Dyke Island."

***

Well, Son, that's how it happened, all that I know of it, at least. I see your tears, but I'm an old man, and I've lived a good life. The time has come for you to do your duty, so I don't have to come back.

I love you, too.

WHISPERS OF THE APOC

7 A SLOW LEAK BY CAMERON SMITH

The ocean beat the shore in rhythmic waves as the nineteen-year-old boy trekked through the cool sands beneath a hazy gray sky. He was dressed in a filthy t-shirt and black jacket, cargo pants and combat boots, and a beaten, blood-stained aluminum baseball bat dangled at his side like a samurai sword from a loop of cord strapped to his belt. A large Ka-Bar was sheathed against the opposite thigh. Otherwise, he was weaponless, and had run out of food days ago, water last night.

Far off down the coastline a figure strolled his way. It neither ran nor lumbered, but walked in the manner of the living. The figure grew and the boy said to no one, "It's not an Eater, man. You can always tell the difference, Billy."

Before long he could make out the figure: older, late thirties maybe, with long, straggly black and silver-streaked hair, full beard. Drawing nearer, he saw weapons—a machete, a few knives, a pistol—along with canteens and a camper's backpack strapped to the man's frame. The economy of his stock and armory betrayed a man accustomed to the new era of survival.

The boy grew nervous but was too curious to turn tail. "I don't know, Billy, what do you think?" he asked aloud, then said nothing more. Both men stopped with twenty feet between them.

"I didn't think you were one, not the way you moved," said the man in a gravelly monotone. "You bit?"

"No, of course not."

"Well there ain't no of fuckin' course about it. What're you doin' out here?"

"Came up from Sac. This town over here has a lot of 'em roamin' around, mostly older ones, not really a threat, you know, but they'll getcha, too. They don't come around the beach much. I think they don't like the water or..."

"There ain't nuthin' here for 'em."

"Right. I know. That's why I came along the coast."

"Ain't nuthin' here for us, either. That's the problem."

"How come you're on the coastline?"

"Buryin' my dog. He was starving. I had to kill him." The man eyed the boy for a reaction. "You ever had to kill anybody you loved?"

"Yeah."

The man nodded and walked closer, extending a hand. "Vic."

The nineteen-year-old shook the hand. "Quentin."

Vic looked inland. "Rumor is there's a fortified town about forty miles east. High fence all around it. The Dead can't get through. They have towers set up to kill any agile ones that try. Town's self-sufficient. Still has livestock, crops."

Quentin's rush of excitement was soon quelled by disbelief. "I've seen a town like that but it got overrun. How you know about this one?"

"I tagged alongside a group for a little while up in Oregon. They'd been there. Probably about three months ago they were there. About a month ago I last saw 'em."

"Why'd they leave the town?"

"Find their families. You got family?"

"No…not…"

"Me neither. My dog was the last thing I had."

"Sorry."

"I'd say we got another few hours of daylight. I'm campin' out here. I need sleep. You're welcome to sleep near me if you want."

Nothing happened that night, except both awoke every hour or so, which was the usual for Quentin. Like a wolf in the wild, he never slept more than two hours at a time, sporadically awakening to check his surroundings then falling back to sleep.

In the morning Quentin's belly pined for food. A button peeled from the cover of one of his pants' pockets sufficed as a sucker. Saliva gradually flooded his mouth, giving the unsatisfactory illusion of drinking.

Vic offered a canteen. "Just sip. We'll get more later from the river." From his pack he brought out a can of peaches. Quentin's eyes grew wide and he had to stop himself from reaching toward it. But Vic shared.

"People don't really share anymore," Quentin noted.

"There's good reason for that. Everybody makes his path out here, though. You trust people, you get trust. No road you choose is gonna be without risk, you know? We start now, we can make that town by night. If they got guards watching from towers they'll spot us right away, let us in. So I heard."

They walked inland, leaving the sand for paved roads littered with occasional abandoned cars, a rare shriveled-up corpse, or bones. No meat was safe. Anything with an appetite scavenged, and anything edible was hunted. Quentin had seen people feasting on dead zombies, even, but he and Billy, no matter their hunger, had never stooped to that. Mostly out of fear of whatever contagion the Eaters carried. But some people didn't care. They'd eat anything. They'd become no better than the Dead themselves.

They found the highway, travelled eastbound. Silent hours passed, broken up by intermittent chatter. Quentin told tall tales of his exploits with Billy, of things they'd seen and done. At one point, he asked if Vic had heard the rumors about why all this had begun.

"I've heard it all."

"Well, you know there was that comet that landed in Russia, and it started there first…"

Vic chuckled. "Same time as that spill in Alaska? Or the strange lights in the sky over North Dakota? There's no sense wasting time thinkin' about why it all ended."

"But maybe if we knew, we could stop it?"

"Stop what? It's not a leaky warehouse full of zombie toxin. If it were, we'd have plugged it. This isn't gonna change."

Onward they marched, winding through the mountains and hills. Quentin watched the road five feet in front of his boots, hungry and lonely despite finally having company again. He yearned for Billy, who whispered cheerful thoughts in his head.

"Eventually, if you think about it, all the Eaters'll die out. It's not a sustainable creature," he smiled.

Vic snickered. "The Dead can't die out, kid. It's an ever-replenished species. The Dead'll always be with us."

Quentin fell back into dark reveries. As they came around a bend in the road, Vic paused. He held out a hand and became stiff. Quentin heard the moist crunching of feeding time. He pulled his bat from the loop at his belt, held it like a katana. Vic unlatched a machete from his leg, leaving the pistol holstered. Making a motion with his head, he and Quentin stepped quietly around the bend.

There was a broken-down car, worn from exposure. One of the Dead leaned in at the driver's door, devouring something. She rose abruptly, sensing them. She wore camouflage pants and shirt, was fresh enough that it was easy to tell that she'd once been attractive, probably yesterday.

She came at them full speed. Quentin swung the bat with all his weight behind it, cracking her across the forehead. As she spiraled Vic brought the machete down across the top of her skull, planted his foot firmly at the base of her back and shoved as he yanked the blade free.

"Hit her again! Quick!"

Quentin lunged forward with another swing that snapped her neck and knocked her head sideways. She collapsed to her knees, roaring senselessly. Vic stepped in again with a chop to her skull. Again he shoved her away, now with a boot to the face, as he pulled the machete from her brain like the sword from the stone. She fell, convulsing and moaning. Quentin's turn was up, and he brought the bat's tip down on her skull with a crunch, caving it in and causing an eruption of brain matter to gush from the cuts made by the machete.

Vic wiped the blade across her camo pants, resheathed it at his thigh.

"I like the way you work, Quentin."

They checked her for supplies, scoured the car. Nothing but a half-eaten raccoon. Vic slung it over his shoulder.

"You gonna eat that?"

"After I cook it."

"I was always afraid you might become like them if you eat what they been slobberin' all over."

"And that's why you're halfway starved to death, kid."

Hours went by and they came across a sign on the highway: SLATE CREEK 23. Below that, WENDVILLE 53.

"Slate Creek, that's the place. It's gotta be," said Vic. "We should eat. Let's get some wood."

The redwoods stretched out around them in every direction. They left the road, and went into the forest. They located the creek by listening.

"This is where they made that *Star Wars* movie with the Ewoks," said Quentin, as they made a fire.

Vic carved up the coon, cutting away and discarding the parts that had been bitten into by the zombie woman. "Put that on the end of your blade and let it cook good," he said, handing Quentin a cut of meat. Quentin stabbed it with his Ka-Bar and put it near the flame.

"You fight pretty good, huh?"

Quentin watched the meat blacken. "I think that's my calling. Me and Billy were like the best team, just how well we worked together. We killed hordes of Eaters."

Vic nodded. "Good. Always use a bat?"

"It's the best for me. Never liked guns. Too loud. And they run outta bullets."

Vic concurred with a grunt. He pulled a pot from his pack and placed it on a little metal stand. He boiled the water, then lowered the bottom of the pot into the creek to cool it. They both drank and ate. But Quentin had to go into the woods to empty his burning bowels. When he came back he was pale.

"Fuck," grumbled Vic. "You need rest."

"Sorry," said Quentin.

"Don't be. Just lie down for a bit. I'll stay on guard. Then you need to guard me for a little while, and then we'll get back on the road and probably make it to Slate Creek by morning."

Quentin lay down by a tree, shivering. Feverish dreams assailed him. The tumult of a giant tromping through the forest then roaring jarred him from his nightmares. Several moments went by before he realized he was awake. A few yards away, two zombies attacked Vic. Vic's hand was in one of the zombies' mouth, blood running down his wrist and forearm. Vic shouted out, writhed and kicked.

Quentin's adrenaline didn't give him any time to think. He was standing, then shimmying up a tree.

The two rotting, lethargic zombies wrestled to consume Vic's flesh. He quickly beat them away and drew his weapon of choice. Before he could throw a single swipe, though, his game changed yet again.

A muscular, bug-eyed man burst out from the woods like a fiend high on PCP and dove recklessly on top of Vic, sending them rolling toward the creek, knocking down the other zombies like bowling pins. Wiry Vic was up, swinging that machete, before they came to rest. He chopped off the hand of one of the slower zombies, then hacked halfway into his neck, so the thing's head lolled over and hung ridiculously, one ear literally resting on its shoulder. He shoved the zombie back and it fell clumsily into the creek and drifted, eyes flicking side to side, body flaccid.

The strong one leapt at Vic like a leopard. The machete cut deep past his clavicle. As Vic tried to yank it free he tripped backwards on a fat tree root in the soil.

Above, safe for now, Quentin gradually came to his senses. Vic was bit—no way to save him. But if he died, the others would eventually discard him, and that would be one more invigorated Eater to contend with. Staying in this tree was a trap.

He slid partway down and jumped, tumbling when he hit the dirt. He pulled out his bat and thunked the back of the most energetic Eater's head, dropping him. He closed in on the one who was coming upon Vic, timed it until the right instant and swung, popping the cretin across the temple. It lurched toward him and he sidestepped and hit it again with a diagonal downward blow followed by another. The zombie dropped, unmoving.

Quentin looked again at the zombie he'd killed with a single strike. "Never done that before," he said. "One hit."

He looked to Vic, who was bit in a few places. The bat rose above his head.

"Don't, you fucker. Don't you fuckin' do it yet." He gripped his hand where the blood gushed, cringing. "I got a little time, so back the fuck up."

Quentin stepped back.

"Fuck," snarled Vic. "Fell a fuckin' sleep. I never fell asleep. Never fell asleep. Why the fuck? Fuck, fuck."

"What do you want me to do?"

"Take my shit and go. Take all of it you wanna carry. Go find the road and go to Slate Creek."

"What about you?"

"What the fuck do you think, kid? I'll deal with my goddamn self. I can't believe I fell asleep. Five fuckin' minutes. It musta been longer than that." He started to cry. "I thought I was gonna make it. I always made it. Everybody slipped up but I never did. Goddammit. Goddammit."

Quentin holstered his bat and gathered up Vic's stuff. He threw on the backpack, but left the machete in the zombie. He eyeballed Vic's gun.

"No. I need that. Now go. Find that town."

"Sorry I got sick," he said, and almost added he was feeling better now. But he hurried away from the creek and back north, toward the road. He wasn't gone ten minutes when he heard the *BANG!* He turned and went back. Half of Vic's outstretched body lay in the creek. The revolver was still in his hand, dry, inches from the water.

"Poor Vic, Billy. We were good partners. Man, poor Vic." He stripped him of the holster and put the gun in it, wore it around his waist. There were only two rounds in the chamber. No more ammo in Vic's clothes or pack.

"Fuck it. Come on, Billy," he said, becoming unnerved.

He travelled alongside the road, remaining in the woods. He felt safer there, with cover.

Around dawn he found the fence line. It reminded him of something from *The Great Escape*, large logs crisscrossing, dressed with bundles of spiraling barbed-wire. He walked alongside it and saw a frill-less tower in the pre-sun haze. Unmanned.

Two desiccated zombies were sprawled across the barbed wire, entangled. Vic's supplies included binoculars, so Quentin fished them out of the pack, descried another tower, and other carcasses. Either shot or starved or timed-out. The Dead had a duration, like anything else, beginning fresh, malleable, fast, strong, and gradually deteriorating, until they finally dried up like mummies. Though the thought of them all disintegrating into dust amused him, he knew Vic was correct: until there was no more life, death would always be replenished.

Nothing in sight moved.

The barrier was about six feet high, maybe six feet from one side to the other.

"What d'you think Billy? If we run you think we can make it? Yeah…just hop across those dead Eaters. Like stones in a creek." With a run and a jump he hurled the pack and watched it soar over the corpses and fall to the other side.

"What? Chickenshit. I'll go first, then."

Carefully he climbed over the carcasses as they crunched and sagged beneath him. It was like a tightrope walk on all fours. A few times his pants got snagged, and he took a few cuts, but made it to the other side with a final feline leap. He stood and brushed himself off, shaking, tired. "See, Billy. Told you."

He found some dried meat in the pack and ate and drank one whole canteen of water. Afterwards, he went to the nearest tower and climbed up, lay down and slept. When he awoke the sun was overhead. He crawled from the tower and walked back to the main highway. Here the boundary was a locked gate, but he was within town limits now. A large, wooden sign had WELCOME TO SLATE CREEK carved artistically into it.

There was a building to his right that said OPEN DOOR CLINIC, with a small tank parked in front. There were sandbags out front like a WWI stronghold. To his left was a gas station, and on the road before it was a large olive-green military truck, and a jeep with a mounted machine gun aimed at the entrance of the town. There were grocery stores and little shops. There were a few vehicles: trucks, cars, all parked and empty.

"Military," he said. He climbed into the jeep. The keys were in the ignition but it didn't start. Same with the transport truck. A label on the dash read, PROPERTY GARY'S AUTO. The plates weren't government. Civilian owned.

Every vehicle he bothered to try had no gas or dead batteries. He walked past Gary's Auto, and saw more vintage military vehicles parked within its gates.

He stayed on the main road until he came to the other end of town, with another fortification guarding the opposite locked gate. Sandbags, a few sideways parked pickups, but no people.

He walked back to the middle of town. Between a bank and a park there was another highway intersecting the one he'd followed from the coast to here. He walked along it, toward the north. There was a police station; a tiny, shoddy motel; an elementary school with a kiosk that read "TOWN MEETING WEDS 6PM." Then there were homes, side roads that led to more homes. Big fields of overgrown grasses, unmanicured yards. Sporadic vehicles but no signs of life except the occasional crow in a tree.

Here and there, on the roads, in the yards, there were bones, picked clean.

And then he was at the other end of town, fortified but unguarded. The river was in sight, to the east. The fence line bordered this side of the water. Fishing poles reached off the ends of abandoned towers, so the townsfolk could fish while the river swept any invading zombies north.

"It's gonna be night soon, Billy. Let's find a house."

Heading back along the highway southward, he spotted a nice home off the road with at least two acres of brush around it.

"See that? Critters could hide there. Edibles, Billy. Vic hooked us up, man. This place is gonna be all ours. I don't know what happened here, it's a good question, but I got a lotta good questions. That don't mean they're gonna get answered."

The house was furnished but empty. Family pictures lined the walls. He gathered them up, and stacked them near the fireplace, face down. The bed in the master bedroom was still made. He slept on top of it after he drank the rest of his last canteen.

"We'll go to the river tomorrow," he said. "Get more water."

Face buried in the pillows, the family photos flashed through his mind, haunting him.

For days he walked around town in search of people but found none. On the third day he came across a zombie rummaging through town, and quickly beat it to oblivion. The next day he found two more, one who was almost starved, another who was probably months old and ambled towards him like a demented geriatric. Both easy kills.

A week went by. He took a bike from a yard and used it to get around town faster. Using his binos he surveyed the stretches of fence line but never saw a gap.

Food was scarce. He caught crawdads with a fishing net set up from one of the towers, found dog food in one house, and caught grasshoppers to eat. His proudest meal was gopher. Traps were simple to devise, but the high grass hid their holes.

One day, venturing up a paved road off the north/south highway, he thought he spotted someone in a window. The house was a single story abode with a high wooden fence set on a hill with acres of land around it. He set down his bike, hopped the fence. He was certain it was a zombie but Billy swore otherwise.

He knocked on the door and called out. He hollered and yelled. An Eater would be clawing through walls to get to him; only the living would hide. He slammed his bat against the door.

"Stop!"

A young man a few years his senior walked around the back of the house, holding a rifle aimed at Quentin's head. Sable hair, dark eyes, thick rimmed glasses, he was tall and healthy, wore a t-shirt, jeans, tennis shoes.

"Why wouldn't you answer?"

"We don't need any company, is why. What do you want?"

"Nothing…"

The man hesitated. "What's your name?"

"Quentin. Yours?"

"Rob. Behind you, that's Thomas."

Quentin turned and saw another one, blonde and also healthy, wearing shorts and a long-sleeved t-shirt and sandals. He casually held a .45 in his hand.

Both men were too far for Quentin to attack even if he'd wanted to, but he didn't. "I'm new in town. My friend Vic told me about this place."

"There's no one here anymore. Everyone left," said Rob, not dropping the gun. But Thomas lowered his.

Quentin holstered his bat. "I'm sorry if I scared you with the banging. But I haven't seen anybody since Vic died. Don't you think it's better if we're together?"

"Not really."

"I'm a superb zombie killer," smiled Quentin. "You know how many I've killed with my bat? Too many to count, obviously. But like, just one hit, guess how many I've killed. With just one blow."

"I don't know."

"Twelve. Vic used to call me Babe Ruth cuz I'd just BAM! One swing and the Dead would drop. That's all I've done. Me and Billy took to it since it happened. He had a sword and I had a bat."

"Look," said Rob. "I don't have any problem with you. But me and Thomas are good on our own. You can respect that, right? I'm not saying you can't live here in town but you don't need to live with us."

"That's fine," said Quentin. "I just wanted to meet the neighbors."

"And you've met them."

Suddenly the door opened. Quentin jumped back and put his hands on the handle of his bat.

A girl at the door, dusty blonde and tall and thin and, Quentin thought, very pretty, said, "Leave it alone, Rob. What'd you say your name was?"

"Quentin."

"Elizabeth."

Rob said, "Get back in the house, Betty."

She ignored him. "Come in and have something to eat with us."

"Goddammit, Betty, what the fuck?"

"Put down your gun," she said, glaring at Rob. She asked Quentin, "Are you good? Or bad?"

"I'm good. I'm useful."

She scrutinized him, as if evaluating his soul. "Come on."

"Goddammit! Betty! I swear to God!"

"What? What, Rob? You gonna shoot? Pull the trigger. Do it."

Rob fumed.

"Go ahead. Shoot him."

Quentin didn't know what to make of it.

Rob swore and threw the gun at the wall, stormed off toward the back of the house.

Elizabeth glanced down at the pistol holstered at Quentin's hip. "That thing loaded?"

"It's got two bullets."

"Then there's two bullets in this whole town, now. Every other gun's been empty for months. Come inside. It's ok."

Thomas brushed by him without speaking. He joined Elizabeth and they went into the house.

Inside he was surprised to find two more young women, one blonde and thin, nervous, and the other with nut brown hair and eyes, with crooked teeth and a pretty smile.

"This is Kelly and Cassandra," Elizabeth said. "This is Quentin. He's our zombie killer."

"We could use one of those," said Kelly, but Cassandra didn't speak. She looked strong, and for that matter so did Elizabeth.

They were all well-fed. It was as strange as it would have been to see people near starvation back in the days before the End. These were the times of hunger. But they didn't resemble the cannibals, who were sickly pallid.

"Where did you come from?" asked Elizabeth. She pointed to a seat, and the girls made some fuss over ensuring there was a plate for him. The table was set like a real dinner, fancier even than anything his mom would have set for him and Billy when they were kids.

"Me and Billy grew up in San Bernadino. After the End, we went up to Sacramento. We were there for like a year, but it started gettin' overrun by cannibals."

They were horrified to hear this.

"So then we came up north a few months ago. I just met with Vic at the beach when he was burying his dog, and he told me about this place."

"So," said Kelly, looking frightened, "where are they?"

"They're dead."

Thomas sat at the table. "You're just in time for dinner, kid. What's your name again?"

"Quentin. How come Rob was so mad I was here?"

"Everybody down south super welcoming?"

"No…"

"We gotta protect ourselves."

Elizabeth said, "Don't worry about Rob. He's… paranoid. We haven't seen anyone in a while. But we're happy to have a new neighbor."

"How long you been here?" asked Kelly.

"A week or so."

"How'd you get in?"

"I climbed the fence."

The answer seemed somehow insufficient to them but they dropped it. They served food and chattered. Quentin felt out of place but was relieved to be with people, and couldn't believe the food they had. He didn't dare ask where it came from, knowing they must have a vast hidden stock.

Eventually Rob joined them, and as he ate he stared coldly at the visitor.

"So, zombie killer. What's on your mind?" he asked.

"I'm grateful. I don't know." He felt interrogated, and spoke quickly, as though Rob knew he wanted to ask about the food. "I'm just happy to see others like me."

"Well, we're not like you. We're just normal people. We're not hardened zombie slayers. How many zombies you killed? Thousands?"

"No. Probably hundreds though. It's easier with a partner. Me and Billy…and me and Vic, when we joined up. We had it down, natural. Just like…tag team, you know?"

"No zombies around here to kill," said Thomas.

"Yeah huh. Sure there are."

Everyone stopped eating.

"Not in this town," said Kelly.

"Well, yeah. I've killed I think three since I got here."

Rob narrowed his eyes. "How'd you get through the gate?"

"I climbed the fence, like I said. There were some bodies, old shriveled up Eaters. I used 'em as a bridge."

"And you think there's some inside?"

"I've seen 'em, but I killed 'em. I'm sure there's a slow leak. A zombie might get through the border now and then."

"They hadn't before you came."

"Well, I didn't hurt the fence…"

"Don't worry about it," said Elizabeth, tension behind her soothing manner. "Maybe you let us know if you see more?"

"Yeah. Of course. I didn't hurt the fence, though." After a while he asked, "Where is everyone?"

The group eyed one another. Elizabeth said, "We don't know. The town's been empty since we arrived."

"How'd you get in?"

"We had a key to the North Gate."

"A key?"

There was a long pause. "Yeah. My cousin left me a key, a long time ago. Just in case."

No one said anything.

Conversation resumed, stilted at first, then light and easy, especially when Rob left the table. Afterwards they cleaned their plates. The shy one, Cassandra, led him to a well out back where he filled his canteen.

"Come back when you need water, please."

"If you think it's ok," he said. They were about to walk back to the house when he grabbed her arm. She looked scared.

"No, I'm not gonna hurt you," he said.

"Ok…"

"I just…I don't have anybody…I just thought we could be friends."

"Of course."

"If you let me come here and eat, I'll make sure no zombies come this way."

"Ok."

"Would you ask Elizabeth?"

"Yes," she said, not averting her eyes. "Just come. It'll be fine."

He let go. "Then I'll see you tomorrow again? And I'll look for any Eaters, first, and I'll kill 'em before I come."

"Sounds good," she said.

The next day he found two more, creeping around downtown. One was fast and darted after him as soon as it caught his scent. Strong as it was, it was uncoordinated, and with a few taps of the bat it went down and he finished it with two hard blows that opened up its skull, brains tumbling out.

He finished the second without a hitch, then went to his new friends' house by late afternoon. He told them about the Eaters, and then he stayed and ate dinner.

This routine continued for another few weeks. Some days he didn't meet any Eaters, and some days he found one, or several. He reported things back almost exactly as they happened, never exaggerating numbers but boasting of his ability to kill.

He became more assured of his role as scout and slaughterer. He was an integral part of the group, he thought, an extension of the family. Elizabeth was kind to him. Kelly ceased to be nervous. Thomas joked with him and slapped him on the shoulder when he saw him. Even Rob would acknowledge him with a nod, though nothing more. And Cassandra spoke gently to him, asking him about his brother, his childhood, which he was more than happy to talk about.

One night during dinner, he pressed the case that there was a slow leak through the fence.

Elizabeth asked, "Have you walked around the perimeter? Maybe there's a gap somewhere?"

"I've looked. I think they're just making their way over."

"I doubt it," said Thomas. "Why would they? They can't smell us or hear us from beyond the fence. They can't see us. They're a path-of-least-resistance animal until it comes to food. But they don't know we're in here."

"Do they know you're in here?" asked Rob.

"No…" But he had seen thousands of zombies and knew that Thomas was right. They wouldn't try to climb the fence unless they sensed food. And not just a crow or a field mouse. It'd have to be something big, and there wasn't anything big except them.

Later, gathering up water with Cassandra at the well, he pressed, "Cass, are we friends?"

"I think so."

"I'm honest with you guys. But I know there's something up. I wanna find out how the zombies are gettin' in but maybe if you told me how you guys really got here…"

"We used a key."

"I know there's some secret. I'll act like I don't know. Please?"

"I'm not lying. But…" She spoke quietly. "We were walking, probably gonna starve if another few weeks passed. And there was this guy in a car, sick. You know how they get, when they've been bit. But he offered us the key. He said there was food, told us about this house. It's got an underground food shelter."

"What else did he say?"

"He said things fell apart here and people were fleeing, but that there was food at this one house. He said he left it because of being bit. He was delirious. He said people didn't kill off their dead and the town was overtaken. We were starving so after another week we risked it, and when we got here, there was no one. No zombies, no people."

"But the gates were closed or open?"

"Closed and locked. But our key worked."

When he was alone he discussed it with Billy but couldn't figure it out. He'd never been much of a thinker, Billy reminded him.

A month went by, and then it happened. He was riding through town when he spotted at least twelve Eaters all sniffing around the shops. He was too far for them to smell or hear, but he spied on them with his binocs.

He considered fighting them now but there were too many and a few looked fresh. Instead, he turned and fled for his friends' house. In ten minutes he was there, ditching the bike on the lawn, looking around to make sure nothing followed him. He hurried across the high grass and then stopped before he went into the house, hearing raised voices within. He crouched down, stepped with stealth to the window, peeked and listened.

The five friends were in the living room: Kelly and Cassandra quiet on the couch, backs straight as Catholic school girls; Thomas lounging, apathetic, in a recliner, head tilted and resting on his fist; Rob and Elizabeth posturing in the center of the room. Clearly, the fight was between them.

"He's not right in the head. Even you admit it," Rob said.

"Who would be? He's been alone out there, surviving…"

"Doing we don't know what the fuck. The kid's a manipulator. And he's using us. For almost three months we've been here and never seen a single zombie or a person, and then he comes in, and says zombies are leaking in."

"We never go downtown, so we can't say he's lying…"

"Either he's lying, or he's letting them in."

"Why would he do either?"

"I don't know. I don't understand his mind," he said, tapping his head. "You've heard him, walking around outside, talking to imaginary people. He's schizophrenic. I know that's really fuckin' sad but it's also dangerous and my caution outweighs my sympathy. I'm sorry he's got brain damage but he's a liability. He's eating our food, which isn't an infinite supply despite what you all think, and there's something about him…if you guys can't see it…"

"I see it," said Thomas.

"He comes one meal a day, never more," argued Elizabeth.

"You can't deny what I'm saying," countered Rob.

Cassandra chewed on her lips.

Kelly said, "He's definitely strange…"

Elizabeth sighed. "Then what do we do?"

Rob raged. "What the fuck? What d'we do? You invited him in. You created this problem. I don't know what to do. He knows where we live. He's a fuckin' psychopath with a bloody baseball bat…"

"Exactly. That is dented and bloodied every day. He's a little bit of a tall-tale-teller but I wouldn't call him a liar."

"So again, say he's really killing zombies. Where are they coming from? How are they getting in?"

"We'll have to go downtown and see for ourselves."

"Fuck that. That's all you."

Watching from the window, Quentin couldn't understand why this fight was occurring, and was flabbergasted Cassandra wasn't defending him. He felt deceived and betrayed, and walked to the front steps of the porch and sat down, head in his hands, staring into the high grass before him.

"What're we supposed to do Billy? I know, but we like them. They could be our family. We're doing what we're supposed to do. What's wrong with us? We'll be alone again, eating grasshoppers and gophers…" And like that, an idea occurred to him.

"Quentin, my god," said Elizabeth behind him.

He stood and spun to face her, stepping away from the porch.

"I didn't even hear you…How long have you been here?"

"I think I know what's happening. I have an idea."

"All right…"

The others came out of the house, stood on the porch and looked at him.

"There's more today. Lots more. At least twelve, some fresh ones, strong. I couldn't kill them, I didn't even try cuz there was so many. It hit me though—gophers. They're always in the same place, downtown. Like they just appear there. And you guys said everything was shut up when you first got here."

"Did we say that?" asked Rob.

"You think I'm a liar, Rob? You think I make shit up? You go out into town, you fuckin' pussy. You never even leave the house and then you act like I'm lying. If I'm lying why don't you leave the house?"

"Cuz I don't wanna be out there with your nutty ass. I don't know what you'd do to me."

"Shut up, Rob," commanded Elizabeth.

"What have I done that's crazy?" he asked them all. "I talk to my twin brother. So what? He's dead. He got his fuckin' arm bit off...so I killed him. What the fuck am I supposed to do? What would you do? I don't have to stop talking to him." He looked at Cassandra tearfully. "How come you don't stick up for me?"

She looked sorry, like she might cry. But said nothing.

"At least you did," he said to Elizabeth, with bitterness. "I was your guys' scout. I was helping."

"I know that," said Elizabeth. "We're all stressed out because of food and—if there really are zombies coming into town—we don't know what to do."

"That's why you have me."

"I appreciate you."

He looked at Rob. "He doesn't."

"No, he doesn't. But that's how it goes sometimes," she said. "Some people don't get along."

Thomas stepped down slowly from the porch, Quentin watching him. Quentin was shaking, his emotions overtaking him.

"I don't understand what you guys want? I don't understand why I'm not good enough for you."

"Calm down, dude," said Thomas, coming closer.

"No, fuck off."

"Chill. Maybe you should go back home for a few days."

"Did you hear me about the zombies?"

"We heard you," said Rob.

"No sense getting riled up," said Thomas. "Remember you're just a visitor. You're a guest here."

The rage swelled up beyond control at that, making Quentin feel like he was garbage flung from a palace. He pulled Vic's revolver out and aimed it at Thomas's head.

"Put that fucking thing down, kid, now."

"No. You guys aren't listening."

"He's only got two bullets," said Rob.

"One for you and one for him," responded Quentin, and he could see the fear in Rob's eyes.

"You're bluffing, you little fucker. Gimme the goddamn gun." Thomas closed the distance and he got a hand around Quentin's wrist. Quentin squeezed the trigger. A blackish dot appeared on Thomas's cheek and the back of his head puffed out. His head jerked back. The life left his eyes and he collapsed.

Kelly shouted in disbelief and covered her mouth and crouched.

Cassandra hollered, "No!"

Quentin marched up the steps toward Rob, who put his hands up, horrified. The gun came up, barrel aimed at his face.

"Quentin, stop!" implored Cassandra. "Please stop!"

Rob quivered before him.

Cassandra and Kelly were crying. Elizabeth approached slowly.

"Quentin," she said, and held out her hand. "Quentin?"

His resolve vanished. He handed her the gun.

"You mutherfucker," spat Rob.

"That's enough," she enjoined. "Quentin. You have to go."

"I'm sorry."

She raised the gun. "I'm begging you, Quentin. You have to go."

He backed away, shocked. He looked down at Thomas ruefully. Then back at them. "Just listen. Please. One last time. And just trust me."

"Go ahead. And then you leave."

"Ok. I think maybe someone died in town, and there was an outbreak. People flee and lock the gates behind them to contain the outbreak. But say there's an underground tunnel. What if somebody got locked in, and ran out the tunnel without closing it off? The zombies follow that guy. You arrive and there's no zombies. But then every once in a while, some leak in through that hole."

"Why now?" she asked.

"Maybe they smell me ridin' around. Maybe it's my fault, I'm leavin' my scent all over town. I don't know. But if I stop it…if I find the hole and seal it…will you forgive me?"

"Go," she said, gun held at her side.

Desperate, he ran through the grass, got back on his bike and pedaled. He rode hard toward the center of town. As he did, he saw the zombies moving in loose formation, sweeping the terrain, heading north. They had sensed him, somehow, found his trail and followed it.

He stopped. "Come on! Follow me! Food time!"

They shifted course. Some ran, some lumbered, and one crawled. Darting down the road he outpaced them easily, but they wouldn't lose his scent. Another mile and he was downtown.

Going to where he tended to find them, he looked around, trying to think. He had been everywhere, except behind the shops on the south side of the road. He rode behind those, dropped the bike and walked along the grass.

"Do you see it, Billy? Help me, come on."

Finally, he did see something in the moonlight.

One of the Dead, rising from the high grass.

Pulling out his bat, he ran to it, swung and knocked the zombie down. His feet spilled out beneath him and he slid down an embankment, landing on cold concrete beneath. Before him yawned the mouth of an underground tunnel at least seven feet in diameter.

He went in.

His eyes adjusted to the darkness. A runner charged through the grass above, dashing into the tunnel after him. When it was close enough he crunched the bones of its skull with his weapon, then ran. More flooded in through the gaping maw, hunting him with abandon.

A zombie caught up to him, grabbing hold and coming in for a chew. But he kicked it and smashed its head against the wall and rushed onwards.

The chase felt like it might last forever. He wanted to give in but Billy begged him to keep running. Then he saw the light up ahead. Faint, but no illusion.

They were behind him, catching up.

He exploded out of the tunnel into the forest. "Come! Come out and get me!" he screamed. He jogged up the embankment, only to see that he was just outside the fence line. The moon illuminated everything, including two large doors, both wide open, at the mouth of the tunnel.

It was a drainage system, large, aimed at the river below. The doors had been built after the fact, to keep the dead out, but when the people had died inside and the plague had spread, someone had come out this way and left the doors open. Eventually all the zombies left the ghost town in search of life. That was the only explanation.

He waited above as the zombies poured out. Seeing him, they clambered up the embankment. He knocked the first down with the bat but it grabbed his ankle and another tackled him from behind. As the bat slipped away he drew his Ka-Bar, punching the blade into both zombies as they riddled him with bites. More piled on and he squirmed and kicked and shoved and lost the knife, but snaked out from the dogpile, raced up the embankment, leading them toward the fence, and then alongside it, and then at the last instant he turned and ran back to the tunnel. With all his strength he shoved one huge metal door shut, and then the other. Just as it was about to close he slipped in. He closed the door, felt for and found a latch, secured it. The Dead pounded and roared against the doors but couldn't get in. Eventually, he knew, they would give up and move on, forgetting why they were even there.

He made his way back into town. Got on his bike and rode to his friends' home. His wounds seeped. "I know, Billy," he said. "I know."

When he got there he was lightheaded but he got over the fence and into the yard, and to the house. He called out to them, and eventually they all came.

From the porch, they stared at him: bloodied, pale, sweating profusely. They uttered words of disbelief.

He walked up the steps of the porch and faced Elizabeth, who remained composed despite her fear. She raised the gun at his chest. "Stay away, please."

Quentin took the gun gently by the barrel, his breathing rapid and shallow. He guided it upwards until it reached his head.

"I sealed it," he said. "They won't come in anymore. I stopped the leak."

"Thank you," said Elizabeth, and spent the last bullet in town.

8 FROM DEAD TO DUST BY T. S. ALAN

There was no antiviral coming. The contagion had spread too quickly for the Centers For Disease Control and Prevention (CDC) and the U.S. Army Medical Research Institute of Infectious Diseases (USAMRIID) to identify the viral pathogen before it spread across the country. Time had run out. The living dead in New York City now outnumbered those still alive.

The Army Sustainment Command that had been set up at the Javits Convention Center had fallen. MEDCOM HQ, which was the Headquarters and Headquarters Company for USAMRIID and the 1st Maneuver Enhancement Brigade (1st MEB), at Madison Square Garden was hastily being evacuated. Command knew they were not going to be able to hold the base for very much longer. Thousands of the living dead had gathered outside at the barricades and along the perimeter fencing of the multi-use indoor arena, all clamoring feverishly to get in and get a meal of human flesh. Brigadier General Ford ordered all operation commands in the city to recall their troops, evacuate and rendezvous at Stewart Air National Guard Base (ANGB) in Newburgh, New York. There was nothing more the military could do for the city; it was time to fall back to the military bases at Colorado Springs, where the virus had yet to reach.

However for the remaining soldiers of MEDCOM Bravo at the 69th Regiment Armory on Lexington Avenue, leaving by land was impossible. The armory was under siege by the living dead from outside as well as inside. The perimeter fencing had failed and there were now hundreds packed into the compound as well as a large agitated contingent at the building's main doorway that were frantically scraping their nails on the heavy wooden entry trying to get in. Inside there was chaos, too. Most of the soldiers of the 1/69th Infantry Regiment Mechanized were sick or had already succumbed to the virus and turned into zombies, all because their CBRN protection equipment had arrived too late.

The armory's commander Colonel Walter Travis had also become afflicted with the virus. There was only one way his remaining uninfected soldiers were going to get out and that was airlift by helo from the roof. MEDCOM HQ informed him that air mission command at Stewart ANGB was going to send a Sikorsky UH-60 Black Hawk to extract them.

Colonel Travis had locked himself in his office. He was writing in a journal again. The colonel had no idea if it would ever be found and read, but he needed to put pen to paper for a record of what had transpired:

It is now 0245 hours and this will be my last journal entry. More and more of the undead have gathered outside our walls. It seems like the entire city has succumbed to the plague... A while ago there had been attempts by my men who are now the living dead to break into my office. But for the last fifteen minutes I have heard no one beating on my door.

Staff Sergeant Becker had called earlier for reinforcements but I could not send any. Though I have not heard from him since, and do not know if he was successful in his mission, I have no choice but to order the last of my non-infected soldiers to the roof for exfil. HQ has informed me that ASOC will send a helicopter to transport them to Stewart ANGB for final withdrawal. I pray that my soldiers make it safely out of the city.

I tried several times throughout the day and evening to get hold of my wife and children, to hear their voices and know they are alive, but I am certain they are dead or worse. All is lost and this illness drains me of my energy and my mind. Before I become too incapacitated I will follow Command's orders. I will kill myself. It is better I die than to become one of the unholy abominations that now roam this metropolis.

Faugh an Beallach!

***

Captain Cullin Arn and her six men never heard the pistol shot that ended their commander's life. They were too busy attempting to make it to the stairwell that led to the roof. The hallways were overrun with the living dead, slowing their progress. Arn was at the front of the fight. The strawberry blonde officer wasn't one to pass off point position to a subordinate. Her fierceness as a warfighter was only outdone by her proactive commitment to getting the job done against a determined and tenacious enemy.

Down the second-floor hallway they went, slowly pushing through the enemy ahead while keeping the ones in the rear at bay. Killing a fast-moving zombie with a headshot wasn't as easy as it was often portrayed in movies and television. Soldiers are trained to shoot center mass, which gives the greatest chance of a bullet landing somewhere in the vicinity of the organs, and so end hostilities by seriously incapacitating or killing the aggressor. However, when you aim small, you miss small, and Arn and her soldiers were expending a lot of ammunition. They were fighting to get to the stairwell that would lead them up to the third floor to the stairwell to the roof.

The stairway from the second to third floor was clear, but the upper level hallway was awash with dead zombies as well as the corpses of Sergeant Becker's team. Becker and his fire team had been sent earlier to the third level to facilitate the eradication of those in the hospital wing that had died and reanimated. There were so many of A and E Company that had "turned" that the fire team had called they were being overrun and needed reinforcements. However, Colonel Travis could not spare anyone; they were too busy with the zombies on the main floor. Becker's team never returned.

The floor and walls were splattered with blood and bits of brain matter and flesh, so much that the hallway looked like an abstract painting by Norman Bluhm. Slowly, stealthily, and one at a time, the team exited onto the floor. It was eerily quiet. Not one zombie roaming about. All the team had to do was travel two-thirds down the corpse-strewn corridor to where the roof access door was located. First Lieutenant Matthew Cooper was the last to come through the stairwell doorway. He cautiously closed it so the noise of the lock latching back into its recess was barely audible. The floor was tacky with coagulated blood and entrails. Carefully, the group moved toward the roof access door in standard military formation, stepping over bodies as they progressed toward their objective.

They had almost made it undetected when one of the corpses reared up from under another and groaned as it grabbed onto Cooper's leg and tripped him. Cooper stumbled and then tripped over another corpse and landed face up, his head landing in the body cavity of a member of the fire team that had perished hours earlier.

For a bullet-riddled zombie with one leg missing and the lower half of the other barely attached, it was swift in getting to the fallen lieutenant. Before Cooper had gotten the boot of his free foot onto the skull of the ravenous monstrosity that had latched onto his other foot, it had started crawling up his leg. Cooper forcefully kicked the zombie atop its skull, trying to beat it off him, but the zombie was unfazed by the boot strike.

Sergeant Anthony Richardson had been right ahead of Cooper when he fell. When he heard the groan he turned just in time to see his superior tumble over a corpse and land on the flesh-stripped corpse of one of his own. Richardson didn't hesitate to come to Cooper's aid. He tried to pull Cooper clear of the crawling zombie, but the creature had been too quick and had latched onto the lieutenant's ankle.

Specialist Emmett Emery reacted immediately to the situation, too. He also grabbed onto Cooper, trying to help the sergeant pull their lieutenant clear of the threat. As Cooper put his boot to the zombie's head for a third time, it bit deeply into his leg just above his kneecap. As Richardson and Emery kept pulling back, the flesh around the bite wound ripped away, freeing Cooper long enough to allow the two to pull the first lieutenant clear before the zombie could get its grip on Cooper again.

Cooper tried to hold back his wail of pain as the flesh tore from his leg, but the agony was too intense. Though Cooper's cry hadn't been extremely loud, it had been audible enough for it to reverberate down the hall and around the corner ahead of them. A loud distant groan came from around the hall. Except it wasn't just the groan of one zombie; it was the collective groans of multiple zombies. A moment later a horde came from around the corner.

When Captain Arn heard the loud moans of the living dead, she immediately bolted for the access door to the roof. Specialist Harold English and Staff Sergeant Patrick Murphy covered their leader's door entry, as Corporal Mark Watson watched down the hall covering the entire team. The narrow stairwell passage up to the roof was clear. Arn ordered her soldiers through the doorway, just as the horde came around the corner.

Richardson and Emery hauled the incapacitated Cooper through the stairwell entry just before the zombie pack reached them. They struggled to get him up the stairs with the zombie horde only steps behind them.

As they reached the top of the stairs, Cooper urgently told Richardson and Emery, "Go. Go!" He knew he wasn't going to be able leave on the helicopter, but he could try to stave off the zombie onslaught so his comrades could escape.

Richardson and Emery tried to pull the lieutenant through the door, but he broke free of them. "That's an order!" he forcefully commanded.

As the sergeant and specialist crossed the threshold and closed the door behind them, they heard the latch bolt engage and then Matthew Cooper cry "Faugh an Beallach!" It was the battle cry of the 69th Infantry Regiment, an Irish saying that meant "Clear the way!"

Cooper had the high ground. It was a tactical advantage that would only last as long as he had enough 30-round magazines for his Colt M4A1 carbine. The stairwell started to fill up with zombie corpses as he ripped their heads apart with the weapon's 5.56mm caliber ammo, spraying blood and brain matter into the air like a wet dog shaking off water. Even with the high ground it took a lot of bullets to stop them. He ejected his third magazine and grabbed for his last one, but when his hand hit his vest he discovered it was missing. He always kept accurate track of his ammo magazines. He had had one chambered in the carbine and three on his tactical vest when he entered the third floor. It must have dislodged when he had tripped and fallen in the hallway. If he had had a hand grenade he would have dove into the oncoming pack with it and taken out as many with him as he could, but hand grenades were not a standard-issue item for his regiment.

Cooper was not going to allow himself to be torn apart. It was one horror he was going to avoid at all cost. He grabbed his M9 pistol, but before he could shoot himself in the head the pack seized him and dragged him down. They tore at him, first shredding his clothes and then clawing at his flesh. Luckily for him it wasn't like a Hollywood horror film; zombies couldn't simply claw flesh away by grabbing at your skin, but they sure as hell could bite and pull. He struggled to keep hold of his pistol as the pack pulled at his arms, trying to tear them from its sockets. A bite to his left hand severed his wedding ring finger, and then he felt his left arm being torn off. First the arm dislocated. Then he felt the flesh and muscle start to give way. With all his remaining strength he forced himself to pull back his right arm, as if he were in an arm-wrestling match, to get the pistol to his head. The pistol went off. The shot echoed in the stairwell. Cooper was dead a split second before his left arm was torn from his body. It only took a few moments for the zombie pack to tear Cooper's limp corpse to pieces. Those that got a part of him retreated with their meal. Several of the group fought over Cooper's torso, dragging it down the stairs as they did, leaving a bloody streak like the slime trail of a snail. For the moment, the smell of blood and freshly mutilated body parts overpowered the scent left behind by the fleeing soldiers. But the ever-hungry mass would soon be drawn back to their forgotten quarry.

***

A temporary reprieve: that is what Cooper's self-sacrifice had earned the six that had made it to the roof. Captain Arn and her team heard Cooper's single pistol shot and they surmised he had taken his life rather than be eaten alive. Arm knew that once the ravenous undead creatures were done consuming their fallen companion, they would turn their attention back to them. She also knew that the door to the roof would not hold the tide of zombies back for long.

The extract helo was late, which for them had been a good thing. It had taken Arn's team longer to get to the roof than anticipated. However, Arn also knew a delayed extract could mean the helo was in trouble or not coming at all.

"Valkyrie One-Nine, Valkyrie One-Nine this is Wolfhound Zero-Zero. How copy? Over," Arn radioed to the helicopter from the 3rd General Support Battalion, 10th Aviation Regiment that was supposed to be coming to extract them. There was no response. She heard some radio chatter stating to rotate right, and then hold. She radioed again. "Valkyrie One-Nine, Valkyrie One-Nine this is Wolfhound Zero-Zero. Do you copy? Over."

"Wolfhound Zero-Zero, standby this frequency," the responding voice instructed over the sound of machine gunfire.

As Arn patiently waited, she could hear the guttural noises from the throngs of the living dead at street level. If they could not be extracted from the armory's roof, they were going to have to make their escape from the adjoining building to their northwest. However, they had limited ammunition and she had no idea if that building had been compromised. The situation was dire.

"Wolfhound Zero-Zero," a voice arose over her radio. "Contact Zero-Six Stewart on Five-Nine-Decimal-Nine-Five-Zero in the red. Read back for check. Over."

Arn had been given Valkyrie One-Nine's radio frequency from Commander Travis, which had come from the air mission commander at Steward. Now she was being instructed to contact the air mission commander directly on a different unencrypted channel. She knew something was wrong if she was being instructed to contact Stewart directly, but she had no idea how bad the situation was at FOB MEDCOM.

"Valkyrie One-Nine this is Wolfhound Zero-Zero," Arn responded. "I read back: Contact Zero-Six Stewart on Five-Nine-Decimal-Nine-Five-Zero in the red. Over."

"Wolfhound Zero-Zero this is Valkyrie One-Nine. Correct. Out."

***

Arn was correct. There was something very wrong. Valkyrie One-Nine was in the midst of a skirmish as it hovered above Madison Square Garden, laying down cover fire so the last of the 1st MEB could be extracted. The only extraction point for the remaining personnel was also from a rooftop position. Though the Garden didn't have a rooftop helipad, it did have enough room for four UH-60 Black Hawks to land on the outer perimeter of the circular roof. Having dropped off a full complement of

MEDCOM HQ medical personnel at Stewart ANGB, Valkyrie One-Nine was on its way back to Manhattan to extract Wolfhound Zero-Zero as ordered. However, as they neared Manhattan airspace, they received a call from air mission command.

"Valkyrie One-Nine, Valkyrie One-Nine this is Stewart Zero-Six. How copy? Over."

"Stewart Zero-Six this is Valkyrie One-Nine, solid copy, go ahead."

"FOB MEDCOM has lost final protective line. Imminent compromise of LZ. Divert to FOB MEDCOM at buster for over watch until exfil is complete. Do you copy? Over."

Chief Warrant Officer 2 Parker Holt confirmed, "Stewart Zero-Six, Valkyrie One-Nine copies. Out."

The four-bladed, twin-engine, helicopter only took a minute to get to Madison Square Garden. As it moved into over watch position, Valkyrie One-Seven was already lifting off from the roof and Valkyrie One-Two was loading their last two passengers.

Pilot CW2 Holt rotated the helo so that the left side M134 Minigun had a direct line of fire on the roof access door. If the enemy broke through, gunner Dylan Jusino would be able to keep them at bay until the last helicopter was in the air.

One of Valkyrie One-Five's crew chiefs helped Lieutenant Morrow direct his fleeing troops to the helicopter. As it readied for lift off, the Morrow began directing the last of the troops to Valkyrie One-Six. A burst of carbine fire echoed from the roof access entry. Six soldiers rushed through the door heading toward Morrow. One of them yelled, "Tangos on our six!"

There was a rapid succession of carbine fire from the last fleeing soldier toward the onrushing enemy, and then the flood of the living dead spilled onto the roof. The hungry mass went directly toward the retreating troops heading to the last helo.

Sergeant Jusino's 7.62 caliber, rotary machine gun whined as it rapidly spat out rounds from its six twenty-inch barrels, tearing the charging zombies into meaty chunks. Though the zombie corpses started to stack up, the sergeant couldn't kill the living dead fast enough. In under a minute he had expended the minigun's 5,000 round belt, and the living dead kept pouring out the access door, charging toward the helicopter.

"Left gun dry," Sergeant Jusino announced over his radio headset. "Rotate 180, rotate 180," he instructed pilot CW2 Holt. As the Black Hawk rotated right to put Corporal Carlos Rojas into firing position, Wolfhound Zero-Zero radioed. Holt knew why Arn was calling; his team was late picking them up. Holt and his crew were in an active fire mission, and ordered to be over watch until all remaining troops were extracted. They couldn't leave, so he told Wolfhound Zero-Zero to contact air flight command for an update.

It only took Holt a moment to rotate the helicopter 180 degrees to get Cpl. Rojas into firing position, but in that brief amount of time a drove of the living dead had streamed onto the roof, reaching Valkyrie One-Two before Capt. Morrow could get aboard. The front of the pack tore into him, as the rest moved to the helicopter just as it began to lift off. The Valkyrie One-Two gunner that faced the oncoming horde had opened fire as soon as the troops were out of the line of fire. But he too couldn't kill enough to stop them from reaching the helo. As Valkyrie One-Two got wheels off the ground the living dead reached them, charging head-on into the crew compartment before they could get the door closed. There was some weapons fire inside, and then the helicopter clipped its wheels on the retaining wall of the roof as it rocked under the extra weight.

A bullet went through the cockpit wall and struck the pilot in the back of his head, piercing his helmet. The bullet tore out the front of the pilot's skull, projecting a thick, crimson splatter of blood and brains onto the windshield. The co-pilot tried to correct the faltering Black Hawk, but two zombies seized him. The flight control stick shifted right, moving the rotorcraft toward West 31st Street above the venue's loading dock, and then the co-pilot's feet came off the pedals. As another zombie pushed its way into the cockpit the co-pilot was thrust forward, pushing the control stick. The helicopter pitched frontward and dove to the ground, crashing nose first to the pavement below. The helicopter didn't explode upon impact. Instead the main rotors shattered as they sliced at the pavement, sending pieces of rotor shrapnel careening in all directions. The Black Hawk banked onto its side, and then spun like a top until the rear rotor and tail assembly tore itself apart. The helicopter hadn't stopped its circular motion before the zombies around the loading dock area swarmed it.

"Break, break," CW2 Holt called over the radio. "Valkyrie One-Nine, Valkyrie One-Nine to all stations. FOB MEDCOM has fallen. I say again, FOB MEDCOM has fallen."

***

The noise from the helicopter agitated the zombies behind the rooftop door. Arn knew the barred entry would not hold for long. Her men scrambled up the Black Hawk's ladder as quickly as they could. The helicopter was hovering high above them, unable to get any lower due to the tight distance between the buildings. They were also fighting updrafts and cross breezes.

There was a crash of glass from the west. It had come from the building on the northwest corner that butted up against the rear of the armory. Capt. Arn's fear had come to fruition. The building behind the armory had been compromised. The living dead were crashing through the top windows, most falling headfirst. Their skulls split open like over ripe pumpkins as they thudded, the impacts causing blood and brains to ooze across the rooftop. However, there were lower windows that the zombies came through, and when they smashed through and fell, they did not die.

Three of Arn's soldiers were already aboard the hovering helicopter. Spc. Harold English was halfway up the ladder when the first zombie came crashing out the building window. Arn ordered Staff Sergeant Patrick Murphy to follow him, but he refused. Murphy was a heavier man, compact and muscular, and was anchoring the ladder, holding it steady. Murphy told Arn to go, and he would follow.

The helicopter was facing Lexington Avenue, trying to remain as steady as possible above the front of the building, but the cross wind was causing the pilot to make constant corrections. From their position they could not see the nose-diving zombies.

There must have been a hallway window that the zombies had discovered, because there was now a constant flow of the plummeting living dead from one particular window. Arn was slow getting up the ladder; both her heavy daypack and the Mossberg 590 shotgun strapped to it were hindering her ascent. She could have dumped the backpack once the helo had arrived, but it was filled with carbine and shotgun ammo, and her instinct as a warrior told her to hold onto it.

Murphy stepped onto the ladder just as the living dead attempted to rush him. The helicopter began to rise moving toward the street, but an up current caused the Black Hawk to violently jolt and then rotate. Murphy lost his grip and fell, one of his feet caught in the lower rungs of the ladder preventing him from plummeting to his death. Murphy couldn't swing himself upright; the helicopter was swaying him, almost slamming him into the armory's façade. As he hung upside down below roof level, he saw the living dead leaping off the building toward him. They dove at him like stage diving concertgoers into a mosh pit. The first few missed, landing atop the clamoring horde on the sidewalk below. However, as the helicopter attempted to correct itself, it put Murphy parallel to the rooftop.

Arn yelled at the crew to pull the helicopter up the moment she saw her sergeant grab hold of the ladder. When the helo first jolted, causing Murphy to dangle like a piece of bait half on a hook, she knew he was in serious trouble. Then Arn saw the first few zombies launch themselves off the roof in a futile attempt to snatch him. As the helicopter regained control and rose once again, it put Murphy directly in the vaulting zombies' path. Before the rotorcraft could rise to a safe height, six more leapt off the building. Murphy attempted to shoot them with his carbine, but two successfully made the leap. One struck Murphy squarely on the chest, the impact triggering him to drop his weapon and nearly causing him to break free of the ladder. The zombie bounced off Murphy and splatted on the sidewalk below. The other struck the ladder but had no concept of how to grab the rungs to hold on. However, like Murphy, its leg became entangled in the ladder, turning him upside down. It immediately grabbed Murphy's leg and bit into his inner thigh. Murphy cried out as he grabbed for his sidearm. He pressed the pistol against the zombie's head and fired.

Arn had been watching the whole time. She saw the blood splatter as the sergeant shot it, and then she saw him look up to her. Murphy dropped his pistol, and then grabbed his knife. Arn knew what he was about to do.

Though Arn could not hear Murphy's words over the noise of the helo, she swore he said, "Faugh an Beallach," just before he cut himself free. Murphy plummeted to

Madison Square Park below, landing face up and in the lap of the imposing bronze statue of statesman William Henry Seward; Murphy's vertebrae were crushed and his spinal cord was severed on impact.

***

The Air National Guard base encompassed 267 acres and was home to the 105th Airlift Wing, which was comprised of ten units. However, by the time Valkyrie One-Nine reached the base only a small contingent from the 137th Airlift Squadron remained. Five of the airlift wing's eight Boeing C-17 Globemaster III large military transport aircraft had already departed, taking most of FOB MEDCOM and 1st MEB with them. Captain Arn and her team exited the helicopter just in time to see a large group of Boeing CH-47 Chinook tandem rotor heavy-lift helicopters lift off. Sgt. Richardson made a comment to Arn about them, which gunner Rojas overheard.

"That's B Company, Mountain Movers. They're from the 10th AR, like we are," he told them, referring to the 10th Aviation Regiment of Fort Drum, New York.

Richardson asked, "Isn't Colorado the other way?" having observed the helicopter's direction of flight.

A half-dozen army soldiers began to load the Black Hawk with more ammunition before they got in. "They're headed to MRIID with troops and some doctors," Rojas answered Richardson. "We're headed there, too." Rojas pointed at the last of the Globemaster IIIs with its load ramp down. "You better hurry. Those are the last Moose out," he told them, and then warned, "As soon as they are wheels up, fire support for the base will terminate." As he stepped back into the helo, he saluted Arn, and then slid the door closed.

Midway to the cargo plane, Spc. Emery stopped and turned to look at a few abandoned Humvees.

"Let's go," Richardson instructed, but Emery refused to move.

"No, Sergeant," he replied. "I'm going home."

This time Richardson was more forceful. "That's an order, Specialist. Now move!"

However, Emery no longer cared about orders. There was something more pressing on his mind, and that was to get back to his family. "I'm going home. I got a wife and a four-year-old in Fishkill—that's twenty minutes from here."

The sound of the engines from the three Globemasters began to grow. The transports were ready for departure. Capt. Arn looked to the planes. She saw a crewmember urgently waving her on.

"We gotta go and we gotta go now, Specialist," she told Emery.

"With all due respect, Captain, screw this. I'm not going to Colorado and leaving my family behind. You want to stop me then you'll have to shoot me."

Emery walked away and headed toward the Humvees. As he did, Richardson aimed his weapon at the deserting specialist, but then quickly lowered it. "Maybe he's right," he told the group. "I have a wife and kid, too. So do you, Captain. Maybe—"

Richardson didn't finish his thought. There was a loud roar of attack helicopters flying low overhead, and then a series of air-to-ground missiles erupted nearby. Then the group saw what was happening: the living dead had broken through and were heading toward the transport planes. Arn and the rest dashed toward the Globemaster III just as the plane began to raise its cargo ramp. They made it just in time.

Emery had done what Arn believed they all wanted to do, and if they had had a few minutes more to think it over, she knew it's what they all would have done—desert.

Her team should have gotten off the helicopter and appropriated whatever ground transportation they could acquire to get back to their families as Emery had done, Arn thought, as she and her men got situated while the Globemaster made a quick takeoff before the horde of zombies could interfere with their departure. Although Arn no longer had a spouse to be concerned about, she did have Casidhe, her six-year-old daughter. Casidhe was home in Lebanon Springs, which was 30 miles southeast of Albany, and less than two hours from the air base. Arn had told her parents to get home and secure themselves in the basement. Arn's house was like a fortress; she had made sure of it. She had been deployed to Iraq when her regiment was called to duty for Operation Iraqi Freedom, and then again in 2008, when she was deployed to Afghanistan as part of Task Force Phoenix. She had been witness to the horrors of war and with Hurricane Sandy had seen how a natural disaster could be devastating to families. She knew the importance of being prepared and secure. Arn had turned her basement into a bunker. She phoned her parents to check in. Knowing her daughter and parents were secure and safe for the time being gave her some comfort, but her daughter still needed her mother. Casidhe wanted her mother with her, to keep her safe from the monsters outside. Now all Arn had to do was figure out how she was going to get from Colorado back to New York State.

When she was done with her phone call, she got a situation report (sitrep) from Sgt. Richardson, and discovered they were not headed directly to Colorado Springs. They were first on their way to USAMRIID at Fort Detrick, Maryland, but that was all the information Richardson could get from the plane's loadmaster. Arn went to speak with the Air Force sergeant.

"Sorry, Captain for the indirect route, but we're on a response mission to Fort Detrick for a heavy assets drop," Staff Sgt. John Eller informed her. "Those Special Ops Rangers are jumping in with some of the 3-2 SBCT after we drop their load. That's all I can tell you."

However, that wasn't everything that Eller could tell her. Arn also learned from him that the airdrop was going to be at 600 feet instead of a low-altitude parachute extraction. This was because the noise from the engines of the three Globemasters would attract the zombies, as well as the Strykers' electronic equipment being too sensitive to take such an abrasive impact from a low-altitude parachute extraction. Arn also learned who was in charge of the mission, codenamed Operation Thunder.

First Lieutenant Earlman from Special Operations, 2nd Ranger Battalion, 75th Ranger Regiment was in command of not only his Rangers, but also the ranking officer for the supporting fire units from the 3rd Stryker Brigade Combat Team, 2nd Infantry Division. Both the 2/75 RGR REG and the 3-2 SBCT were out of Fort Lewis, Washington, and though they both had a small supporting presence at the armory, she did not know the mission commander.

"Operation Thunder is on a need-to-know basis," Earlman told Arn. "But if you know the work MRIID does, then you know why we're on this response mission." Earlman then offered, "You want to know more, then you and your team need to join us."

It didn't take any guessing on Arn's part to understand what they were trying to accomplish at USAMRIID. Colonel Travis had told her before he sent her team to the roof that all the research data collected on the virus from FOB MEDCOM was being transferred to MRIID's Biosafety Level-4 facilities at Fort Detrick. Included in this transfer was the return of half the remaining MRIID doctors and some CDC virologists. All other operations were being transferred to Colorado Springs.

Maryland was certainly closer to New York than Colorado, but Arn was certain that she would be literally jumping back into action against an ever-growing enemy that might not be stoppable. However, her choice was clear—Fort Detrick was closer than whichever Air Force base they were headed to in Colorado Springs. She told Earlman she would get back to him after she spoke with her team. He told her to hurry because shortly they would be over the drop zone.

Sergeant Richardson was torn between fighting and fleeing. He had joined the 69th New York National Guard, like his father and his grandfather before him. His reason was to prove himself to himself, wondering what he would do under fire. He had trained for anti-siege, and had been in numerous firefights with bullets and explosives being shot at him. But it was a world of difference when it was an exponentially growing, relentless enemy horde that had to have their heads blown off in order to kill them. In the last three days he had seen they were fighting a losing battle. If there was any hope for the salvation of humanity, then perhaps MRIID could find it. It was also closer to his home in Middletown, New York, than Colorado Springs. He was in.

Specialist Harold English had only been with the 69th a few years. He lived and worked in Manhattan, but his parents and siblings lived in Binghamton. He too wanted to go home. He was certain that if he stayed with his captain and sergeant he would have the best opportunity of seeing his family again. He said yes.

Corporal Mark Watson said no. Although he also lived in New York City, he had no family or girlfriend there. He originally hailed from Great Falls, Montana. He was better off taking his chances on going to Colorado. He was out.

Arn went to tell Earlman their decision. He ordered them to gear up for a low-level static line jump. But the plague had something else in mind.

***

The three transport aircraft were flying in a 3-ship, multi element formation, when the lead plane suddenly dropped in altitude, and then popped back up higher than it had been. Though the lead did not cross into the vertical space between the planes to left and right wing position, the abrupt altitude dip and climb was concerning to Captain Jenny Moore, who was piloting the Globemaster left of the lead. She asked her co-pilot, First Lieutenant Amy Hellinger to radio the lead.

"Thunder One-Three, Thunder One-Three this is Thunder Two-Three. How copy? Over."

The lead did not respond. Hellinger repeated her radio call, but there was still no answer.

Once again the lead plane quickly dropped altitude and popped back up. This time, though, the aircraft began to move left, crossing into Thunder Two-Three's flight path, and then right into the flight path of Thunder Three-Three. The lead's wings sharply tilted as it banked. Then the plane's cargo door opened.

Hellinger radioed the third aircraft to warn them of the loss of radio communication. "Thunder Three-Three this is Thunder Two-three. We have no joy on Thunder Leader. I say again, we have no joy on Thunder Leader."

As Hellinger was about to tell Three-Three to break formation an object came falling out of the cargo door. It was a person. Then there was another, but no parachutes opened. Thunder Three-Three broke right, getting out of the way of the falling bodies.

Thunder One-Three sharply climbed, and then rolled left, tilting hard, almost with its wing tipped toward the ground below. More bodies fell out the cargo door with no parachutes. Captain Moore made an evasive maneuver, attempting to take the plane out of harm's way, just as a stream of parachutists exited the aft cargo door. The plane was at such a precarious angle that the jumping warfighters' chutes didn't properly deploy from the static line. Several men tangled in their chutes plummeted toward the plane.

***

The plane banked left abruptly, and then there was a loud crash on the roof. Eller radioed to the cockpit, but before he got a response there was another loud impact. This time an explosion followed it.

***

The first parachutist to hit the plane did so on the roof of the forward portion of the cargo compartment, and then bounced off. The second jumper to make contact with the plane was sucked into the outer right engine, the chute getting stuck and flapping over it. While the engines were robust enough to be bird-strike resistant, they could not survive a whole flock or a human body being sucked into them. Engine four erupted in fire, and then the turbine disc failed. Hellinger quickly shut the fuel off to the engine as the automatic fire detection system activated to extinguish the flames. At the same time, the captain adjusted the thrust of the remaining engines and the aircraft's bank to keep it level. The Globemaster III could fly on three out of four turbo-fan engines, but the loss of 25% thrust was a serious matter with a full cargo load.

The lodged fluttering parachute began to come free. Captain Moore needed to get rid of it before it got sucked into neighboring engine three. If they lost another engine on the right wing the transport would go down. She pitched the plane left, so that the right wing was tilted up. The chute shifted direction. For a moment it flapped in the wind. Then it partially opened, catching some air. It was enough to pull the chute free and send it streaming away. Moore leveled the plane once again.

A warning alarm sounded. There was a problem with engine three on the right wing. It was running above the normal operating temperature. Moore knew that something must have struck it when the warfighter got sucked into engine four. Moore knew that if she sustained the high thrust load on the engine it would fail. She had no choice but to order the payload dropped, even though they were fifty miles from the drop zone. Moore told the loadmaster that his crew needed to immediately drop the two Stryker Fire Support Vehicles (FSV).

**

Staff Sgt. Eller had remained on the radio with the co-pilot, and was aware of what was happening. When the order came to drop the payload, Eller's crew went into immediate action. When the aft door began to open and the Special Ops Mission Commander was informed of the emergency, Earlman demanded to speak with the pilot. Capt. Moore told Eller she would have no problem with speaking directly to Earlman, and to prep the load for discharge. Eller wanted to let out a big grin when he handed the comm set to the mission commander; he knew what his captain was going to say to Earlman, but he kept his grin to himself.

Earlman was on the radio with the captain for less than thirty seconds. After he reminded Moore that he was mission commander and then ordered her to make it to the drop zone, Moore told him that he was only mission commander once on the ground. She also reminded him that she was the ranking officer of the flight mission, and the payload was going to be dropped for the safety of everyone aboard. Earlman grumbled, "Son-of-a-bitch," as he pushed the comm set back to Eller, and then returned to his mission members to let them know the heavy assets and Stryker teams would be jumping and the Rangers would continue to the drop zone.

***

The first sled rolled to the end of the cargo compartment. A small drag chute ejected out the door and then opened. A moment later the drag chute pulled out three larger chutes, followed by the first Stryker FSV sliding out the back of the plane, the three chutes pulling open ten larger parachutes. After the first Stryker was clear, the second rolled to the end. Less than fifteen seconds later

Stryker Two was on its way. The two five-member Stryker teams followed afterward, and then Captain Arn and her two team members jumped next. They jumped without Earlman's consent.

Airdropping the load had worked. Captain Moore reduced the thrust on the engines, and engine three returned to a normal operating temperature. Thunder Two-Three caught up to Thunder Three-Three and took the flight lead to the drop zone.

Earlman's Operation Thunder had begun with six Strykers, six Stryker teams, and a platoon of Rangers— eight per plane. Earlman didn't know how many warfighters had escaped from the lead transport before it nose-dived toward the ground, but he hoped that whoever made it out had made it safely to the ground and without a carnivorous enemy awaiting them. Nonetheless, the loss of life and equipment was significant, and now, with two more heavy assets not getting to the drop zone, the lieutenant was concerned that the losses would critically jeopardize the mission's ability in helping B Company, 4th Light Armored Reconnaissance Battalion/Marine Corps to keep the USAMRIID facilities at Fort Detrick secure. However, the mission commander was confident that if the two Stryker teams could get their vehicles to Fort Detrick quickly, the mission could still be successful.

***

Captain Arn saw an opportunity and she seized it. She and her two subordinates had been tethered to the static jump line on the same side of the plane as the 3-2 SBCT members. As soon as she heard Earlman notify them about the situation, she knew it was imperative they jump right behind the two teams. Arn, Richardson, and Emery were out of the plane before Earlman could stop them.

Before jumping, Arn had informed her two comrades that they needed to keep eyes on one another so they were situationally aware of where each of them were landing. She also told them they needed to steer clear of the Stryker teams. Spc. English had never done a parachute jump and he asked how the parachute was steered. Arn had to whisper an explanation to him that steer clear was not to be taken literally, because you couldn't steer a T-11 military parachute like you could a civilian skydiver's chute. She told him he just needed to stay away from the Stryker members and join up with one another as quickly as possible.

When Captain Moore had ordered her crew to dump the payload, she did not think Earlman would be so reckless as to order the Stryker teams out of the plane in order to recover their vehicles. Eller had tried to warn the mission commander that the vehicles were being dropped over terrain that was not conducive to asset delivery, and that in all likelihood the vehicles would be unrecoverable due to impact damage upon reaching the ground. However, Earlman informed the loadmaster that his assessment of the situation was unacceptable and that if he closed the aft cargo door before the Stryker teams could jump, he was going to shoot the loadmaster for refusing to obey an order during wartime. Eller took Earlman's threat seriously. He kept the door open even though he was certain Earlman was ordering the Stryker teams to their doom.

***

Both Stryker teams landed in a small open area off Pretty Boy Dam Road, a short distance from the Pretty Boy Dam. However not every member of the two teams landed without incident. Two members missed the clearing and ended up in a forested area. The parachute of the driver from the first Stryker tangled up in some tree branches, but he didn't land too high that he couldn't release himself safely, and there were no zombies waiting for him. However, the vehicle commander for the second Stryker team wasn't as lucky. He too became entangled in some tree branches. As he hit the branches the chute ripped causing him to swing into another tree, and into the jagged point of a short dead branch. The branch pierced his larynx, impaling him. For a moment he twitched, and then the dead branch snapped. The vehicle commander fell. He was dead before he hit the ground. One of his team members knifed him in the eye to be sure he didn't reanimate.

Although the loss of one member from a team was tragic, it was not devastating. All members of a Stryker Combat Team were familiar with the Stryker's systems and could take over another member's duties when needed. There would be one less person in Stryker Two to do air guard duty from the rear air guard hatch that opened to the roof.

Both teams would not have a problem with locating their vehicles. Each team had roughly seen where they landed. Plus Strykers were equipped with GPS locators for exact positioning. The roadway was clear and both teams double-timed it to their vehicles. They knew it was only a short time before the zombies would smell them.

***

The first Stryker landed on top of a farmer's barn a half-mile northeast of the Pretty Boy Dam on the outskirts of the town of Parkton, Maryland. The 16.5-ton, eight-wheeled armored fighting vehicle crashed through the barn roof, ripping a large hole in the structure, slid across the wooden floor, and finally came to rest halfway out the main barn doors it had destroyed. Miraculously, the Stryker FSV suffered little damage on impact. Unfortunately, the loud crash attracted almost every zombie to it in a half-mile radius. The first Stryker team had barely begun to unstrap the vehicle from its pallet sled when they found themselves under siege. Luckily for the team, not all of the 7,000 plus inhabitants of Parkton had succumbed to the virus or had been in the immediate area. The two air guard sergeants kept the zombies at bay while the other three members got the vehicle operational as quickly as possible. However, a growing horde of living dead surrounding them was the least of their problems.

The Stryker FSV had crashed through the roof from back to front, destabilizing the building by destroying or fracturing the barn's main support columns. There were no warning creaks or splintering sounds that the building was going to give way: the only undamaged wood support just snapped and the barn collapsed, crushing the driver and gunner who had just finished unstrapping the vehicle from the sled.

The two air guard sergeants standing on the front of the vehicle that protruded across the barn's threshold were also struck by collapsing debris. The first sergeant was killed immediately, crushed under broken lumber. The second air guard sergeant wasn't as lucky. He was knocked off the vehicle after being hit by the collapsing debris. He landed unconscious on the ground and nearly at the feet of several zombies. He abruptly awoke in horrific pain as the ravenous living dead bit off his face.

Vehicle commander SSg. Axel Grant had been inside the vehicle getting the Stryker's systems online when the building gave way. He had also been on the radio to his driver, who was giving him a sitrep on the vehicle's readiness. Grant heard the thunderous collapse around him, and it was evident from the noise that the damaged barn had given way. After unsuccessfully attempting to make radio contact with his crew, he struggled to exit the vehicle but found all the doors and hatches blocked by debris. Though he knew the Stryker would be impenetrable to zombies, he couldn't stay trapped in the vehicle forever. It was only equipped with three days of food and water for five people. Also, he needed to know if his crew was dead or just incapacitated. The only way he was going to find out was to see if he could get the fire support vehicle out from under the rubble.

The second Stryker did not crash into anything. It missed landing in the reservoir behind the dam by several hundred feet, and came to rest just downstream of the spillway. The water wasn't deep, only a few feet, but it was rocky, and tree-lined inclines bordered the waterway. It would be slow in traversing.

Stryker team two did not know the fate of the other Stryker team, not at first. They were too busy attempting to get their vehicle operational, and the flowing Gunpowder Falls waterway was hindering their progress. They too had a zombie menace to deal with, or so they first thought. The living dead had gathered on both embankments, but they made no attempt to come any closer. The two air guard sergeants who were on over watch duty atop the vehicle at first hadn't noticed the zombies' odd behavior. The air guards were ready to kill any zombie that attempted to traverse the water, but none tried. The living dead stood ten feet from the water's edge, groaning. Every once in a while an additional zombie would join the group. It would move close to the bank and then turn around as if it had seen something that frightened it. At first the air guards thought the zombies had figured out that if they got too close they would be shot. However, after the seventh or eighth time the strange behavior occurred, the two over watch soldiers realized the zombies weren't looking at the guns aimed at them; they actually feared the water. It was the damnedest thing they ever saw from a zombie.

***

The barn-crashed Stryker had struggled to get free from under the collapsed outbuilding, and it took all of the diesel engine's 350 horsepower to get the heavy fire support vehicle out from under. A one-man Stryker Fire Support Team was not a combat team. SSg. Grant needed to rendezvous with the other team. It was best he take command of their vehicle and get to Fort Detrick post-haste. He radioed the other team. They would come to him.

***

Captain Arn and her two warfighters had made it safely to the ground, although Spc. English did get his feet wet when he landed in a farmer's pond. Arn didn't know exactly where they had landed, though she had seen a dam nearby and the Stryker teams landing on the opposite side of it. The closest farm and two nearby homes were vacant and lacked vehicles, but did yield information in the form of an address on a piece of mail. They were somewhere in the town of Parkton, Maryland, though from the ample space between the residences, Arn surmised they were not in the main part of town. Luckily, Arn's cellphone still had an internet connection. She knew the internet would be as extinct as humanity would be if the war against the living dead wasn't soon won, so she quickly jotted down the route they needed to take to get back to New York. They were approximately 215 miles southwest of their first and closest destination of Middletown, where Sgt. Richardson resided. That was if they stuck to the main routes, which they knew would be more risky. They would have to take the longer, more rural roadways to avoid the heavier populated areas, which meant a much longer trip. They needed to acquire transport. They headed northeast toward the dam, hoping the town of Parkton would have a suitable vehicle.

As they crossed the dam they observed a Stryker team in the water below. From what they could assess the team had unharnessed the vehicle and was getting ready to depart. However, there were a whole lot of zombies waiting on both sides of the water's edge for them. It was imperative Arn's team avoid contact with the 3-2 SBCT. Any interaction with the vehicle crews could risk their freedom. They crossed the dam unnoticed and continued toward town.

The team was just about to exit a dense tree-lined section of Pretty Boy Dam Road into another residential area, when SSg. Smith caught a glimpse of a Stryker coming around the bend from behind them. A Stryker had a low acoustic signature, which was part of the reasonthat the vehicle was a formidable combination of mobility, stealth, and lethality. The team ducked into the woods for cover. Arn was certain it was the Stryker they had passed shortly before, but she couldn't figure out why it was going in the opposite direction of Fort Detrick. The speeding eight-wheeled vehicle passed, not detecting their presence. After Arn was sure the vehicle was clear of them, she again moved her team forward, checking the nearby residences for suitable transportation. When they moved to the second home along the roadway, they heard a vehicle running from inside a closed garage. When they opened the side door a blanket of car fumes billowed out. A working car was exactly what they were after, but the garage was filled with toxic fumes, too much for them to make an immediate entry. Then the Stryker returned, but Richardson was keeping an eye on the front property line for any threats, and saw it in time before it could get close. The fire support vehicle stopped just past the residence. It stood idling for a moment and then moved away, heading back toward the dam.

If it hadn't been for Sgt. Richardson's quick thinking at closing the side door before they bolted behind the garage for cover, the billowing exhaust fumes would probably have drawn unwanted attention. Richardson was sure the smell of the fumes had drifted to the street and the two air guards had probably smelled it, and that is why the Stryker FSV momentarily paused. After the armored vehicle departed, Arn and her team moved back to the garage entry. When the fumes had cleared enough for them to enter, they discovered a family of three inside the vehicle with one end of a hose attached to its exhaust pipe and the other in the partly opened rear window. The team assumed the family must have contracted the plague and feared they would turn into zombies. Except the family hadn't realized that suicide by carbon monoxide asphyxiation wasn't going to prevent them from turning into the living dead. Arn and company departed in search of another vehicle, leaving the zombie family trapped inside the car.

A few more residences away, the team saw a Stryker sitting near the road. Unsure of why it was sitting there, and with a bunch of zombies lurking around it, Arn decided to err on the side of caution. She moved her team around the back yards of the residences and onto the rear of the property that the Stryker was on, and came upon the destroyed barn.

There was another small group of zombies wandering around in the back of the property. The zombies immediately smelled the approaching team and went after them. Arn didn't want the living dead from the front of the property being attracted by gunshots, let alone making their presence known to whoever was in the Stryker. She ordered the use of knives against the half-dozen zombies. As they moved through the half pack of zombies, blading them through the eye socket to puncture their brains, Arn came to one with a chewed off face and a bite-ravaged body. It was one of the 3-2 SBCT. There was a corpse of a soldier on the ground, too. That soldier had been nearly cannibalized to the bone, leaving little left to be reanimated.

Arn figured the Stryker had crashed into the barn, collapsing it, and the two Stryker soldiers must have perished in the process of getting the vehicle out from under the debris. She didn't know there were two other bodies buried under the rubble. The reanimated Stryker soldiers were not visible. However, her conjecture didn't explain why the vehicle was sitting on the edge of the roadway in the front of the residence. Nor why the other Stryker had gone up the road toward the second armored vehicle and then back the way it had arrived shortly thereafter.

There were eight or so zombies around the Stryker and on the road, and no vehicle air guards doing over watch. Arn and her team repeated the killing process without incident, although Spc. English nearly got bit when a zombie tripped him up and he fell. Richardson came to his rescue. With all the living dead dispatched, the team cautiously approached the eight-wheeled vehicle.

It was too good to be true. The Stryker was abandoned. But why? Arn wondered. Had it been damaged to the point it was undrivable? After all, it had crashed into the barn and was still decorated with broken pieces of lumber. It was the optimal transportation. The Stryker could run on four or eight wheels. It had a range of 300 – 330 miles with a top speed of 60 mph. Plus this vehicle was equipped with a M2.50 caliber machine gun as the main armament for the remote weapons station and a M240 7.62mm machine gun for its secondary weapon. Even if the weapons were inoperable, the vehicle was secure enough to be impermeable to the living dead, as well as heavy and powerful enough to run over a small herd. After a quick undercarriage inspection revealed no damage, Arn and team decided to see if the vehicle was drivable. Most of the vehicle's electronic systems were on, though the vehicle's engine was turned off. Spc. English was the designated driver, since he was one of the armory's personnel who drove their medium tactical cargo vehicles. The vehicle started without a problem. English slowly moved the Stryker off the property and turned it to the direction they needed to be headed. Arn stood in the rear air guard hatch watching their surroundings as the truck picked up speed. Without incident, they would make it to Middletown, New York, in a little over four hours.

***

Without incident, Spc. Emery would have made it to his Cooper Road home in Fishkill from Stewart ANGB in under thirty minutes. It wasn't just the living dead that had hindered his short trip; it was also the living.

The main roads leading to and from the base had been mainly clear. Emery believed it was because of all the active combat fire happening around the area to prevent the living and the zombies from breaching the base. However, after he crossed over Route 87, traffic on the inbound side of Route 84 began to grow heavy. There were still people in cars who believed they could get to the air base for safety.

Route 84 remained relatively clear of vehicles on the outbound side all the way to the Newburgh-Beacon Bridge that spanned high above the Hudson River. He hadn't made it half the way across when he believed a large horde of the living dead was running directly toward him. He had to get across the bridge and no damn zombie horde was going to stop him. He depressed the gas pedal and sped up, charging toward the oncoming pack. The zombies moved out of the way. At least that is what he thought, until one person stood in his path attempting to wave him down. He realized the running zombies weren't actually zombies but the living, fleeing in panic from some unapparent threat. It wasn't until he neared the end of the bridge, almost to the toll plaza, when he understood the significance of what he had witnessed.

There was a huge pile up of cars blocking both the inbound and outbound lanes near the outbound toll plaza. Some of the vehicles were on fire. The living dead were everywhere, feeding upon their victims. The living were fleeing in all directions, trying to stay alive. He attempted to find a way around the congestion, but the zombies took notice. If he wanted to get through, he knew he needed to clear the way, and that meant engaging the enemy as well as getting some of the cars out of his path. Emery squeezed over the front seat and into the back to get to the roof hatch and the pintle-mounted M249 light machine gun on top of the roof. He checked the cartridge box that held the 200-round belt of 5.56x45mm NATO ammunition. It wasn't a full belt, but he believed if he used the ammunition frugally there would be enough to eliminate the oncoming threat.

Even being prudent with the ammunition he didn't have enough to expeditiously eliminate them. Heads made for small targets, and there were many. When the ammo belt went dry, he changed to his M4 carbine with its 30-round box magazine. Luckily, there had been several discarded full magazines on the floor of the front passenger seat, for he had only one full magazine remaining from the armory. By the time Emery had eliminated all the living dead, he was down to a magazine and a half of ammo, and there was still another eight miles to go.

With the zombies being cleared from the immediate area, he knew it was prudent for him to get the blocking vehicles out of his way before more threats showed up. However, the impasse proved to be too challenging. He had quickly come to the realization that the only way through the condensed motor vehicles would be by foot.

By dusk Emery had reached the abandoned Verplanck Tenant Farm House, which had been used as a visitor center for the Stony Kill Farm Environmental Education Center. He took refuge there until dawn. He was now less than 4 miles away, and had no way of contacting his wife to tell her he was almost home. Cellphone service was now nonexistent.

It took Emery until midafternoon to get to his residence. The curtains were drawn and the doors were locked. Seeing the house had not been breached, he had high hopes that his wife and child were safe. He found both of them in the bedroom.

His four-year-old daughter Melissa seemed very content making a meal out of her mother. Her protruding, over-filled belly was proof. She had eaten a good portion of her mother's torso. However, seeing and smelling fresh meat was more appealing to her. Emery was sickened to the point of vomiting from the discovery he had made. He quickly fled to the dimly-lit kitchen and threw up in the sink. He heaved several times, wondering how he had expelled so much when he had eaten so little the night before.

Eating was still on little Melissa's mind. She shambled into the kitchen, groaning, with outstretched arms. The weight of her consumed mother slowed her attack. Distraught and teary-eyed, Emery raised his M4 and took aim. "God, forgive me," he sobbed and then pulled the trigger. It was a clean shot to the forehead that blew out the back of his daughter's skull.

Emery had not given much thought to his dead wife. He sat on the kitchen floor weeping over what he had done, and for the guilt he felt at not getting home sooner. His reanimated wife crossed the threshold and lunged toward him before he noticed her presence. If it hadn't been for her stumbling across their dead daughter, she would have seized him before he could react. Emery grabbed the carbine that lay next to him, and let loose with a barrage of bullets. His wife did a macabre dance of death, but none of his bullets had struck her in the head. When the gun went dry she came for him again. Emery grabbed an 8" chef's knife from the wood knife block upon the kitchen counter, and drove it hard through his wife's right eye.

Emery collapsed back to the floor. Overwhelmed by the loss of his daughter and wife, he could not bear to live. He reloaded his weapon, and then placed the barrel of his carbine under his chin and pulled the trigger. However, as he did the barrel shifted. The 5.56mm bullet ripped through the side of his face, missing his brain. Emmett Emery would die from blood loss an hour later. Seven minutes after that he would return as one of the living dead.

*　*　*

The living dead were everywhere, just not as many in the rural populated areas, as Arn had surmised. There were some zombies that got in the path of the vehicle, but there were no hordes to deal with. The few zombies that had the misfortune of getting in the Stryker's way were mangled under the large steel-belted tires, and spat out the back in a twisted mess as it rolled over them. The trip had already taken six hours, and they had only made it to the Delaware Water Gap Recreation Area north of Stroudsburg, Pennsylvania, when the vehicle slowed to a stop along Federal Road just twenty feet from the turnoff to Dingmans Campground. Spc. English was slumped over in his seat, sick and sweating profusely. English had not told his captain or sergeant that he had actually been bitten back in Parkton.

When Richardson tried to give English some water because he was complaining of extreme thirst, English became panicked and fearful, as if the water was poisoned. His water fright struck Arn as peculiar and alarming, and then she remembered observing the zombies along the dam's waterline. It was as if they had an aquaphobia. Was English's agitated state over the water related to the zombies' bizarre behavior at the Pretty boy Dam? she wondered.

Arn and Richardson discussed what needed to be done about the specialist. They both agreed that he was infected; the proof was the bite wound on his arm. However, neither wanted to execute him. He was a member of the 69th Regiment and had survived the siege of the armory. English also had been an important mission member in their fight for survival. No, they both agreed. No killing Spc. English.

They didn't want to leave the specialist sitting on the roadside up against a tree. The least he deserved was a place where he could be comfortable for whatever amount a time he had left. Seeing the large campground road sign that stated there was a general store, they left him inside the log cabin store with his M4 carbine in his lap.

"Nár laga Dia do lámh," Arn said to him in Gaelic before she left: May God not weaken his hand. Spc. English understood his fate was now in his hands.

Richardson simply told him, "Faugh a Beallach. See you on the other side, kid."

***

Just before the turn off to Route 84 East in Matamoras, Pennsylvania, Arn and Richardson had no choice but to stop and refuel the Stryker. Even in four-wheel drive mode, the trip had consumed nearly all 53 gallons of diesel. It was a risk getting out in an urban area, but if Arn wished to get to Lebanon Springs after they made it to Middletown, they had to refuel. It took longer than they wanted. Richardson had to hook up the vehicle's high-power generator to the station's pumps, because there was no longer electrical power. With the exception of two living dead, which Arn dispatched, there was no horde of zombies to deal with. They were underway in less than an hour. They reached Richardson's home shortly before dusk. The family SUV was gone, but there was a note from his wife on the inside of the entry door. His family had bugged out. They had received a call from the commander's office at Camp Smith, the military installation of the New York State Guard in Cortlandt Manor near Peekskill, offering her refuge, as she was a spouse of a New York State Guardsman who had been called to active duty. They had left for the military installation on the second day of the outbreak.

Captain Arn told Richardson they should go to Camp Smith immediately. It was only 35 miles northeast via US-6 E. However, Richardson knew Arn was anxious to get home, especially since she had not been able to reach her family after cellphone service went out. Richardson knew if there was a chance of his family surviving the plague and the zombie uprising then it was at the military base. He took Arn home and went on to Camp Smith alone.

***

Arn came home to find her father inside the house, sitting in the dim candlelit living room, very much alive, and not a zombie. He had become ill and, according to news reports before the electrical blackout, he had signs of the zombie virus: extreme fatigue, profuse sweating, high fever, extreme thirst, and dehydration. He had exiled himself from the basement so he didn't put his wife and granddaughter at risk. But he had not died and had not turned into a zombie. He didn't know if it was the luck of the Irish or if he had just contracted a different viral infection, but whatever it had been, it had passed.

He had known his daughter Cullin would return, no matter what. She would not leave Casidhe motherless. So he had waited. He had been right.

Arn's mother and daughter were alive and well in the basement, and that is where they would all stay hidden and locked away. She had enough food, water, and sundry items to last a family of four for three months, and solar power to keep their bunker lighted.

***

Sergeant Richardson made it to Camp Smith, but the military base had been abandoned. He did not find his wife and son anywhere on the installation, but he did find his SUV in the parking lot. For whatever remaining days he had left, he would make it his sole purpose to find his family. He left the base with a full stock of food and water, and a lot of weapons and ammunition.

***

Capt. Jenny Moore and co-pilot Amy Hellinger got 1st Lt. Earlman and his 2/75 RGR REG to the Fort Detrick drop zone. Earlman and his warfighters along with the 3-2

SBCT, including the one unit that Air Force National Guard pilot had parachuted into Parkton, would join the Marines of B Company, 4th Light Armored Reconnaissance Battalion to defend MRIID in hopes that the doctors there could develop an antiviral. Fort Detrick would fall less than 24 hours later.

Thunder Two-Three and Three-Three successfully made it to Schriever Air Force Base in Colorado Springs. Upon disembarkation, Watson spent three days at the base with the rest of the flight crew, and a whole lot of other military personnel and their families, sequestered in a hangar that had been set up as a quarantine area. Once he was cleared, he was then sent to the Cheyenne Mountain Air Force Station. He never saw any of the flight crew again. He didn't know they were not going to Cheyenne, but staying at Schriever in its underground facilities.

Along the 25-mile bus trip to the mountain, Watson didn't see any living dead, though there was a high military presence along the route. Later, he would discover from a corporal in the Colorado Army National Guard that the Colorado Springs area had no outbreak, though the guardsman had heard rumors there had been a few reports of infections and they had been expeditiously dealt with.

The crackpots and conspiracy theorists would have had a field day with what was happening at Cheyenne Mountain. After being boarded at a heavily guarded checkpoint three-quarters of the way up Norad Road, and having everyone's identification checked that had been issued at Schriever, the bus continued on. The official, guarded entrance station was about 1.5 miles away from the famous mountain entrance, the north portal. Halfway from the guarded entry was the Cheyenne Mountain Fire Station, which was being utilized as a base camp for A Company, 1st Stryker Brigade Combat Team, 4th Infantry Division from nearby Fort Carson that had been assigned as force protection for the mountain complex. Upon reaching the legendary entrance, the one that had gained most fame from the replica used in the television series "Stargate SG-1," of which Watson had been a fan, he disembarked at another checkpoint.

Seeing the north portal entrance for the first time, Watson had expected to be wowed at its grandeur, but he wasn't. It was in disrepair and only foot traffic was being allowed through it. Watson didn't know that in 2013, there had been a mudslide that deposited 7,200 cubic yards of mountain debris in front of the entrance. Although the 721st Civil Engineer Squadron from Peterson AFB had cleared the majority of the debris, there was still much repair work to be done before vehicle traffic no longer had to be diverted to the south portal.

After being processed at the guarded entry, and being assigned a sleeping accommodation and a duty assignment suited to his military occupational specialty of truck driver, he was allowed into the parking lot area where a billet area of tents and trailers had been set up for all non-Air Force personnel and their families.

Day one at the facility was mundane. And as in some cruel punishment for his total disappointment in the north portal entry, he was duty assigned to dump truck driver, helping the 721st with their repair work. Day two at the facility was better. He was re-assigned as a driver of a medium tactical cargo vehicle transporting supplies from Peterson AFB.

Day three at the facility, and ten days into the plague, Watson was inside the south portal tunnel making a drop off when all hell broke loose. The plague had come. Whether it had been transmitted from an undetected carrier or it had drifted in on the air currents, all the precautions the military had taken to prevent infection hadn't mattered.

Fortune was on Watson's side. Not only was he near the open 23-ton blast door between the main tunnel and the office buildings complex, he got into the facility before the door was shut. It wasn't just mere luck that allowed him past the guarded entry; it was the Colorado National Guardsman that he had befriended who let him in when the other assigned sentry assigned was distracted. There was ordered chaos inside the complex. Watson made sure he was out of everyone's way as he began to cautiously explore the 4.5-acre excavated chamber.

There were 15 buildings inside the mountain—one mile inside from the opening and 2,000 feet down from the top of the mountain. The office complex was made up of thirteen three-story buildings and two two-story buildings. The buildings were freestanding, connected by hallways and ramps inside, as was the lower level where crew quarters, maintenance, the mess hall, and the cooking facilities were located. All of the buildings were on large springs, and built away from the rock walls in the mountain, so they could move independently if there was an earthquake or a blast. There was also a high-tech air filtration system in case of a bio attack. But it was too late; the virus was inside the facility. At first they believed the spread of the virus could be contained. Those infected were taken to an isolation area. Upon confirmation they had contracted the zombie virus, they were terminated. However, the viral agent spread quickly and the infected began to outnumber the healthy. Then there was a coup d'état once those who were ill heard that they were being killed to stave off the viral spread.

Eight hundred personnel could survive in the Cheyenne Mountain Complex for 30 days completely cut off from the outside world. The bunker was self-sufficient with its own power generators and five inside lakes, one that held the fuel needed to power the underground generators, one for drinking, and three industrial lakes used as part of a backup heating and cooling system. Thirty days later there were only 19 persons remaining.

***

Thirty days wasn't a long period of time, unless you were hiding in a shelter that had no view to the outside world with the exception of some surveillance cameras. By day eighty-seven the Cheyenne Mountain survivors were becoming claustrophobic from being confined so long. They wanted out of the underground bunker. They knew what was waiting on the outside world for them. They had plenty of cameras on the outside property that showed the grounds, but it didn't matter. They also knew that once the blast door was open there was the possibility the living dead could get in, but they were confident that they could eliminate the threat in the immediate area to get the door closed once they were out. On day 100 they had had enough.

From what they could tell on the security monitors the perimeter fencing had not been breached. The only living dead had come from those contained inside the grounds. A dozen warfighters were assigned as a part of the elimination team; Cpl. Watson was one of them. Seven stayed behind in the facility to monitor the kill team's progress. There weren't that many zombies in the tunnel, and with the firepower the team was carrying, it only took a few minutes to terminate those that were lurking about. However, the billet area was a different story.

When they exited the main tunnel there were two Strykers still standing guard at the entry. Even though none of the team knew how to operate their remote weapons stations, the vehicles could still be used in their assault, providing they could get them started. They were only able to get one armored fighting vehicle running, so not everyone would be able to utilize the vehicle for protection.

There had been over three hundred people living in the camp, and it appeared that half of them had reanimated and the other half had become their food, leaving their skeletal remains spread over the compound. Watson walked beside the vehicle as three warfighters stood in the roof hatches, keeping watch and being the front line of defense. As they swept through the camp, it appeared that none of the living dead were runners, just shamblers. The odd thing about them was it appeared they were dehydrating instead of decaying. From what Watson knew of zombies, they always rotted as they got older, not mummified. However, his knowledge of zombies was limited to what he knew from watching George Romero films.

It took them nearly an hour to eliminate all the zombies in the billet area, as well as the Stryker base camp and those along the road right down to the main entry. The group suffered no causalities. However, there were others roaming about the gated facilities, those not in the immediate area of the complex proper. These were zombies wandering the fringes near the perimeter fencing. The survivors needed to not only eliminate them for their own safety, but also they needed to check every foot of the fencing in case there was an unseen breach.

Watson discovered during his first encounter with one that those along the borders were not the feeble living dead. The corporal and his Air Force partner had come upon three of them feeding on what appeared to be a family of rabbits. Once the zombies had gotten a smell of the two of them, they turned their attention away from the furry critters they were devouring and set their sights on them both. The three zombies came full speed charging toward them. Watson's partner was not a seasoned warfighter; he was one of Cheyenne's food service specialists, meaning he did the cooking as well as operating and maintaining the base's kitchen equipment, and had only been in the service for six months.

The Airman Basic would have pissed his pants if he had had the chance. All he had to do was kill one of them; the other two had gone after Watson. However, the airman could not get a shot to the rushing zombie's head before the zombie took him down and bit into his throat, ripping off a nice-sized portion of flesh. Watson had no choice but to put the gurgling, blood spurting airman down after he killed all three zombies.

With the elimination of the living dead, and seeing that the perimeter fencing was in proper order, life at Cheyenne Mountain became routine and mundane. Cpl. Watson had stayed on the Globemaster III instead of parachuting in with the Rangers for a reason, and it was to get back to his hometown of Great Falls, Montana, to see if any of his family had survived the zombie apocalypse. Now that the base was relatively safe from incursion, he wanted to leave.

As he drove out the main entry checkpoint, he surveyed his surroundings. There were still many of the living dead, some more mummified than others, but most of them still very much ambulatory.

For dust thou art, and unto dust shalt thou return. That is what Watson had learned as a child, and that is what came to his mind as he drove down Norad Road. Except that was no longer how death worked. From dust thou art, and unto the living dead shalt you become, and unto dust shalt thou return, Watson hoped.

As he sped up he cried, "Faugh an Beallach!" to the 900 miles ahead of him, and then wondered if any of his former 69th Infantry Regiment team members had made it home themselves.

9 Needs Must by John L. French

"He must needs go that the devil drives."
William Shakespeare, *All's Well That Ends Well*

She had brought her sons to the beach for a vacation. With what was going on in Europe, Asia, and North Africa, not to mention parts of this country, it might be the last one ever, for anyone. Still, she had to work. So she sent the boys outside to get some sun and play on the beach.

"Stay out the water," she told them. "Remember, I'll be watching you two from the balcony."

Not that she would be able to see them that well, or that they would listen to her. They were boys, their father's sons, and they had inherited his defiance and daring. But maybe her warning and their belief in their all-seeing mom would keep them from going too far in.

So after they put on their suits and she smeared more than enough sunscreen on them, she let them loose on the Ocean City beach. Then poured a glass of wine, set up her laptop on the balcony table, and went back to tracking what might the world's last, great plague.

***

The first thing anyone on Maryland's Eastern Shore knew about what was happening to the rest of the world was when the dead washed up on the beach at Ocean City.

First it was one body, then two, then a dozen. By noon there were hundreds, maybe thousands of bodies on the sand—all dead; the living had retreated to the boardwalk or their hotels and condos. The smart ones had gotten in their cars and headed home. Some of them may have made it.

By five o'clock there were thousands of corpses littering the sand. When the sun went down they rose up, some moving slowly, others more rapidly. Some were dazed, some were confused, and all were hungry. And the town was full of tourists.

I was with the Fifth Regiment of the Maryland National Guard. We were called up, together with the Army Reserve, and stationed in Stevensville, on the west end of Kent Island, just hours after the undead appeared in Ocean City.

I had heard rumors, whispers, hints of a plague ravaging faraway places, but I hadn't given them any thought. I worked in Baltimore and was always too busy to keep track of anything but the Ravens, the Orioles, and the ever-growing crime rate. Looking back, I should have been paying more attention.

Some people in government, both in DC and Annapolis, had been paying attention. So they had a response plan in place for exactly what had happened on the beaches of the East Coast. Maryland, at least, was ready.

Colonel Angela Weng was the CO. She was a small Asian woman who would have scared the hell out of Patton and convinced MacArthur never to return. She took the news of the zombie invasion calmly, as if she had accepted the inevitable and was ready to deal with it. We waited for her orders, all of us sure that they would be pack up, load up, move out, and prepare to repel the invaders.

Instead she quietly said into her headset, "Take out the bridges."

"What bridges?" I said, stopping just short of yelling at a superior officer. I was her sergeant, her aide, in fact, and so had a certain leeway. But that didn't include questioning her orders.

"You know which bridges, Baldwin."

I did, the old Ocean City Bridge, the newer one over the Assawoman River, the Route 54 Bridge across the Delaware line.

"We are also taking out a large part of Fenwick Island. Delaware's governor isn't too happy about that but neither am I, so that makes us even." She looked at her watch. "Three, two, one ... The missiles are launched. Ocean City is about to become an island."

"Begging the Colonel's pardon, Ma'am, but the people, the tourists, there must be ..."

"Two hundred fifty thousand of them, Sergeant, at least. And right now you're wondering why we're not going in, wiping out the enemy, and rescuing them." Weng paused, lifted her head toward the ceiling, and closed her eyes as if asking whatever gods she worshipped to forgive what she was about to say and do.

"It's likely that some, who knows how many, of the tourists were attacked. We don't know much about the undead but every indication is that any bite is 100%

infectious. The incubation could be anywhere from two hours to two days. Now if you get bit, to whom do you run?"

Before I could reply, Weng answered her own question. "To your family, to your friends, to your parents. How many of these were in turn bitten? One becomes two, two becomes four, four becomes, well, the math is not pretty. And since we can't tell who's infected and who's not, universal precautions are called for. Anyone in Ocean City at the time of the invasion is now considered one of the enemy. There will be no attempts at relief or rescue. In addition, those quarter of a million people will keep the undead busy until we can come up with a way of stopping them. That is, a way that hasn't been tried before and one that has a chance in hell of working. But just in case...

"The bombers are next," she said. "In a day or two, as the enemy begins massing at the western edge of the city, the Air Force gets its turn. Nukes are out. They might do for the undead but it could also create radioactive zombies, in addition to contaminating the Eastern Shore and the mainland. But I'm assured that by week's end Ocean City will be a wasteland. But just in case..."

Weng thumbed her mike again, gave more orders. "Plant charges at the Nanticoke and Kent Island bridges. If any of the enemy survives and gets near, then take them down as well." Colonel Weng looked at me. "In case you're wondering, Baldwin, both spans of the Bay Bridge will also be mined. If the enemy crosses the Nanticoke we yield the Eastern Shore and set up in Sandy Point Park."

In Baltimore I wear a different uniform. I'm a cop, a detective. Despite things being as bad as they ever were and getting worse, no one ever thought to "yield' the city to the bad guys. So I had to ask Weng,

"Why?"

She looked at me. Her eyes softened and for a second I may have seen a touch of sadness in them. The second passed and she said, "This is war, Sergeant, war against an enemy we don't know how to stop. For the most part they can't be killed. But we can. If we fight, everyone one of us who falls adds to their ranks. So the cold equation is that some die so that others can live, plan, and fight. And we pray that sooner or later we find a way to win."

To my mind, action was still called for. It was simple— go in, do a search, destroy any of the walking dead, and save as many as you can. Quarantine the ones you bring out until you're sure they've not been infected.

Soon I learned that no one could be saved, that all of us were damned.

***

She needed someone, anyone. The boys had not returned. The mother in her wanted to rush down to the beach to look for them, to try to save them. The practical part of her told her such action would be useless at best, and more than suicidal at worst. She dug deep into her childhood and dredged up prayers to Saints Anthony and Jude that someone had found them and taken them in. Or that they were safe and hiding and would soon come back to her. But then the dark part of her worried that even if they did, would they still be her boys, or something else?

But even as she considered the what-ifs and what-thens she remembered her duty. Not to her sons, but to the world. She made a call, said some more prayers, then looked for her second wine bottle. Finding it empty, she turned to the mini-bar, knowing it was unlikely she'd ever have to pay for the high-priced, too-small bottles.

***

Colonel Weng took the phone call. "Yes, sir. I understand, sir. Yes, sir, twenty-four hours." She listened for a few more minutes, said, "Yes, sir," again and thumbed off her phone. Then she began swearing, starting in Chinese then shifting to English, Spanish, and what I was later told was Creole.

"The dead are rising," she announced to everyone in the room, "and not just those animated corpses east of us. This ... plague, or whatever it is, has infected the whole world. You die, of anything, you come back, hungry for more victims."

She paused, letting that sink in. Finally someone, I think it was Javier, asked, "What's the plan, Colonel?"

""What else?" she said coldly. "We fight. We follow orders." Then she issued new orders. "From now on, everyone goes armed and no one is alone. Bed, meals, the showers, even the latrine; at least two people together at all times. If someone dies, whatever the reason, empty a clip into their head. Destroying the brain is the only sure kill for these things. Now pair up and go about your work. Sergeant Baldwin, I need a word."

We went outside. "Ma'am?" I asked. I was hoping she didn't need me to accompany her to the latrine.

"I've been told there's this professor, a Doctor Tarquin from Johns Hopkins, who's been studying how to combat this enemy since their existence was first reported. We've been given orders to extract her."

Even knowing the answer, I still asked, "From where?"

Weng just pointed east toward what had been Maryland's favorite vacation site.

"I thought you said no relief or rescue."

"Needs must when the Devil drives."

She asked for volunteers and wasn't very happy when I was the first to step forward.

"Sergeant, I need you here."

"Begging the colonel's pardon, but it doesn't seem like you have much choice."

Or many volunteers. This was not an ordinary combat mission, on which the worse that could happen is you could get wounded, killed, maimed, or disfigured for life. On this mission, if things went south you were looking at being killed by your own troops, being torn apart and devoured by mindless zombies, or becoming one yourself. If they were mindless. Who was to say that you didn't remain fully aware of but unable to control what your body was doing?

Of the men and women under her command, only five other than myself opted for a day at the beach. She still would have had me stay behind if I hadn't been the highest ranking volunteer.

Doctor Tarquin and her two children were staying on the sixth floor of the Barbary Coast Hotel. Command was in cellphone contact with the professor. The plan for getting them out was simple. Just before going in, the Air Force would send in its gunships to clear the beach. A chopper would drop us off in front of the hotel. We would go in, get the professor and her boys, and catch a ride back out.

Like I said, simple. Except that the beach might not be fully cleared. Even if it was, there might be undead in front or inside the hotel. And getting out would be worse. Command and the colonel expected that any number of civilians, uninfected or not, would want to hitch a ride off the island.

"The chopper has a limited capacity. Anyone, and I do mean anyone, comes close, you are to treat them as hostile and take the appropriate actions. And, Sergeant, the only one we need to get on that chopper is Doctor Tarquin. Is that clear?"

It was perfectly clear. Six soldiers, two children, and any number of civilians were less important than one woman everyone hoped could kill things that were mostly already dead.

I did what every soldier was supposed to do in that situation. I nodded, saluted, and said, "Yes, Ma'am."

"Are you okay, Jack? Can you handle this mission?"

I noted Weng's use of my first name and the worry in her voice. I didn't know if was concern for the mission or for me, but it was my way out. All I had to do was to indicate some doubt and I'd be off the hook.

Instead I said, "I'll be fine, Colonel. After all, I'm from Baltimore. That city's been plagued by mindless zombies for years. But that's our own fault for electing them."

***

Gunfire woke her from her stupor. At first she thought it was the TV and was about to shout at her sons to turn down the noise. Then the haze parted and she remembered. The she looked out and knew they were coming for her. She wished them luck. She wished for her boys to be back. And she wished she gave a damn to whatever happened to her.

***

The drones went in first, some with cameras, others with guns. When they didn't do a complete enough job, Apache Longbows were sent in. Within fifteen minutes, whatever had been on the beach, living or undead, had been cut to ribbons.

Drawn by the gunfire, zombies and hopeful civilians had begun gathering as soon as our chopper set down. We landed as close to the hotel as possible, but there was still some beach to cross. Along with Javier, I provided ground cover for the others, watching to make sure no one or no thing got too close, all the while trying to ignore twitching limbs searching for their torsos. Our chopper took off.

We gained the lobby unopposed except for one guy behind the desk. When six armed soldiers all point their weapons at you and shout "Don't move," you should not move. The poor bastard moved, and it wasn't to hit the deck. Instead he came toward us. Kelly's shotgun took his head off.

"Ride or walk?" Taylor asked, standing by the elevators. We had discussed this on the chopper. Both stairs and lifts had their good points and bad. In the end we chose the climb, none of us liking the idea of being trapped in a box.

We took it slow, floor by floor, alert for noise or movement. Were there zombies on any of the floors? From what the Colonel said, it was possible. We knew Tarquin was safe in her room, that is, she would be if she had followed Command's instructions to lock her doors and not let anyone in.

The sixth floor. Tarquin's floor. The door to the hallway opened inward. Jackson held it while the rest of us rushed the hallway. So far, so good. No zombies. Nothing except heads peeking out of other rooms trying to see what was going on.

We ignored them, banged on the door of Tarquin's room. No answer. We banged louder. Still nothing. Winder was about to put a size sixteen to just below the lock when I tried the knob. The door swung open. Weapons at the ready, we went in, Winder and Jackson standing guard outside.

Weng had told us that Tarquin had two kids, boys, ages eight and ten. With the opening of the door and the rush of soldiers into the medium-sized room there should have been screaming. Instead we were met with silence. No professor, no kids.

Before I could ask, Javier said, "Right room. Sarge."

I looked around, searching the room with cop eyes. No bodies on the floor. No blood on the walls, no damage, no ransacking except for one seriously depleted mini-bar.

"She's out here, Sarge," Taylor said, looking out on the balcony.

She? Not they? That was not good. I didn't want to go out there but when Taylor opened the door I did.

Doctor Beverly Tarquin was alone on the balcony. She was sitting in a plastic chair with empties from the minibar scattered around her. There were also two proper-sized bottles that had once contained wine. I looked at her. She was wearing a one-piece swimsuit that in most circumstances would have been flattering to her red hair and trim figure. This was not one of those circumstances.

"Doctor Tarquin?"

She looked up at me, tried to focus. After a few blinks she gave up and settled for a blur. Then she pushed herself up out of the chair. She wobbled, almost fell forward, then sat back down.

The potential savior of the human race was drunk on her ass and worse yet, I thought I knew why.

"Where are your sons, Professor?"

Tarquin looked at me with that blank stare that comes over a lot of drunks as they process a question. Answers to "What's your name, where do you live, how did your car wind up in the harbor?" take the back roads of their minds before replies come out of their mouths.

In this case Tarquin just pointed to the beach. "I sent them out to play. I had to work and watched them from here. Watched them as the dead washed up. I yelled, but everyone was yelling. Then they were all running. Then they were gone, and so were my boys."

Tears came next. I wiped mine away and said, "Let's get you out of here."

"But my boys …"

"We'll look for them later," I lied. She was drunk enough to believe me.

Then came shouting from the hallway.

"Sarge," Jackson yelled, "we got company. The hallway's filling up."

"Living or dead?"

"At this point it don't matter."

Jackson was right. Word was out that there might be a way out of OC. We should have planned for this, I thought, but there was no time for what-ifs.

Jackson and Winder had retreated into the room. Together with Javier the three had their weight against the door, locking it against the crowd.

"What's it like out there, Winder?"

"Looks like what's left of the hotel's guests. I think most want to go home with us. Others might be wanting to eat us but will probably settle for munching on the crowd. And before you ask, we could probably fight our way out but not without taking a bite or two."

I took a peek outside. The beach was filling up. Soon they'd be coming inside—living and undead, the former risking all for a chance of escape.

Time for Plan B. I got out my radio.

"Baldwin to base. Tarquin is here but alone. Hotel and beach not secure. Repeat not secure. We need extraction from the sixth floor balcony."

Weng's voice came over. "I've got your room on one of the camera drones. Your balcony doesn't extend out far enough to get a chopper in."

I had been afraid of that. "What about the roof?" I asked. "If need be we could fight our way up. But not without casualties."

I watched Weng's eye in the sky ascend past me. Minutes later, she said, "The roof is not good as an LZ. What isn't slanted is covered. Can you fight your way to ground level?"

I thought about the growing crowd outside the door. Then I eased a look over the balcony. The news had spread even further and the beach was even more crowded than when we landed. If she were sober I'd ask our zombie expert if the undead put out some kind of odor when there was fresh meat around.

"It's possible, Colonel, but not without heavy losses. And before you ask, that would probably include Tarquin."

"What about her children?"

"They were on the beach when the dead washed up. It might be that they're part of the group that's knocking on the door."

I let that sink in, then prodded. "So do we fight our way out or make a rope out of bedsheets?"

No answer, not right away. Then Weng came back. "Hold your position. We'll come up with something. For now, Sergeant, remember your orders."

Weng didn't sound too confident. Even her "remember your orders" had an implied "for as long as you can" about it.

My orders. Nothing mattered but Tarquin. No way could she climb a ladder if they could get one to us. We'd have to carry her. If there was a "we" by the time it got here. How long would the door hold? How long could we hold them when it failed? What did the Colonel call it, the cold equation? Some die so others can live. It was also, I realized, our job description.

I gave the orders I had to. "Javier, Winder, put your weight against the door. Keep it closed. If it looks like it's going to give, start firing through it. If it opens, stand your ground as long as you can.

"Jackson, Kelly, move that dresser behind Javier and Winder and get behind it. If the crowd gets past them, do what has to be done. Taylor, you're with me. Help is coming, but its ETA is uncertain. And it's coming for Tarquin. Anyone else is a bonus."

There was nothing more to say. We knew our jobs. The target first, then us. Leave nothing for the enemy. I had a clear view of the backs of my team's heads. I had my shotgun and a sidearm, the latter not Army regulation but the one I carried on the streets of Baltimore. I had more than enough ammo to do what might need to be done, with enough left over for me. We would deliver the target. We would not be taken.

Javier and Winder held their ground against the pounding of the door. The rest of us waited, for the door to give way, for the chopper to come. I imagined the hallway crowd getting larger, putting more weight on the door from outside.

"Sarge," Taylor said, looking down at the mostly unconscious Tarquin. "You know there's no way she's getting in that chopper alone."

I looked at the balcony, checked the clearance. Weng was right. There wasn't a helicopter built that could come close enough for a pickup without sheering off its blades. It might be possible for a line to be sent over—might. If the chopper could stay in one place long enough. It was starting to look like the only option was for a drone to be sent in to pick up Tarquin's laptop and the rest of us to die heroes.

"So we'll throw her in." A bad joke but the best I could do.

She snorted. "No way in hell we can make that toss." She saw the same thing I did. "Maybe a ladder or a line. Something. If she's as important as you say, they'll have some kind of plan."

Taylor looked down at the still-drunk professor. "And I thought Javier could tie one on. This lady is well jarred. Well, whatever they come up with, someone will have to carry her. And don't look at me to do it."

So we waited. To give Javier and Winder some relief, I had them switch, one at a time, with Kelly and Jackson.

The door held, with no signs of cracking or giving way. Not yet, anyway. And sooner or later someone would find some tools and start putting them to use. Then it would be all over but for the shooting. And the killing. And the dying.

My field phone rang. Weng. Command had come up with a plan, two plans actually. Normally I wouldn't bet on any plan put together by anyone above the rank of lieutenant, but this time all our chips were on the table with no chance of buying back in if we lost.

Then she told me what the plans were. And suddenly we were all in with an unsuited two and three with four aces showing after the turn.

Strapping Tarquin to my back and rappelling down the front of the hotel seemed like the lesser of two dumb ideas. If the beach and balconies below us could be cleared. I hoped the hell hey could because I didn't want to try Plan B.

I saw them before I heard them. Specks in the distance that got bigger as I watched. Two Apaches and a transport. The transport was smaller than the chopper that took us in. Too small for six people, maybe too small for four.

"I'll need someone to piggyback the professor when they shoot the rappel line over."

No one spoke. They looked one to other then back at me. I saw their answer in their eyes. They had already accepted that they were not going to leave the room alive. They had made their peace with whatever form of God they prayed to and had decided on what to do in the last moments before meeting Him.

***

Through her haze she knew they were talking about her. Something about a rescue. Maybe they found her boys and were bringing them up to her room. Or maybe they'd bring her to them. Either way they'd be all right, she thought. Boys are tough, they can survive anything. She looked out over the ocean, then down at the beach. It was as crowded as it always was. But why, she wondered, was everybody looking up at her and not at the water. The thought came to her that they should not be out there at all, not with what was happening. Or maybe it's over, and things weren't as bad as we thought they'd be. With this happy thought and the prospect of seeing her boys again, she let herself drift off. They'd wake her when the boys got back.

***

The transport chopper came as close as it could, then it gave way to the Apaches. Knowing what was going to happen, I yelled, "Get her inside and down."

Taylor dragged the professor out of her chair and into the room just as the Apaches started firing into the rooms below us, clearing the balconies of anyone hoping to catch a ride or maybe just wanting to see what all the noise was about.

The gunfire wasn't so loud that I couldn't hear that the pounding on the room door was getting worse.

"How we doing? The door holding?"

"Good news and bad news, Sarge," Jackson said. "The door's doing great but the frame's starting to give way."

I should have expected that. I've worked enough B&E's in Baltimore to know that a strong door and a good lock mean nothing if they're attached to a weak frame.

"How long?"

"Long enough for you to get the doctor out of here."

That wasn't my plan. "Kelly, stand down. I'll take my turn at the door."

"Like hell, Sarge. We took a vote." The rest nodded.

A nod and a "thank you" wasn't enough, but it would have to do. My phone rang again.

"Sergeant Baldwin, this is Chopper One. We can't clear the balconies. As fast they go down more take their place. Stand by for the package."

A large quad drone was released from the rescue chopper. As it approached us, it trailed a long black tube, maybe wide enough for two people strapped together.

"They've got to be fucking kidding," Taylor said, once she realized what Plan B was.

"When the drone gets here we have to secure our end of that tube to our balcony. Then Tarquin takes a ride. Once she's safe, then we go one by one for as long as it holds."

The banging was getting louder. Not much time left. "Who ordered pizza?" Winder said as the drone dropped its end of the tube.

Setup was quick. We strapped it down, the rescue chopper lowered itself to make a 45 degree slant, and we were ready.

"Time to go, Doctor Tarquin."

***

She barely heard the words. Time to go where? With her boys, but they weren't with her. She couldn't, wouldn't leave without them.

Hands on her wrists, dragging her from the chair. Not without the boys. She starting kicking out, trying to break free.

***

"Not without them, not without my boys."

It was the worst time for the professor to begin sobering up. She starting fighting us as, behind me, I heard wood breaking.

"Sarge, go now. You have to," someone shouted.

Tarquin went limp as Taylor slugged Tarquin from behind. As I caught the doctor, Taylor said, "He's right, only this one matters. Go. We'll be right behind you." She held the tube open.

I bear-hugged Tarquin and dove into the blackness of the tube which immediately collapsed around us.

Damn, I thought. Dying was one thing, dying stupidly was another. But then gravity and the silicon slickness of the tube's lining did their work and we started downward. I had a vision of Chevy Chase in *Christmas Vacation* careening out of control on a snow disc, a vision that was dissolved by gunfire all around us. The Apache's clearing the upper balconies, I told myself but knew that wasn't all. By now the room's door frame would have given way and the other five would be fighting for their lives, or maybe their true deaths. I hoped at least Taylor would make it.

***

Blackness, like a womb, like a rebirth. Where were my boys? Will they be waiting for me? Is that them? No, it's not. It's nothing human.

***

We slid into the rescue chopper and were grabbed by rough hands. Soldiers in full body Kevlar pointed their weapons. One of them said "Cut it loose" and their end of the tube fell away.

Shouting "No!" I moved toward one of them, only to be pushed back. Part of me wanted to look out but I was afraid that if I did I'd see Taylor falling out of the tube into the crowd below. Another part of me was sure that if I got too close to the open door someone would push me out.

"It was only supposed to be the target," a different voice said.

"Change of plans. Doctor Tarquin didn't want to play."

Guns were on us, guns with trigger guards removed to allow for the heavy gloves. One of them said, "You move, you're dead. You resist, you're dead." Then to someone else, "Secure them."

As they were tying me up, the chopper turned to let the Apaches move in. Missiles were fired into the room, our room. I screamed and cursed them, even knowing why they did it. The new rules of battle—kill your own for the good of all, even them.

Our arms, hands knees, and feet were strapped; leather hoods covered our heads. The professor and I made the return trip back to base as just so much baggage.

When we landed, more armored people stripped us and checked for bite marks. Despite not finding any, we were still put into separate observation cells as men with guns waited to see if we stayed human or turned zombie.

No one ever told me why Tarquin was worth the cost of five good soldiers. I heard one story that had her with the CDC trying to weaponize maggots and flesh-eating bacteria. Another had her escaping custody and heading back to OC to find her boys.

An hour after our chopper landed, as reports came in that some of the undead were gathering at the edge of the Assawoman River looking like they were ready to take another swim, the Air Force sent in bombers. They stopped short of going nuclear, but by the time they landed, Ocean City was a wasteland, its only visitors helicopters carrying cold-eyed snipers, taking down stragglers, both living and undead, with well-placed head shots, leaving it a land of ghosts where brave men and women died and lost boys searched for their mothers.

Dashing into my apartment on the fourth floor, I slammed the door behind me and knocked my tablet off the table, causing it to kick on. "This sucks!" was all I could think. I was going to turn into a mindless, flesh-eating monster. The torrential music of the Violent Wasps blared through the portable speakers, adding to the chaotic thoughts in my mind. "This can't happen to me! I'm a vegan for God's sake!" It was true. I had not so much as looked at a piece of meat in months. My girlfriend Jennie was a vegan, so by default I was a vegan too. You do that when you are hard up for a girl and trying to impress her. "Oh, God! Jennie!" What the hell am I going to tell her? Who am I kidding? I'll be a biter within an hour or two. She'll get the hint when I try to suck her brains out... and not in the good way.

Moments earlier, I had been downstairs on the stoop waiting for my buddy Pete. I was going to wingman for him down at the Venus Purse this evening. I was standing there, watching the last shadows of the sun drop below the crowded urban skyline. I took another slug from a fifth I brought down with me and tossed my cigarette butt over the stair railing into the rubbish pile below. That's when it got me. The thing jumped straight up and latched onto my left arm. It must have been slumped down in the garbage. Rubbish had gotten stacked so high lately there could have been a undead orgy going on in there and I wouldn't have noticed. I couldn't even smell the thing because the whole area already reeked of filth and rot. Before I was able to pull my arm back, the rotter chomped down on my forearm. I smashed it across the head with the bottle in my free hand, cracking its skull and causing one of its eyes to pop from its socket. The decaying beast let go and stumbled backwards. Still holding the broken end of the bottle, I stabbed at its face several more times until it collapsed. I had killed it, but it had essentially killed me as well. Only after looking at my bloodied arm did I finally feel the rush of pain and the realization that I was doomed. Panicked, I ran back into the building.

"Downtown is a terrible place to live," I had been told over and over. "You got to get yourself out of there." But, did I listen? No. The zombie apocalypse breaks out and I'm in a run-down, five-story brownstone by the tracks. Sure, it was incredibly dangerous, but living near the club scene downtown made me the envy of the "in" crowd. The danger factor made this place all the more popular. I was on the bleeding edge of existence. Hipsters everywhere would give their left arm to live in this neighborhood. Ironically, things had become rather literal for me now.

I never took this zombie problem issue too seriously. I mean, sure, undead corpses shuffled around these days, craving human flesh and all that. But, it's not like they were hard to run away from, or you could cave their skulls in with a handy metal pipe or even set them on fire. I watched Pete once set a rotter ablaze using nothing more than a lighter and a can of hair spray. "Biter Bar-B-Q!" he exclaimed as the zombie lit up like a dried Christmas tree.

You don't realize how flammable these things can be when they've been out in the sun too long. It was awesome to watch but got out of hand when the flaming corpse wandered over and set Pete's car on fire. That's also when I learned that insurance doesn't cover zombie attacks. Stingy bastards!

So, it was never that big a deal in my mind. I was more worried about the rats in the halls of the building than the occasional rotter shambling nearby. The cops did a decent job of clearing out the biters when reported and the military would napalm the shit out of areas where heavy mobs were found. Hell, I felt safer in the inner city, since the government was hesitant to bomb out large populations of the uninfected. Burning up large portions of the voting public always caused a significant dip in the polls. But the feds wouldn't think twice about bombing a rural farm or remote survival encampment.

I did my best to calm down and consider my remaining options. I was about to become one of "them." A menace to the people around me and a danger to the neighborhood at large. Not that I gave a damn about most of the losers around here, but I really didn't want people seeing me all slacked-jawed, drooling, and wandering the streets for meat like some kind of homeless junkie. The way the rotters smell, their grotesque hair style, and all their clothes eventually becoming so dated that it would be impossible to stay fashionable. Hard to stay hip when no one cares about the band name printed across your shirt anymore.

I thought I should do the right thing and end it all before I turned. A quick note to anyone who might find my body and a gunshot straight through the head, simple and effective. Now, if I only had a gun… or bullets… or the balls to carry it out. "Time to grow a pair," I said aloud, trying to instill some courage in myself. "But first I'll need to write a note!" I began to scramble around for paper and something to write with. Tossing through a couple of drawers filled with junk, all I was able to find were some note pads with kittens on it that Jennie had left behind. Kittens definitely do not provide the gravitas you expect in a suicide note. I'd have to find something else.

Yeah, stall and let the inevitable happen. Everyone would understand. "Seems like he was going to kill himself but he just couldn't find the proper stationary to write his note before he turned": that's what they'd say. Bullshit!

Then came a heavy pounding at the door. "Oi, mate?" a voice called from the hallway. "You in there?" Before I could move an inch, Pete threw open the door, his hulking frame filling the entryway. In one burly arm he held a wholesale-size tin of pork and beans that was now half empty. In the other hand he wielded a spoon more appropriate for serving than dining. Pete ladled huge helpings into his mouth even as he spoke. "What gives? I head downstairs, look around, and you're still up here. You flakin' on me tonight?" He noticed the deep gash marks and blood running down my arm. "What's that? Biter get you or somethin'?"

I didn't know how to answer or even if I should. I had seen Pete twist the head off a rotter like he was opening a beer bottle. Not sure if he wouldn't do the same to me. It would, however, solve my current dilemma. Meekly, I answered, "Yeah… got bit…"

Pete furrowed his brow and paused. It appeared as though he was sizing me up to see how easily I would fit through the window he was about to toss me through. Instead, he responded, "So, you are flakin' on me tonight?"

"What am I going to do, Pete? I'm going to die!"

"Don't worry, mate. You'll come back," he joked, as he let himself in and headed towards my kitchen.

"Oh, thanks. I won't exactly be myself by then." I was in no mood for jokes.

Pointing the sloppy spoon at me, "You thought about killin' yourself before you turn? That's what most people do. I can help you with that."

"What do you think I've been doing? Updating my status on social media?"

I was cut off by a terse rapping noise emerging from the floor. It was our troll of a landlord, Mrs. Vanderhoff. She was a crusty old woman who had inherited the building from her husband when she lost him to the zombie scourge. She was just under five feet tall and built like a bowling ball. She had no patience for younger folks like Pete and myself, cursing our entire generation as the cancer that put an end to the human race. You couldn't hand in your rent without a lecture on the ills of society today: "In my day, we had people, doctors, scientists, people who got things done! Guys who would find a cure for these diseases. And what do you people do? Nothing! Drugs, sex, drinking, more sex, that's all you people know. Worthless kids these days. You're all worthless!"

I had the extra special privilege of being located in the apartment above hers. She had no tolerance for loud noises, strange smells, or anyone she didn't recognize in the building. Yet the place was infested with rats. I could only assume they were her pets, as she did nothing to get rid of them. The pounding continued until I managed to turn off the music.

"Fucking bitch, that Vanderhoff," Pete grumbled. "I still haven't doled out to her on me flat for last month. Rotters I can handle, but that woman gives me the creeps. She's like a human tick, all bloated in the middle but with these spindling arms and legs. I can't stand to even be in the same room as her. Swear I've actually seen zombies move away from her. Becoming a rotter could only improve her looks. Betcha the old bag's somehow immune." Opening the fridge, Pete began to fill his arms with my precious stash of crafted micro-brews. "Seeing as you are not going to be needing these anymore…"

"Hold on, wait a minute," I began. "What if the bite didn't take? What if I'm not infected? Maybe I'm immune? It could happen, right?"

Pete briefly thought about this possibility. He took a second look at the vicious bite on my arm. "That bite there, hurt much?"

Surprisingly, while it did before, I no longer noticed any pain. This was odd, as I have been known to cry over a splinter in my finger. "It's not that bad anymore," I noted.

"Sorry, mate, you're turning," Pete stated matter-of-factly and returned to raiding my refrigerator.

"No, no! This can't be happening to me. I've always been careful. I'm cautious about everything."

"That's for certain," Pete added, his voice echoing from within the fridge. "How many times you hook up with that same bird... ah, Jeana..."

"Jennie," I corrected him. "We've been taking it slow. I wanted more than just some hook up. I was changing for her. I bought her clothes, I ate her awful cooking, and I even rummaged up that specific brand of makeup she demanded. Things were going to be different with her. I gotta give her a call." I searched the room for my phone.

"Special?" Pete pulled the armload of loot from the fridge and piled it onto the kitchen table. "Seriously, mate. No one is into that anymore. Have you not looked around, it's the fuckin' apocalypse out there. Ain't no one got any time for a relationship. Chicks are willing to hook up with any man who still has a pulse and looks like they can fight off a rotter, if only to have a safe place to sleep for the night. You've been setting yourself up for heartbreak." A quick scan across the cluttered apartment: "Oi, that tablet there, I'm claiming that, too. Oh, does that have your collection of Sweat Party on it? That'd be epic."

"You're not taking that." I pointed at the digital tablet as I grabbed the two-way off the table. "I want Jennie to have it. Something to remember me by." Pete shrugged, twisted open one of my brews, and commenced to finish off his tin. "Jennie, you there. Pick up!" I yelled into the receiver. I called for her again and again. What if I couldn't get hold of her in time? Answer, please!

"Hello," Jennie's sweet soft voice came across the radio.

"Jennie! So glad I was able to get a hold of you." My heart pounded, the urgency in my voice was evident.

"What's going on?" she asked. "You sound terrible. Were you in an accident? You didn't wreck your car, did you?"

"Jennie, I don't know how to tell you this." I hesitated. The news would devastate her but I simply didn't have the time to ease her into it. "I've been bitten."

"Oh, God!" she exclaimed. "Is it bad? How long do you have?"

"I don't know." I turned to Pete, who had more experience in zombie-related matters, "How bad am I? How long do you think I have?"

He gave me the once-over. "You're starting to look a little pale. I've seen this happen way too many times. I would say you've got about an hour. Hour and a quarter tops before you're fully ripened."

"I've got just over an hour," I repeated over the air waves. "Honey, this is it. If you see me again, I won't be the man you remember."

"Well, that's for sure," she answered, surprisingly unfazed by the dire update I just gave her. "Is that Pete I hear? Is he over there?"

"Um, yes. He's here with me." I imagined that she was thankful that there was someone familiar to be by my side during my final hours. At least that's what I wanted to believe.

"Ask if he can pick me up tonight and take me to the Venus Purse with him?" she said, without a hint of alarm.

"What?!" My heart practically stopped.

"Yeah, tell her I can swing by her place about nine," Pete piped, easily overhearing the conversation. "I'm gonna need the keys to your car, mate. I'm kinda light on wheels these days. Heh, remember that night? Zombie Bar-B-Q!"

"What the hell, Jennie?" I couldn't believe what I was hearing. My body hadn't even turned cold yet and she was already making plans. For Christ's sake, I was still talking to her on the phone! "I love you and you're already moving on?"

"Aw, don't be that way," her voice cooed. I had heard this tone before, often accompanied with another crazy explanation as to why she absolutely had to have some new shoes or some brand of jeans she saw in a store window that was teeming with biters. "I loved you too and we had some fun times together. But you're a zombie now and I just can't see a future with us, especially once your skin starts to fall off. I mean, what am I supposed to do? Introduce you like, 'Here's my undead boyfriend. He doesn't talk much, kinda gross to look at, and terrible in bed but, hey… he's a keeper!' I don't think so." Her cold sarcasm hurt more than the thought of joining the ranks of the walking dead.

"So, that's it? It's been swell but time to move on? Is that all there is?" I was devastated.

"I guess so," she summed up, before adding, "Tell Pete nine tonight would be great. Oh, and have him bring me your vinyl collection over since you won't be listening to much of anything anymore."

"I'm on it," Pete yelled back and immediately headed towards my box of mint condition records.

"Great!" Jennie replied over the radio. I wasn't even part of the conversation. I had already become a ghost in my own home. "Gotta run, babe. Thanks for everything. Love you! Bye!"

That was it. Jennie was out of my life for what little remained of it. Our life together was so meaningless that she was able to move past it during a two-minute phone call. On the other hand, maybe I should have been happy that she wasn't suffering. I didn't know what or how to think.

Pete hefted the crate of albums with a grunt. It had taken me nearly a decade to build that collection, filling the crate so full that I struggled to drag it across the room, and now here was Pete balancing it on his shoulder with one arm. I ignored everything, standing there staring at the black screen of the phone. Pete ported the cargo out and dropped it off in the hall. He then returned to the beer he had opened and stood next to me, placing his heavy hand on my shoulder. "How you feelin'?"

Overall, I didn't feel much of anything. I wasn't overly cold or warm. My arm didn't ache and the confusion and panic in my head began to clear. The realization that Jennie so easily moved on without me should have brought me to tears, but there was nothing. My heart wasn't beating hard anymore, I wasn't flushed with anger and frustration as I would have expected. There was nothing save for a small twinge of hunger in the pit of my stomach. "I'm a little hungry."

"Yeah, you ain't got much time. You come up with a plan yet?"

"I was thinking of doing the honorable thing, save myself from infecting anyone else. That was the plan before, but now... now, I'm not sure what I want to do." I was dumbstruck. So many things left undone, where to start.

"You better come up with something quick. How about I take you up to the roof? One jump and it's all over. Bonus points if you land on that big crab Vanderhoff, taking her out as well. I'd owe you for that one."

I wasn't listening. Instead, I wandered over to the couch and slumped down on its worn cushions. "This isn't how I thought things would end for me," I heard myself moan. "I had plans... dreams. I wanted to be remembered for more than... well, for something. My life sucked. My unlife will probably suck as well."

"Listen, mate, I hear you. Not everyone gets what they want and people rarely get to write their own ending." He crossed the room and towered over me on the couch. "What you want? To go out with a bang, be remembered? It's still not too late for you to make a lasting impression." He polished off the beer in his hand, downing nearly all of it in a single swig. "Now if it were me in your situation, I would accept my new role. If I am to be a rotter in this new zombie land, I'd bloody well be the scariest fuckin' rotter this city has ever known. I'd doll me up in some heavy gear, helmet and all to protect me soft noggin. Toss off one last time before me prick fell off and then go place meself in an area where no one would suspect a biter to be. Wait for the turnin'. It would be epic!"

I didn't doubt for an instance that zombie Pete would become a menace to society. I could picture his hulking build in riot gear terrorizing what remained of the living. Those huge arms of his tearing into helpless saps like myself, rending the flesh from their bones… rending flesh from their bones… "What's left in the fridge?" I asked.

"Not much," he replied. "I saw some ketchup packets, jars of green stuff, and what appeared to be a container of tofu or some veggie shit. All of that rabbit food you've eating."

The vegan diet, the crap I put up with to try and impress Jennie. What a wasted effort. "You got anything more substantial at your place? Something more… well, meaty?"

"There it is." He bent over to get a closer inspection of my face. "Your eyes are beginning to glaze over now. Won't be long before that 'meaty' urge consumes you and you start sizing me up like a steak dinner. Tell you what, you should put on some shredded jeans and that heavy leather jacket you were wearing last week. Slick up your hair and head over to the Purse. That pale skin guise you've got going on is the dog's bollocks. Head into the mosh pit while you still got a mind to do so and dance the rest of your life away. You turn there, start tearing into those pricks and posers. It would be a good hour before anyone knew what was going on and by then it would be too late. They would all be zombified. Brilliant! Fuckin' legendary!"

"Sure, that would be cool." I tried to sound enthusiastic but I didn't pull it off. "But that's not for me. Sure, most of the people there are douchebags, but I can't see myself feasting on them."

"Yeah, they all do seem like they would be a bit greasy," Pete mused. "How about you head downstairs to Vanderhoff's lair. Knock on the door, she lets you in and gets started on one of her famous rants. Before you know it, you turn on her like a lion on a wildebeest. You could dine on that sizable chunk for a good month and I'd be livin' rent free for a year or more. Fuck, you'd be a bloody hero to everyone in the building. It's win-win, what do ya say?"

"I wouldn't mind that too much. I'm not sure she wouldn't pop like a balloon when I bit into her." The thought made me smile, albeit briefly.

Pete smiled back. "That's the spirit! I'm sorry that it has to end this way. Like you said, it sucks. This world is fucked and most everyone knows it. That's why people are living like it's their dying day. The rotters are eventually going to get everyone. You can be as cautious and careful as you want. Shit, you can lock yourself in a fucking vault with years of supplies but it's still a matter of time. They're going to get us all. Myself included. Eventually, you gotta remember that it's nothing personal and learn to accept the apocalypse as it comes."

Pete's simple philosophy on the times we lived in did ring true. The rotter that got me, it wasn't personal. It was just doing what any rotter does. Eventually, there might come a day when the world was nothing but rotters. My number had come up and it was time to join the new in-crowd. First of my group to sign up, I was on the bleeding edge of existence.

"Car keys?" Pete asked. I motioned to the set on the kitchen table. He scooped them up and slipped them into his pocket. He then gathered up the collection of micro-brews and stacked them on the crate just outside the door. He hoisted the whole stack of music and beers up to his chest. His big… beefy chest. Before exiting the doorway, he recommended, "Oi, if you do stay here and turn, appreciate it if you lock yourself in the bathroom. I may be coming back for the couch tomorrow."

"Aar… Urr…" was all I could manage, along with a droplet of drool. The words were there in my head, but my lips and tongue were not cooperating.

"Thanks, mate. Cheers!" and he strolled off with his loot.

I sat on the couch for a time contemplating my final act. So hungry now… so hungry. Who was I to stand in the way of the new world order? Eventually, I rose from my seat and walked over to a drawer in the kitchen. It was full of mismatched utensils, rubber bands, push pins, and assorted junk. From it, I pulled the spare key to my car that I kept there and shambled out into the hallway.

Outside the building, it was dark and the night air was cool. The first stars had begun to shine. It had been six months since the first zombie uprising began to change the world. There were far fewer people these days, barely any cars on the road, more space in the town, cleaner air to breath. None of the animals seemed to mind the slow-moving corpses; they made for easy meals. Each day had actually become better than the last. A world without humans was coming to pass and who could say that it wouldn't be a marked improvement?

I unlocked the car and climbed into the back. The rear floorboard would make for a nice quiet resting place. I cleared my mind and let the virus wash away my trouble and anxieties. If my timing was right, there should be a very nice meal or two stopping by in a little while.

WHISPERS OF THE APOC

11 In the Valley of the Dead, Johnny Rotten is King by Alexei Kalinchuk

His white tee said "Tad" in handwritten letters. The T and D looked more carefully printed than the A, blackly scratched in chisel-tipped, permanent marker. Classic Anarchy A in a circle. I drew it last year as a senior in high school to piss off my parents, who bought me these white tees to wear under my dress shirts when I went looking for a job because their bitter divorce had eaten through my college fund.

Who are you? I asked this small Asian kid wearing my twice-defaced tee in my parents' summer cabin.

He's cute. Can we keep him? Marisol cracked.

I'm Tad, he said, pointing at the shirt. Then he told Marisol, I'm not a house pet.

How did you get in? I asked, noting that beside the baseball glove on the couch, there was a wooden baseball bat.

Stop interrogating him, Bill. He's not here to steal your parents'—well, whatever that is. Marisol pointed at an end table where a stuffed jackalope stood on its haunches, sniffing the air for danger.

***

I decided against explaining anarchy and punk rock and my anger at my parents to Tad. Whatever the state of things, I knew some things mattered more now; like food and fuel. If this was anarchy, Johnny Rotten could keep it.

Salivating, I busied myself opening a can of sardines from the pantry, after tossing another can to Marisol.

I used a ballpoint I found to write my name, Tad told me, smiling, still pointing at the shirt.

That he was still able to smile with dental brochure teeth wasn't the strangest thing about him—that would be the baseball cleats, baseball socks, and pin-striped baseball pants. Was it so long ago I was in that world of little league with its pizza celebrations and parents bragging about your nonexistent fielding skills to other parents?

Have you eaten? Marisol asked Tad, still trying to mother him after my "interrogation."

Tad blinked several moments before responding to probably the only Latina with a Mohawk he'd ever seen.

Um, no. I'm real hungry. Hey, you speak good English.

Are you shitting me, little man? Marisol said to him.

You're Mexican, right?

Uh, I'm not. Are you Chinese? Malaysian? Nice English.

Korean. I'm sorry.

Shaking my head, chewing fish, I went to get the jersey I saw through the patio window. It hung on a deck railing. Although Tad had washed most of the blood out, leaving it drying out here where the wind could carry a blood smell out to the bears was a bad idea. Also, this drying shirt advertised our presence. I decided not to say anything when I walked in, ready to hang the ruined jersey from the shower rod.

11 IN THE VALLEY OF THE DEAD, JOHNNY ROTTEN IS KING BY ALEXEI KALINCHUK

Marisol stopped explaining Reagan's Central American sins to Tad when she saw me. We'd been friends since high school so she could read me. She raised an eyebrow.

It's nothing, I said, shutting the patio door.

Don't nothing me. What's up?

I looked at Tad, trying to think of how to describe the risk of those things being drawn here, but without alarming him. Maybe my attempt at calm was amateur, maybe it was misplaced concern for a polite kid who had already laundered his own bloodied baseball jersey, maybe I should've said nothing.

But that's when Tad broke.

Did I do something wrong? he asked, his eyes wet and watering down his cheeks. The happy kid in half a sports uniform was now unmasked, scared, just like the rest of us.

***

Over canned peaches, Tad told us how he'd found the key under the potted plant on the deck. Marisol told him that was very smart of him to look where lazy people hid their keys, smiling at me over his head. I shrugged, my heart not in our usual teasing. She understood because she stopped, and in that moment, Tad asked about her Mohawk.

Oh this? Marisol flapped a hand at her hair.

It's fallen a bit, I said.

Well, Bill, Marisol said, it wasn't like we could've stopped for hairspray.

It sorta looks like a dinosaur back fin, Tad said, ignoring Marisol's remark. Like a dimetrodon maybe?

Marisol and I didn't know what a dimetrodon looked like, but I remembered a set of encyclopedias we had here for those moments when my parents wanted me to study in the hostile quiet we all enjoyed on our family vacations. After paging through the dark brown D volume, we found pictures of a stegosaurus and a t-rex, but no dimetrodon. I tried to cheer Tad up.

It's okay, at least we have encyclopedias until TV comes back. Hey, worst comes to worst, we can rebuild everything from the ground up. These will be blueprints to start over. Build engines. Purify water. Grow crops. Just tear out the pages we don't want to replicate in the New World.

Goddamnit, Bill!

Goddamnit, yourself. I'm not treating him like a kid if he's probably already seen a lot of crazy shit out there.

Goddamnit, Marisol said one more time, then launched herself out of the chair and out of the room. That's when I understood that she didn't want to protect Tad from reality.

She wanted to protect herself.

***

Last night our journey out of the city wasn't easy. I'd driven us here after the concert broke up. Or rather the scheduled bands didn't show and the few punks there weren't even talking about Fang or Flipper's cancellation.

They were sharing cannibalism rumors.

I walked away from these stragglers outside the chained doors of The Yard, wondering where all the scenesters were when Marisol approached. I usually drove her home from shows.

Let's get out of here, she whispered.

I put a finger to my lips. Some gutter punks might have wanted a ride, too, and after one vomited in my car last year, I was less tolerant, even if that made me "a suburbanite poser."

When we pulled away from the curb, some of the gutters sneered at us in my rearview for not inviting them.

And I did try to drive Marisol home, which brought us to a National Guard checkpoint.

That wasn't here when I left earlier, Marisol said, both of us so still as we slowly pulled up.

The Guardsmen assumed alert postures behind a sawhorse. Under a sodium lamp casting orange light down on their faces, they looked as mythically menacing as tomb statues.

How long was it that you left? I asked in a soft voice.

I took the bus, transferred, so, forever ago.

Beyond the checkpoint was the part of the city where Marisol lived with her aunt and uncle and cousins. Her parents were "disappeared" last year when they made the mistake of going back to visit El Salvador, a country in the middle of a civil war. Now, anyone in a uniform flat-out scared her.

The Guardsmen walked toward us.

That's when Marisol jumped out of my car.

The Guardsmen raised their assault rifles and started shouting orders. Marisol yelled back that she needed to go home and what was going on.

My trance broke. Jumping out, I announced in a calm voice that I was trying to take my friend home.

They lowered their weapons and relaxed upon seeing me, I noted. I'd grown out and cut my blue hair off a week ago. I looked normal enough. They told me the street was closed.

What am I supposed to do? she asked those pale faces atop their camouflage uniforms, their eyes squinting at her Mohawk, her leather jacket and her jeans.

No one gets in, a Guardsman said to me, ignoring Marisol.

Gunshots rang out from nearby.

The Guardsmen yelled at us to get back in the car and turn it around, their weapons held again in a fighting stance. Their radios hissed and crackled with excited voices.

We got in the car and drove off. We didn't say anything about Guardsmen or gunfire. We didn't discuss alternate routes into this area of pawnshops and discount stores and Latin supermarkets and tire repair places. Minutes later, she spoke.

Have a good night, sir, Marisol said in her whitest voice. She was mocking me for how the soldiers had treated me.

C'mon, I said, my voice flat

How about a pat on the back and a blowjob, sir? After we shoot this Mohawk bitch, how about it?

She was sobbing, so I said nothing.

Minutes passed.

Can we stop somewhere? she asked at last, as we drove the night streets without a direction. I'm thirsty.

There's a gallon of spring water in the backseat, I told her. I brought water and a shirt to change into when I went to shows, in case I sweated up slamming in the pit.

She found the water. After sucking down several mouthfuls, she was putting it back when she found my spare shirt.

She unfolded it to read the front.

NO SKATE HARASSMENT, it said.

I used to hang with a lot of skate punks. She snorted at the shirt and rolled down her window and tossed it out.

I almost complained, but someone stumbled out into the road in front of us. Someone in a mask. It reminded me of those carnecerias in Marisol's neighborhood. Those meat coolers stacked with flensed heads, the bare eyeballs fixed on you. Goats. Lambs. More naked-looking than the pig heads because the pigs still looked smug, but bodiless. This masked person slapped at the car's hood although I'd had to slam on the brakes to keep from hitting him. Half his face was gnawed off, the white of a cheekbone protruding. Blood splashed down from his eye orbit to his chin and pasted the collar of his shirt to his body. Some crazy mask.

Hey! Hey! Move out of the way!

Instead of minding me or my hand waving over the steering wheel for him to move his ass, he crossed over to

Marisol's open window. She just managed to roll it up when he slapped a hand to the glass. Marisol shouted for me to drive.

Shadows detached themselves from the roadside in a jerky stagger toward us. They beat the sides of the car until I gunned it out from under their stink. I don't know how many of them there were. Then we saw more. What I thought was civil unrest or some out of control costume party was something very different. And those weren't masks.

And I drove through stop signs and red lights, sometimes around those freaks as they milled in the street.

The sound of their clawing at my car, palms slapping it, made me think of the beating wings of some terrible beast.

***

He probably let them die, Marisol said, halfway to the cabin. He probably let them die.

Who let who die? Even already knowing what she'd say, I felt that letting her talk might take some of the chill out of her guts. I know I felt like I was all ice cubes myself.

The president talks to the governor, he decides parts of the state, they aren't worth saving, but some are.

Marisol named places. Moneyed places, white places.

Normally, we went back and forth and I asked a lot of questions about these things. I didn't now. I knew Marisol's family were somewhere in a city we were deserting.

My own parents were in Europe.

303

They were doing divorce rehab with new lovers and they were supposed to call me at home every night. Before they'd left the country to go sleep with Ugly and Boring near ruins where people spoke modern languages, they both asked what I wanted from Europe. Like that could've fixed our brokenness.

Just look over the Berlin Wall, tell them I said hi.

That was what I told my parents, lying on my bed, fetal position, staring at a wall of a room in a house that was put up for sale just days before. I said goodbye to my parents with a stupid joke and now I wished I could take that back.

***

Over more canned sardines packed in tomato sauce, Tad told us how he'd come to be in my parents' cabin. He'd been sleeping over at a friend's so they could get up and go play in a little league game the next day. But that morning after they suited up, Tad's friend said he couldn't go.

Tell coach I'm sorry, Keith said.

You're burning, Keith's mother said, touching the back of her hand to his forehead.

Tad said goodbye to his friend and left and started riding his bicycle to the ballpark. His friend was sweaty and looked so awful Tad didn't think he'd show later as promised.

I didn't know who was going to play first base, Tad said.

But riding down his friend's street, he forgot all about games. A few houses away, a dog was barking beside a car parked in the drive. The car quaked and Tad almost stopped to look. He saw two people in the car.

I just thought they were kissing, he said.

But the dog, an Irish setter leaping and planting its paws on the car door and barking, that puzzled him.

I didn't have time to think about it after I saw these people in the road in front of me, Tad said. There was something wrong with them, how they were moving.

Then they knocked Tad off his bike and grabbed at his clothes and tried to bite him.

And then Miss Florence ran them down with her car. I didn't know her, Tad said, but she looked like my science teacher. She was black with freckles and glasses. I was scared and when I picked my glove and bat off the street, I saw that the ones that tried to grab me were still crawling for me with broken legs like it didn't even hurt being hit by a car.

Little boy, you better get in this car, she said to him.

And before he got in her car, Tad looked behind him.

And then he saw that whimpering Irish setter being torn apart and eaten by three strangers in the road.

There was no going back to Keith's.

And Miss Florence drove us out here, Tad said.

I asked where Miss Florence was and that's when Marisol tagged me hard in the shoulder, which hurts a lot if the puncher wears a goddamned horned demon ring.

We didn't mention Miss Florence again.

***

The cabin's fuse blew our first day. We didn't have another, and anyway, reception in this valley meant meaningless static on radio and TV. Two mornings after, before we'd even eaten breakfast, there was Marisol going through the pantry and piling everything up on the kitchen counter. Tad helped. When I saw her with a legal pad and pen from my dad's study writing things down, I had to investigate.

Two jars spaghetti sauce, I read over her shoulder.

She ignored me while Tad lined up packaged food like he was going to open a store. Even facing jars and cans the same way.

Are you playing Grocery? Look, you even got the kid in on it. Hey Tad, what aisle's shampoo on?

We have to do the bathroom, too, Marisol said to Tad.

Besides how she avoided eye contact with me, I also noticed her hair. Not only was her Mohawk down, like it might've been after sleeping on the couch with Tad—-she refused the spare room—-but it was a different kind of off-black color. The bleach streak was gone.

You must've found my mom's stuff, I said, surprised that she used my mother's hair dye.

I think it gets less attention, Marisol said.

You always wanted attention. Your bleach streak.

If we have to run somewhere on foot, I won't stand out. Those goddamned freaks will see a bleach streak in the woods.

Why run anywhere? We have a car, I reminded her.

With a half-tank of gas.

You checked? Listen, we can't panic. That's a mistake and so is all this inventory shit.

Is it?

Marisol lost her parents to a junta or whatever and she lived in a part of town where cops treated the residents like criminals. That made her paranoid, I told myself. And she didn't say anything else to me that morning and she and Tad played Grocery and then they inventoried the bathroom and closets and every last thing we had.

***

I wanted grilled Spam for dinner, but Marisol said we needed to ration food. Anyway, we could eat America's favorite potable meat product out of the can without cooking. I said a little char on the Spam made it taste better.

Then we should grill during the day, Marisol said, so nobody can see the fire at night.

We'll grill dinner in the garage. I have charcoal.

Charcoal makes carbon monoxide fumes, she said. We'll be poisoned if we use it in a closed space.

I can use some old newspaper then.

Paper won't get hot enough.

Or I can break up a chair or something. Anyway, I'm not asking your permission. It's my cabin, Marisol.

Marisol and Tad just looked at me then.

***

11 IN THE VALLEY OF THE DEAD, JOHNNY ROTTEN IS KING BY ALEXEI KALINCHUK

I had a secret. It didn't appear on Marisol's inventory either. My father liked to keep a fifth of second-rate whiskey in the den behind a volume of Gibbon's *Rise and Fall of the Roman Empire*. His sense of humor. It reminded me how last year he started staying out late at comedy club open mics because he thought that being an accountant wasn't his true calling. Staying out didn't make him a standup sensation, but his marriage to my mother did start falling apart.

And now I was slugging his cheap whiskey and my mood was getting fouler and fouler on account of something Marisol had said to me earlier that day.

End of the world isn't so bad, I had joked, trying to get past the awkwardness of our Spam Argument.

You think?

We'll have to repopulate if everything ends up falling apart, I said, not really believing the world was ending. At least we have that to look forward to.

Repopulate?

Yeah. You and me. Tad can get some brothers and sisters.

Fuck you. I'll wait until he's old enough, have his babies. That or humans can die off.

Tad? Really?

Anyone but you.

It hurt. I could see she really meant it. And the rest of the day there was that wounded quiet between us and a holding back in their faces and voices around me. Hell, Tad who was there during the argument was probably trying to figure out how sex was supposed to work.

So the Repopulate Argument drove me to whiskey in this cabin where my parents once had so many of their arguments.

And that led to The End.

***

We were on the deck grilling Spam in broad daylight and Marisol was making stink-faces at me because I was using batteries in my boombox to play a Social Distortion tape. It made me feel better, being a little secretly drunk, listening to some tunes, and having a half-assed barbecue.

Bill. We need the batteries.

What? I said, trying not to slur.

We can drive out of the valley tomorrow and see if we can get radio reception.

I didn't reply for a moment, thinking that my car radio was broken, so using the boombox to listen to the news wasn't bad as far as plans go. But it also bothered me.

You're not my boss, Marisol. By the way, I need my keys now that you're done inventorying my things in my car.

Goddamnit Bill, don't be a dick. Marisol sniffed me. Are you drunk? Where did you find—?

Never mind your inventorying head. Here's another thing your inventory didn't catch.

And then I produced a softball I'd found and I grabbed the baseball bat. I was still mad that Marisol said she was making babies with Tad and now I wanted him to see me knock this ball out into the middle of nowhere. I was originally going to play catch with him to cheer him up, but now fuck them both.

And then I tossed that softball in the air and smacked it with the bat, but I pulled my swing at the last second.

I guess I knew I was being an ass.

They didn't say a word to me as I hopped the deck railing to go down the slope to where I had pop-flied the ball. Save me some Spam, I shouted over my shoulder. I heard them shut off the music before I went ten steps. I'd make it up to them. Their faces told me I'd gone too far. Goddamnit, Marisol was right. We'd have Spam tonight, but tomorrow we'd leave the valley to listen to radio news. I used the bat as kind of a walking stick, muttering these promises to myself and still enjoying the warmth in my head of Canadian whiskey.

But the sounds of shuffling ahead broke through my haze. Someone approached. This possibility had always existed, but I guess I just now recognized it.

I dropped back behind a tree and waited.

She came into view then. I clenched the baseball bat tightly by my side, studying the torn flesh in her neck. Her track suit was ripped and blood-soaked and dried stiff. I didn't know what surprised me more; that she was still walking or that she had that much blood in her to begin with.

In front of her, like a holy icon, she held the softball, glowing white. Her eyes were glassed over and her chin looked sticky with blood. She walked up the slope toward the cabin.

She didn't see me, but the guy behind her did.

He was lanky, older, with mutton chops, a comb-over, and wearing a mint-green, three-piece suit. He turned his head, then put out a shaky long-fingered hand for me. I smashed it down with a swing of the bat, but also noted that blank look in his face and the blood on his clothes. Hitting him had no effect, no howl, no changed expression; he put out his other hand for me and I smashed that one down, too. And then he put both those flopping broken hands out for me and opened his mouth to bite. Somehow I shoved him back and then I swung for his head and he went down, blood sprinkling the front of my clothes on impact. Now was not the time to consider what I'd just done because the woman dropped the softball she was holding and came for me. She was one of them. And I broke her head, too. Then I heard rustling in the underbrush behind me and there were several more freaks limping my way.

Even if I'd wanted to lead the freaks to the cabin—I didn't—I couldn't run back up the slope because another of the freaks had cut me off.

Then I got busy swinging. I swung until sweat ran down my face along with the freak blood. I shoved them back and swung until I thought my arms would break. I never hurt so bad and swung so hard even when I used to play little league. Then the bat broke. Now I stabbed with it, but nothing took them down except a blow to the head. Not a heart stab or strike to the neck or groin, nothing. They didn't feel anything, like people on a drug. Filthy and bloody and trying to bite me, they were like no other addicts I'd ever seen.

JUST SAY NO, YOU ASSHOLES! JUST SAY NO! I shouted, and speared their heads.

When I finally managed to break past the ring of attackers around me, I bolted to the cabin. Blood-drenched and sore-limbed, I found a broken-headed freak sprawled on the deck and pieces of Spam scattered underfoot. No sign of Marisol and Tad. Cursing, I found a cast iron pan and raced back down the slope and I smashed in their heads as they climbed the single-file path to the cabin. I don't know how long it took, but I got them all at last just as the sun went down.

I found the note the next day, taped to the fridge.

I'M SORRY.

Tad and Marisol didn't leave empty-handed. The car, the batteries, and half the food—gone. I told myself they would make it out of the valley and send help. It's been a week. I've since rolled all of the dead freaks into a ravine. Into the ravine for the birds and critters to eat, all of the Johnny Rottens and Ritchie Daggers and Janie Joneses. Hah. I live alone. I read encyclopedias by day, then I sit to wait for the stars. Last night I heard gunshots from a few miles off and watched what must've been somebody's vacation home burning in the distance. Eating pineapple chunks out of a can, I shook my head and watched the blaze flicker a long time, inhaling the cinder smell, that smell of all vacations past and to come.

12 Stuck in the Middle with You by Lou Antonelli

It had been over a year since President Trump made the last emergency broadcast, and the electricity failed.

When the zombie plague first struck, I lived in the Oak Lawn neighborhood of Dallas. For some reason, it burned through the gay population there especially fast, and after a few weeks there were only three of us in our apartment building.

I had been able to plunder a nearby bodega and I had canned food to last me a long time. Thankfully, the water line from the tank atop the apartment building had been turned off by someone when the crisis first struck, and there was still water.

Every morning I went on the roof and drew off cans of water. I tossed buckets of shit and piss out the window.

Even after the power went off, satellite cell phones still worked for a couple of weeks, and I was able to talk to my brother in the small town in east Texas two hours east of Dallas.

Our parents had died early on—he'd had to euth them—but he seemed to be one of the lucky people with natural immunity, same as me. He was holed up in the small town we grew up in, where a militia defended it against all intruders. He said if I could make it there, they would let me in and protect me.

On our final call, the crackling on the cell phone indicated that the satellite system was failing, too. I vowed to him I would work my way back home and meet up with him.

"Great plan, dude, but be careful sneaking out of Dallas," he said.

I was safe where I was holed up. But...

"Yes, I know. I figure if I wait a while the zombies are going to rot and fall apart, and I'll have better odds. How are thing there?

(Crackle)

"The sheriff is a 'muni, and he's got a good posse, but the shamblers are streaming out of the big cities and into the country looking for fresh meat," he said. "They're not only coming from Dallas, some are coming south, from Houston."

"How are y'all holding out?"

"We dynamited the bridges into the county last week, across the Red River and the Sulphur River, but that is only slowing them down."

He said something else but I couldn't make out what he said.

"Everyone has their own little hideout set up. If the shamblers infest the county, we all have some place to retreat. Or will have," he said. "I'm still working on mine."

"If you are not at the old home place, where will you be?"

The connection was fading and he asked me to speak up.

I shouted. "If you're not at home, where will you be? Speak up, I think the phones are finally going down."

"If I have to abandon the house, I'll…"

(Crackle)

"What? What?" I shouted.

"I'll hide someplace and leave a clue only you will recog…"

The line went dead.

I held the cell phone in front and stared at it. Somebody had done a great job keeping the system operational as long as they had. I put the cell phone down on the table. Despite all I had gone through, I felt so lonely right then.

I looked outside the window. There were a handful of "jerkies" propped up in doorways and alleys.

The handful of us left in the neighborhood after the first year picked up the term—which apparently had proliferated across the remains of Dallas—because of their appearance after the Dallas summer heat.

The zombie flu had started during the late winter, and as things warmed up the rotting increased exponentially. That summer the temperature was between 90 and 100 degrees from June through August in the daytime.

Some of the dead were left as writhing piles of maggots in the streets and sidewalks, looking like heaps of boiling rice. Some days the swarms of flies almost blotted out the sun.

What were left after the summer were called "jerkies" —not only because of the way they moved, but because of their appearance, like dried-out beef jerky.

' Munis like me then faced the problem that the zombies that were still mobile after the summer were that much tougher to kill. There had been three other people holed up in their apartments in the same building as me by last September—but they had been killed that fall by shamblers as they went scavenging.

By New Year's I was the only one left there.

Now it was July 4th, a year after President's Trump pathetic last address on Independence Day. I never knew what to make of the man—people had mocked and excoriated him—and he seemed so over his head as the disaster had spread earlier in the year. But who could have handled such a catastrophe? I remember thinking, "Happy Birthday, America. Good-bye, America."

Trump's last Presidential Order was to dissolve the federal government and disperse its resources to states and local governments as they tried to fight the disaster at hand. That wasn't a bad move for Texas, with all its military bases.

The City of Dallas itself tried to maintain order as long as it could, but the sheer number of zombies overwhelmed its efforts. The only reason the few of us 'munis survived in the apartment building was that we did the obvious thing, the same thing my brother said he was doing back home in Pittston.

We set up our own defensive position. We demolished the staircase and disabled the elevator. We only lowered the fire escape to enter and leave the building. It was secured by a chain with a strong combination lock.

Zombies can't fly, climb walls, or work combination locks, thank God. Or figure out how to pull down a fire escape, for that matter.

Still, people were getting ambushed when they ventured outside their rat holes to scavenge for supplies. That's why the other people in the building had died by the end of last year.

But now it was July 4 and the city was heating up again. The only reason I survived the previous summer heat was because I had all the water I needed. There were times I lay for days in a full tub of water and thought cool thoughts.

But all indications from the flow at the spigot on the tank on the roof was that the water supply was going to run out soon.

It was time to vamoose.

***

The morning I left the building to head out of Dallas there had been a cool snap and the temperature at noon was only 95. My plan was to try to get at least outside the city and into some leafy suburbs by nightfall.

I packed some of the last canned food, three full canteens, and, most importantly, a half dozen shotguns and rifles. This being Texas, it had been easier to scavenge for firearms than anything else in the wake of the zombie apocalypse.

The jerkies tended to roam alone now, simply because there were so few of them. There had been vicious packs of zombies right after the outbreak, but I hadn't seen a pack of any kind from my window for months.

Still, I ran into a jerkie just three blocks away as I headed towards the interstate. She has been a large young lady, with bleached hair. The remains of a t-shirt lying across her deflated breasts said "Jars of Clay." Her shorts had rotted away.

The only sound a zombie would usually make was a loud sniffing when they got a hold of your scent. I heard that before I saw her, as she came around the corner of an old diner. It was unnerving to see something had once been human—up close—turn its head like it was looking at you, but with dead sightless eyes.

It made what would pass—for a zombie—as a charge towards me, barely able to stay upright. As it lurched and staggered at me, I pulled out a handgun.

I also had scavenged a bunch of handguns, and I wanted to save the ammo for the long guns if possible.

The best advice I had gotten, when I was part of the neighborhood posse fighting off the zombies in the first months after the outbreak, was from a former Marine sergeant.

You didn't find many veterans in Oak Lawn, but he had been forced to retire when the military brass learned he was gay.

He said, "When you know you have to shoot someone coming right at you, don't panic but hold your fire until they are close enough that you're sure of your shot."

A variation of "Don't shoot until you can see the white off their eyes," I suppose.

I had seen people panic and start shooting when the shamblers were far away, and if they missed, they'd get so nervous that by the time the zombie was upon them they couldn't have hit it with a howitzer.

Then we'd have to shoot the zombie—and shoot the victim, too.

As the Jars of Clay girl came at me, I popped a shot square at her face. You could see the black remains of her brain shoot out the back of her skull. She had actually been staggering forward fast enough that she continued forward a few feet and dropped not six feet from me.

Dammit, that was too close for comfort, I thought.

Unfortunately, the reverb from the gunshot was sure to attract other zombies, and I was at least a mile from the interstate.

I reholstered the gun. "Time to try for the four-minute mile," I muttered to myself.

I began to jog south to where I-30 was. It only took me ten minutes to get there. Thankfully, I only saw a couple of zombies, and they were far enough way I don't think they even detected me.

After running up the ramp onto the highway, I saw the vista of the blacktop extending off into the distance. Wrecked cars littered the side, and bones were scattered everywhere. Many people had been attacked as they had tried to drive out of the city.

I noticed that there seemed to be a clear lane extending down the middle of the highway, and it was obvious that some cars and trucks had been dragged out of the way.

Was the highway still in use?

I learned soon enough. I began to walk eastward and soon saw a police car blocking the center lane. When I got close enough for whoever was in the car to see me, its lights went on.

A real live cop stepped out.

I picked up my pace and smiled as I came up to him.

He had his hand on his gun in its holster, but smiled back.

"Finally leaving Big D?" he asked.

"Yep, I've been holed up since the outbreak," I said. "I didn't know there were any police still around."

"The police department administration collapsed a long time ago—well, fuck, the whole city did—but there's still a group of us in our own militia, and we try to keep the highway open during the day."

I looked up and down the highway. "I didn't know there was any travel between cities anymore."

"Not much," he said. "But we get maybe three convoys a day, mainly from the East Coast. Even with a 'muni survival rate of only ten percent, that left like 800,000 people in New York City alone."

He followed my gaze. 'Of course, the shamblers have largely reduced that number, but there are still thousands of people trying to work their way west," he said. "We have the farms and resources to support them."

"Are the motherfuckers ever going to go completely away?' I snapped.

"It won't be much longer," he said. "I know a fellow who was a mortician, so he knows the rate of decay of a human corpse. He said in about three more years none of them should be ambulatory."

"What about the recently bitten or dead?"

He actually laughed. "Most of the people stupid or reckless to have been bitten have already been turned," he said. "Folks like us—we had the sense to survive."

He got a serious look. "Where are you heading, son?"

"A small town in East Texas, called Pittston, near the Arkansas border."

"I know of it. That's a long way. You planning to go on foot?"

"I have to get a start. The only possible living family member I have may be there," I said.

"If there is an eastbound convoy, maybe they'll have room for you," he said. "Problem is, not many people are heading east."

He waved a finger. "If no eastbound convoy appears, stay with me until we gather up and head to our place at sundown. You can come back out tomorrow. It's probably safer."

"I have plenty of guns."

He turned me around and looked in my backpack.

"Son, I got more than that in my back pocket. Besides, what will you do when you have to sleep at night?"

"Climb up a tree, I suppose."

He laughed as his radio came on.

He reached into the patrol car.

"This is Silly Jack, over."

"Silly Jack, this is Ten of Spades. We have eyes on two jerkies heading north on State Fair Avenue towards you. Over."

He walked over to the side of the highway and pulled out binoculars. He leaned on the concrete wall and peered into the distance, then walked back to his car.

"Ten of Spades, this is Silly Jack. Target acquired, will terminate with extreme prejudice, over."

He took a high-powered hunting rifle from the patrol car and walked back to the wall. I joined him.

He peered again through his binoculars and pointed.

"See the fuckers up the road?"

I peered and could just see through the shimmering heat distortion two human-like figures walking away from the ruins of the Texas State Fairgrounds.

"Yes. Do they have any clothes on?"

He kept peering. "Not any more. Look like real jerkies."

He held up the binoculars with one hand while extending the other one sideway to me.

"By the way, the name is John, John Sillman."

I shook his hand. "I'm John Joseph Adamcek. My friends used to call me Adam."

"You can call me Jack," he said. "When I still had living friends, they called me that. I know how that goes."

The zombies kept walking towards us. "You want to take a crack at them?"

I shook my head. "I don't have as large a supply of ammo as I'm sure you have."

He smiled as he put the binoculars down on the wall and picked up the rifle.

"You're sharp, kid. I know why you're still alive."

He loaded the magazine, peered through the telescopic sight, and pulled the trigger.

You could see the large dark puff of ejecta as one zombie got it in the head and dropped down.

"You're good at this," I said.

"I've been getting a lot of practice lately," he deadpanned. He took a second shot.

You could see the small white puff as the bullet struck the pavement behind the second zombie.

He growled. "Fuck, I have to waste a shot. Yeah, we have all the ammo that the Dallas PD had, but God know when there will be any more."

He looked through the sight again. "Steady, steady," he said to himself.

Another crack. This time the zombie went down.

"You're still a crack shot," I said.

"I was a sniper in Afghanistan," he said. "That was one good thing I brought back from that war."

I looked across the landscape. "Hey, where is your spotter?"

He pointed with the rifle barrel. "Straight ahead, top booth on the Ferris wheel."

I looked and saw that at the top of the Texas State Fair Ferris Wheel one booth was rocking ever so slightly.

"Wow, that's a great idea! But how does he climb up there?"

"He doesn't. There is a flywheel you can turn manually with a chain," he said. "It was a failsafe in case of a loss of power, to get people off the wheel. Each morning we pull up a fire engine and give the wheel a half turn."

He turned and stashed the hunting rifle back in the patrol car.

"But we don't supply cotton candy."

***

As Jack supposed, there were no eastbound convoys that day. There were a couple going on west, to Fort Worth and Odessa. It was good to see clusters of healthy, live people—albeit dirty and often very, very nervous.

One convoy had started in Atlanta. The other had originated in Newark, New Jersey.

After the second convoy left, Jack shook his head.

"God only knows what they saw," he muttered. "It was really, really bad in the northeast."

As the sun began to set behind Fort Worth, we got into his patrol car and went to the "fortress," which was a sturdily-built Sears Roebuck store on Ross Avenue that had been shuttered a few years earlier. It had the advantage of having its own parking lot and was the largest building in its East Dallas neighborhood, so it was easily defended with clear lines of sight.

It was also reinforced by being surrounded with 20 fire engines—an impressive sight.

Generators and propane kept things humming. For better or worse, all the men in the militia that defended the interstate were either single or had lost their families and had no other attachments.

When I sat down to dinner with them, they were genuinely curious to hear of my experience hiding out in Oak Lawn.

"I cain't believe you had enough food for over a year," one said.

"I don't know why, but a bodega nearby wasn't looted in the initial riots. I think the Hispanic families left to get back to Mexico, and the white people didn't even know what it was," I said. "The signage was in Spanish."

Everyone agreed that I should be able to catch a convoy eventually heading east on I-30, but getting from there to Pittston would be a problem.

Pittston is 40 miles north of the interstate.

"That's gonna be a rough hike, 40 miles through the Piney Woods," said one officer.

"From what I've heard, there are hardly any shamblers in the Piney Woods and Big Thicket," said another. "The black bears came out of the creek bottoms and ate them. The cougars also ate the shamblers."

A third snorted. "Thank God the virus doesn't affect animals."

"So I'm more likely to be eaten by a bear, then?"

There were grunts of affirmation all around.

I pushed my plate away from me. "Well, I'll die well fed, then. Or the bear will have a good meal himself, I suppose."

One officer spoke up. "What kind of firepower do you have?'

I told him. He reached under his chair and handed me a small burlap sack.

I smiled and reached across the table to take it. "What's in here? It's heavy."

"Hand grenades. You know the saying, close only counts…"

I peered inside and saw he was telling the truth. "Damn, you all have everything!"

Jack winked and me and said to the others, "Should we tell him about the nuke in the basement?"

I didn't know if he was joking or not.

***

As hoped for, bright and early the next morning a convoy came down the interstate that had started in Albuquerque and was headed towards Shreveport—specifically, Barksdale Air Force Base.

Jack asked the Captain in charge if they could take me to Mount Vernon—about sixty miles west of Texarkana. I would be on my own the rest of the way to Pittston.

We shook hands as I climbed into the Buffalo.

"Good luck, youngster," said Jack. "I hope you make it safe."

"Thanks for everything," I said. "Maybe some day I'll be back, when things come back."

"Things will come back," he said. "But it will never be the same."

He looked sad as he turned away. One of the officers back at the fortress had told me Jack had had a wife and five children—and he'd had to euth them all.

The Captain of the convoy said the Buffalo truck leading the convoy had seen service in Iraq and was being refurbished at the Red River Army Depot when the zombie plaque struck.

Riding in that truck was the most secure, comfortable feeling I'd felt in two years. A Buffalo is a six-wheeled, 38-ton, armor-plated supertruck designed to set off EODs by driving over them. A zombie Godzilla couldn't have bothered us.

But that was only 90 minutes. Then we reached Mount Vernon.

As I got out, the Captain came to me and asked if planned to go to Pittston on foot.

"What choice do I have?" I felt it was a stupid question.

He smiled in a knowing way and pointed to a ruined building on the frontage road. The sign read, "Piney Woods Bicycle Shop."

"That place is still full of bicycles," he said. "Grab one, it will get you on your way a lot faster."

I thanked him and walked onto the frontage road as the convoy pulled away. I went over to the building.

There were the usual bones and signs of carnage, but it didn't appear to be looted. To anyone who had to travel any kind of long distance, I would think a bicycle would seem insufficient transportation. But I only had to go 40 miles—probably less, since my brother had said the bridges into the county had been demolished.

Still, a bicycle could get me to the county line.

I found a tandem bicycle with its tires still supple and inflated. I took the front seat and headed up the road towards Pittston singing "Daisy Bell."

***

There were few abandoned vehicles along the way, and no signs of life—or zombies. There were still the occasional piles of bones along the roadside, but that was such a common sight as to be hardly noteworthy.

"This is like the way the pioneers found the landscape," I thought. "Pretty much empty."

Except now the emptiness was littered with roads and abandoned homes.

Ten miles up the road I saw a brick house that looked fortified. I didn't slow down, and I saw a rifle pointing out a slot in a bricked-up window. A hand-lettered sign was tacked on the remains of the mailbox and said, "Move on."

Twenty miles up the road—halfway to Pittston—I reached the county line: the Sulphur River. The main span had been a heavy reinforced concrete bridge. I don't know how they blew it up, but they had. I would have to swim across. Because of weight, I would have to leave most of my firearms behind. I put a Ruger SR22 in a watertight pack I had packed, and stowed it in another watertight bag I had brought along, where I stashed my clothes. I would swim across naked.

The water was filthy and full of silt, but the current was weak and I was able to swim and splash myself across fairly easily. Once on the opposite bank, I used a towel (thanks for the reminder, Douglas Adams) to dry off, and I got back on the highway.

I left the bicycle, plus a backpack of firearms and canned goods, behind on the far bank.

My luck ran out at a small crossroads community called Nealey. There had been one store there, which I saw was a burned-out ruin as I walked up.

Three shamblers seemed to come out of the ruins—one woman and two men. I was startled to see how fast they moved.

I pulled out the Ruger and cursed as I saw they were "newbies"—recently turned zombies. The poor bastards must have held out there for years and then someone—or something—had finally gotten to them.

The woman had dark long lustrous hair, like a Native American, and her clothes were all still intact. The men looked enough alike that they were probably father and son. They both wore heavy-duty farm work clothes. None of them showed much signs of decay at all.

Like I said, because of their condition, they moved fast enough that I looked around quickly for a defensive position. Thankfully there was a burned-out gasoline tanker truck right there.

I climbed the ladder and got on the top. As stiff as he was, the "father" still tried to climb the ladder. Since I was overlooking him, it made for an easy shot into the top of his head.

The "mother" and "son" staggered over his body and also tried to climb the truck. My next shot hit the mother in the chest. I took a deep breath and aimed again, and my next shot went into her forehead.

The "son" groaned and sniffed loudly. He raised his head and reached for the ladder. My shot went through his left eye.

I slid down the side of the tank and jumped onto the parking lot.

I looked at the dead "family."

"Poor bastards," I thought. "To make it so long, and still end up like this."

Their appearance told me that there might still be shamblers wandering around, so I kept my guard up as I walked the rest of the way into Pittston.

As I neared the town, I could see a recent grass fire had spread unchecked and burned many homes. I walked into the downtown and saw no signs of life or activity there.

It was clear there had been some kind of battle. The skulls of zombies with bullets holes in their brains were all over.

Lots of zombies. Enough that I supposed the small population of 'munis left in Pittston might have been overwhelmed, or at least had retreated.

I found our home. It was ruined, but unburnt. There was no sign of my brother, but also no sign of fighting or violence. He must have retreated to some fortress of his own making. But where? I didn't see obvious clues. He probably had left in a rush—the kitchen cabinet doors were all open.

I walked back to the downtown area and walked to the White Oak Creek which ran through the city. It was large enough that it really should have been called a river—but it was a creek compared to the Sulphur River to the south and the mighty Red River to the north. There was an old railroad bridge across the creek. It was an old rusty steel girder thing, and it had been dynamited, also. The remains poked out of the water on both sides of an abutment in the middle of the creek that remained. I looked and saw that the small shack that had been in the middle of the bridge, on top of the abutment, was still intact. It had held railroad switching equipment.

When we were kids, my brother would fish on the banks of the creek. The shack had been there as long as we could recall. It was tin, perhaps six feet wide and twelve feet long. The only concession to modernity was that, a few years earlier, the tin roof was replaced by panels of solar cells so the equipment inside could still operate during a power outage.

I squinted in the dwindling light. There were pieces of the old steel trestle sticking out from both sides of the abutment. As I peered, I realized there seemed to be graffiti written on the rusty girders.

I walked down the bank of the creek to get a better look. I could just make out the writing, spray painted in white on the right side.

"JOKERS," it said. I looked on the left side of the abutment.

It read "CLOWNS."

I took out the Ruger and shot into the air. The door opened and my brother stepped out.

He waved his arms and yelled. "Hey, I see you found me, little brother!"

I walked so I was opposite the abutment. "That was a good clue!"

Our father had grown up in the 1970s, and one day, when my brother and I were called on the carpet for some stupid shit we did, he looked back and forth at us, and quoted that song by Stealers Wheel.

We never forgot it, and every so often, even as adults, we'd bring that moment back up again and laugh.

"How do you expect me to get to you?" I shouted.

"Same way you got across the Sulphur River," he called back.

After I swam to the bottom of the abutment he threw down a rope and hauled me up.

I walked inside the shack and saw he had gutted it. It was tight but he had a hot plate, a small refrigerator and a radio. A bed was propped up against the wall.

A light was plugged into an outlet. "All the comforts of home," he said with a grin.

"How long have you been holed up here?" I asked.

"Fifteen months. Even with the bridges down, we had too many zombies infiltrating, and after a real hard-fought battle downtown, the sheriff said we should all go to our own hiding places. I told him I was willing to hide out here. He said 'It's cramped. But you can have it if you want it,' and as a last favor, he blew this bridge up, too."

"You mean you've been here all this time?"

"Sure. I have plenty of water, obviously, and all the fish I can catch. Thanks to the solar panels, I have power, too."

"But can we both sleep in here?"

"Sure, head to foot, a little diagonally." He reached up into a cabinet on the wall. "I even saved a sleeping bag for you."

He patted me on the shoulder. "Don't worry, we won't be here all that long."

"What do you mean?"

"I have a radio. Regular broadcasts have started up again, from D.C. The government is getting back together. The military is conducting mopping up operations against the zombies. General Mattis is now president."

He plugged in the hot plate. "I'll start cooking dinner."

I grimaced. "I suppose it's fish, then."

"Nope, I saved something special for this day," he said with a big smile as he took a can out of the cabinet.

Grilled Spam never tasted so good.

WHISPERS OF THE APOC

13 A Walk in the Park by Chad Vincent

Gilbert Grant pulled himself out of his worn-down Chevy Malibu. His knees creaked almost as loud as the rust-riddled door as it slammed shut. Dangling from his finger was a yellow plastic bag from his night shift as a stockman at the local CPS Pharmacy. Reaching in as he walked, he peeled open a box of rat poison and threw the blocks through a gap in the trailer's skirting that was poorly hidden by a tall tuft of weeds. It was a difficult shot under the one working street light. Two of the four brown bricks missed the hole and bounced back into the yard like an evil pair of house dice. He did not care. His chair was calling him by name through the door and walls.

The grainy groan of cinderblock steps accompanied him to the door, which looked as thin as tinfoil. Wiping his hand on his pants, he flipped through a motley ring of keys. Dangling off the ring in blackened metal was a sharp-edged letter A, an eagle head cut through the background. A similar tattoo showed on his forearm, an artistic variation of his 101st Airborne patch permanently embedded on his skin and mind. That life was long ago, yet still fresh enough to haunt his memories and dreams. Now he worked part-time, got one monthly social security check and one disability check, and drank just enough to coast through life.

With a flick of his finger, a set of lamps burst to life in mismatched wattage. On the base of one lamp, ceramic wolves hunted through the snow, while the rest of the pack circled on the lampshade in attitudes of chase and silent howls. The overhead bulb smiled through blackened teeth from above.

The living space was sparse. Milk crates served as end tables, one draped in a camouflage hand towel. A wolf tapestry hung on the far wall, and a single La-Z-Boy held together with military grade engineer's tape along the arm rests filled in the room. Gilbert plopped into the chair and set his feet up on a footlocker that served as a coffee table. More accurately, a beer table. Cans towered upwards like a ziggurat. Beside his chair he slid out a can of Blue Beard from between sheets of cardboard. The can and its winking pirate were room temperature, yet he popped the top and took an "I'm off work for two days" guzzle. With his other hand, he clicked the TV to life. This was not the flat screen with usb ports type, but the set in a yard with a "free" sign type. His one splurge beyond the cases of Blue Beard was cable. Gotta have huntin' and fishin' shows.

Things were better when his wife was alive. She followed him when he joined the Army and stayed for nine years, and then through some under-the-table construction jobs until his knee gave out the rest of the way. It was her strength and vibrancy that kept life worth living. She was a good woman. Then the cancer took her, took her quick. The last two years had been, well, blurry.

Outside, the neighbor's dog began barking. Four a.m. and the dog was going bat-shit crazy. Not unheard-of in the trailer park but unappreciated each time it happens. Meth heads, alcoholic blackouts, and other deformed addicts came out at all hours, more so at night, sending canine home defense systems into full alert. No Brinks or ADT here, more like German Shepherd, Rottweiler, and Pit Bull incorporated. That's why there was a .38 hiding in the beer box at his ankles, a boot knife behind the curtain, and a replica police baton on nails above the front door. Those were just the quick grips. Other measures were in place throughout. Inside the locked footlocker was his money pit, his arsenal. One .12 gauge for birds, a Russian 7.62 for illegal venison, a .22 for rabbits and squirrels, and a .9 mm with one box of hollow points. This one was not for animals. There was plenty of ammo for all. For years, he had supplemented the table with animals from various local state parks, conservation lands, rivers, streams, and other heavily wooded areas within a short drive in his worn-out Chevy.

Outside, the dog barking turned from fierce warning to engagement, biting at something or someone. Gilbert considered going to the window, but a commercial with a shiny red truck climbing over a field of boulders sucked him back. Dream, dream, dream.

The dog yelped and fell silent.

Gilbert pressed the show to mute and pulled the .38. The chair swiveled to face the door, barrel resting along his bad leg, forward. A moment passed with nothing but an eerie silence. He heard his neighbor open the door and scold the dog in a loud rant from the front porch. A very short, quick scream, and he too grew silent.

This is getting serious, he thought. Time for wishing on commercials was over.

As he started to stand, the window near the kitchen shattered under a single slap of a hand. Gilbert raced over. Four hands surprised him, slapping and grabbing at the weak, slatted opening, slivers of glass scattering onto the thick carpet and raking into the hands' own skin. The weak metal of the trailer's window mold bent just a little with the continuing blows of the hands. Coming out of the dark tree line were two more figures, falling in right behind like inconsiderate Black Friday shoppers.

Behind him, causing him to pivot once more, the front door began to reverberate from slap after slap, as if there were more than a few drunken callers. Putting his back into the short hallway he eyed both locations, not sure where to point the barrel. Turning, he rushed to the three rooms back in the darkness of the hallway and locked each one shut. He returned to the edge of the living room to the increasing commotion of beings trying to gain entry.

A short, dreamy time passed and the door began to wobble. With an appalling crunch, the lower hinge gave. The aluminum entry bent inward like a giant doggie door. One creature slid in to its waist, pawing at the dirty carpet, then another two wriggled their way in behind to knock over a pair of dirt-caked work boots. Their arms worked feverishly at pulling down some invisible curtain that spread out before them.

Blam! Blam! Blam! The first three intruders went down and he seized the break. Scattering cans to the wind, he kicked the bodies back outside, slid the footlocker to the door, folded it back down into a semblance of cover, and braced the footlocker at the floor. Drawing the keys out of his pocket, he fitted the key in the lock; the lid flew up and away. The .12 gauge was pulled from its leather wrappings. He knew it to be loaded and fingered the safety off. The rest of a near-full box went into his right front pocket.

He kicked over the La-Z-boy onto its back beside the locker, which added weight to help keep the door closed. This was unorthodox, but so was having three dead bodies on his makeshift steps. He edged to the back window and held the stock to his shoulder, double-checked the safety, and looked down the sights to take in as many targets as possible. Blam! Blam! Just to left center and right center. Four more dead. Another two approached from twenty feet away, tearing through a worn hedge. He waited until their shadowy shapes overlapped in his sights. Blam! One fell, one staggered. Blam! The second toppled across the weathered air conditioner. Backyard secure.

"I hope those weren't just some drunks passing between the hedges," he said, in hindsight, but he felt little concern.

The front door now was about to fall behind more slamming hands and pressing bodies. Gilbert reloaded as he turned. Crunch! The door began to fold from the top down. The sound of the intruders drummed in his head.

"Crappy, coreless, aluminum doors," he muttered.

There were at least five outside now, but the fallen door and footlocker were still in the way, even if only as obstacles. Blam! Chachink. Blam! Chachink. Blam! He took care of the front yard with three well-placed shots. Five bodies fell. He racked the chamber and fed the loading port from his pocket.

Stepping to the doorway, he saw nothing stirring. Stay? Go? He'd always harbored a plan of paranoia, figured he'd just hunker down, but now that it was here? No, not really. Acting fast, he threw every scrap of food, every beer he had left into the footlocker. Shotgun on his back, he grabbed the cracked leather handles, and dragged the locker over the wrecked door and down each cinderblock step. The locker's corners dug parallel ruts in the yard and then it went into the back seat. One body with a gaping neck wound raised an arm towards his ankle as he passed, but he did not notice in his haste. Two bodies rounded the far corner, returned from death beneath the back window. Something lifted its head from the neighbor's porch; blood and tissue glistened in the street light.

The .12-gauge was slung in the seat beside him as he got in. The .38 hung just below the dashboard in his left hand. He started the engine with shaking hands, and the car sputtered before cranking a hit. Two bald tires sprayed gravel and dirt over the garden of dead bodies as it snorted onto the road.

"Where to, where to?" he asked himself. Hundreds of locations sprinted through his mind, grocery store, pawn shop, gun store, police station, water tower.... That last thought was pressed aside as four wanderers stepped into his path on the road. *Stepped* might be the wrong description—more like *ran* with hands out like claws. His initial inference of druggies was losing to out to roaming bands of alcoholics. He felt better shooting people smacked out of their head with drugs, not drunks like himself. Gilbert slammed on the brakes, of which at least three gave protest and very little pressure. Mrs. Norris from two doors down stepped beneath a lamp pole light in the middle of the street. Her shoulders slumped over her walker without regard to his screeching halt.

"Gladys, I almost hit you," he said angrily over the dashboard.

A hand palmed onto the window behind his head, dividing his attention. While he paused but a moment, switching his focus from Mrs. Norris to the hand behind, a crowd had encircled the car from the rear. These were some fast drunks.

"Gladys, get out of the way," he yelled through the glass over the increased hammering at the windows and the sound of rusty panels giving way at his rear.

Gilbert made an executive decision. He slipped the shift into reverse and not-so-gently pressed through the throng. At some point *through* the throng became *over* the throng.

Wham! Out of the darkness, as he was looking over his shoulder while in reverse, another car jumped onto the narrow trailer park road. Mrs. Norris was no match for the compact's bumper and neither was the Malibu when taking the metal monster full on the nose.

The impact jerked Gilbert sideways and backwards, causing him to drop the .38. In the back, the footlocker rattled and remained relatively in place, but the shotgun slid onto the floorboard, in the darkness. Steam hissed from beneath the crumpled hood. Pistons ground and whined in contorted protest, but a strange absence of sound replaced everything in Gilbert's foggy mind.

The breaking of glass soon penetrated the nothingness in a slow progression of sound. Glass struck his collar, his neck, and hands reached in behind. He slid away, feeling the floor for either weapon. With luck, he found one resting atop the other. When he came up with them, the driver's side window was a crowd of hands and dark faces pressing through.

Out the passenger door with a kick, he didn't even attempt to close it. Before him was a single assailant, arms outstretched towards his face. The pistol rested in his waistband, so, raising the shotgun to his shoulder, he fired. Never shoot from the hip when you could aim.

"Meth head drunks!" he grumbled, and rushed forward into the dark. Something deep inside him knew it must be more than a rampant outbreak from a tainted batch of hooch or ill-prepared batch of painkillers, but his mind needed an explanation, even a poor one.

Before him now was the only building that wasn't a trailer for another mile or more. The pool house and manager's office looked like a fortress compared the the thin-walled trailers everywhere else. Locked. The butt of the shotgun opened the door with two strokes. Quick, shambling footsteps behind warned that figures were closing in, too many shadows to count beneath the parking lot light and front motion sensor. He ducked inside and hit the lights. Thinking fast, he wedged a chair under the handle and leaned a long couch partly across the window for good measure. Hands found the door as he took a step backwards.

He glanced at the window. Instead of seeing the rowdy degenerates outside, his own dirty stare and part of the couch glared back at him in a tell-tale reflection created by the light in the glass. "How stupid, Gil, turn on the lighthouse. Bring 'em all in," he said shaking his head, abusing himself with sarcasm. With a snap, the lights were out again and he was done with self-accusations and focused on living.

A look around revealed nothing that hadn't been here two days ago. The backyard light shone in from the rear above the pool outside, giving all the light he needed to explore the room. He started rifling the paper-littered desk, and gazed across four windows, the door to a closet that held pool supplies, the front door, a back door leading out to the pool, and rear access to thirty mailboxes.

His mind brought him to another place, one his body fought to forget. An interior of a darkened building, a weapon slung across his back, he was transported back to a shelled-out dwelling. Separated from his platoon, an unknown number of adversaries controlling the immediate area, and he was all alone. Fear drizzled down his Kevlar vest quicker than the sweat ever would. Some internal strength beckoned him back. He kicked back against the wall and listened to the grind of fingers on wood, metal, and plastic as he returned to the world.

Tonight he was only one beer in and still had his whole mind. How depressing. What a way to attend such an event, completely sober.

Wheels turned; he took inventory. That was just what you did. No need to give up yet. In a flash he was past the interior door, tearing through pool supplies, looking for the "flame" symbol. Hefting a heavy 5-gallon bucket, he dragged it along to the door. Outside, hands were already drumming a persistent cadence on the door and around the window.

He flipped out the box knife he carried from work and cut open the hard, plastic top. Before pouring anything, he rammed a dust pan under the door. This was to ensure that most of the liquid would flow outside and under people's feet. He was still relatively sure they were people, even if part of his mind protested the thought. The broken top leaked eye-burning vapors into the room, but Gilbert held his breath, pinched his eyes closed, and poured the bucket's contents under the door.

Throwing the empty bucket into the far corner, he took a long-nosed grill lighter from a hook on the wall beside a restroom key. It slid beneath the door and he clicked. This set off a whoosh of flames that lit up the night. Yet, to his dismay, in spite of all the flames at their feet, the mob persisted. They ignored the flames completely: no screaming, no running in pain, just a sickening barbeque smell mingled with heavy chemicals. A small flame licked on this side of the door and he suffocated it with an old denim jacket from the back of the desk chair. Eventually, the front would burn through. This would be a concern soon.

Gilbert grabbed the shotgun and moved towards the door at the rear which led to the pool. Pungent aromas of cooked meat seeped into the room, as at the entrance of a reputable steak house. Strange, it didn't smell half bad if you could have cut out the underlay of hot chlorine and hints of nose hair burners in it. Beyond the pool door, the sight was grim beneath the yellow security light and high-set backyard light. The pool had been closed all summer for various reasons, namely laziness. The concrete bowl of the pool, which was poured about the time President Kennedy had the worst day ever, was low on water and what was there was full of trash and debris. Luckily, the whole thing was surrounded by a privacy fence.

The fence, the locked door, all kept these supposed crackheads at bay. It also had kept the manager inside. Rather than being asleep in the adjoining trailer, the little old man with "super" stenciled on his right lapel rose from the knee-deep water of the deep end. A deflated pool raft from two seasons back hung off his shoulder like the edge of a rainbow cape. Rising from the water like some lake monster, his eyes locked onto Gilbert with ferocity.

That feral stare cut Gilbert's bravado to the bone, and momentarily muscles twitched to sight the shotgun down on poor Mr. Danson. But years of practice prevailed. You never alert the enemy to your position with unneeded sound. This reasoning had kept him alive in the field and would do so here.

During that night in the bombed-out shell of a home, the same one that still sneaked into his nightmares, when a dark figure had entered the building with a Chinese model AK-47, it was silence and cold steel that had kept him safe. So when his focus returned from the land of terror, it was the cold steel of his box cutter that wavered before him to keep him safe from Mr. Danson.

The ex-superintendent of the park splashed the scummy water to a froth, but the slant of the slick, blue walls of the deep end ensured that there was no escape. Still, never leave an enemy at your back, or in this case, your backyard. Gilbert made the decision that, under the circumstances, Mr. Danson had to go.

Taking down the flimsy rod of a cleaning skimmer from hooks on the fence, he hefted it as if judging a blacksmith's blade. Gilbert whittled the plastic end into an elongated point. It made an excellent spear point. With a thrust, Gilbert speared Mr. Danson in the his shoulder. Mr. Danson didn't seem to care. After taking another thrust into his chest, Mr. Danson ignored the fact that he should be bleeding to death. Instead of slowing from terminal blood loss, the arms thrashed with the enthusiasm of a cheerleading squad on homecoming night.

"That should have cut through the heart," Gilbert said, confused and frustrated, and also soul-wretched that he felt compelled to kill the man who had helped him clean up his little yard when the last windstorm had swept through the neighborhood. He punched the long pole downward, puncturing somewhere between an eye and the nose cavity. The stick came to rest within the eye socket, stuck fast and refusing to pull free. Mr. Danson had finally found the slumber which his new state had refused. Thus Gilbert realized that the brain was the critical organ to destroy.

Grabbing an extension cord, he tied the doorknob off onto a spigot, sealing the office from the pool area. Moving along the fence, he then ensured a second time that the gate was locked. With little else he could see to do that would further barricade the pre-fab dwelling, he took a seat at an umbrella-topped table and just breathed. The shotgun lay across his lap, pointed towards the door, finger flickering atop the trigger guard like a nervous cat's tail.

Most people at this point would have passed out from sleep deprivation, physical exhaustion, and multiple chemical dumps that delivered the highs and lows, but Gilbert lived and worked at night. So when the soft moans grew behind the corner of the wooden fence, he was not only awake, he was primed. This travelling mob reinforced his belief in the drug and alcohol basis for this abysmal early morning. After Mr. Danson, Gilbert was done giving normal excuses to anything that happened.

Survival had always been something he was fortunate with, or rather he was good at getting by. Despite the muddied illusions of fate and luck, Gilbert had every intention of being prepared to make it out of this thing alive. Once again, he sized up the situation. Multitudes of people were out to get him. Luckily, very stupid people. He did not have the mental energy to question this new situation that had become his world. It just was.

"Ok, remember the basics," he said to himself. "Water, food, security." With each of these he flipped out a finger to count them off. Patting himself down, he mentally made a list of anything that would fit into the three categories. First, gather anything useful out here. Then he would start checking the room inside.

Peering into the trash can, he saw that Mr. Danson had actually done his job. It was empty except for a single plastic bottle. Good enough to hold a bit of water, though.

He lifted it out and a sloshing gave him hope. Germs be damned if there were a few ounces of some sugary drink. But his hopes were dashed as he lifted it to the light. It contained not a few swigs of soda, but the thick juice of tobacco spit that clung to the sides like motor oil. Mr. Danson was no junkie but he did have his habits. No thanks.

Last summer there had been a vending machine; now nothing remained but a rusted, rectangular line where it had left its residue from years in the weather. Probably sold and the money spent that same day. A few cleaning supplies, an abandoned towel with one mouse-shredded end, and a stack of ash trays. He took a bottle from among the cleaning supplies, a near-empty bleach container. This could be used to purify water, though the bulky bottle was a hindrance.

He peeked through the rear window into the office, as the pool area was now empty. The door, though slightly warped, had held from the fast-burning chemical fire. He entered, noticing the quiet after the recent terrible rhythm on the door. The search began. Behind the desk, covered by trash boxes and a cheap printer, was a mini-fridge. It delivered half a sandwich in a brown bag, four packages of cheese and crackers that could outlast the average human in shelf life, and a half-consumed off-brand sports drink. Checking his pockets, he counted eleven shells.

"Dismal," he said, shaking his head. "Sure could use that footlocker. Sure could use a beer."

As his head moved back and forth to spot anything else of importance, his eyes landed on another set of keys on a peg further down from the grill lighter's now-vacant spot. Hidden beneath a fly swatter were the keys to the maintenance truck. It was a junker, but it had to run better than his car. He tore them down while taking a bite of cold sandwich.

Scouting the window, he downed the last of the neon-green drink. The people outside had abandoned the door, except for the few charred bodies that slumped like fallen trees, and the burnt exiles were chasing a screaming lady into the darkness that led away to the back of the park. One stood beneath the light outside, swiping at a fat moth that seemed to perpetually elude capture.

It was dark and quiet enough outside but for the swatting of one and far-off cries that settled themselves into the night. Closing his eyes, he relied on his hearing, which told him the group around the side of the pool fence were on the move. Another idea came to mind as his hand rested on a long stretch of wall switches. He glanced outside through a near window. Slumped bodies leaned against the door: the reason the fire had not burned through was that it had been smothered by bodies. Two of the burned husks pawed with malformed hands. Legs churned, their motion burned to little paddling gestures. One burned finger snapped off on the door like cracked clay. On the far end of the building was the old truck, but who knew what hid in the darkness beyond.

His free hand counted shells once more and made sure the shotgun was full. The cheese crackers went into his other pockets as he swallowed the last bite of sandwich. Tapping his belt, he reassured himself that the .38 was still stowed. The near empty bleach jug was held alongside the truck keys in his left and the shotgun suspended steady over his shoulder.

With the lid of the jug, he began flicking switches by the door. Lights flared all along the edge of the building. At the opposite end, overlooking the road, a floodlight shed its unnatural light on a crowd bent over in the street. Sounds began to match the scene: tearing and ripping of cloth, the shredding sound of something being rended apart. The thought streamed through his head as to what it could be: that bath salt guy in Florida, who he had seen on the news.

"Murderers! Cannibals?" His mind was unable to process the scene. It reverted back to self-preservation.

Quiet and careful, he sneaked out the door to the pool. With a final glance towards Mr. Danson, his body floating in the flotsam, he went through the back gate. Rounding the corner, he had to duck beneath a row of untrimmed bushes along the fence and building towards the truck. Something gave him pause.

"Mrs. Norris," he whispered to himself, as he hit the corner nearest the truck.

There she stood. No walker, no cane, standing straight and strong as never before.

"Mrs. Norris," he whispered again. "Get in the truck, we're getting out of here." As he said this, she turned into the spectral light at her back. The side of her jaw was not only broken, but hung open, slack in perpetual awe. Through all the confusion of the night, the memory returned to him. "You were hit by that car." That was his last thought before she lunged with the speed of one of her cats.

With the shotgun shouldered and the pistol behind his back, he had a split second to react. He smacked her with the bleach jug, but it did little to divert her charge. As they toppled, he threw out his hands and the jug nestled beneath her chin, allowing her only to bite at the air above his chest. The fall knocked him on his back, the shotgun digging into his spine. With a howl of pain fueled by fear, he rolled to his left, then reached back and pulled the pistol while with his other hand he pressed the jug below the vicious gnashing of teeth. The jug slipped from beneath her chin like an oily piglet.

Just as the teeth were coming down, the plastic grip crashed into the side of her head. It did not knock her out, or even hinder her attack, but it did smash her head enough to the side that she bit uselessly into his sleeve and the air beneath his armpit. Without even thinking, he wrapped his arm around her neck and beneath her chin, closed off the airway and compressed the carotid to cut off blood to the brain. Little did he know, she needed neither to live. Still, the headlock was well suited to keep her teeth at bay.

Gilbert rose to one knee and wrenched the hold as tight as he could, so tight that her writhing strength toppled him backwards yet again. Falling to his back, he kept his arms in place. His one thought was the wish for her to pass out soon. Yet when they fell, he hit his back again and she crashed hard, forehead first, with a crunch of bone. On impact, she stopped moving.

Thinking she had finally succumbed to lack of oxygen or blood, he slipped from beneath her clawing hold. Her body did not slide off as it should; rather, her head stuck fast to the edge of the concrete. Leaning low, he saw the truth of it. She hadn't passed out at all. She had landed on a protruding piece of rebar that stuck out of the ground. What once held a parking block in place now held Mrs. Norris to the crumbling edge of the concrete. Revulsion skewed his face, but the sound of more people moving and groaning in his direction sent him back into survival mode.

"Sorry, Mrs. Norris," he said, but still scuttled to his feet and ran towards the truck without looking back.

None were near enough to intercept him, and he got to the driver's door an instant before any others. The key fit, but first he pressed on the clutch so it slid backwards. Chuga, chuga, chuga, vroom, it started with some reluctance and he churned broken asphalt all the way to the wreck of his car. There was just enough time to grab the footlocker from the back seat and throw it in the back before the pack of bipedal wolves got too close for comfort. More gravel flew and the road became nothing but a blur that evolved into a breath of light at the eastern edges some distance down the road.

Her customers craved a fix and Mara did her best to make sure her supply kept pace with the growing demand. It was nerve-racking, demanding, and deadly work but she was driven and determined to survive.

Mara crouched, concealed and waiting, with her finger on the trigger. A trickle of perspiration began a maddening insect-like crawl down her neck. She ignored the urge to move and waited for her target to step close enough for a sure shot. The zombie lurched past her as the bait squealed and strained at its bonds. She had been three years into her neurosurgical residency when the zombie outbreak had altered the world. In moments like these, her experience steadied her hands. At the last possible moment, she squeezed her rifle's trigger. She saw a blossom of something that resembled raspberry jam seeping down the back of her prey's neck. It was, by some quirk of fate, near the same spot that sweat still tickled Mara's neck.

The zombie collapsed. Mara scrambled to the fallen zombie, focused on getting it off the street and into the safety of her workshop before she encountered anyone. She crouched beside the zombie. The bullet slug had shattered two neck vertebrae and severed the spinal cord. It gazed up, paralyzed. A few inches higher and she would have wasted a bullet.

Someone groaned. It was not the zombie.

"Shit." Mara looked up at the bait. The man she had gagged and trussed to the splintered wooden light pole jerked his body within the confines of the ropes. He had been one of those irritating bleeding hearts who insisted that zombies deserved limited rights as citizens, and be confined to secured areas, but under no circumstances should they be killed. She endeavored to see things from this point of view but could not. Not that she had tried too hard; zombies had killed her husband and daughter.

The bait's bulging eyes seemed even less human than the zombie's as he fought to break free. Mara mentally chastised herself for botching the job. Hunted relentlessly by armed bands of survivors, zombie numbers had dwindled as a result. The hunters did not realize the zombies' secret potential. As far as Mara knew, she was the only person to have discovered the value in harvesting from incapacitated zombies. She made her living off the recently resurrected. Thanks to their contributions, she could almost say she thrived.

But now she had a loose end. Mara usually waited, letting the zombie bite and infect the blood of the bait first. Then she made the paralyzing neck shot, dragged her prey to safety, and returned to free the newly turned. Kill a zombie; create a zombie—that was her motto in what she had dubbed this Crave New World.

Today she had let herself get careless. She had screwed up. Royally. She sighed, knowing she couldn't let him go.

The bait met her gaze, accusation in his eyes. He tried again to cry for help but the gag she'd stuffed in his mouth rendered his words inaudible. Mara chambered another round and shouldered her rifle.

This time the slug tore straight through the brain, leaving behind it a path of irreparable destruction. Like the zombie outbreak itself, she realized.

The report from the shot echoed once and faded. The tang of gunpowder lingered much longer.

***

"Mommy, can I have another popsicle?"

Mara frowned. She twisted in her lawn chair and regarded her daughter. "Skylar, you already ate a popsicle. One's enough."

Skylar's shoulders sagged but her voice rose. "But, Mommy, why can't I have another one?"

"Because I said so," Mara said. As an afterthought, she added, "And because I don't want you to get cavities in your pretty teeth."

Keith returned from the grill and sat down across from Mara. "Come on, hon. It's summer. What better time to—"

"Keith, please. I'm being a good parent here, okay? I need you to back me up, not run me over."

Her husband's mouth drew into a straight line. "No more popsicles, Sky." He leaned back and stretched out his legs. "How about you pick me a bouquet of dandelions instead?"

The girl beamed up at her father. "Okay, Daddy. I'm gonna pick you some daddy-lions."

"We can't spoil her," Mara said after their daughter was out of earshot. She felt defensive, and the summer heat had her on edge.

"One popsicle isn't going to spoil her," Keith replied.

"She needs to learn that if I tell her 'no' she can't go running to you in hopes of getting a different answer."

Keith gave her a measuring look. "But what if I don't always agree with you?"

Mara felt her cheeks flush. "Are you trying to pick a fight now?"

Her husband rose, and for a terrible moment, Mara expected him to strike her. But Keith, unlike her father, did not express anger with his hands. Instead, he knelt at her feet and took her hands in his.

"Mara, listen. You're being too hard on her. She'll be grown up and moved away before we know it. You'll think back and wonder where all the time went. You are a driven, determined, and intelligent woman, and I love that about you. But learn to relax and enjoy time spent with Sky, okay? Every memory, every giggle fit, every scraped knee, every birthday party, every Christmas morning... those are memories you'll treasure. When she grows up and moves away, and it's just you and me and the newspaper, you'll wish you'd given her more popsicles, believe me."

Mara sighed. He was right—up to a point. "Fine. But when she starts to run wild, you can't always be Good Cop to my Bad Cop. I need you one my side."

"We'll present a united front," he said, nodding. Keith's cell phone rang. Mara knew from the ring tone that his work was calling. Keith was as a camera operator for one of the three local TV news teams. Some breaking news story needed his attention.

"Fire? Car crash?" Mara asked after he ended the call. She had already resigned herself to losing him for the rest of the afternoon.

"No." Keith shook his head, frowning. "It's an angry mob, down by the shipyards." He stood. "They disembarked from a freighter that just docked. Then they just started attacking people."

**

Mara loaded the incapacitated zombie into her battered but functional wheelbarrow and steered down an alley toward her current safe haven.

She had selected a location close to the home she had fled and not yet revisited. She wasn't sure she could face the memories head-on and had forfeited all her earthly possessions as a result. Instead, she had set up her base of operations in a ground-level apartment adjacent to downtown.

She encountered no one on the return expedition, and for this, she felt thankful. Had she run into one of the gun nuts, she would likely have gotten nothing more than a high five for eliminating another zombie, but in their enthusiasm, they often asked too many prying questions. A zombie rights activist, on the other hand, might accost her—not physically but with words. They often gathered to chant and carry signs with slogans like "Zombie Lives

Matter," "Shame on Zombie Killers," and her personal favorite, "Jesus: the Original Zombie."

The zombie's eyes rolled in their sockets as she wheeled him into her workshop area. Whether he felt angry, afraid, or simply craved sustenance, Mara could not say. She paused to lock and bar the door. Then she dumped the zombie onto a rocker recliner and eased the blood-drenched back of the chair to a 45-degree angle. She fired up a generator she had salvaged from an abandoned auto body shop and dragged a wooden straight-backed chair behind the recliner.

Mara plugged her most cherished possession into the generator. She had stolen a cranial bone saw from a mortuary. Like the auto body shop, the abandoned mortuary had not been entirely empty. Though any cadavers lying on the prep room's embalming table when they reanimated were long gone, she heard several zombies still locked inside the coolers pounding on their trays. She'd listened to the sounds as she'd gathered all the tools she thought necessary for her survival, then fled the building, heart pounding.

In the months that passed, Mara became adept at capturing and harvesting zombies, just as Indian snake charmers know how to handle cobras safely.

***

"Mommy, will you keep me safe?"

Dark circles hung like nesting bats beneath Skylar's eyes. Her six-year-old daughter sat on their couch with her knees beneath her chin, hands clasped protectively across her shins.

"Of course I will, honey." Mara took inventory of their jugs of filtered water and cans of food. She thought they had enough vegetables, but the shortage of fruit concerned her. If they had to stay locked down for longer than two or three weeks...

"What about Daddy?"

"What, honey?" She had heard her daughter's question but automatically stalled.

"Where *is* Daddy? Did something bad happen to him?"

As it turned out, Keith had been one of the first people to encounter, in person, the city's earliest zombies. After ensuring that she and Skylar were safe in the house, he'd driven to the television station. He and his assigned reporter had driven to the shipyards in a station van. They'd gotten a better camera shot than their competitors but had paid for it with their lives.

"Yes, but it's going to be okay because he's with Jesus now."

"In Heaven?" Skylar picked at a hangnail. Mara looked closer and realized her daughter had bitten all her nails to the quick.

"That's right."

"Why can't Jesus come down here and help us? Everything will be all right in Heaven while he's gone."

"He'll be around when you need him most," Mara lied. "As long as you believe."

***

The man standing just inside her door acted skittish and overcompensated by running his mouth.

"Have you ever tried your own stuff? You must have. It's the best—better than anything."

Mara didn't reply. Instead she gave her customer what she hoped passed for a warm smile. They had completed their transaction: a Rolex for her and something that resembled a dead night crawler cut into pieces and stored in a plastic sandwich bag for him. Now she wanted him gone. He stank of flop sweat and unwashed feet.

The man dragged one hand through his greasy hair and giggled, chirpy and porpoise-like. Mara wondered how much longer before he cracked. Suicides now outnumbered confirmed zombie kills, according to the crackly AM radio broadcasts she picked up during her all-too-frequent sleepless nights.

"I tried a lot of stuff in the old days." The man giggled again. It was a sound tinged with madness and sorrow. "I made a lot of money in the stock market and really took advantage, y'know? Coke, mushrooms, heroin, even mescaline; but this stuff beats it all. It's mind-blowing, like having an orgy up in Heaven with a bunch of hot angels."

Mara mumbled her vague assent. She had never tried her wares, but had heard similar colorful analogies. One professorial man had explained, "It is like introducing absinthe directly into the bloodstream, yet there is no hangover whatsoever, only a feeling of disappointment when the euphoria fades." A barefoot, dreadlocked woman had confided, "It's pure bliss. After I eat one of your 'shrooms, I feel like my brain is drizzled with THC gravy." Mara mentally filed these descriptions, and even used them on occasion with prospective customers. She had to admit "like an orgy with angels" had a certain allure to it.

"It's an escape from the hell this world has become," the former stockbroker said. He raked his fingers through his hair again. Mara wondered how soon he would start balding if the gesture became a habit. Not that it mattered; she didn't think he'd tough it out much longer. Most of her customers seemed to be that way. Turning to drugs to escape the horrors of the real world was only a temporary coping method. She guessed most of them either ran afoul of zombies, or took their own lives, swallowed up in tar pits of hopelessness and despair.

"What is it exactly?" The man's eyes glittered. "Shrooms, right? But laced with something."

Mara did not intend to give her secret away. "You deserve a break. You need this," she urged. "You have a chance to soar up above this rotten world for a while."

The man gave her a look of surprise. "Yes… yes, I do." He turned toward the door. Now that he'd been reminded of the gift in his hands, he seemed anxious to be gone, and for that Mara felt thankful. What would she have said if he had pressed her? She knew someday she would have to defend her secret. She kept a loaded handgun among other precautions against this eventuality.

"Make sure you go somewhere safe."

"Of course. Always." He left her apartment at a brisk walk and Mara chained and barred the door behind him. The warning had become her standard disclaimer. Mara concluded that some of her customers had died while taking the drug based on the uncomfortable fact that none of her customers returned more than twice despite their praise. She did not think it possible to overdose, but surmised the out-of-body experiences left users in such a helpless state that zombies sometimes attacked and killed them without their ever being aware of impending danger.

***

Zombies craved brains. So did the living.

After making this discovery, Mara had managed to live well—at least by modern standards. The world had changed. Though money had become obsolete, many still clung to it, stubbornly waiting for the day when things would go back to normal. Mara knew that day would never come.

She played all sides. She found this to be the best way to survive. Mara traded for goods and services, and kept herself on friendly terms with all factions, yet insulated herself against potential attack.

Life was good but there was so much death. Mara, always a realist, knew that death was inevitable, as was suffering, hardship, pain, and grief.

She grieved the deaths of her husband and daughter. She still grieved the deaths of her parents, though they had passed on long before the zombie outbreaks.

However, she did not grieve the deaths of the others. The ones she killed were necessary for her own survival.

Death was a bitter pill, one she swallowed out of necessity every day.

Only nagging memories of her daughter truly troubled her. She envisioned Skylar swinging at the park, stuffing popcorn into her mouth at the movies, drawing pictures at the dining room table.

In every one of Mara's memories of her daughter, Sky looked up and asked, "Why did you lie to me, Mommy? Jesus wasn't there when I needed him, and you left me. Why did you let the zombies find me?"

***

"Skylar, come here. Right now!"

Her daughter ignored her command. "I want Daddy!"

Zombies roamed downstairs. Mara had counted at least six of them as they burst through their home's front door and into the living room. Mara had raced upstairs to Skylar's room, knowing that more zombies would likely follow the first contingent. If she and Sky climbed down the vine trellis while the invaders shambled below, she thought they could lock themselves in the garden shed or the garage until the zombies grew restless and left the neighborhood.

But Skylar wasn't cooperating.

"Sky, get out of the closet. They're coming upstairs!" Mara cast a frantic glance over her shoulder. She could see the shadow of a pair of filthy bare feet through the crack between her daughter's bedroom door and the floor. The figure began pounding on the door. Mara's heartbeat seemed to match the pounding's tempo and urgency.

"We have to GO!" Mara's voice cracked on the last word. Four years of undergraduate school followed by four years of medical school meant nothing to the zombies. Three years into her residency, all hell had broken lose. What good were her skills as a neurosurgeon when just finding food, water, and shelter had become nearly impossible tasks?

The pounding became incessant and the door began to splinter on its hinges; other zombies had joined the barrage. Her years lost on a now-worthless degree weren't even the worst of it. The worst, Mara realized, was that after Sky had been born, finishing medical school and starting her residency had kept her away from home. Skylar had grown up very much Daddy's Girl. It had never bothered Mara—until now.

"Sky, baby, you have to listen to Mommy. Daddy's not here and we have to leave..."

"I only want Daddy to carry me!"

Sky's words, though muffled by the hanging clothes, wounded Mara. She knew she couldn't afford to wait any longer. She crawled on her hands and knees into the dark depths of the closet. Sky screamed and kicked out, mashing Mara's nose against her face. Fireworks filled her field of vision and she withdrew. Liquefied copper seemed to be melting down the back of her throat. She gagged and spat blood.

The door exploded inward and a trio of zombies stumbled into the room. Panicked, Mara reached far into the closet and seized her daughter's foot. She yanked, turned, and dove for the window as desiccated hands clutched at her clothing and hair.

Mara forgot about the trellis. In a moment of raw terror, she kicked off against the windowsill and dove onto the roof of the garden shed. Blackness enveloped her senses.

She awoke in the weak gray light of the pre-dawn sky lying in relative safety above the reach of any zombies. Her nose throbbed and the tissue and nerves surrounding her left shoulder howled their dismay. She assumed she had dislocated it in the fall. The pain from something else hurt worse, however. In her right hand, Mara clutched one of Skylar's shoes.

***

Mara heard the woman's screams and crept to her door, her rifle ready. Through the peephole, she recognized her latest customer. So much for getting somewhere safe before you got your fix, she thought. She threw open her door and shot a look in both directions. Seeing no zombies, and no apparent danger, she hurried over and crouched beside the writhing woman.

"Dear God! Kill me!" The woman shook as if suffering a seizure. Saliva dribbled from her mouth onto the filthy hallway carpet.

"What's wrong?" Mara looked the woman over, but refrained from touching her. "Where does it hurt?"

"In my soul!" The woman's eyes bulged from their sockets. Her hands shook. "So much pain, so much sorrow."

"I don't understand. From what?"

"What the fuck did you give me?" her customer moaned. "Pain, isolation, regret. I ca-ah-ah-ah-ah—" Mara guessed the woman had suffered a psychotic break. Blood vessels had burst in her eyes, creating bloody red clouds that encroached on the blue skies of her irises. Her pupils had become pinpricks.

Mara stood, realizing her assumptions had been wrong. She thought zombie attacks accounted for the customers who never returned. It had never occurred to her that users suffered bad trips. Perhaps it was possible to overdose, after all. Her harvested tissue provided a temporary ascent to ecstasy—or an unbearable descent into agony. Unfortunately, she had no way of knowing which experience awaited the user.

In a rare act of mercy, Mara aimed and pulled the trigger. Then she slung the rifle onto her back. Her ears rang from the report as she dragged the dead woman by her wrists down the hallway and out into the alley for disposal.

***

"I hear you're the woman to see about a drug that puts all others to shame."

Her latest customer stood nearly a foot taller than her. Mara bet he outweighed her by at least eighty pounds. He grinned as he spoke. She did not like his grin. There was no warmth in it, not even a look of desperate merriment.

"I may have something that fits the bill." Mara edged away from her visitor, affecting a coolness she did not feel. "What do you have to trade?"

"Don't you take cash?" The man cocked his head sideways as if confused.

"Not much use for it these days. I usually trade for watches, jewelry..." Mara paused. The man had strolled between her and the handgun she had left on a shelf. Her rifle stood against the wall by the door. She cursed her carelessness. "But I immediately trade those items for food, clean water, and supplies."

"You're lying." The man pocketed her handgun and gave her a hyena-like sneer.

"I'm not! And that's mine. You can't take—"

"Hush up and listen." The man put a finger to his lips. "I'm not here to hurt you. I want you to hear me out without getting all defensive and waving a gun in my face, okay?"

The four chambers of her heart thundered like the hooves of a galloping horse. She prayed her voice wouldn't crack. "Okay."

"Good. Now here's what I propose. You could use a business partner, someone to watch your back. You need someone to protect you from robbery—and worse. That person is me."

"You're saying you'd be my bodyguard."

Anger darkened the man's features. He shook his head. "No! I would be your partner. I get fifty percent of the take and you get to keep on keepin' on."

Mara considered and took a step forward. "That has potential. What's your name, anyway?"

"Don't worry about it."

"Okay, Don't-Worry-About-It, you've got a deal. I have a question though. How do you feel about sex?" She bit her bottom lip and lifted her eyes to his. "I've been on my own for a looong time."

The tall man's eyes widened. "Get over here." His voice sounded husky and ragged.

Mara strolled across the workshop floor, sizing up her chances. When she reached the man, he withdrew her handgun and she recoiled, eyes wide.

"Just relax," the man said, "and don't try anything stupid."

Mara studied his face for several moments. Then she knelt and unbuttoned his jeans. She unzipped his fly and his erection sprang out at her like a sausage jack-in-the-box. She felt her gorge rise as a pungent odor hit her. The man apparently had not showered in weeks. She overcame the urge to gag and circled her fingers around his erection.

Mara felt a cold circle of metal on her skin. The man had pressed the barrel of her handgun to her forehead.

"Don't be a tease, darlin'. You know what to do."

Mara gazed past the gun and looked into the man's eyes. She opened her mouth, wide and inviting, her tongue resting within like a pink satin pillow. She lifted her left hand as if to brace her right wrist and pressed a small switch instead. A dagger blade shot out of her sleeve and severed his erection as it slid into place. The man yowled and pulled the trigger. She heard the gun dry-click against her forehead. He tried again.

Mara tossed the deflated penis over her shoulder. Blood spurted from the raw stump in gouts. The man swung the barrel of the handgun against the side of her head and her surroundings blurred. He turned and stooped to retrieve his lost manhood. Still seeing double, Mara raised the dagger and dove forward. She slashed the blade against his Achilles tendon. The man sprawled onto the floor, bellowing obscenities. Mara leapt again but her attacker swung his elbow, caught her forearm, and knocked her away. Pain lanced through the limb, but she had endured much worse. She scrambled onto the man's back and buried the dagger partway into his spine. Knowing she was running on waning adrenaline, she thrust the blade into his spine below the neck twice more, finally damaging his spinal cord enough to paralyze him.

She collapsed to the floor beside her attacker and lay there panting. "Next time you steal... someone's gun, you... ought to check... if it's loaded or not."

After another minute she regained her feet, stooped, and rolled the man onto his back. He gazed past her at the cobwebbed ceiling. Mara could see shock taking hold. "Ever hear of something called a Gambler's Draw? It was a bitch to make, and it's dangerous to wear, but it sure saved my ass today, didn't it?"

"I only wanted to be your p-partner," the man whined.

"I've got a different position in mind for you, asshole," Mara said. "Zombie bait."

***

Two weeks and three successful zombie kills later, Mara crouched in an alley behind an overflowing dumpster. She watched a band of survivors march past, patrolling the streets. They were all armed, and she knew if they encountered any zombies, they would shoot to kill without hesitation.

And they'll make a mess of things while doing it, Mara thought. In most cases after these groups made kills, she couldn't salvage anything from the cadavers. The brains had to be removed intact.

Mara visualized her harvesting process. She used the cranial saw to remove the top half of each zombie's skull. Then she severed the brain stem at the base of the skull. She removed the entire brain, flipped it upside down, and removed the temporal lobe. This allowed her to access the much narrower limbic lobe. This she always extracted with utmost care. In life, the limbic lobe regulated emotions. According to her customers, in death—or undeath—it contained a lifetime of happiness in concentrated form. She hung the harvested lobes on a rustic wooden clothes-drying rack until they dehydrated. There was a method to it, like drying fruit or smoking jerky.

Much to her frustration, bullet slugs—and even the occasional crowbar or baseball bat—did too much damage to zombies' brains. Out of necessity, she hunted alone.

Mara wished these roving bands would find somewhere else to patrol. They inhibited her livelihood. She watched in silence as this latest group trailed away down the street and disappeared around a corner. Her eyes slid to the other end of the block in search of prey.

A door opened in her subconscious and a mental image came to her with such force that she fell back on the dirty concrete, stunned. Pain lanced up from her tailbone, but she pushed the feeling away. She'd visualized a revolving door. A man and zombie chased each other in an endless circle. The man fled the zombie, yes. The man could also represent one of her customers seeking escape from real-world troubles. And what helped him escape? Zombie brains, specifically the limbic lobes.

The zombie, in turn, chased the man. Everyone knew the undead craved brains, but no one knew why. Could it be for the same reason? Mara trembled with excitement. Did zombies instinctively try to escape their futile existence by ingesting new memories and emotions found in the brains of their victims?

Mara rose to her feet, intent on returning to her workshop to consider this new idea further. She turned and stopped cold, confronted by a nightmare she never thought possible.

A zombie had shambled to within arm's length. It stood there, glowering up at her through milky eyes. Half of its face had been torn away. Dried gore had congealed around the zombie's gaping maw. A once-pink t-shirt was now torn, grimy, and encrusted in dried blood. The zombie's fingernails had all sheared off, leaving bony stubs protruding from filthy, desiccated fingers.

Still, Mara thought she recognized those fingers, the nails chewed away by a scared little girl huddled on a sofa and asking about her daddy and about Jesus. Mara glanced down and confirmed her fear.

The diminutive zombie still wore one tattered shoe.

Tears blurring her vision, Mara knelt and held her arms open as Skylar stepped closer.

***

Time crawled, a snail laboring through molasses. Seconds passed like minutes, minutes felt like hours, and days masqueraded as weeks. Mara lived her life in a haze, hunting zombies on autopilot, and dispensing doses of ecstasy—or insanity—with curt brevity.

Embracing her daughter, only to betray her with the twist of a blade had been the hardest thing she had ever done. Nevertheless, the decision she had made next had pushed her resolve further than she had ever thought possible. She needed to see, needed to know, and the only way to know was to experience the memories herself.

Mara had brought Skylar home in the wheelbarrow and eased her into the recliner in the workshop. Skylar had looked tiny nestled in the recliner. Mara had stroked her daughter's cheeks, no longer fearful of being bit and infected. Violent sobs shook her until her tear ducts gave up, unable to keep pace with her guilt and sorrow. At last,

Mara had plugged the cranial saw into the generator and sat down to her task.

Bone dust and the odor of burned hair had permeated the room by the time she'd finished. Mara had removed her daughter's brain, extracted the limbic lobe and had left it hanging in the drying room apart from the others.

That had been a month prior.

Now Mara sat alone in the same bloodstained recliner; a dealer about to sample her product for the first and last time. She fingered the dried brain matter, so mushroom-like in texture. It looked and felt enough like hallucinogenic fungi that she understood how so many of her clients could have missed the truth. Or perhaps, deep down, some of them had known but had not wanted to acknowledge the inconvenient reality.

"They're encephaloshrooms," Mara muttered. "That's marketing gold." She laughed without mirth.

In carrying out the details of the sentence she had handed down upon herself, Mara had intentionally left her door unlocked; if someone living came to rob her, so be it. If one of the undead intruded upon her while the drug swept her away, so be that as well. She had made her peace with both possibilities.

Right now only one thing mattered. Mara needed to see herself through her daughter's eyes. She would witness what kind of life Skylar had lived. Had she been happy or miserable? Had she felt loved or ignored? Mara would experience it firsthand in one concentrated dose. But would the revelation bring her jubilation or retribution?

Mara pressed the dried shred of brain onto her tongue like a communion wafer and closed her eyes. She chewed, swallowed, and attempted to prepare herself for whatever came next.

15 Blood in the Water by Emmet O'Cuana

Tom kept one eye on his son in the back of the car as he drove. Stanley slept through most of the journey. Occasionally he would stir to the sound of Tom's wife crying. Charlotte made a soft and wet keening sound that made broke Tom's heart.

Tom's son slept and dreamed faraway dreams, his wife sobbed, and outside the family vehicle the living hid in their homes, motionless, terrified—and the dead walked.

When morning came, he watched as Stanley awoke and rubbed his eyes, squinting out the window in the morning light. The car was now crossing a bridge across a grey, choppy sea. A thick mist obscured the road ahead.

Tom was exhausted. He had driven all night without a break, fear chasing him to this remote island off the west coast of Ireland that he had a dim memory of from a childhood holiday. It was a mad hope that had brought them here, but then the world had become mad.

He realized he was gripping the wheel so hard he was fixed into his seat, tensed, vibrating in concert with the engine.

Charlotte looked hollowed out by shock. She had said little else over the night except to mention the thought of eating made her nauseous.

But Stanley had slept through the worst of it. He had not seen the bodies by the roadside, the burning homes near the motorway, or the train swarmed by a horde of those things. He had slept and dreamed, while Tom and Charlotte had not been able to close their eyes all night. The car engine had muffled the screams. The memories would remain for them.

"Where are we?" Stanley asked. The voice of his son almost made Tom drive through the guard-rail into the sea. The spell was broken.

"You remember I showed you the map of Mayo?" Tom replied before prompting, "It's a safe place for us."

"We're on a holiday, Stanley," said Charlotte, giving her husband a meaningful look.

Ahead was the island. There was a man standing at the end of the bridge. The car slowed to a stop.

***

Minutes passed. It felt like hours to Tom. Was this one of the creatures? He sat frozen in his seat, his foot resting on the clutch. If the island was not safe after all, he had no idea where else to go. If the things were here, too, there was nowhere left. Had he dragged his family across the countryside for nothing at all, survived against all odds only to meet a lonely end here? The stranger raised his right arm and waved. Time relaxed.

***

Stanley watched Charlotte give his father a reassuring squeeze on the arm. It was a private moment between them that was strange to him, a child, used to having their undivided attention. He did not like it.

Tom unbuckled his seatbelt and exited the car. The fog was so thick he seemed to vanish for a moment. Then a gust of wind cleared the way. His father and the stranger were only a few feet apart, speaking to one another.

"Mummy, who is that?"

"Shhh!"

Stanley knew enough to be quiet, but leaned forward, squeezing between the driver and passenger seats to watch. His mother reached back and gripped his right shoulder, hard. Her fear was being broadcast within the confines of their car with her every ragged breath, each shivering twitch of her arm, but to Stanley it was all just noise. He had always been a poor observer of the world outside of his own immediate concerns.

The man waved to the car and then walked back the way he had come. Stanley watched Tom turn and smile grimly at him and his mother.

"Oh," Charlotte said simply. "Oh." She rubbed her belly tenderly.

"You've gotten fat, mummy," said Stanley.

***

Charlotte promised herself she would tell Stanley that she was pregnant when she knew they were safe. He was a jealous child. A brother or sister would not be made welcome by Stanley. The world had ended, the dead were killing the living, and nothing much made sense anymore.

If her son's frequent emotional outbursts were added to all of this, any hope of keeping her calm would be destroyed. She felt so tired.

Only a boy so self-absorbed could have slept so soundly in their car that night. Charlotte loved her son. He was her flesh and blood. She had made peace some time ago that he was a little shit.

***

Mick had lived on the island his whole life. Before the Trouble started—he had reclaimed that particular expression for the mass slaughter of the living by the rotting dead, now that they had done for Catholics, Protestants and everyone else in the country—he had rarely visited the mainland.

"Not likely to ever again now, eh?" he said cheerfully, as he threw another lump of peat on the fire.

His guests huddled together on the thin carpet by the fire to warm themselves. Mick's home was a small stone building with a thatch roof. The man himself looked every inch the Man of Aran, postcard-friendly stereotype Charlotte remembered from regional news programs on national broadcaster RTE. She and Tom had that softness in appearance of a comfortable city life in Dublin. Standing by the fire, dressed in a woollen geansaí, raincoat and worn jeans, clean-shaven and with kind eyes—Mick could have been the romantic hero of a Maeve Binchy novel Charlotte had read as a teenager.

"Yes, haven't seen anybody here for a while now. Your car was the first across that bridge since this whole business started. I understand, I suppose. Some felt they could defend their homes when it started. They thought it would all be over soon. But I knew it wouldn't be. Not Trouble like this. The dead and all," he chuckled, "that's too much trouble for anyone."

Mick was all alone on the island. There had been others, old families like his, descendants of fishermen that had lived here for centuries. But the homes of his one-time neighbours were empty now. The dark inflection in his voice brooked no further questions on the matter. They were not likely to come back. Charlotte made a note of that. The strangeness of this situation right now was less of a priority than the dead rising.

"But you are safe here," he said, with those kindly brown eyes lit by the fire. "Safe as a marquess in his castle."

Charlotte smiled tightly, her husband hugging her to him. Mick gave the boy a brief glance, and for the briefest moment his expression changed from a welcoming smile to a frown. Charlotte had no idea what that meant. Why did Mick feel sorry for Stanley? Hadn't he just said they were safe?

After the family had warmed themselves sufficiently Mick served them dinner. Fish stew. "Get used to it," their host laughed.

***

The island quickly became a home and, until the day by the rock pool, Stanley continued to be oblivious to the disaster that had overtaken their lives and was not afraid.

He found the island to be an ideal playground. Stanley was not lonely and did not miss the company of other children. He had always been a solitary child. When his schoolmates had chased each other around the yard, or kicked a ball around, teachers used to find him tucked into a corner of the classroom reading a large book he'd lugged about in his bag. He was oddly proud of his bookishness, saw it as an achievement of sorts. He chose to ignore that the other children did not want to play with him. The books he read did not have pictures or large type. He read stories that he assumed grown-ups would read. He did not meet many book-readers.

On the island, in the absence of any other children and with a paucity of reading material, Stanley discovered the joys of running, of hiding, and exploring the rocky grassland of his new home. This island was his schoolyard now and, without the distraction of the printed page, he began to invent games for his own amusement.

Sometimes his mother Charlotte would come and find him before dinner. That in itself was a game for Stanley, hiding and giggling as his mother shouted herself hoarse. Every now and then, Mick would be the one to track him down. Mick was always smiling, friendly, happy to see a child at play once more on the island. He didn't mind looking for him. But he gave Stanley a stern warning.

"Stay away from the beaches and caves down by the water, son. It gets rough out there and the sea could take you away in a jiffy!"

There was a cluster of empty homes on the raised hillock of the island, perfect for looking down on the wide blue ocean and affording a good view of the bridge to the mainland. In the mornings Mick would sit on a stool outside, smoke some of his quickly diminishing store of tobacco in a favorite pipe, and gaze out across the sea.

Stanley's family moved into a small house near Mick's. They received food and clothing salvaged from the other homes. Stanley did not think about the missing people, or ask his parents where they had gone.

He would see Tom staring at the bridge as though trying to see something, sometimes standing on his tippy-toes. Eventually his father stopped after Mick began laughing at him so hard he had a coughing fit. "Sure we're protected here," Stanley heard Mick say to Tom, and then "the neamh-mairbh have never set foot on this island." Only then did Tom unpack the car. Stanley did not ask what that word in his native language meant. He was not interested.

Stanley did notice that Mick would vanish sometimes. He would vanish, usually just before the sun went down, then reappear, all smiles, often with the evening meal of fresh cod. The light of a fire would be seen from inside his home, a few repeated bars of an old sea shanty echoing out into the warm night, the smell of peat smoke, and shortly afterwards they would hear his call to dinner.

One evening, when the smiles and laughter came more easily to Stanley's parents, Tom asked Mick if he could join him fishing someday.

"Oh now, don't worry about that," said Mick, knocking his pipe against the table to dislodge ash and embers. "Let me take care of that. You get comfortable and take your ease for a while longer yet. We'll have plenty of chores before winter, I assure you!"

"But we'll be home by then," said Stanley, laughing.

The adults all stopped and looked at the boy. Their faces were fixed in expressions of sadness. He only then in that moment knew the truth.

"We're not going home, are we?"

"Darling, it is just not safe," Charlotte said. She reached out to him and he jumped out of his chair, staring at her like a hunted animal.

"Don't be mad…something very bad is happening back home," his mother said. "Some very bad people were hurting our neighbors, Stanley. It was too dangerous for us there, so we ran away."

"You're safe now, son," said Mick. "You are all welcome to stay here for as long as you want. The bad people won't find you here."

Stanley started to shout at them at the top of his lungs. His head was hot with rage and he felt sick in his stomach like he was about to vomit. They did what they could to calm him. He hated Tom then—Tom who was weak, who would flutter his hands like a shirt on a clothesline in the wind and only make Stanley angrier; Charlotte the woman who could barely raise her voice even when she tried. He had been trapped with these two weaklings and now they were stuck on an island in the middle of nowhere. No more books, no more movies. It was all so unfair! When he stopped, Stanley just fixed Tom and Charlotte with a stare full of hate.

Awkward goodnights followed, the adults trying to extricate themselves as politely as possible following his outburst. Mick was mortified. Stanley didn't care. He wanted to go to the home they had left behind, to his own bed with its warm blankets, instead of the small cold room waiting for him in a cramped island cottage. That night he lay still for hours and listened to the waves.

***

Tomorrow he would tell them, Mick told himself. Tomorrow. For the boy's sake. He looked at the worn sack he used to bring the gift of fish back up the hill. The time would be coming round again soon. He decided to give them another day. He knew Tom and Charlotte would make the right decision, break the cycle the island had been trapped in for so long. The dead were walking on the mainland, but an older evil had claimed this place as its home long before. There was a price to be paid for safe refuge.

***

Stanley left the house in the early morning. His parents were still in their room. Mick was nowhere to be seen. He made for the sound of the waves, walking down the hill. The path led down to the rock pools.

It was cold and crisp. The dew on the grass made him slip and lose his footing once or twice before he began to step more carefully. Sharp rocks jutted out from the boggy ground. Stanley had a vision of sliding down and smacking his head against one, cracking his skull open. His parents wouldn't find him for hours. He imagined them seeing the blond hair of a cold corpse matted with blood and the island winds snatching away their miserable sobs. The thought of their grief made him smile.

He made slower, more careful progress, grasping the long grass and emerging rocks to balance himself. The smell of sea air filled his nostrils and he felt excited to be exploring by himself. Mick's warning about the sea rang in his ears, but he didn't care. This small rebellion felt good. Life on the island was remaking him and he walked with a more confident step. Sucking cold air down into his lungs gave him a sense of exhilaration that movies watched from his bed had never matched.

He followed the little dirt path at a quickening pace, glad to be free of the treacherous soft and slippery earth of the slope. Round the bend it went and then he saw it—a small inlet, with sheer rock faces on both sides, a stretch of white sand and rocks in between. It was low tide and an outcrop of rocks ringed the beach containing a small pool of stagnant water.

And there was something in the rock pool. Stanley thought of a scarecrow cut down from its post, but he knew what this was. A body. The body of a man washed up on the pale sand.

Stanley started running towards it—gulls shrieking in the sky, the wind threatening to knock him off the path and down to the crash of waves below—he ran until his chest hurt and his nostrils were stinging from the abrasive salt air.

Stanley the bookish nerd would have run and called for an adult. Stanley the boy reborn on the island saw the opportunity for a real-life adventure

He jumped from the path down to the beach and there it was. But the body had been moved. It was on the dry sand, further away from the receding tide. At first Stanley thought a wave had caught it, thrown it forward on to the beach.

But the water was calm, a placid wet surface. The sand was darkly stained, tracking from the body to the water's edge. And the body had no legs. It was a torso with arms, and no legs.

"Hello?" Stanley said, quietly, gently, not expecting an answer.

And it reared up on its two arms, a ruin of a face, eyeless sockets and a bloodied mouth, a howl of recognition from its throat. Stanley screamed. The gulls joined in.

***

He heard his father shouting. He did not understand the rush of words; their meaning escaped him. The roar of anger was so alien to the kindly, too-gentle man he knew. A stranger was yelling with his father's voice.

Stanley was disappointed to find himself in the small, now familiar, cottage bedroom. He was sure it had all been a nightmare, that he would wake up back at home, safe from the fears left unspoken by his parents—the "bad men" that had forced them to leave everything—safe from the monster on the beach. The memory of the dead man who came crawling for him rushed back. Stanley moaned and outside the room there was a sudden hush. The door opened and his mother appeared.

Her face, red eyes and pale teary cheeks, hair wild like she had been running her fingers through it and pulling hard, was a picture of complete shock.

"Mum….?" Stanley whimpered, and no other words came, he felt a pressure on his chest, a sense of rising panic and then tears. She rushed to the side of the bed and cradled him to her as he sobbed.

"You're safe, you're safe, it's gone now, you're safe with me," she said, rocking him, his face pressed up against her jumper, tears soaking the woolen fabric, a mother's warmth and a boy's wet cheeks.

He heard his father enter the room.

"Charlotte…?"

"Deal with him!" she said in a hiss.

Tom left the room, his expression a flux of concern and anger. Stanley let sleep take him, hoping that maybe he would wake up back at home this time. He no longer wanted to take part in any adventures the island had for him. He did not wonder where Mick was.

***

"No, no, no, no!"

He woke in the middle of the night to the sound of his parents whispering, crying, pleading with one another. Their fright, their sadness, compounded and became magnified within him. He could not tell if it was his mother or his father whose words had woken him. One was begging the other, but he could not understand what they were saying.

***

Mick did not appear for several days after that. Stanley assumed his father visited him, because now in the evenings he would come home with a fish for dinner.

Without Mick the prospect of meals became more difficult—neither of Stanley's parents knew how to properly prepare a fish. Back in Dublin fish came battered and wrapped in grease paper, or crumbed and frozen in a cardboard box. Stanley eventually got used to detecting bones with his tongue and leaving them on the plate.

"Eat up, Stanley," his mother said each evening. "Eat everything on the plate. You need your strength."

She encouraged him to go out and play, but Stanley was still too frightened. He thought of the man, the dead man, on the beach. And he remembered something else. The bite marks on the face, large, not like a fish's, but still smaller than a shark. He had pored over pictures of these constantly moving predators of the sea in a school textbook, measured the diameter of a shark's jaw with his ruler during a lunch break spent hidden away in the library.

After a week, Stanley and his mother left the cottage together. They went for a walk across the island, staying well away from the beach. Instead, they followed a narrow stone path, large enough for a horse and cart. Stanley's mother held his hands and told him stories about the island she had learned, about how it had been settled by fishermen who sold their wares on the mainland to pay their rent. He imagined growing up here—well he guessed now he was—but back then before the monsters, when there was the option to one day leave. Few had apparently. Life on the island had been a comfortable one for its small population until the Trouble had started. His mother told him about that, too. That the bad men they had run away from were not just bad men, they were dead men who walked and ate the living. To hear her speak it sounded like a bedtime story.

"Zombie" was a new word for Stanley. Knowing the name of the thing he had met gave him a sense of control. It was just another monster.

She was still talking when he saw the girl. She appeared just over a rise, dark black hair and a pale face, looking right at him. "Mum," he said, "Mummy!" tugging on her arm and pointing. His mother followed his outstretched hand—she had to see the girl, had to. There was a sudden rush of movement and the girl was gone.

"Was that a zombie, mummy?" Stanley said.

"I didn't see anything, dear," she said.

"Mum! She was there, a girl." His mother shook her head and Stanley impatiently let go of her hand and ran across the field, up towards the small rise. He was almost there when he heard the roar of the ocean. He stopped, and that now-familiar tightness in his chest seized him. Stanley turned around and walked back to his mother.

"It was probably a bird, Stanley," she said. "The dead can't come here. We're safe, remember?"

***

Stanley went out for walks more often, but now finally alone. His mother didn't seem to mind. He saw Mick, too, briefly. Stanley noticed the faint traces of a fading black eye. The adults were not talking to one another anymore. Whatever had happened, his parents and Mick kept it from him and did not even pretend at civility. But one thing Stanley was sure of was that it had been Mick who saved him from the zombie at the rock pool.

Mick was strong. He had lived here all his life, survived even after the start of the Trouble, and still he was not afraid. Stanley was certain Mick had rescued him and was the real reason they were safe on the island. Maybe Tom and Charlotte would leave the island, once the dead had rotted away entirely, of course, and Mick could be his father.

He did not see the girl during his walks, but he looked for her. Perhaps there was another family somewhere, hidden away.

One afternoon the sky became overcast and just as suddenly rain began pouring down. Stanley ran, half-blind, across a muddy field. The winds that swept down across the low island buffeted him, soaking him in sheets of rain. He made it back to the cottages and saw Mick, standing alone and unbent in the wild weather, shielding his eyes to look out at the bridge to the mainland. Stanley turned to try and make out what the man was looking at. Through the rising mist and the wet he saw them. There was a mass of bodies, slowly making their way across the steel bridge. Zombies.

"Go inside to your parents, boy," said Mick. "Go inside and get yourself out of those wet clothes. I'll take care of it."

"We should hide—maybe down in the caves!"

"No! You stay away from the water, Stanley. You don't go down there. Be a good lad, help your family, they'll need you now. They'll make the right choice for you—they're good people, your parents. Not like the people who lived here."

Mick spoke firmly, but without anger or sadness. Stanley did not know what the man could do, why he was so sure of himself. He did not know what Mick meant about the people who used to live on the island. Of course his parents were good. They were his parents. It was Tom and Charlotte's job to be kind to him. He heard Mick whisper "This is impossible," and then—

"Go inside now!"

With that, Mick set off, down the path towards the bridge.

Stanley turned and ran in to the cottage. "They're coming," he yelped, and his parents hugged him, brought him through to their bedroom and asked what he had seen.

Charlotte fetched a towel to dry him while Tom paced the room nervously. The storm broke across the island in earnest, but over the crashing of the sea and the howling of the wind Stanley could hear the creatures moaning in the distance, getting ever closer.

"Did he say anything to you, Stanley?" Tom asked. He looked up at him, this man who was looking at him in an odd, almost nervous way, as if he could barely bring himself to meet his own child's gaze. "Did Mick tell you what to do?"

"No, Dad…he just said to help you." And Tom let out a sob and ran his fingers through his son's hair.

A loud, crashing roar shook the cottage. Mother, father and child screamed. It felt as if the island was about to be swept away by the storm. A shriek of metal cut through the bellowing confusion—and something else, a high-pitched wail that chilled Stanley to hear.

Hours later the storm and its unnatural violence passed, the winds died, and calm descended.

Charlotte left the bedroom. Stanley heard the sound of the front door creaking, his mother's boots scuffing the stony path outside and then the strangest sound—her throaty laughter, the sound of birthdays and Christmas. Stanley and Tom emerged out to a changed world. The sun was shining, the waters around the island were calm and blue—and where the bridge once stood was a wreck of torn steel.

Of Mick and the zombies there was no sign.

***

Tom let his hand rest on her stomach, felt the kick. He smiled down at Charlotte and they laughed together, that old familiar sound they used to share as one. "We have to do it," she said. And he knew she was right. He hated that she was right. Mick had saved them all once again, using the darkest rite in the island's Commonplace book. Now the only living souls left on the island were Charlotte and himself, their unborn child—and Stanley.

***

As his mother's belly swelled, Stanley tried to do what Mick asked of him. He scavenged for supplies from the neighboring houses, helped around the house, made his mother hot water boiled over the fire in an ancient black pot, and went out with his father to cut turf. He stayed away from the sea. But even though he tried to be helpful, nothing he could do seemed to make them happy. His mother was given to short blasts of anger that Stanley could never predict. His father's moods were dark, constant, and the air seemed to hum with resentment whenever he was nearby. Stanley learned to stay outdoors most of the day.

Having to please his parents was a new and unusual activity for the boy—not as much fun as the games he had begun to enjoy before the storm tore down the bridge, running and hiding and teasing the adults to distraction. He was trying to be a "good boy"—and he was not very good at it.

The balmy weather and calm seas that had followed the strange night when Mick had vanished held for weeks. In the distance Stanley would see the occasional zombie wandering across the mainland peninsula. They would appear lost, sad even, aimlessly shuffling through the wilderness—hunters without a home to return to, a family to feed, or a fire to sleep beside.

Mick never returned. And Stanley's parents did not go out to look for him. They pretended otherwise, but Stanley was certain Tom and Charlotte knew exactly what had happened to the kindly man who had welcomed them to the island. Their hostility towards him made Stanley feel truly alone for the first time and he had begun to consider his situation here on the island a little more carefully. Mick was dead, Stanley was sure of it.

Tom brought the fish for dinner. He had no rod. Stanley did not ask about it, but not because he had not noticed. Now he knew not to speak if he could help it. Questions just made his father angry. On the days when he walked across the island by himself, the air growing colder with each day, Stanley could feel he was being watched. He knew it was her, the strange girl with the pale skin and dark hair. And in the distance he would hear the sea pounding on the rocks and taste salt on the air, like a promise made that was still to be kept.

***

In the end it was Tom who did the deed and performed the sacrifice. The cold night air announced the approach of a bitter winter. The time was set. Mick had prepared Charlotte and him for what had to be done on this evening, explained each step of the ritual. He went to collect the rope from Mick's house, the home of the island protector where it had rested for generations. He woke his son after midnight and made him get dressed. Then he led Stanley out into the night. The boy was unusually quiet. He did not ask where they were going. Instead he seemed to be listening. When they found the coastal path Stanley began to tug on Tom's sleeve, urging him to go back the way they came.

He picked his son up, held him over his shoulder and kept walking. He ignored Stanley's shouts and only grunted once when a flailing foot connecting with his chest. Tom remembered the morning Mick came back carrying Stanley and shouting about the pact with the people below the waves. He remembered the sick realization of where he had brought his family, and how the man he thought was their friend offered no resistance as Tom beat him. How many generations before Tom's family had tried to fight against the island before realizing there was no fighting the doom of that place? The island was safe. It always had been a refuge for those with nowhere else to run to in the wider world. People found their way there. More would come, perhaps with a boat. It had happened before, during times of war, occupation and famine. Zombies were simply the latest suffering to strike Ireland. Ochón agus ochón ó and all that.

Tom had agreed to the sequence—Stanley, himself and his wife—a deadly and torturous arithmetic demanded by the Commonplace book. And then, if there was no one left living on the mainland to be drawn here, the people below the waves would come for the child three winters hence.

Mick had done right by them. He had kept the pact and eliminated the threat from the mainland into the bargain by offering himself up as sacrifice. The allotted season had rolled around again too soon. The price would be paid twice this year.

Stanley was screaming again, but in a panic now, as the sound of the ocean came ever closer.

Tom made fast work of it. He had hammered in the stake the week before, to let the island's masters know what he was planning. He threw the body of his still-screaming son to the wet ground, stunning the child, and then tied him securely to the stake. Trussed up like a deer after the hunt. Another year of food. Another year of safety. He had bought his family time.

Tom walked away from the boy's cries and followed the path back up to the cottage where he would spend the rest of his life. He got undressed in the dark and slipped into bed beside his wife.

"It's done," he said, and kissed her shoulder. Charlotte took his hand and pressed it to her belly.

***

They came for Stanley before dawn. Dark hair, deep eyes and pale skin. He saw the girl. She smiled at him with her sharp teeth.

"I don't know, Ray," Allie said, as she lowered her binoculars. "It pretty looks quiet to me. There are two or three shambling around the mouth of the railroad tunnel."

"Two or three we can handle," Ray whispered, out of habit, as he fingered the handle of his katana. "But do you remember that tunnel in Westport?"

"How could I forget that shit storm? I miss those mountain bikes. They could haul ass," she said, as she slowly slid back down the embankment on her belly. She quietly drew her own katana as she got to her feet.

"There is a bike shop just on the other side of the train trestle in Harpers Ferry. If we're lucky, it won't be empty," Ray said, as he started to quietly move. "We'll follow the C&O towpath along the Potomac here and bypass that tunnel. It will loop around to the bridge."

The two moved along in the silence of experience. All their gear was stowed and padded for stealth. When they rounded the bend and saw two of the undead on the towpath ahead they didn't miss a beat. Without even breaking pace they decapitated them both.

One was a woman in a filthy yellow sun dress that was incongruous in the cool autumn air of late October. The other was a man in a state of long decay and desiccation.

As always, Allie quickly and efficiently searched the bodies as Ray watched for threats. The woman had a purse still hanging across her shoulder diagonally. Allie dumped it out and discarded everything except a full tube of Chapstick and a quality fingernail clipper.

The man's pockets were empty but he was wearing a policemen's gun belt. The holster was empty, but the belt had a single .357 magnum round still secured in it.

Allie drew it out like it was made of glass or gold and held it up to the light to examine it. When her eyes shifted to Ray, his smile was wide.

"Three," was all he said as she stood and drew her stainless steel Ruger SP101 from its holster and expertly opened the drum. It contained two rounds. This addition made three.

Allie reholstered as they began to move.

"Don't say it," she whispered.

"Say what?"

"You always say it. 'Save the last two for us'."

"I don't always say it."

"When it comes to my .357 you do." Allie shook her head. "We each have 12 rounds in our ARs and you still have like fifty rounds of 9mm for your Glock."

"I don't always say it."

Allie fell silent then because the train trestle bridge came into view. "Ray, look."

In the center of the bridge were four train cars about three hundred feet from each end of the bridge. Allie looked through her binoculars. There were two tankers of some kind, a passenger car, and a freight car.

"Looks like we can get across. We should get moving. We need to find a place to bed down before dark," she said, and Ray nodded.

***

"Dammit," Ray cursed quietly. "There used to be stairs that went up to the trestle here for the Appalachian Trail crossing." They looked up farther. "We'll go to the tracks up by this end of the tunnel and double back."

Ray led the way and as they moved the wind picked up. Autumn leaves were filling the air as the breeze turned into a constant wind.

They emerged onto the tracks before they realized that not all the sound was from the rustling leaves. They were only a dozen yards from the gaping maw of the tunnel when *they* began to emerge. First a few, then a dozen, and suddenly hundreds.

They didn't wait to count.

They moved carefully so they didn't stumble on the railroad ties. On the bridge the eight-inch gaps between the ties had nothing but air below. These gaps forced them to be careful but drastically slowed the hungry horde behind them. The front line would trip and fall over and over again. The ones too slow to rise would be overrun and crushed into the path.

A few hundred feet onto the bridge, someone had nailed plywood onto the tracks between the ties, allowing them to move fast.

Until they saw the words spray painted on the bridge:
WARNING: Trap ahead.

They came to a section where two sheets of plywood were painted with faded orange spray paint, outlining the edges. In the center it said: TRAP: Don't Step Here!

They could see on the outside of the rails that the ties were gone here. The rails had "SAFE SAFE SAFE SAFE SAFE SAFE SAFE SAFE" written along the tops.

A sign to the side said, "Use the Rope."

There was a rope hanging down from high above, on the trestle, on the far side of the trap. But it was tied off loosely near their feet. Allie lifted the rope.

Behind them they could hear feet, now on the plywood, coming their way.

"GO!" was all Ray said, as he turned toward the zombies moving toward them.

With the help of the rope to stabilize her she moved quickly across the rail like a balance beam.

Ray only had to dispatch one zombie before he turned and began across the rail without the rope. Allie swung him the rope just as the first zombie set foot on the trap.

As he slipped through the trapdoor like a chute he got a hand on Ray's ankle and dragged him off the rail just as he got his hand on the rope.

Like lemmings, dozens of zombies fell to the shallow river far below. The trap door was counterbalanced and reset whenever another zombie set foot on it. Ray and Allie stood there like bait as they fell, one after another, to the river below, their bodies drifting away in the strong current of the shallow rapids.

After about fifteen minutes all the zombies that were still able to move had fallen into the trap.

"That's brilliant," Allie said as the trapdoor reset for the last time. "It's quiet. It resets automatically without power. Brilliant."

"I bet there is another one at the far end," Ray said. "Look at this." He drew away a blue tarp. Underneath was a dolly made to roll along on the rails. There were about twenty-five cases of canned food under the tarp. "This would roll right over that trap with supplies."

"Come on," Allie said. "Let's go find this genius."

The freight car was closest to them. The sliding door was slightly ajar and they peeked in as they walked by. More dusty cases of canned food filled half the car.

The passenger car was next in line but the stairs on the end had been blocked with corrugated metal panels. It looked like an enclosed passage had been established into the freight car on the end.

The first tanker car was for water. Above, a large inverted canopy, hanging upside down from the train trestle, functioned as a huge rain catchment system.

"Ray, this last tanker is propane," Allie said. "And there is another one of the twelve-feet-long cargo dollies under that tarp. And bikes!"

There was a lean-to style tarp set up over a rack with a dozen or so bikes.

"I think we are going to stay here tonight," Ray said.

***

The passenger cars had curtains drawn all along both sides. And no easy and obvious way to enter. They went back to the freight car and slid the door open enough to climb up. It was dark inside. Cases of supplies filled most of the end toward the passenger car, including tools and 55-gallon drums of fuel.

An arch had been cut into end of the car with a chainsaw. The door to the passenger car was just beyond.

They both held their AR15s at ready. The door slid easily open and revealed a very clean and organized club car. Closest to the door were bathrooms to both left and right marked *LADIES* and *GENTS* in art deco brass. There was a bar next with a large selection of booze. Bookcases in the area opposite the bar were well stocked with canned goods of all kinds. There were café tables and chairs, sofas, and overstuffed leather recliners, as well as booths along the same side as the bar.

There was another door at the other end about 40 feet along. They opened it with rifles ready and were hit by a stench they were not prepared for.

"What the fuck is that?" Allie gasped, as she buried her face in her elbow, still looking straight ahead.

"I have gotten use to smelling rotting zombies, but what the hell could that be?" Ray said.

There was a bed at the far end of the room. From it came a quiet, raspy voice.

"That would be me."

***

"My name is Henry Danton," he whispered.

The smell was a man lying in his own shit and piss. But that was not the worst of it. A massive leg wound had gone septic. Rancid puss soaked the mattress. Some kind of flesh-eating virus had opened and blackened the wound, exposing the man's femur. Gallon jugs and various cans littered the floor around the bed.

"Be careful when you go in the bathroom. Martha is in there and she has turned," he whispered weakly. "I think she killed herself."

Allie pushed the door to the bathroom open with the point of her sword. A different, more familiar smell flowed out. Martha was there, hanging from a noose made from an extension cord.

Without pausing, Allie stabbed through her eye socket and out the back of her cranium. Her thrashing stopped.

"She felt guilty for stabbing my leg," Henry said. "It was an accident. Her machete was... covered in gore."

Allie noticed his ankle was tied to the bedpost. It was a beautiful Victorian four-post bed.

The room was lovely in its Old World style. Ray was busy opening windows.

"I couldn't do it while I was strong enough." His hand patted a Beretta 9mm. "I'm a coward. Plus the whole Catholic thing. Asking Martha to help was the last straw for her. Can you send us to the river together? Please?"

Ray picked up the Beretta and checked the load. "I'm sorry this happened to you. Did you build all this?"

Henry just nodded slightly, his eyes drooping.

"We'll take care of everything," Allie said in her kindest voice.

His eyes slid shut and Allie severed the top of his head with a single sword strike on the bridge of his nose.

***

They did as Henry Danton wished. He and his wife Martha were laid to rest together on the soiled mattress and with the help of the cargo dolly Ray was able to say a few words over them at the trap door.

"We are going to rename this the Danton Bridge. Thank you, Henry. We will pay it forward."

With those words, they tipped the mattress and the bodies onto Henry's trap. The water was deeper at the Harpers Ferry end. Their bodies disappeared into the green water straightaway.

Screams made them look away and they saw below in Harpers Ferry a teenage boy and girl running out of an alley with several dozen zombies in hot pursuit. They were wearing red matching T-shirts that said *Thing 1* and *Thing 2*. They must have been in one of the tourist shops. They had no gear, no backpacks, and had been caught unaware.

"Some of those are fresh and can still move pretty fast," Ray said, as he raised his scope to his eye and waited. "Looks like some of their pals turned without notice."

Allie put two fingers in her mouth and whistled an amazingly loud blast. The tiring teens saw them and began running their way.

Ray held his fire until one zombie got too close to the panicked girl and he shot. The zombie dropped, tripping the three directly behind it. The crowd of zombies increased to about fifty by the time the teens got to the trap.

"It's a trapdoor. Hold onto this." There were two ropes at this end of the bridge. "Use the rail like a balance beam." The girl just grabbed the rope on the run and swung the distance as rotting arms stretched out for her.

They watched, out of breath, as the entire horde plummeted to the river below.

"I'm Ray. This is Allie." Ray reached out his hand to shake. "Are you guys hungry? I was about to make dinner."

"Ever watch *Star Trek*? Didn't anyone ever tell you what happens to redshirts…?" Allie smiled.

About the Authors

If you would like to contact one of the authors please email us at: info@tannhauserpress.com

Acknowledgments

I'd like to thank Donna Royston for all the heavy lifting with the editing chores associated with this project. I'd also like to thank Heidi Sutherland for the cover design.

As always, I'd like to thank The Hourlings writers group for your support and encouragement as well as your participation in the anthology.

I want to thank my excellent wife Brenda Reiner for continuing to be generally awesome.

Mostly I want to thank my childhood friend, Ray Clark. We were friends when they were still a real thing. We would plan sleep overs based on the Creature Feature TV schedule in TV guide, to be watched on my Black and White TV. Zombies were chief on the priority list then. Followed closely by Godzilla and Hammer Films.

Ray Clark, my childhood friend, died in the mid 80s.

It's almost 40 years later and I still have not visited his grave. When were were kids he swore he'd reach up through the dirt and grab my ankle if I ever stood on his grave.

Maybe I'll have the courage soon... maybe.

Made in the USA
Middletown, DE
19 January 2018